THE EPIMETHEUS TRIAL
BOOK FOUR
A CONCEPT BEYOND

I0591150

E. A. SETSER

"A Concept Beyond"

Book Four of "The Epimetheus Trial"

Cover Art by Ashley Greathouse, Mellody Stout, and E. A. Setser

Editing by Gail R. Delaney

The Epimetheus Trial

Elder Blood

Into Antiquity

Beyond the Veil

A Concept Beyond

This is normally where
I put my dedication but
I don't have anything new to say
So if you're still here
After all this time
We'll say it's for you

Prologue

Worlds beget worlds

Just as life begets life

Enlightenment exceeds the binary

Falsehood and truth

Dark and light

Death and life

Better bookends than dichotomous

Spectrum both between and through

Truth of self lies beyond the self

Between ego and others

Within instincts

Within lost memories

Between id and self

With one another

For life begets life

Just as worlds beget worlds

Chapter 1

Two figures drifted along an arching spire bridge, surrounded by numerous groupings of entities in their own exchanges. One, crowned in crimson, was nebulous in form, but it grew static as it spoke of its past, even if it was faceless. The other was framed in purple and constant in shape, but no matter what it divulged, it remained amorphous and nondescript.

Crimson drifted aside, flowing through the bustle of entities as it moved to the underside of the spire. Purple saw a figure highlighted in cerulean perched on an outcropping. It flicked pebbles into a stream of prisms and fractals, studying the way they reemerged elsewhere, often instantly.

Perhaps Cerulean thought it might come to understand the nature of this river and how its ripples folded over on themselves. Or, more reasonably, it only looked to pass the time. There was plenty of that to be had here. Besides, most were quick to give up on understanding the river and contented themselves with accepting it as yet another curiosity.

Its intentions were far from the most important thing about this figure, however. No, what caught Purple's attention was its form. It was constant. It had structure, a body. And if Purple were to guess, a face.

Purple hurried over beside Cerulean. She looked down and exhaled at the sight of hands taking shape. She looked at the figure and smiled pityingly.

"Well, I'm not happy about the circumstances," Eytea said, "But it's nice to see a familiar face."

"Eytea," Galo said, smiling as he flicked a rock into the river, "I was wondering when we'd find each other."

"How long have you been here?" Eytea asked, nudging him with her hip as she gestured to the upcropping.

"I…" Galo trailed off as he scooted aside, "I don't know anymore. I lost my sense of time, well, I don't know how long ago."

"Of course you don't. If you did, you wouldn't have lost it," Eytea mused, sitting beside him, "That happens to everyone though. It's merciful."

Galo nodded absently, watching the river. "The reincarnation cycle," he said, "Seven times your last lifetime, and you're due to go back."

"Right. If we could keep track of time, we'd know when we're going back."

"Which would feel like knowing the day you're going to die."

"That's my take on it, too," Eytea said, "So. Do you wanna talk about how it happened?"

Galo closed his eyes and shook his head. "I don't think I can."

"It's okay," Eytea assured, "You'll get there when you get there."

"No, it's not that I don't want to," Galo refuted, "I'd love to."

"Then what's stopping you?"

"I, well, can't remember how it happened."

"Well then," Eytea said, hunkering down in front of the rock, "Tell me what you can remember."

"Morbid curiosity is a new side of you," Galo snickered, "Does the afterlife bring that out in everyone, or is it just you?"

"Our deaths are our last story from that side," Eytea said, "Telling it is a rite of passage. It means you're ready to settle in here."

"Yes, I can see how this place could be, well, difficult to get used to if you haven't come to terms with your death."

"Definitely," she said, "It's also a good way to get to know people, and well, I... You know."

"I don't," he said, "You what?"

"It's not important right now," she dismissed, "Now you. Go on. What do you remember about how you died?"

Galo cupped his hand over his other fist, resting his mouth and chin against it. His eyes darted about the river as he pondered. After a bit, he raised his head and gaped his mouth as hesitant words issued forth.

"We were in some kind of factory. Laboratory. Research center? I'm..." he said, "I was... fighting MalVek, and —"

"Hold up. Hold up! Hold! Up!" Eytea cut in, "MalVek?"

Galo nodded.

"Stocky supergenius well-meaning misanthrope MalVek?"

Galo nodded, arching an eyebrow.

"Wait, so Sinkua was right?" Eytea realized, "One of The Coalition did turn on us. Or... Oh shit! Was it all of them?"

"No, just him," Galo assured, eliciting a heavy sigh from Eytea, "And he never turned on us. He was always plotting against The Coalition. NalSet went missing, and we're pretty sure MalVek killed him. He abducted Nikasu, but we got her back. He took Phylus's eye. And he masterminded this whole brainwashed zombie thing with that arising that The Avatars were always on about. That one he abducted Sinkua for."

"Is that when he killed you?" Eytea asked, watching the tics in his face, "When you went to rescue Sinkua?"

Galo exhaled his confirmation. "It was this whole elaborate rescue mission. Days to plan out. But he threw one wrench after another in it, one of which was trapping me in single combat with him."

"You've fought him before though," Eytea said, "I mean, yeah, he had to hold back, but so did you. I can't see how he could get one over on you."

"I don't know if he did."

"You remember all that stuff he did, but you don't even remember if he killed you?"

"I thought I killed him," Galo protested, "Leviathan and I put a hole through his abdomen. His lower digestive organs were gone."

"Then… How did—"

"I don't know!" Galo exclaimed, throwing his hands up, "Next thing I know, I'm waist deep in the Southland Sea. I'm talking to… someone. I hear someone else apologize. Another someone else is laughing. And then I'm here."

"That's…" Eytea trailed off, "That sounds… difficult. I'm sorry I pushed you."

"It's fine," Galo sighed, smearing his hands down his face, "Vielle also died while Sinkua was being abducted. Killed by The Harvester, of all people. I'm surprised she hasn't told you about MalVek."

"This is actually the first I'm hearing that she'd died."

"Hmm. Well, I'm sure she'll turn up."

Eytea watched the river with him for a stretch, reflecting on this bombardment of developments since her death. She had never doubted Sinkua about a member of The Coalition going turncoat. And MalVek was a prime candidate by all reasoning except that he was too obvious.

But that he could have sabotaged them for decades was baffling. On top of that, he had overpowered so many people who she knew could take him in a fight. The more she thought about it, the more absurd it all sounded. It was like he'd been hiding something.

"So, does MalVek have powers or something?" she blurted out, "I mean, is he a secret Faux Hybrid? Y'know, like Yahsek, but better?"

Galo gave a hesitant crooked shrug. "He has powers," he said, "But they're all tech based, like with wires and—"

A familiar voice stole Eytea's attention. She slapped Galo's shoulder to stop him as she looked over her shoulder. Galo went silent and joined her in looking for the source. It rose from behind and well below.

"No, no, no, no, no, no, no! Shit!"

Another voice cut in.

"Stop! Don't go in there!"

The two voices faded, but Eytea and Galo had heard enough. They pushed off the rocky upcropping and hurried back to the spire bridge. Down in the chasm, they found their friend speaking with Crimson.

"Sinkua!" Eytea called down, waving.

Sinkua snapped his head up, emerald eyes wide and brilliant. He smiled with a tinge of sorrow as his eyes met hers.

"Eytea," he sighed, "Galo. I'm…" He trailed off and shook his head. "I'm sorry."

"It isn't your fault that we're here," Galo said, "We all did what we could and what we had to."

"No, I mean I was hoping we'd get back together under better circumstances," Sinkua corrected, "Hey, what's the quickest way up there? I feel like an ass, yelling like this."

"Jump?" Eytea shrugged, "Just, y'know, shift your weight upward in the air, and gravity will flip around or... I don't know how to explain it, okay?"

Sinkua spoke with Crimson, clearly more familiar with it than Eytea was. He motioned for it to go first, and the wisp rose in the air a bit, paused, then rotated as it continued to the underside of the bridge.

As it came around to the top, Sinkua thrust his fists upward as he leapt. He flailed his arms, grasping for purchase on the nothingness around him, as he drifted along the same trajectory as Crimson.

"Well," Sinkua said as he came to the top of the spire, "This sucks."

Eytea stared agape at Crimson, baffled as it, well, returned the gesture. They looked each other over, tilting their heads as they took in the revelation of one another's corporeal forms.

"Where do I know you from?" Eytea asked.

"I met Sinkua on a ferry to Quarun," he said, "He was collecting contact information. For what, I can't remember."

"That must have been when he was looking for backup for Parliamentary ArcNos," Eytea said, "Oh shit! Does that mean...? Wait, no. Were you on a cruise liner when you died?"

"No, I escaped that grisly of a fate at least."

"Of all the first encounters you could've had here," Galo said aside to Sinkua, "you got someone you met once in passing?"

"Actually, a prior one of my incarnations has been looking for him," the man said, "He's sort of compelled me to seek him out. If you could just give me a moment."

His sense of form and distinction faded. What emerged in its place was blurry and nondescript. Still, he had a more distinguishable presence than when Eytea had talked to him on the bridge. For one, she could confidently guess he was a Northlander. For another, he was quite older than the ferrygoer Sinkua had met in passing.

As this vague older man turned to him, Sinkua underwent a similar transformation. He became less distinct, recognizable only by his eyes, and half a head shorter. He also looked a fair bit slighter in frame. Any difference in age was either too little or he was too indistinct to tell.

They spoke at length in a language that Eytea couldn't understand. She regretted having passed up on the chance to learn Harkzanian and Mberhali from BeiLou, and now she hadn't seen her in she knew not how long. She had yet to even cross paths with Gijin either.

As though to save her from her own introspection, the older man returned his attention to her. Sinkua reemerged through the vague shorter man who had taken prominence.

"Pardon us. Mister Drukoa hasn't had time to learn Ouristihran," the man said, "Listening in on us will make for a good foundation. And grant him practice at dual prominence. Hence the two faces."

"Mister Drukoa?" Eytea asked, "Is that the other guy's name?"

"Yes, Tetsen Drukoa. I just needed to know what became of his voyage to sea."

"Oh! You must've been looking for him for a long time. I'm glad you found him."

The man chuckled both ruefully and pityingly. "It hasn't been that long. At least not this time," he said, "Priors don't retain knowledge. He and I could have found each other none or a dozen times."

"I'm confused," Eytea said, shaking her head, "Who are you?"

"Lhangat Leyessen. And you?"

"Eytea. That's Sinkua. Tetsen Drukoa's other guy," she said, "And that's Galo. He's working through some things."

"All monoymic?" Lhangat observed, "Did the Mberhali take over after I died?"

"I don't think that's far from the truth," Sinkua said, then returned his attention to Eytea and Galo. "Hey. So, listen. I had this plan to get all of us out of here. But, me being me, I fucked it up as soon as I got here."

Eytea reached out to him and pulled him into a hug that could have drawn breath into their illusory lungs, only to squeeze it right back out. She buried her face in the crook of his neck, basking in his corporeality. He was here. He was whole. She could place her hands on him. And with that, so too did she have form and substance.

"It's okay," she assured, "You're here. We're all here. We'll make the best of it. And if we need it, you'll come up with a backup plan."

Sinkua pulled back, holding her shoulders as he looked her over. He sighed and shook his head.

"It's not okay," he said, "There is no backup plan. And now we're stuck here, knowing all the bullshit I left behind."

"He believes he found a way to circumvent Phoenix's limitations and return the three of you to the world of the living," Lhangat said, drawing a look of deepening confusion from Eytea, "Alas, his plan depends on Epesol, which he dropped in the river upon his arrival."

"Okay. The river thing, I understand," Eytea said, "But what are Phoenix and Epesol, and what are the limitations? Sinkua. What is he talking about?"

"Phoenix is my Etherworlder," Sinkua said, "What Leviathan is to Galo and Yggdrasil to Vielle."

"And Odin is to you," Lhangat said, looking her over quizzically, "I assumed you knew. You bear the mark."

"The whole Hybrid thing was pretty murky when I was alive," Eytea said, "So how did you and Tetsen Drukoa know each other? Were you a family friend? Maybe an uncle?"

"I was his father-in-law," Lhangat said, "Well, I was going to be. His sea voyage saw the end to that."

Galo looked aside at Sinkua, eyes twitching as his throat snagged. He looked away and sat next to the spire bridge with his legs dangling.

"Oh!" Eytea exclaimed, "I must be the reincarnation of your daughter. We just couldn't see each other because I forgot that I'd been the Odin Hybrid before."

"Son," Lhangat corrected, "And no, you're not Kanet's reincarnation. I saw him some time ago, but I haven't come across him since then. I do wish we had spoken when we had the chance."

"But we're both the Odin Hybrid, right?" Eytea puzzled.

"You are, but that doesn't mean you're the same soul."

"You mean Etherworlders have more than one Hybrid?"

"Not that are alive and active together," Lhangat qualified, "But of course they do. You don't think they'd wait seven lifetimes without a proxy in the Omphaloworld, do you?"

"That's our—" Sinkua cut in.

"No, I got it," Eytea interrupted, "Thank you."

"Tetsen is the exception," Lhangat continued, "He is Phoenix's one and only because he does not have to wait to reincarnate. Or perhaps it is that he does not have to wait because he is her one and only. Which brings me to wonder…

"Sinkua, right?" he beckoned, "Epesol will return to the living world when you reincarnate. If we can send a message to your new self, you might have another chance at your plan."

"That wouldn't work," Sinkua refuted, "I cut the bond with Phoenix."

"You've done what?!"

"We're still Hybrid and Etherworlder, but we're not as tightly bound," Sinkua explained, "I can still use the powers and wield Epesol. But when she's ready to find a new host and go back, I won't get taken back unless my seven lifetimes are up."

"Well, what was your plan, then?" Eytea interjected, "Maybe we can figure something out."

"Eytea, you know you can't go after anything that fell in the river," Lhangat scolded, "If you jump in after Epesol, you'd be astronomically lucky to not get hurt. And if you manage that, you'd be even luckier to surface anywhere near where you jumped in. Not to mention finding your way back here."

"I've been here long enough to know these things," Eytea bit back, "But it's not like it vanished."

"And that's assuming you don't fall into the Netherworld."

"Uh huh. Sure. I get that this place is stupid big and weird as shit to navigate," Eytea said, "But stuff that falls in the river doesn't disappear. It's somewhere.

"So. Sinkua," she continued, "What was your plan?"

"Phoenix can resurrect the dead—"

"Is that why I haven't seen BeiLou in a while?"

"It is," Sinkua said, "Anyway, Epesol is a sword that works as an extension of her powers. But we can't resurrect Hybrids, and we don't know why."

"You think you could use it on us from this side and cheat the system," Eytea gleaned, "Well, that sounds like it would've been worth a shot."

"Not on you. I was going to, well, cut a hole to the living world, and we can go back through that."

"I'm sorry. Cut a hole?"

"Tetsen told me that Sinkua believes there to be some manner of membrane between the afterlife and the world of the living," Lhangat provided, "Like with some sort of portals or, ah, hyperspace prison?"

"I know what half of that means, and that's all I need," Eytea said, "So we find Epesol. You make a door. And we walk out."

"More or less," Sinkua said, nodding, "I imagine something similar happened when I revived people, but it was more, well, cut-to-fit."

"In that case, we'll just have to be on the lookout for a sword bobbing in the river," Eytea beamed, cupping her hands over his cheeks, "With any luck, we'll go back together and pick up from where we left off. But in the meantime, let's try to enjoy the time we've got together."

Sinkua sighed disdainfully, leaning into one of her hands as he cupped his own over it. "I can't leave things the way I did for long," he said, "But I guess we don't have any choice."

"Exactly how did you leave things?" Galo asked, neither standing nor looking up from his spot.

"After I killed The Harvester, Odin and Sleipnir sacrificed themselves to destroy the Veil. Phoenix and I killed Seriamus, and Nikasu joined us in the fight against Pandora," Sinkua recounted, "We got pinned down pretty bad though. So, I broke Phoenix out of the Ruby, and we burned up together to bring Odin and Sleipnir back. We were careful to keep the fire away from Nikasu of course. So, if Pandora somehow survived the fire, Odin should've been able to finish her with Nikasu's help."

"So Nikasu is the last living Hybrid with only Odin, Sleipnir, and Nemesis to support her—"

"Pandora killed Nemesis."

"—with only Odin and Sleipnir to help her, and we don't know whether Pandora is dead," Galo said, "How desperate were you that that was your best plan?"

"Extremely," Sinkua bit back, "And it was more of a long-term gambit than I made it look like. But as you might recall, I hit a snag."

"What about MalVek?"

"He was still alive when I died."

"You're right then," Galo said, coming to his feet, "We can't leave things how you left them. We need to find…"

He turned to face Sinkua but trailed off in quivering dumbfoundment as he made eye contact. Sinkua's hands became incorporeal, ethereal soon after. A sense of immaterialness crept up his arms like lichens, rendering his illusory body translucent and amorphous.

Eytea reached for him, but her hand passed through his arm with shimmering ripples trailing her fingers. As the dematerialization consumed his torso and moved down his legs, the spectral shape of his arms started unravelling. Like ropes formed of smoke and light, they frayed and unbraided. Eytea cupped her hands against his face, the last corporeal remnant of him.

"Stay with me," she pleaded, "Sinkua. Stay. I can't… I just… Please. I need you to stay."

"I..." Sinkua gasped, "I'm sorry. It's too late."

His face became immaterial, reducing his presence to a bundle of shimmering smoky ropes in a humanoid shape. At his core, a ripple formed, coming more from the essence of this place than within himself. A light pierced it, halting the strands of Sinkua's ethereal remains.

His voice, urging, manifested in Eytea's thoughts.

"The ring."

The light snapped back, taking the luminous strands with it through the ripple. When the air settled, nothing but memories remained of Sinkua.

"Did.... Did he just..." Eytea trembled, "Was that ... a reincarnation?"

"Hard to say. They don't look the same for everyone," Lhangat said, sounding far more curious than concerned, "But that was something new."

"What about the Phoenix Hybrid returning?" Galo asked.

"I've never seen one," Lhangat said, narrowing his eyes as he gave Galo a quick once over, "Though I wouldn't suppose they're particularly unique."

Eytea stared at the ground as she gritted her teeth. She swallowed hard and looked up.

"He said something. Right before he disappeared. 'The ring,'" she said, "What do you think he meant?"

"I should think you would know better than I," Lhangat deflected, "You did know him most recently after all."

"Your engagement ring," Galo said, staring into the bustling of spirits below, "It has a piece of the Phoenix Ruby in it."

"He thinks it came here with me," Eytea realized, "But I didn't have it when I arrived. And I haven't seen it either."

"He must have supposed that, if you find both, you could use Epesol," Lhangat suggested, "Even if just long enough to cut your way out of here."

"It's one long shot on top of another," Eytea said, shaking her head, "But, if we're going to help everyone else, it's the best plan we've got. Maybe even the only one."

"It isn't a plan," Galo refuted, "It's a desperate gambit."

He stepped down the curvature of the spire bridge, turning askew from Eytea's and Lhangat's perspective. Eytea reached for his shoulder, not to save him from falling, but to beckon him back to her.

"Galo," she urged, "Wh... Where are you going?"

Galo sighed and looked back. "We need to go our separate ways," he said, nudging her hand off his shoulder, "There are, well... I have things I need to figure out."

"Then let me help you," Eytea pleaded, "Please. I've been alone so much here. Whatever it is, I can help you figure it out."

Galo shook his head. "No. You can't. I need time away from everyone I knew."

"What about the ring? And Epesol?"

"You actually think there's merit to his plan?"

Eytea looked down, clenching her eyes shut. "I… I have to," she choked out, "I want to go back. It's lonely here. And it sucks."

"Yes, well, I…" Galo said, trailing off into a defeated sigh, "If I find either of them, I'll look for you."

Galo pushed off the spire and floated to the field far below. As he settled near the river and began to walk alongside it, Eytea watched her hands become incorporeal.

"Will you be well?" Lhangat asked.

"Now you're concerned?" Eytea snipped, "Weren't you just chastising me for hoping we'd find Epesol on a riverbank?"

"You share a bond with my son," Lhangat said, "Your pain is familiar to me, even if you are not his reincarnation."

"I don't need another father figure who's disappointed in how I was born," Eytea scolded, "I'll take my chances on becoming immaterial."

With no further acknowledgment, Eytea drifted away from him. As she approached the rock where she had found Galo, her body became increasingly insubstantial. Though her mind remained intact, her form was reduced to a luminous cloud of wisps.

Floating along the riverbank, Eytea reverted to an entity framed in purple.

Chapter 2

Dull pressure bore against Sinkua's torso. His throat churned with a scrambling of his equilibrium. His forehead struck supple ground on beat with a distant eight quarters rhythm.

The last thing he could recall clearly was Eytea reaching for him. Now he was prostrate and being shaken, perhaps punched. Whatever had happened, whatever was happening, this illusory body was incredibly convincing.

"I see you will be rejoining the world of the wakeful," a familiar voice greeted.

He didn't know anybody else who sounded like that. But it shouldn't have, couldn't have, been him. Unless the illusory body was no longer illusory.

It would certainly have explained why someone was so adamant about waking him. A world with no societal obligations, a place where the perception of time went to die, didn't exactly beget impatience.

But returning shouldn't have been possible either, especially not as himself. He had loosened the bond between himself and Phoenix. Breaking her out of the Ruby had seen to that. And even if he were wrong, he should have been reborn and had no recollection of having been Sinkua. He might even have been Nikasu's child, making him the reincarnation of his own uncle, had there been happenstance truth to his bluff.

"There is clothing is in the saddlebag beside your head," the voice continued, "Your dagger is in there as well, as is your morningstar. Repaired. Though you may wish to seek a blacksmith to reinforce it."

Sinkua groped about until he found a burlap sack. He moved his other hand along the surface, finding coarseness with musculature underneath.

This wasn't ground. It was the small of Sleipnir's back.

"Odin," Sinkua said. He came up with a belted tunic and a cloak and pushed himself upright. "Where are we?"

"Bealstilla," Odin said, "I have banished Pandora to the Netherworld. Am I to suppose you defeated Seriamus?"

"Yeah," Sinkua said, his voice distant as he dressed himself, "So, am I alive again?"

"You are."

"How? And why?"

"This is a failsafe placed upon the Phoenix Ruby," Odin explained, "Should you sever the bond and sacrifice yourself for noble means, you may reconstitute from the ash."

"I have to go back," Sinkua pleaded, "I had—"

"Indeed, you do. I am seeing to that," Odin said, "MalVek is in the wind and could still become the new God of Chaos. You need —"

"No," Sinkua cut off, reaching around to press the tip of his dagger to Odin's throat, "I need. To go. Back."

Odin pushed his hand away. "Ungrateful whelp," he grunted, "I have seen to your return, and you would squander it by rejoining the dead?"

"You've seen to…?" Sinkua said, shaking his head in annoyed bewilderment, "I had Epesol. I found Eytea and Galo. We were going to find Vielle and all come back."

"Impossible," Odin scoffed, "Only by such effort as you put into my resurrection could you revive Hybrids. Absent the Phoenix Ruby, however —"

"Don't tell me what's impossible, you purulent fuck blister," Sinkua scolded, pulling the morningstar chain across Odin's neck.

Odin twisted the chain in his hand, pulling Sinkua off balance, and pitched the weapon aside. "You must regroup with Nikasu and destroy MalVek before he becomes the God of Chaos," he ordered, "She alone will not endure against him."

"The two of us wouldn't do much better," Sinkua insisted, "Send me back so I can get everyone else."

"I cannot do that," Odin refused, "If I kill you —"

Sinkua cut him off with a punch to the back of his head.

"Open a fucking portal and —"

Odin reached back and seized Sinkua's wrist with such vigor as to silence him. "And what?" he challenged, throwing Sinkua's hand to his side, "Do you think it is so simple as opening a door for you to walk into the afterlife and walk out with your little friends?"

"That's not my plan," Sinkua said, "But of course, a spiteful jackass like you can't even imagine Omphaloworlders thinking of anything better."

"Eytea, Vielle, and Galo are dead, and dead shall they remain," Odin said, "Should you wish not for yourself or Nikasu to join them, you will obey my orders."

"I don't take orders from you, Odin," Sinkua barked, "If you were worth half the shit you talk, you'd protect Nikasu while I get the others."

"Whatever ridiculous plan you've conceived is nothing but childish wishes," Odin derided, "Speak no more of it. No longer will I entertain such drivel."

"Fine! I'll do it myself then," Sinkua snapped, reaching for the spear.

Again, Odin caught him by the wrist, only this time he pulled forward, lifting Sinkua and yanking him aside. Odin pulled back on the reins, halting Sleipnir as he held Sinkua aloft.

"Insolent."

With Sinkua clawing at his forearm, Odin pitched him away with a backhand fling. Sinkua tumbled through the air and struck ashen dirt. He bounced and rolled for several meters, halting barely within shouting distance of Odin.

At least, so he figured, as when he called out to him, he either wouldn't or couldn't answer. Believed dead by all who knew him, Sinkua stood alone in a barren landscape that everyone else didn't know existed.

Many spirits became distinct as Galo came within conversational distance. Those most vivid were Masnethegeans, mostly victims of the Triad Titan, it seemed. They regarded him in passing, leaving him with growing feelings of trust in them and fear for them.

Some appeared as two different people, sometimes strikingly different. The two incarnations of one spirit overlapped but moved asynchronously.

He turned most of his attention to the river. Despite his misgivings, he took pause at any glint of light longer than the width of his hand.

The plan was absurd. Ridiculous even. And that was before Sinkua dropped Epesol in this confounding river. Now, on top of the sword, they also had to find a ring that might not have even been findable because it might let them carry out the plan without him.

But no matter how stark raving asinine this gambit was, Galo felt compelled to watch the river, just in case. Because as much as he didn't think it was feasible, Eytea did have a point. It was their only shot.

He looked to a sky of roiling crystal clouds. Dotted throughout were countless expanses of land, many linked by bridging structures of a multitude of shapes. Most were too distant to make out any distinguishing features, though. Wisps of light flowed between them as spirits moved to islands above and below.

As he moved into the shade, the island he had arrived on obstructed his view. Crystalline formations covered the underside. Most likely deterrents, so he reasoned.

Yet, upon leaving the shade, he saw that most of the islands didn't have these structures on their undersides. There even looked to be spirits milling about on them.

"What a rare sight this is," a warm sagely voice said, "A twice-served Chieftain Sage."

The spirit before him appeared as two people, just as Galo apparently did to them. Standing still, the two incarnations flickered between an otherwise simultaneous presence. One was that of Gijin, his grandfather as he knew him. The other was Takmet, judging by his resemblance to that statue, right down to the copper sheen. And the extra pair of arms.

"Grandfather. Ancestor," Galo said, "It's been a while. We've all missed you in Masnethege."

"I had hoped it would be much longer," Gijin said, beckoning Galo to join him by the riverbank, "But as I understand, you were unable to fulfill the last thing I asked of you."

Galo sighed as he accepted the invitation. "Don't let this go any further than it must," Galo parroted, "No. I wasn't. I'm sorry. There were more complications than any of us could mitigate. We were all just, well, figuring it out as we went."

"You met The Coalition, yes? My understanding was that one of their operatives would ensure that you and Sinkua crossed their paths."

"We did. They worked with us as much as they felt necessary," Galo said, "But that turned out to be the root of many of the, well, difficulties. One of their own plotted against them and us."

"I see," Gijin said, "So not only did CreSam's corruption go farther than they intended, its repercussions ran deeper than they could manage."

"Sinkua told me that CreSam was a Coalition mole," Galo confirmed, drawing a quizzical stare from Gijin. "Malia recovered some Avatar security videos."

"At least she was able to escape. With Nikasu safe and alive, I hope?" Gijin asked, to which Galo nodded. "Splendid to know. But as I was saying, I hadn't considered how much Coalition intel CreSam may have leaked to The Avatars. Perhaps I should have worked with them more directly."

"You did what you thought was best with what you knew," Galo assured, patting his back. His attention drifted to the river, focusing on no particular presence until he shook himself out of his introspection. "But we've gone off on such a tangent that I'm almost afraid to tell you that that's not who I meant."

"Oh?" Gijin prompted, drawing back with a look of fearful curiosity, "More moles that went bad?"

"Actually, he might be why any of them went bad at all," Galo said, "MalVek was never on the up and up. He'd been siphoning intel to The Avatars and disrupting their operations since they arrived here."

"Arrived…?" Gijin puzzled, a relieved smile spreading as he came to understand, "I see. You've learned of their origins."

"I'd say you could have told me that before you died," Galo chided, "But I guess you figured that would come in time."

Gijin laughed. "I did indeed," he confirmed, "Some knowledge is best accepted when found on one's own."

"Ten years ago, I wouldn't have believed you as much as I do now," Galo agreed, slipping into that same river gazing introspection, "But some things, I'm still struggling to come to terms with."

"Like that Sinkua and Phoenix could not resurrect Eytea?" Gijin probed, "Or me, if I might be so bold as to presume?"

"That body didn't have much time left. It was an unspoken agreement that we'd be better off letting you stay dead," Galo explained, "Besides, he brought back BeiLou, and she'd been dead much longer than you."

"No matter how much time he spent with us, his bond with her would always be stronger than his with me," Gijin said, "Because its foundation was a lie. Or an omission of truth. My own doing by any name. Thus, he could circumvent limitations for her that he could never hope to defy for me."

"Yes, well, I think cheating the system has gone to his head."

"Oh? Do explain. Should I suppose it pertains to your awkward silences as you stare at the river?"

Galo let out a rueful chuckle "It has everything to do with that," he said, "Sinkua sacrificed himself to stop Pandora. But he also had this plan to use Epesol to cut a hole for all of us to escape through."

"Well," Gijin exhaled, "that would be unprecedented."

"Not to mention unviable."

"You have no faith in this plan?"

"This plan has no merit to it," Galo deflected, "Even when he was here and had Epesol, it was asinine. Now, the sword is in the river, and he's alive again, maybe as a baby. Which I think means the sword is back in the living world."

"Perhaps. Perhaps not," Gijin said, shrugging, "But as much as I never thought I'd hear you cast doubt on a desperate Phoenix Hybrid, I suppose this is more Galo talking than Metkhal. What with the environments which molded you."

Flashes of memory bombarded Galo's thoughts, glimpses between MalVek's deceptive death and his own. A name resonated. Tsenukoa.

"Do you mean that…" Galo trailed off, "… I was possessed by Metkhal? Like how you possessed Gijin?"

Gijin laughed. "I thought you had figured it out," he said, "Nothing so elaborate as that. No Galo, you are the reincarnation of Metkhal. Thus, I, having known you as Metkhal's father and posing as Galo's grandfather, see you as both. Just as I should suppose you see me as both Gijin and Takmet. Unless he's choosing not to emerge, though that isn't always an option."

"Your Takmet side still looks more copper than flesh," Galo said, "But yes. And that does explain a lot. Right before I died, I had visions that felt like someone else's memories."

"Oh? What happened in these visions?" Takmet beckoned, "I could corroborate whether these were Metkhal's memories or Galo's fears."

"If they were memories, they happened after you became a statue, and you weren't close enough to hear us," Galo said, "But I was standing in the water with someone named Tsenukoa. Ouristihra was flooding, and he was setting out in search of other lands. Ones that hadn't been impacted by the Etherworlders."

Takmet nodded. "And what did you say of Tsenukoa's plan?"

"I promised to keep his belongings safe while he was gone. Including… Gungnir? …for Kanet," Galo said, his reflection splitting between the embedded memory and meeting Lhangat, "But I refused to deliver a message for him."

"Why?"

"Because I believed he would make it back safely," Galo said, "Even if I doubted he'd fare better than all the explorers before him, I knew he'd find his way back to Mberhan."

"Much of Metkhal's world was the stuff of fairytales in Galo's world," Gijin said, "Thus, Galo would much sooner cast doubt on anyone returning from so ambitious a journey."

"Kanet's father said Tetsen Drukoa was engaged to him. To Kanet, I mean. So Tsenukoa is Mberhali for Tetsen Drukoa, isn't it?" Galo confirmed, "That's where you derived Sinkua's name from. His last incarnation you knew."

"Well, not so much derived. My memory of the mononym we had given to Tetsen Drukoa had become muddled," Gijin said, chuckling to himself, "I misremembered Tetsen Drukoa's honorary Mberhali name as Sinkua. So, I thought calling MeiLom that might help him tap into some of those old memories."

"Did we give mononyms to all our visitors?" Galo asked.

"Only those we declared honorary Mberhali," Takmet said, "But since the flooding didn't let up after I was copperized, I suppose that came to be anyone who took shelter there."

"I remember telling Tsenukoa it might be the last bastion in Ouristihra," Galo said, "And you told me that Masnethege was the oldest standing community."

"Well, this has all been quite a roundabout way of making my point," Gijin said, "But if Metkhal could focus on rebuilding and believe Tsenukoa would find his way home…"

Galo sighed. "I can focus on finding what we need in Sinkua's absence."

Eytea paused as a flicker of green in the river grabbed the corner of her periphery. That color was of no particular curiosity. After all, any conceivable color could appear in the iridescent waters. Rather, it was the concentration that caught her attention. It was, from what she could tell, a sizeable patch and quite bright at that.

But in the split second it took her to turn her head, the flash had dissipated into the usual multicolored ripples. Another came at the upper edge of her periphery, only to elude her once again as she tried to look straight at it.

Having seen it twice though, she confirmed one of two things. Either it really was there, or her incorporeality was finally breaking her mind.

She closed her eyes, as much as that was possible. The smoky form had no eyes. No anything, technically. But it had the same capacity for sight as her body. So, she shut that off.

Eytea reasoned she ought to have been able to expand her periphery beyond bodily limitations. If she could see in all directions all at once, the green flickering couldn't hide from her. It would just take a bit of concentration.

But as she opened her eyes, as it were, her vision was still just as limited. Either her assessment was wrong, or there was more to it. The green flickering taunted her a third time. She didn't try to catch it.

As though to reassure herself of her amorphousness, she looked to where her hands might have been. Two smoky appendages appeared from the luminous cloud, the ends tapering off into some crude imagining of hands.

Somebody was perceiving her.

She looked around, focusing on other spirits only as long as it took them to pass across her field of vision. They churned and rippled as they interacted with each other, sharing experiences across countless lifetimes.

But none of them had any semblance of shape to her. Just as it had been since she arrived. Everyone else caught up on lives since the ones they last shared, but she had yet to find anyone she knew from a prior life.

Now though, that isolation might no longer come packaged with constant incorporeality. She had lost too many people who had let her retain formfulness. First it was BeiLou. Then Sinkua and Galo. Vielle, she didn't so much lose as find out she should have been an option. Lhangat was her own doing, but she stood by that choice.

If she could find whoever was perceiving her though, she'd have another chance. Maybe this would finally be the one to stick around.

"Eytea!" a voice called out.

It was behind her and tragically familiar. Her body reformed, Eytea spun about to see her mother looking up and straight ahead from a perpendicular island.

"Eytea!" Elemeno called out again, "How are all of you walking on that wall?"

Eytea shook her head and laughed. "From where I'm standing, you're the one on the wall."

"I suppose it would look like that," Elemeno conceded, "Could you come to me? I've been looking all over for you, and I'd hate to think we're stuck at different angles."

Eytea pushed off with her wings and leapt high, suspending a few meters off the ground. She turned sideways to orient her body parallel to the ground she had jumped from.

Her feet now aligned with the perpendicular island, she folded her wings back and focused on that patch of ground. Her gravity shifted, and she fell toward the island. She pinned her arms down and pointed her toes, quickening her fall before she could lose her concentration and drop on her back.

Despite her rapid descent, her landing was no hotter than if she had glided down on spread wings. She lit upon the island, straight into a bear hug from her deceased mother.

As saddened as she was by her passing, Eytea couldn't hold back her elation. No longer would she have to endure incorporeality. Her mother had no reason she knew of to wander off without her. But she was no less confused about the circumstances.

"Mom!" Eytea remarked as she pulled back, "How did you end up here already? I thought The Avatars would have lost interest in you after they got me."

"They might have if I had lost interest in them," Elemeno mused, "I may have coerced my way into helping The Coalition. You might be surprised to hear that I was quite the asset to them."

"After how you handled The Geneticist, that doesn't surprise me at all," Eytea said, "So, when and how did you die? Was it before Sinkua sacrificed himself? Or did you let your guard down in the aftermath?"

"Actually, I died when we were trying to rescue Sinkua from MalVek," Elemeno said, "Oh! I suppose that warrants its own explanation. Let me see if I can make this brief."

"I already know. Galo told me."

"Oh. Oh dear. That is dreadful that he didn't make it out alive," Elemeno mourned, "Well, Sinkua had been pushed into a pretty bad episode. This new friend, Uro, MalVek brainwashed him into pushing me down a tall stairwell. Did Galo tell you MalVek can control people with his voice? Well, it turns out it works over a PA, too."

"That must have been terrifying for both of you."

"Truly. But I hope Uro doesn't think it was his fault. None of us could resist MalVek's will," Elemeno said, "In any case, I landed at Sinkua's feet. The last thing I remember was him staring down at me. He looked so haunted and... empty. I suppose that's what led to the sacrifice you mentioned."

"I don't have all the details, but I'm sure that factored into it," Eytea said, "But for now, let's head to my home to talk things over. I feel self conscious talking about this out in the open."

"Oh! You have a home here?" Elemeno puzzled, "Like an actual indoor living space with furnishings?"

Eytea panned the barren landscape and laughed. "I guess there's not much here to look at, is there?" she said, "We all just occupy pockets in the ground. Or they might be in the crystals. I'm not sure."

"Well, where's your pocket? Is it far from here?" Elemeno asked, "Not that we need to rush."

"It's wherever I want it to be," Eytea said as she crouched and pressed her palm against the ground, "A lot of how we interact with this world has to do with intentions and willpower. It think it's how we adapt to there being four spatial dimensions. That's why everyone you never knew looks like glowing puffs of smoke. I think."

Eytea parted the ground as she dragged her hand along. A sheet of fractalized light stretched over the hole as she drew back.

"My home is right through there."

"Oh, it's like the portals," Elemeno noted, "But would that mean we're moving across the fifth dimension?"

Eytea shrugged, straddling ignorance and apathy. It made sense that the portals took people across the fourth dimension. But she'd never thought about whether these islands were three or four-dimensional. Much less if there was an imperceptible fifth dimension.

All she knew was that the door would close if she lost her concentration. So, she grabbed her mother's hand and pulled her along as she hopped into the hole.

Elemeno surveyed the rustic living space. It resembled an efficiency apartment, not much larger than her room at Country Living. A record player filled the space with an ambience of acid rock. Two armchairs sat angled toward each other with their lines of sight converging on a rabbit ear television.

Where the media for the record player and television came from, she couldn't be sure. She had yet to see any other signs of technology and industry. She chalked it up to, as Eytea had put it, matters of intentions and willpower.

The real curiosity was the chairs. They looked like a matching set, but one was faded and indented, while the other looked factory new.

The reason became obvious as Eytea settled into the well-worn chair.

"This place was supposed to be for you and Sinkua, wasn't it?"

"Am I that transparent?" Eytea asked. She scratched her upper sternum. "Nope. Still got a body."

Elemeno laughed and folded her arms atop the backrest of Sinkua's chair. Eytea probably wouldn't have minded her sitting there, but it felt intrusive to be the first to use it.

"So, is the second chair a recent addition, or…?" Elemeno asked, "Because you mentioned Sinkua sacrificing himself."

"No, I made both chairs as soon as I knew how."

"Well, can I ask where he is? Or have you two not found each other yet?"

Eytea sighed. "We found each other, but he's not here anymore," she said, "There's a lot to explain. Give me a few minutes to make a chair for you, and I'll tell you as much as I know."

"Is there anything I can do to help? Maybe conjure up some drinks? Extend the room?"

"I don't think you can, since you didn't make it, but you're welcome to try," Eytea said, "But maybe while I'm working on the chair, you could tell me what you know about Etherworlders? Sinkua told me a little before he disappeared, but I want to know more by the time he gets back."

"Oh gladly. Matter of fact, I have a lot to catch you up on."

Chapter 3

Sinkua's hand went for his ruby, only to find the scar where it had fused into his chest. A four-pointed star of ridged flesh adorned his sternum with keraunographic scars blooming in all directions. His reconstitution had been remarkably faithful, complete with all the aches and marks he had died with.

He felt his face to find his facial hair was still gone, and his cheeks were still sticky with the Project Cerulean substance. That was perhaps a blessing, seeing as he had no reason to think the ordeal had cured him of his episodes.

Wounded buildings dotted the horizon like a firing range for milystic rage. His and Phoenix's sacrifice hadn't completely leveled the Bealstillan ruins. He conjured a flame with the flick of his wrist, just to assure himself, and set out towards them.

"What are your intentions, Sinkua?" a voice asked.

Sinkua scrambled into a defensive stance. After a second of mounting tension, he realized nobody was trying to get the drop on him. The voice came from within.

"Phoenix?" he asked, speaking aloud despite knowing it wasn't necessary.

"Yes," Phoenix said, "Again, what are your intentions?"

"First explain how you're inside my head," Sinkua insisted, resuming his walk, "I thought I separated us so you could go home."

"I thought the same. That was my understanding of the ruby and dagger," Phoenix said, "However, it would seem our reconstitution has bound me more intrinsically with your soul."

"An unforeseen side effect?" Sinkua asked, "Or are you thinking sabotage?"

"Neither would surprise me. Even the most skillful craftworkers are not infallible. And Pandora had thralls to spare, any of whom could have disrupted the crafting processes," Phoenix said, "Now, I implore you to stop dodging my question. What do you intend to do in Bealstilla?"

Sinkua sighed as he sorted his thoughts. His idea was absurd, and he knew it. But with options being in shorter supply than resources, he had to resort to the ridiculous.

"I'm looking for bodies," he said, "When I impaled The Harvester with Epesol, you were able to revive the souls he had fed on. Sort of."

"I would not be capable of reviving any of the Bealstillans," Phoenix insisted, "I also doubt they'd be glad to see you."

"Not that I'm new to people on this island being unhappy to see me," Sinkua said, "But that's not what I'm getting at. Aren't you in my subconscience? You should know what I'm thinking."

"I've isolated myself in order to keep us as distinct of entities as I can," Phoenix explained, "It's burden enough for me to house the memories of so many of your lifetimes, and I fear that a total binding would impress them as well as my own onto you."

"You're blockading the memories that were in the ruby?"

"I am, but I apologize my defenses may not be impenetrable," Phoenix said, "Now, what do you plan to do if we find bodies?"

"I'm going to gather them in one place so you can attempt to revive them all at once," Sinkua said, "It doesn't matter if you can. It might be better if you can't. I'm hoping that the strain will open a tangible gateway to the afterlife."

"You're right. That idea is absurd."

"What? I never…" Sinkua puzzled, "I didn't tell you that, and I thought you were cut off from—"

"It's gray, in a word," Phoenix said, "My access to any part of your mind is not best described in the binary."

"Well…" Sinkua hesitated, trying to comprehend the nature of his neural passenger, "Will you help me? I can tell you have some misgivings, but I can't read your mind."

"You should know that I have little confidence in the viability of this plan."

"I've been hearing that a lot lately, and I haven't had time to get used to it."

"I know," Phoenix said, "I also know it would do you well for someone to see it through with you despite those doubts. Especially after the indignation you faced from Odin."

"Does that mean you'll do it?"

"As best as I'm able."

Sinkua drew his morningstar and looked it over. Phoenix's mentioning of Odin had reminded him to check what sort of condition it was in. He might have, as Odin had suggested, needed to take it to a blacksmith. But until then, he just needed to know how durable it was.

He also couldn't dismiss the possibility that Odin meant to sabotage him.

"So," Eytea said, her voice drifting as she fidgeted, "What do you think?"

"Well, it's um," Elemeno said, flapping her elbows between the armrests, "It's bigger than I was expecting."

"I know! I know. I can," Eytea fumbled, "I can work on that. It's just that my memories are sort of, well, cloudy. Distorted. I don't know."

"Your memories?" Elemeno asked, "Wait. Didn't your grandparents have a chair like this?"

"When I was a kid, yeah," Eytea said, "They got rid of it when I was seven or eight. I figured it was from when you were growing up."

"And you wanted me to feel like a kid when I sit in it?"

"Uh, sure. We can pretend this was on purpose. That's what I was going for," Eytea joked, "No, I haven't seen it since I was a kid, so my sense of scale is out of whack."

"Well, until you muster up the strength to shrink it, I guess I've got the biggest chair in the house," Elemeno said, "Of course, I could always just learn how to make my own place with décor to my liking."

"You don't need to leave any time soon."

"Eytea, you've got about a hundred and sixty years here, and I've got three hundred and…" Elemeno said, trailing off into mumbles, "We'll have plenty of time to reminisce, but we should both get out there and mingle with the other dead. Reunite with people from our past lives. Learn or relearn some history. You know? Make the most of our time here."

"Yeah, about that. You know how I was joking about being transparent and still having a body? And how most people look like weird clouds?" Eytea asked, "That means you never knew any incarnation of them. If you have a mutual connection, you can learn to perceive them as you get to know them. It can also help if you're with your mutual connection."

"Well thank you. That'll be useful to know," Elemeno said, "But what does that have to do with my staying here?"

Eytea sighed as she organized her thoughts. "The longer you go without being around people who can perceive you," she managed, "The more imperceptible you become to yourself. And eventually, you become intangible."

"You look like a cloud ghost even to yourself?" Elemeno asked, "How do you deal with it? I mean, how do you get back to normal?"

"Coming here helps," Eytea said, "Sometimes, I'll happen across a casualty of the ArcNosian Civil War. But they're generally not that chummy. Actually, they make me nervous. I feel like maybe I should keep my distance. You know? Like I'd be bothering them if I hang out with them."

"So, you need me around so you can stay tangible?" Elemeno asked, "Well, I guess I can't say no to that. I can't leave knowing you'll be unsafe without me."

"I'm sorry. It's just," Eytea said, "I know you've got great things to look forward to out there. But I'd like you to stick around a little longer."

"It's fine. Really. I'm used to our neighbors thinking we're a little co-dependent," Elemeno insisted, pushing herself out of the comically oversized chair, "But what about people from your past lives? Have you met any of them?"

"No, but not for a lack of trying," Eytea grumbled, "I'm starting to think I don't have any."

"Well, that sucks. I mean sure, of course there are people here after their first life," Elemeno considered, "But you'd think they'd at least be able to perceive each other."

"I don't make the rules," Eytea said, throwing up her hands in resignation, "But hey, what do you say we head out? Maybe you can find some people you knew and introduce us."

"All this talk of past lives does have me curious about mine."

Eytea pressed the wall until it felt like putty. The imprint glowed, seeping blue light between her fingers. She swiped downward, parting the wall into a sheet of fractalized light. Elemeno joined her, and they stepped through together, their orientation rotating as they emerged.

Before the ground settled, they found themselves staring down a trio of spearheads.

Galo perked up as the water shimmered and churned. He reached aside for Gijin.

"No way," Galo gasped, "Did Epesol just—?"

A swishing pulled at his attention as he wrestled with his assumptions. He looked to Gijin, only to find an empty space followed by a voice bursting from behind.

"Get back!"

His sleeves pulled against his shoulders as Gijin yanked back on the collar. Galo tumbled back into a reverse somersault, scarcely sooner than a rush of iridescent water erupted from the river. Droplets spattered on shins, sizzling into steam on contact.

His nerves settling along with the water, Galo looked back to see the dual form of Gijin and Takmet looking past him.

"What was that?" Galo asked, "Why does the water burn?"

Takmet tilted his head to acknowledge something behind Galo. As Galo got his feet back under himself, someone addressed Takmet in a language he didn't understand. It sounded nothing like what little Mberhali he had learned and even less like the handful of Harkzanian words he'd picked up from Nikasu.

As he turned to find a minotaur towering over him, Galo receded and passed through Metkhal as he relinquished presence.

Elemeno tried to put Eytea behind herself just as Eytea shoved her back and assumed a defensive stance. By the time any of that happened though, the bearers withdrew their spears and relaxed their own stances. Slightly at least.

"Sincerest apologies, Hybrid of Odin," one of the women professed, bowing her head with her right fist over her heart. The two flanking her gestured likewise. "We sensed an unfamiliar soul in your vicinity."

Mouth agape, Eytea's eyes darted along the three of them. She didn't recognize them. But she could see them.

Even more curious, they also had wings. Purple ones, at that. And their spears bore an uncanny resemblance to her halberd, were the axe blade to be removed.

"Are you three…" she gasped, "Are you also Hybrids of Odin? Do you know Lhangat Leyessen?"

"No, we serve Odin in a different capacity," the same one said, "You do not know of us?"

"It is as I told you. The new Omphaloworlders forget the ways of old," the one to the right insisted.

"Yes well, most of the Etherworlders died a few thousand years ago, and nearly all the historical records have vanished since then. I assume that's what you three are? Etherworlders?" Elemeno cut in, drawing ireful glares from the winged trio, "Sorry. I'm Elemeno. Mother of Eytea, your Hybrid of Odin."

"Elemeno. Pleased to be acquainted," the middle one said, "It's been ages since we needed to introduce ourselves, but I suppose it cannot be helped. My name is Eir. These are my sisters in arms, Sigrdrifa and Randgrid. We are the last of the Valkyries."

"We are now, yes, but we had the dishonor of being slain in our sleep by Vuordevaltene well before most of our sistren," Sigrdrifa corrected, "Only to now have been cast into this wasteland of an Omphaloworlder afterlife."

"The threshold of the Etherworlder afterlife was recently broken," Randgrid said, "Perhaps by Phoenix, but I've not known her to be capable of this."

"She is not, but she would try if asked," Sigrdrifa said, "Her Hybrids have long had an unhealthy fixation on saving everybody."

"Everyone has their obsessions," Eytea said with a shrug, "But that does sound like something Sinkua would do."

"Well, be that all as it may," Randgrid continued, "we seek to return to duty."

"And now that we have found you, Eytea, we are ready to serve," Eir said, "Have you any candidates for our consideration?"

"Candidates for…?"

"Ahh. I see. Your kind truly has forgotten everything."

"I told you," Sigrdrifa interjected.

"Well, you can think of us as…" Eir trailed off, looking aside as she exchanged rapid mutterings with Randgrid, "… employees of Odin. When he or any other Fjarthursk Etherworlder loses their Hybrid, we scout this afterlife for replacements. His Hybrids are most helpful in this search. The most recent one, especially so."

"It would seem Fjareskjon is now known as Ferya," Sigrdrifa said, "Fjarthursk and all other languages have converged into this singular Ouristihran."

"I must say, however," Randgrid cut in, "that you are a most peculiar sight. It has been ages since Odin selected a new soul. Never mind that none of us recall nominating you."

"When you say new," Eytea said, "do you mean I just lived my first lifetime? Or that it's my first time being his Hybrid?"

"The latter," Randgrid said, "Ever since his sixth Hybrid, he's been keeping a rotation of the same five souls. Though I suppose this having been your first life would account for why we had no say in the matter."

"I'd wager being dead was a factor," Sigrdrifa snarked, "What are you getting at, Randgrid?"

"It's suspicious," Randgrid insisted, "Odin straying from his five is cause for concern."

"We have not sensed all of them here," Eir said, "It would appear he willingly passed them over in favor of a neophyte."

"Arestor," Takmet said, "I've warned you to be careful when you surface."

"Deepest apologies, old friend," Arestor professed, "I know as well that others cannot endure these waters as you do that I cannot resist making an entrance."

Arestor hunkered down to face Metkhal at eye level.

"Did I splash you, child?" Arestor asked.

Despite his stature, those bovine eyes filled Metkhal with a sense of hope, fearful and laced with misgivings as it may have been. This beastkin who endured the river could just as soon be a font of power and wisdom as a herald of dread and mayhem.

"I do not trust this one," Arestor muttered, "Keep him around as long as he is useful, but do not put your back to him."

Metkhal stepped back and looked to his father. Takmet gave nothing. Arestor stood upright, regarding him from the difference in their heights.

"I see," he said, "That is how you saw me."

"What? I..." Metkhal stammered, "I didn't... Father. What is he talking about? How does he think I saw him?"

"In death just as life, you hesitate to speak with him directly," Takmet said, "Do all the beastkin frighten you, or is it only the minotaurs?"

"I... I don't know. They're just..." Metkhal grasped, "So many of them joined Mawakouteza. It was easier to be wary of all of them."

"Many of my brethren did, I concede. But I did not," Arestor deflected, "You know this to be true."

"I also knew many of your brethren to have not joined," Metkhal countered, "Right up until the day they sacked Skjarvestad."

"We could be at this until sunlight finds its way here," Arestor dismissed, "Tell me, Metkhal, what did you feel when you looked in my eyes?"

"What? Well, I..." Metkhal trailed off, "Cautious optimism."

"Would you care to elaborate?"

"Obviously, you're powerful. And Father trusts you. I hoped you'd be a good ally, but I was also afraid of what you might do if you decide you don't want to work with me."

"You feel these things because of the nature of this place," Arestor said, "The phenomenon is not constant, but we often feel toward others how they felt toward us in life. Do you understand now?"

Galo's disappointment pulled at the back of Metkhal's thoughts. Metkhal knew Galo couldn't understand their conversation, as they had been speaking Mberhali, but the universal language of emotions seeped through. As much as Metkhal tried to justify his subhumanization with their semi-human forms, Galo had seen the truth of his discrimination. Metkhal saw the beastkin as unwieldy tools at best, volatile weapons at worst.

"You saw hope in me?" Metkhal asked, "And I hated you. I thought I was just indifferent, but I despised you. I just never realized it. Is that why you were afraid?"

"No. But we need not discuss that now. I have something to ask you," Arestor beckoned, "Did Tsenukoa return alive, or did he never depart for Durasarzim?"

"He left in search of Chizambal soon after the sea took you. He never returned," Metkhal said, "Why do you ask?"

"I sensed him shortly before I was freed from my copper prison. Rather, I sensed someone much like him," Arestor explained, "He did not carry the cordial spite that he and I harbored for each other. In fact, if I thought such things possible for Phoenix, I might think he was trying to free me."

Metkhal closed his eyes as he considered a tugging at the back of his thoughts. Galo couldn't understand them, but he sounded like he'd gleaned something from the mention of Tsenukoa and Phoenix.

"Galo says that was Sinkua," Metkhal said, "He was trying to free you."

"To what end?" Arestor asked, hunkering down to look into Metkhal's eyes as though he might see through to this other entity.

"That, I don't know," Metkhal said, "Galo and I don't yet speak each other's language."

"I see. Well thank you for what you could tell me," Arestor said, "I would also thank this Sinkua for his intentions and hope we might reconcile our differences."

A hand settled on Metkhal's shoulder, and his senses passed through Galo's as they receded and faded.

"Sinkua worked with Odin after I died," Eytea said, drawing confused looks from the Valkyries, "You might have known him as Tetsen Drukoa."

"I am afraid that name is unfamiliar," Eir said.

"He and Lhangat Leyessen must have been from a time after our deaths," Randgrid surmised.

"Sinkua and Tetsen Drukoa were both Phoenix Hybrids," Eytea clarified, "Lhangat's son was the Odin Hybrid in Tetsen's time."

"Then this Sinkua," Eir said, "He was your lover, yes?"

"He was," Eytea said, side-eyeing the Valkyrie, "Do the Odin Hybrid and Phoenix Hybrid always end up together or something?"

"It's more of a compulsion," Sigrdrifa interjected, "Destiny is no matter of absolutes."

"I see. Well, Sinkua was here for a while, but then he vanished."

"As the Hybrid of Phoenix is wont to do, given the nature of their reincarnation," Eir said, "Did he have any pertinent insights as to Odin?"

"Not particularly. He did say that he and Phoenix resurrected him and his horse by sacrificing themselves."

Three sets of eyebrows flew up.

"Perhaps Phoenix did bring us back," Sigrdrifa remarked, "Glory be to the fiery avian."

"Glory, indeed," Eytea said, "But Lhangat said the way he disappeared didn't look like any reincarnation he'd seen. So, I'm hoping that maybe he just got brought back to life, and he's trying to find a way back here."

"To what end?" Randgrid asked.

"To bring Galo, Vielle, and myself back to the world of the living," Eytea said, "We still need to find Vielle though."

"Galo being Leviathan's Hybrid," Elemeno provided, "Vielle is Yggdrasil's."

"Right," Eytea nodded, "Odin killed Pandora with Nikasu's help. But she has followers who need to be dealt with, and the two of them need our help."

"Nikasu is Nemesis's Hybrid," Elemeno said.

"Vielle will prove difficult to locate," Eir said, "I hesitate to say impossible, but I wish not to digress any further."

"Are you offering to investigate Odin's behavior?" Sigrdrifa asked, "Your generosity is admirable, but your ignorance is great. We can enter the living side of the Omphaloworld as we please and thus can ask him ourselves."

"We must consider that Odin's integrity has been compromised," Eir countered, "It would be safer for Omphaloworlders less familiar to our kind to speak with him, lest we expose our suspicions prematurely."

"True as that may be, Phoenix could no better resurrect a Hybrid than Sanngridr could tame her own fury," Sigrdrifa insisted.

"We assumed she couldn't resurrect our fellow Etherworlders, but the exploits of this Sinkua have proven us wrong," Randgrid said, "I see no better explanation for our presence here, and we have no reason to suspect Eytea of lying."

"I would love to believe she can help us, but her help is contingent on miracles," Sigrdrifa said, "If she could aid in investigating Odin, she and this Sinkua would have already had a plan in motion. Never mind that we have no frame of reference for when or if Phoenix could even repeat such a feat."

"Eytea," Eir beckoned, stepping between her and Sigrdrifa, "I would hear your proposition."

"Well, when Sigrdrifa said you three can go to the living world, I thought about asking you to bring Sinkua here," Eytea said, "But I'm guessing you'd have to kill him, wouldn't you?"

"You would guess correctly," Eir said, "I suppose that would not be conducive to his plan."

"I don't think so," Eytea said, "He was going to use Epesol to cut a passage to the living world. If he comes back here dead, he'd almost definitely reincarnate before he can pull it off. Especially if we don't find Epesol first."

Eir spoke aside with Randgrid and Sigrdrifa in a language unfamiliar to Eytea. Fjarthursk, she supposed. She grew more uneasy the longer they spoke.

"You suppose he intends to return here alive, then?" Eir asked at last.

"I know it sounds ridiculous, but it also sounds like the kind of thing Sinkua would try," Eytea said, "And I know him better than anyone except for maybe Galo."

"Ridiculous describes it lightly. However, it would be safer for us if you and your friends were to investigate Odin's behavior," Eir conceded, "To that end, what would you ask of us? Do you seek to arrange recompense for this investigation? Or do you believe we can help in executing Sinkua's plan?"

"The second one," Eytea said, "Right before he disappeared, he told me to find my engagement ring. He had it made from bits of silver and ruby from his necklace."

"Phoenix lived in the ruby," Elemeno said, "Nobody had told him it was the, well, Phoenix Ruby."

"Right. So, I think he thinks the ring will let me use Epesol to carry out his plan without him," Eytea said, reconsidering her understanding of his plan, "But maybe he meant it'll help him get back. Or help me find him when he does."

"Well, housing an Etherworlder in a gemstone is unprecedented, but if her power is ubiquitous within it, a fragment could grant limited usage of Epesol," Eir pondered, "That, however, is a moot point. Epesol would have returned with him."

"What if he dropped it in the river?"

"That… might complicate matters."

"I thought so," Eytea said, "Do you think you could help me find Epesol and my ring, then? In return, we'll look into what's happening with Odin when we get back."

"Before the Grand Genocide, this would have been a far easier task. Unfortunately, the Shrines appear to have vanished with each Etherworlder's death," Eir said, "We have happened across traces, however. If we can identify the Harkzanian or Dragon Family Shrines, we ought to find Epesol among them. Your ring, be it not with them, ought to be among the Fjarthursk Shrines."

"Then we go forth to seek the Sword of the Sun?" Sigrdrifa asked.

"And repurposed fragments of this Phoenix Ruby?" Randgrid added.

"We do indeed," Eir announced, brandishing her spear, "I cannot promise our success, Lady Eytea, but I swear our most earnest effort."

"I know I'm asking a lot. And I really appreciate your help," Eytea said, "It was great meeting all of you. Come find me any time. I'd love to get to know you better."

The trio of Valkyries bowed their heads and saluted with a fist to the chest.

"We will seek you once we have news to share," Eir professed.

With that, they turned and launched themselves skyward in streaks of purple.

"Grandfather?" Galo said, pausing to acclimate, "Did I understand right? He wants to thank Sinkua for trying to free him?"

"Yes. And to move past any disagreements he had with Tsenukoa," Gijin clarified, "But Sinkua might know this by the time you find each other."

"Why not?" Galo said, "Did Metkhal promise to bring Arestor back with us?"

"No, he know that isn't his place," Gijin said, "We saw Sinkua vanish, Mortvill and myself. Mortvill suspects he was resurrected, rather than reincarnated, and that he'll find his way back here."

"Truly?" Galo asked, "So finding the ring might just be a backup plan. But why would you assume Arestor will see him first? Can he help bring him back?"

"It's more that he can scout for him farther than anyone else we know," Gijin said, "The river connects to other spiritual realms, namely that of the Netherworld. Arestor can endure the sufferings both of that place and of the river itself."

"How does he do that?" Galo asked, "Brute strength? Or is it a beastkin thing?"

"It could be a result of his soul eroding and reconstituting. Or this could be his mutation as the son of Vuserah," Gijin said, "Be it as it may, Mortvill has asked Arestor to scout the Netherworld for both Sinkua and Epesol."

"I see," Galo said, bowing his head to Arestor as he spoke aside to Gijin, "Tell him I said thank you. And do you think you could teach me Mberhali? It'd be good if I could speak with him more directly."

"It would be my pleasure."

"Maybe while we're at it, you can explain what Mortvill thinks he stands to gain by currying Sinkua's favor."

"That, I will attempt to the best of my abilities."

Chapter 4

Frayed string catching his eye, Sinkua crouched before a scorched frame of a house. He followed the string to dig up a cracked medallion etched with some four-legged animal. Another piece of ruined string extended from the other end.

"A family lived here," Sinkua said as he rose to his feet, "with children."

"Which I suppose means more chances to find a body," Phoenix added.

"Sure," Sinkua nodded, crossing the threshold, "if that's how you want to look at it."

Phoenix was right though, both in her observation and her priorities. And he knew this. But the thought of exploiting the souls of children filled him with apprehension.

Worse still was knowing that Pandora had destroyed this place because of him. Or rather, one of his past selves. Rationally, he knew Pandora's actions were her own. As were those of his past incarnations. He could no better be accountable for them than he could resurrect people long enough dead to have reincarnated.

He took pause at that thought. Bealstilla fell centuries before the Trifecta erected the Veil.

"Sinkua," Phoenix interrupted, "There's most of a torso under the kettle."

"Right," Sinkua sighed, "Thank you."

"You sound like you're having doubts," Phoenix said, "In fact, your apprehension has been becoming more apparent since you saw that toy. What's troubling you? Do you feel sorry for the children?"

"I feel guilty about them," Sinkua said, "I hated The Avatars for exploiting children, but now I'm about to pull on their souls so maybe I can see my fiancee and my best friend again."

"We both know your intentions go beyond serving your own emotions."

"Do we though? Or are we just telling ourselves that so we can sleep better?" Sinkua asked as he hoisted the overturned kettle, "Besides, you even said that you doubt the viability of this plan. And I'm starting to see why."

"Certainly not because of your own misgivings," Phoenix said, "No, I think I interrupted just as you were realizing the logistical issue."

"They've all been reincarnated," Sinkua said, "What happens to a living person when we try to resurrect one of their old bodies?"

"Hopefully nothing," she said, "You should be used to hearing this by now, but none of your past selves ever asked me to do anything like this."

"It is becoming familiar," he said, running his fingers along the desiccated flesh, "So, if their soul is in the afterlife, we're going to pull on them from across multiple lifetimes. Might unravel them."

"I hadn't considered that, but I can't dismiss the possibility."

"And if they're alive, maybe nothing happens on either end," he continued, "Or we could play tug-of-war with someone's soul and cause who knows what kind of harm."

"Unraveling is also a possibility, I'm afraid."

"This is ridiculous," Sinkua said, thrusting to his feet.

He stormed out of the house and on to the communal courtyard. The stone and bronze rubble looked to have once been a large fountain, perhaps surrounded by benches. Sinkua dropped onto a mound of it and buried his face in his hands.

As he sat, he glimpsed his own reflection, only to do a double take as he realized something wasn't quite right. He grabbed the bronze fragment to investigate and found that he didn't have the Project Cerulean substance on his face anymore. His skin was just still clammy from it.

This compounded his misgivings. If he had an episode from the strain, there was nothing to stop him from going brimstone and nobody to bring him back.

"Sinkua," Phoenix implored, "Listen to me. I can't promise that your plan won't hurt anybody. Or that it'll work. But it is more viable than what you suggested to Eytea."

"The engagement ring won't let her use Epesol?"

"Not to the extent you're after, I don't think. Which means you need to at least try your plan."

"But what about the—"

"Unraveling souls?" she cut in, "I said I can't say it's impossible. But that doesn't mean it's probable. Besides, you've endangered lives to fight The Avatars before."

"That was different," he protested, "And that doesn't make it okay anyway. I was asking people to risk their lives to fight an obvious threat. This is risking unwitting souls for my own agenda."

"Well, if it makes you feel better," she said, "I did detect Arestor just before we returned. He had reconstituted and was no worse for wear."

Sinkua lifted his head and looked upon the arc of ruined houses. If Arestor could recover after so much time unraveling, most people could do it after a few minutes of pulling. The pain might be excruciating, but it would be brief. And they would recover. They might not even have time to feel anything.

"Wait a minute," Sinkua said, his face twisting with confusion and offense, "There's a separate afterlife for Etherworlders. How would you know what kind of shape Arestor is in?"

"…Damn."

"What?"

"You didn't know that," Phoenix said, "Not as Sinkua."

"Meaning it slipped through from a past life."

He felt Phoenix nod in affirmation.

"So, you lied to me to get me to go through with it?"

"Yes. I'm sorry," Phoenix said, "But you are correct that the pain would be brief. Mortvill used to pull on souls as a means of torture, and the survivors always recovered in short order."

"The survivors?" he asked, "Meaning people did die from it?"

"I knew I shouldn't have said that," she muttered, "Only in the most extensive of cases. This far removed, we'd need to be at it for hours for that to even be a risk."

"Well," he sighed as he got back to his feet, "I guess it was a pleasant lie. And you could be right about Arestor."

"We're deep in guesswork territory, and the only way to get answers is to try something," she said, "If you're ready, there are two bodies under this rubble. A man and a woman."

"Probably a couple."

"Their lives are foggy, but they appear to have only been neighbors."

Sinkua chuckled. "Another pleasant lie?"

"Believe whatever will move you forward."

Galo settled on a rock as Gijin sat on one across from him. At Galo's insistence, they had found a spot well removed from the river. The irony of his discomfort near water wasn't lost on either of them.

Galo closed his eyes as he tuned out the noise of spiritual bustle. Speaking in far more languages than he understood, the only thing more consistently indistinct than their forms was their words. Hopefully, that would change soon.

"I picked up a couple of new words when Metkhal was talking with Arestor," Galo said, "Durasarzim and Chizambal. Were those both Mberhali words?"

"Durasarzim is Pukoqeyen. It originated in Pukoqet, which is now Poravit," Gijin said, "Chizambal is Mberhali, however."

"Oh! Do you also know Pukoqeyen?" Galo asked, "Or does Metkhal? I might want to learn that one next."

"I know enough to ask for directions," Gijin said, "But unless he took to it after I first passed, Metkhal knows quite a bit less."

"Well, I should just be grateful that you can teach me Mberhali," Galo said, "I'll ask Arestor about Pukoqeyen. Or maybe I should go for Harkzanian next. It could be a good way to honor Sinkua's memory."

"It would be," Gijin said, "Now, getting back to Durasarzim and Chizambal. Those both translate to Distant Lands or Outer Lands."

"You mean there are islands outside of Ouristihra?" Galo asked, "Or there used to be?"

"I'm afraid I can't say for certain," Gijin said, "Names like that were speculative. Given the calculated size of the planet, it's unreasonable to think that all the landmass was in this one continent. But if anyone found more, they never came back to tell anyone."

"Okay… Okay," Galo said, his eyes wide as he took everything in, "I'm sorry. You were never open about this stuff when we were both alive."

"I'm sorry, but I had a façade to maintain."

"Oh no, I understand why you did it. But now, knowing what sort of things you know, I just want to dig into it."

"You always did have a thirst for the scholarly," Gijin laughed, "Now then, can we focus on learning Mberhali? And just Mberhali?"

"Of course. Of course!" Galo said, "Let's get to it. Teach me to say stuff like Mawakouteza and Chizambal like I know what I'm saying."

Gijin set into the basics of Mberhali compared to Ouristihran. He opened with the differences between the alphabets, more subtle than some other ancient languages but still necessary to know. Pukoqeyen, for one, had all but nothing in common, even being written from the right rather than the left.

Gijin was quick to move on from mentioning that before Galo could pull them onto yet another tangent. Not that they were short on time, Gijin considerably less so. Willing as Galo was becoming to accept that Sinkua's plan had a bit of merit, he had to work under the assumption that he would be here another hundred sixty years, give or take.

Malcontentment crept up in his thoughts, bitterness hijacking his focus. The urge to lash out, to prove himself superior, grew stronger. But when he looked to Gijin, the urge didn't feel as though it was directed toward him.

He considered that this could have been unreconciled spite for Sinkua, residual from The Prophet's influence. After all, he had died trying to save him. But he knew that wasn't Sinkua's fault. He no more set out to be captured than Vielle set out on a suicide mission.

"Grandson!" Gijin called out.

Galo snapped his focus back to Gijin.

"Are you still following?" Gijin asked.

"Sorry! Sorry, it's just…" Galo fumbled, "That forced empathy thing. Does it work even if you can't see the person?"

"I can't say for certain that it does for everyone," Gijin admitted, "But I have experienced it. Why do you ask?"

"I'm feeling spiteful all of a sudden. Like someone thinks they're better than me," Galo said, standing for a better view of his surroundings, "And I need to prove them wrong."

"Well, if you're that aware of your spite, I can assert you have indeed caught it from someone else."

"Well, well," came a third voice, "I've waited so long to find the two of you here."

Gijin rose as well, his face consumed with a level of concern previously unknown to Galo. They looked around for an origin, but nobody among the crowds of souls was looking their way.

"I don't see anyone," Galo said, "Where are you?"

"Wait there. I'll come to you," the voice said, "Get back from the stump. I have no reason to hurt you. This time."

Galo stepped away from his seat, and it wriggled and sank. He considered who the voice could have been, who could have been spiteful toward him because of feelings of inferiority. The fact that nobody came to mind worried him almost as much as how accustomed he was becoming to the feeling.

The stone stump vanished, followed by a rumbling under his feet. An upside-down spirit emerged through the hole, apparently from a patch on the underside not covered with crystalline structures. As it crested the edge of the hole, it flipped upright to reveal the face of the first person who Galo had ever truly hated.

"The Hunter," Galo snarled.

"Stay your hand, boy," he said, "I've got no use for quarrels with you or anyone here. And just call me Amirione."

"Okay. Amirione," Galo said, steadying himself, "What are you doing here?"

"What am I doing here? I was dead first. From the looks of you, I'd say by about ten years."

"Closer to seven. And that's not what I meant."

"I know what you meant, boy," Amirione said, "So how'd you go out? Which of them got you?"

"MalVek," Galo said, "I don't know if you know he was working with The Avatars. But he captured Sinkua and killed me when I went after him. I don't remember how."

"I know him but only by reputation. Never talked to him," Amirione said, "Doesn't surprise me he killed you."

"What's that supposed to mean?"

"Not what you think, obviously. Despite the quivering mess that you were when your masquerade granddad died, you were a tough little shit. Course it took someone with MalVek's reputation to get rid of you."

Galo regarded him for a moment. "So?" he drawled, "Is that all you wanted to know? Who killed me?"

"Nah, that wasn't all," Amirione said, "But it does bode well for why I've been on the lookout for you."

"Which is?"

"Did you ever cross paths with The Geneticist?"

"Crossed paths and fought him," Galo said, "My uncle threw me through a high-rise window. But Malia helped me stick the landing, and then we watched Leviathan eat him."

"Should've known Malia couldn't be trusted," Amirione muttered to himself. "Well, I was hoping you'd say the bastard'd been killed. Much as I don't expect you to care, you've made me a very happy man, Galo."

"I… have?" Galo puzzled, "I don't follow. Was Ebralgi a traitor? Were you?"

Amirione laughed pityingly. "Nothing of either sort," he said, "You know we all have our own lives and opinions, right? Avatar. Coalition. Imperial. Parliament. Doesn't matter. Not a monolith among them."

"Drop the monologues and get to the damn point."

"The short of it is that Ebralgi fucked me over, and I was hoping to live long enough to see him taken to task. Short of taking him myself."

"Okay, now I'm intrigued. What did he do to you?"

"Takes a bit of backstory, but I'll give it to you abridged," Amirione said, "I contracted some brittle bone thing. Forget what it was called, but it was terminal. Found The Avatars of Fate, figured I'd spend my last few years making a difference with them."

"And they gave you the bone reinforcement treatment?"

"You got it. But turned out that was terminal, too. Don't know if that was design or defect, but it doesn't matter now," Amirione continued, "The Harvester said if I got rid of Gijin, he'd have Ebralgi work on a cure."

"That's where his shifting state power came from?" Galo guessed.

"You're a quick one," Amirione said, somehow with as little sincerity as sarcasm, "Yeah. He tested it on himself and was so smitten, he forgot he was making it for me. Acted like I had nothing to do with it when I asked. Sure, it wouldn't have saved me from Spril and EshCal. But it's the principle."

"Damn," Galo muttered, "I didn't know there was so much in-fighting in The Avatars. And I guess I never considered that they could've coerced you into working with them."

Amirione laughed again. "I wasn't coerced, you dumb shit," he said, "Did you forget the part where I found them? I liked their social vision. Their aggressive political reform. All that shit. I wanted to spend my last years making the world I wish I could have lived in."

"If you saw what MalVek started, you wouldn't feel that way."

"Maybe not. Maybe so," Amirione said, shrugging, "All that matters now is that that shitstain Ebralgi is dead."

As Amirione turned back to the hole, Galo called out to him.

"Is there anything else you need to say?" Galo asked. Amirione shrugged. Galo gestured to Gijin. "Something about how you killed him?"

Amirione shot a glance toward Gijin, then turned back to Galo. "Why would I say anything about doing what needed doing? I didn't know Ebralgi would renege on his promise any more than you knew you were doing me a service when you killed him."

"I should've known an apology was too much to ask," Galo muttered.

"One common enemy doesn't even make us acquaintances, boy. Best I'll say is that if you leave me be, I'll reciprocate," Amirione said, "And if I feel like it, maybe I'll make—"

His face went blank, and his eyes rolled back as he stopped speaking. His face contorted, and he doubled over, screaming and babbling incoherently. More souls followed suit, the island speckling with shrieked gibberish.

Galo looked to Gijin, only to find his grandfather just as confused by the sudden madness. Galo turned his attention inward, consulting Metkhal. The closest thing to an explanation was that the apparent gibberish was an old language, but Metkhal couldn't pin it down, much less speak it.

Amirione came upright with an unfamiliar face, looking at least as fearful and confused as Galo felt. A new voice came with that new face, speaking in what sounded like the same unknown language.

"Grandfather?" Galo beckoned, "Does this have anything to do with why he was on the underside of the island?"

Gijin just shrugged and shook his head.

"Sin—"

Dim withered threads lashed through his thoughts. Decayed bones cracked against his fingertips.

"—inku—"

Crimson flashes blurred his mind's eye. Bloody bits of tongue sloshed through his teeth.

"Sink—"

Incomprehensible voices cried out in fits and bursts. Searing air ensconced him as every muscle tightened.

"—nkua!"

Disparate strands flashed as they reached for one another. The air thrummed before him. He opened his eyes only to see the last split second of an ephemeral rippling.

"—ku—"

His left eye twitched. A vein in the side of his neck pulsated. Cracks of milystic heat zigzagged down his arms.

"Sin—a!"

With a spiteful grunt, he slammed his fist through the gathering of bones, scattering them in a spray of sparks.

"—kua!"

Patches of flesh between the milystic cracks charred to a murky brick red. He ground his teeth so aggressively, he flaked off palpable enamel dust.

"Si—"

He threw his head back as a primal roar erupted from the depths of his lungs, unleashing a concussive heat wave that further scattered the remains.

"—nku—"

Flames parted the skin between his shoulder blades, spreading into a pair of wings. A single beat suspended him a meter off the ground. He twisted his brimstone body, aiming away from the sun.

Leaving a wake of scorched soil, Sinkua launched himself westward. Phoenix's voice within his mind fell silent.

Eytea and Elemeno watched with cautious regard as crowds of souls scattered. Panicked voices called out with words that Eytea couldn't understand, and she assumed neither could her mother.

Fear and confusion pounded Eytea's thoughts, overwhelming her with rusty orange flashes as the voices kept shouting. She huddled down and covered her ears. But though it dulled the voices, the flashes persisted, and the emotions grew so pressing that they became all but tangible.

A hand settled on her shoulder. Her mother's, she reasoned. But any comfort she found in that assumption dissipated when an unfamiliar voice disproved her.

"Stand, Odin Hybrid."

This voice, somehow, radiated equal portions nurturing and scolding. Grace and indignation. Gentleness and ferocity. It reminded her of her mother, had she had an upper-class upbringing.

Eytea looked up to find a svelte woman standing over her, well taller than Sinkua yet slenderer than herself. Curly blonde hair flowed down to just below her butt. Silverish blue feathers adorned with black markings draped from her shoulders to her knees.

"You understand me, yes?" she asked, "I am speaking your language, I do believe."

"Yes. Yes! Sorry," Eytea professed, reining in her emotions as she got to her feet, "Are you also a Valkyrie?"

"I am not, but that unburdens me of one question," the feather-adorned woman said, "Has a man named Bragi come through here?"

"I'm sorry, but I don't know who that is," Eytea said, "Do you think he had something to do with all of this?"

"I see Sigrdrifa spoke true," the woman muttered to herself. She regarded Eytea with an air of thin patience, "Such mischief as this is unlike him, but he is capable of such exploits as an Etherworlder of the artful word."

"There's an Etherworlder of, what? Stories and poems?" Eytea mused, "What's next? An Etherworlder of floral arrangements?"

"You would be not far from the truth," the woman said with that same indignant grace, "I am called Freja, Fjarthursk Etherworlder of love and fertility."

"So, you're literally a sex symbol?" Elemeno piped up from behind her.

Freja turned and regarded her with chilling pity. "Yes, I suppose the word fertility does have different meanings depending on the connotation," she said, "Luck be with you that both apply to me, else I might be just as offended by your misattribution as by your coarseness."

"Lady Freja?" Eytea beckoned, "Do you need us to help you find Bragi?"

"I do not. But I would know your name."

"Eytea. And that's my mother. Elemeno."

"Eytea and Elemeno. I see," Freja noted, "No, I have sought other Fjarthursk Etherworlders since I emerged here. I noticed Omphaloworlders speaking a Bealstillan dialect and thought he may have been responsible."

"I don't know what he looks like, but I didn't notice anyone acting sketchy," Eytea said, "So, when you say you emerged, do you mean out of the Etherworlder afterlife? Because Randgrid said something about somebody breaching it."

"I do indeed," Freja said, "Even those of us who fell victim to Pandora's Box went to the sanctuary of milystic souls. But something recently pulled me to this more tsoran plane. I thought the Etherworlder afterlife had thought to reject me."

"Randgrid thinks it was Phoenix," Eytea said, her thoughts calming as the crowds settled to curious murmurings, "She and Sinkua, who you might know as Tetsen Drukoa, resurrected Odin. Three of the Valkyries came back, too, but I don't think he knows he did that."

"A curious theory indeed," Freja said, "Should you meet any more Fjarthursk Etherworlders, you will tell them you and I have spoken, yes?"

"Sure thing."

"And tell me of them when next we cross paths."

"Of course," Eytea said, "I'll tell Eir, Randgrid, and Sigrdrifa that I met you when they check in with me."

"Thousand thanks, neophyte Odin Hybrid," Freja professed, "I take—"

"Wait!" Eytea beckoned, "When you say neophyte, do you mean… Well… I asked Randgrid already, but—"

"She told me," Freja interrupted, holding Eytea's shoulder, "You were hoping I might have some perception beyond hers, yes?"

"I was, yeah. So… Can you see my past lives?"

"I have no such capabilities as that," Freja said, "I can, however, tell that you have lived only one lifetime."

Eytea's jaw tightened. It wasn't the answer she was hoping for. But it was an answer, and that was as much as she could ask for.

"Thank you," she said, "for the closure at least."

"Open yourself to finding comfort in your truth," Freja said, "Now then, I take my leave. My warmest regards to your lover Sinkua."

"I'm sorry," Elemeno cut in again, drawing an impatient glare from Freja, "I have to ask. How do you and the Valkyries already speak Ouristihran if you've all been in the Etherworlder afterlife since before the language even existed?"

"What are you talking about? Most of us need only brief observations to learn Omphaloworlder languages," Freja said, "Yes, even those of us who lost our powers to Pandora's Box."

"Sorry, I didn't realize that was a stupid question," Elemeno defended, "Weird though. You speak cleaner Ouristihran than Odin did after a month in the living world."

"Curious indeed," Freja noted, her brow furrowing, "Though the abandon with which you asked so foolish a thing has me less embarrassed to ask what has nagged my thoughts since I came here."

"What's that?"

"Why is everyone walking on the bottoms of these islands?"

Chapter 5

Salty steam whipped around his brimstone body, suspended in flux between clinging to him and dissipating in the wind. Clusters of threads shimmered and faded beneath him as he passed. The odor of burnt fish persisted.

"Hold on," Eytea beckoned, "What are you talking about?"

"You understand you can walk at any orientation here, yes?" Freja asked, "This place has no objective sense of your up and down."

"Yeah, four spatial dimensions. I get that," Eytea said, "But what do you mean we're walking on the underside? Everybody's been on this side since I got here."

"If there's no up and down, how can there be an underside?" Elemeno asked, "There's just what everyone agrees is the topside."

"The bottoms are covered in crystals, anyway," Eytea argued, "They keep the islands in place."

"Is that what all of you believe?" Freja asked, "They do nothing of the sort. Those are ruins."

Galo peered into the hole. Bits of crystal rattled along the depth center, failing to gain enough momentum to fall through in either direction. He swiped some upward, and it shot out of the hole and scattered.

He consulted Metkhal through mental charades and broken Mberhali. The crystals had covered the bottoms of the islands after his lifetime. The mass conclusion at the time was that they balanced the islands. Galo found it hard to argue with his reasoning.

Galo asked about Amirione walking on the underside through a shared mind's eye visualization. Metkhal showed his altered presence as being Bealstillan, at least judging by his clothes.

Galo considered that the age of Amirione's soul might have allowed him to walk on the underside. The man was ancient from his ancestor's perspective, after all. Of course, it might have been that the crystals had always been safe to walk.

Galo rubbed a handful of the dust between his palms. It was coarse and warm, but nothing of particular concern happened. His hands felt heavy, but he chalked that up to the tingling sensation being reminiscent of extremities falling asleep.

Seeing no use in further pondering, Galo stepped into the hole.

The buffeting air dried. Scorched vegetation replaced the smell of burnt fish. Dust filled the cracks in his brimstone form. Some melted and dried on him. The rest scattered in the scalding wind.

"The Valkyries mentioned Shrines," Eytea said, "Is that what the crystals are?"

"They are the remains of them," Freja said, "If they remember our constructs, they ought to have drawn the connection to the crystals."

"They said they died long before the others," Elemeno said, "Maybe they just didn't witness the Shrines being destroyed?"

Freja regarded her out of the corner of her eye. "Meaning they last saw this place in its once splendor?" she asked.

"Exactly!" Elemeno said, "They died when this place was still intact and woke up in the aftermath."

"I… suppose that is not the worst hypothesis," Freja conceded, "They would be embarrassed to learn of their mistake, to be sure."

"I think they thought the rocks sticking up out of the ground were Shrine ruins," Eytea said.

"Those are the bottoms of the foundations," Freja clarified.

"Yeah, I figured," Eytea said, "But if everyone reincarnates every seven lifetimes, how does nobody here remember them?"

"Ooh yeah, that's a good question," Elemeno said, "Souls don't die, right?"

"Some which fall to the Netherworld are never to return," Freja said, "Though such a fate is exceedingly rare."

Eytea looked out to the clusters of souls. The panic had died out, and they looked to be going back to whatever they were doing before. Well, most of them did. A few kept wandering, drifting with purpose toward their own personal horizon.

"You said they were speaking Bealstillan, right?" she asked, to which Freja nodded, "Would they remember how this place used to look?"

"They would. The extinction of the Bealstillans precedes the destruction of the shrines. It was Pandora's first conquest in your world," Freja said, "You sound as though this thought has given you concern."

"It's just that I think they're trying to go to the underside."

"This is good. They look to reclaim and rebuild."

"… They won't fall off?"

"Of course not," Freja laughed, "Neither would any of you. They are simply old enough to remember."

"Well, that's a relief, I guess," Eytea said, "But it still leaves the question of why they all suddenly returned."

"Yes. I also worry for the shock they might experience when they see the crystal side."

"Why would they be in shock?" Eytea asked, "Haven't they seen it like this before? Like during other times here since their lifetime?"

"For perhaps the same reason others do not recall the shrines. Prior incarnations only remember their afterlife from their own lifetime," Freja clarified,

"Now then, I can speak not of your intentions, but mine are to help rebuild. Perhaps I might come to—"

Elemeno interrupted with a single gasped word. "Mortvill."

Galo hung in the air as he crested the hole on the underside of the island. His sense of balance flipped, causing him to feel upside down. Recalling Eytea's instructions to Sinkua, he leaned and willed himself to turn.

The crystals, it turned out, were harmless. Even standing on an entire landscape strewn with them caused no harm.

"Grandfather!" he called down the hole, "Come down here. It's safe." He looked out upon the stretches of prismatic shimmering. "And incredible."

Gijin emerged moments later. He and Galo shared their fascination at the long neglected crystalline field. As Takmet, he pondered with Metkhal how and how long ago this side came to be thought forbidden. Galo could only guess at their theories though, as he listened primarily for exposure to conversational Mberhali.

"Well, well," Gijin said, gesturing into the distance, "It would appear that Amirione gave others the same idea."

In every direction, souls emerged from the horizon.

The ground sank below him, the stink of burning vegetation giving way to scorched savory florality. Scores of mangled clusters of threads gathered. His wings dissipated to smoke, and he dropped into their midst.

The threads jostled as he landed. The ground softened against his feet. He reached for the nearest cluster.

Immense pressure coursed through his body as he set the threads aglow. As he withdrew his hand, the cluster receded, leaving an odor of searing flesh.

He reached for another, a stabbing sensation running down his torso. Just as before, this one came alight and retreated with a smell akin to undercooked meat.

Over and again, he rejuvenated the dimmed threads to the same consequence. Pain, the clearest sensation since he had set out for this place, rippled through his body, and the threads retreated.

Still, the faster he restored their spark of life, the deeper the surrounding air thrummed. Fractalized glimmers seeped through folds in the air. He reached for them as a cluster of shimmering threads retreated.

But he only buffeted the luminous ripples, and they settled into still air.

"What, pray tell, is Mortvill?" Freja asked, "And what might it have to do with any of this?"

"Mortvill is a who, not a what," Elemeno said, "He's the Tiamat Hybrid."

"Not the one I knew," Freja said, "But I suppose that is to be expected. The curse ought to have claimed the one I knew ages ago."

"Curse? What curse?" Eytea asked.

"It is not my place to discuss, but it is more that I wish not to digress further," Freja said, "Elemeno, what bearing do you suppose the Tiamat Hybrid has on this Bealstillan renaissance?"

"Yeah, and when did you get so much more familiar with him?" Eytea said, "Hell, I'm just now learning he was a Hybrid, but you sound like you got chummy with him."

"I worked with him. We teamed up to rescue Nikasu," Elemeno said, turning aside to tell Freja of Nikasu's Hybrid status, "and to expose a traitor in his ranks."

"You did what?!" Eytea exclaimed, "Okay. I need you to tell me everything as soon as possible."

"The quick version is that The Omnimath and The Harvester are both Mortvill, but The Omnimath came from the future to undo the damage that The Harvester caused," Elemeno said, "He brought MalVek, NalSet, and Chekov with him."

"The Tiamat Hybrid harnessed the power of Bahamut?" Freja asked.

"I don't know what that is, but I don't think their time travel was a Hybrid thing," Elemeno said, "But anyway, we're going off on a tangent here."

"Yes, of course," Freja said, "Apologies of my own and on her behalf as well."

"Okay, so Mortvill had been consuming souls to keep himself young," Elemeno said, "What if he took all the souls who existed before the Grand Genocide? Or at least before Bealstilla was destroyed? And now that he's dead, they're coming back."

"That would have to be millions of souls," Eytea protested, "There's no way he took that many. My being a neophyte wouldn't be so strange if he did."

"The logistics do not quite pass muster, as they say," Freja said.

"Yeah, like the fact that they had reincarnated since then," Eytea said, "Unless they, what? Somehow got imprinted on other souls here?"

"Your hypothesis is a decent enough starting point, however," Freja said, "He would only need to consume enough for those remaining to be strangers. But might I ask how he died? Particularly at whose hand?"

"The Harvester killed The Omnimath," Elemeno said.

"And Sinkua killed The Harvester," Eytea said.

"The Phoenix Hybrid, yes?" Freja confirmed, "Well I suppose that could have some bearing on this. As I said though, there are logistical issues to your idea, but they would no be impossible to resolve."

"Well, you speak Bealstillan, right?" Eytea asked.

"Of course I do, and I see where you are taking this thought," Freja said, "Come, join me in rebuilding with them. I will ask of their prior whereabouts."

Glimmers of grand architecture flashed through Galo's mind. Metkhal pulled at the rear of his thoughts, but this had a greater sense of depth than previous times. It felt like his consciousness was being coaxed toward something beyond Metkhal's presence.

He closed his eyes to consult Metkhal. Unfortunately, he still didn't know enough Mberhali to be even piecemeal conversational. Whatever Metkhal was trying to show him, Galo couldn't make sense of it from mental charades.

When he opened his eyes, the architecture flashed stronger than before. The luminous burst set Galo wincing back into consultation with Metkhal.

He opened his eyes slowly this time. The crystal architecture wasn't as bright. Nor was it opaque anymore. But it had persisted much longer than before. And all the while, that pull from deeper in his thoughts remained steady and strong.

"Galo?" Gijin beckoned, "You appear unwell. Would you like to go back?"

Galo shook his head. "Metkhal's trying to show me something. Or tell me something. I don't know," he said, "He needs to talk to Takmet."

Flames roared across the basin at the sweep of his arm. Muffled screams rippled through the pounding noise of thoughts. Shimmering clusters of threads dulled and collapsed.

Fire sprouted between his shoulder blades. The ground vanished. The wind howled. A fallen cluster moved beneath him.

Dull pain pulsated throughout himself. The cluster came alight again.

Another rush of wind. Another rekindled bundle of threads below his feet.

And another.

And another.

Every time with that same throbbing pain, bearing down more and more with each repetition.

The air rippled more aggressively. Fractalized light pierced it more starkly.

But it fell apart like cobwebs when his hand passed through.

The ground rushed at him. And as it struck his feet, the whole basin came ablaze. Another howling of wind, and the darkened threads atrophied within his thoughts.

Eytea paused at the edge of the island to let her mother catch up. They stepped off the edge and, with a sensation quite like leaving her crafted den, flipped around to the underside of the island.

Down here, souls bustled about with the same sense of purpose but a lesser sense of harmony. They gathered the crystals into piles, but the piles never persisted. The souls appeared unbothered though, moving on to the next often before the crystals finished scattering.

"Oh goodness," Elemeno gasped. She stumbled and grabbed Eytea's shoulder, pulling her into a sudden crouch.

"Yeah, it's really something," Eytea said, hoisting herself and her mother back upright.

"You... You don't see that, too?"

"All the people trying to make crystal sandcastles?"

"No, the..." Elemeno hesitated, "I keep seeing buildings. It's like I'm imagining what they're building."

"Must be the Shrines that Freja and the Valkyries were talking about," Eytea reasoned, "Being around the Bealstillans must be triggering flashbacks."

"But if I knew them, why didn't I turn, too?"

Eytea shrugged. "We don't even know for sure why they turned," she said, "We just have a theory that Mortvill and Sinkua have something to do with. Oh, and also Mortvill."

"Well, we can't talk with them like Freja can," Elemeno considered, "But maybe I can make sense of it while we build with them."

"I can't imagine what you're trying to show him that the two of you don't have the words for," Takmet said, "Did I overestimate how much Mberhali I've taught him?"

"No, it's at least as much my fault," Metkhal admitted, "I know less Ouristihran than he does Mberhali."

"Well, Leviathan and I have already had more of an impact than I'm comfortable with on his mental state. I'd ask that you not make matters worse for him," Takmet said, "Now, what were you trying to show him?"

"I have memories of how this place used to look. But they're not mine."

"Another of your past selves?"

"One of Tsenukoa's."

"Oh? And how have you come to have their memories?" Takmet asked, "Could this be a residual effect of safekeeping the Phoenix Ruby for him?"

"That's not what—"

"Though were that the case, I should think I would have experienced the same by now."

"I don't mean—"

"Unless being in copper protected me from it."

"Dad!" Metkhal exclaimed, "I don't literally have their memories. It's from one of the books."

"Oh! You should've said so in the first place," Takmet said, "Which one?"

Metkhal pinched the bridge of his nose, opting to ignore that comment lest they go even further off course. "Rhobhan Porywyd. Ninth in the collection."

"You know, I thought about skipping to that one," Takmet recalled, "I spent so long making so little progress on Leatinia Kuvrakh's book."

"Ёžoraci is a tricky language," Metkhal commiserated, "But it was Motanos in the second half."

"Who's Motanos? Her son?"

"No, Motanos is Leatinia."

"Ah, how interesting," Takmet said, "Well then, after you finished with, ah, Mister Kuvrakh's book, what did you find in Mister Porywyd's?"

"Someone that Rhobhan resurrected drew pictures of shrines made of crystal. The sky looked just like it does here," Metkhal said, "He included them in his book."

"The closest thing to photographic evidence of the afterlife."

"Photo-what?"

"Ah right, I suppose that technology is, well, after your time," Takmet said, "In any case, I'll clear this up with Galo."

"Thanks. I'm hoping we can use what I remember to rebuild them," Metkhal said, "At the very least, having landmarks ought to make it easier to search for Epesol."

"A daunting but noble task, indeed," Takmet said, "Although we haven't accounted for how these people reverted to their Bealstillan incarnations."

Metkhal closed his eyes for a moment. "Galo says Sinkua killed ... Mortvill? The Tiamat Hybrid in their time," he said, "That could have something to do with it, all the souls that he freed."

As he neared the stench of seared bronze and stone, he changed course to zero in on the lingering odor of his own burning flesh. No hope was to be found in that wasteland. Nor in any other.

Visions of Seriamus consumed his thoughts.

And the air grasped his neck with thorny fingers.

The Bealstillans proved standoffish toward outsiders. Especially ones who spoke a language that they didn't recognize.

Eytea considered they may have also found her wings off-putting. Neither Odin nor his Hybrid had destroyed their homeland. Nor had they shut them out of surfacing here with later incarnations. But they had failed to protect them from either.

In fact, after so thorough a genocide, the Bealstillans would have been justified in looking at all Hybrids with disdain. Only two had destroyed them, but nobody else helped them. Eytea, or any Hybrid, must have looked quite audacious showing up like nothing was wrong.

Then again, they could have been put off because a mass of amorphous schmutz just sat down and started stacking crystals with them.

Still, the more she fortified their mounds against a spiteful sense of gravity, the more they warmed up to her. Well, the less cold they were, anyway. From what little she could distinguish of their faces, they weren't completely averse to brief eye contact.

"Honey!" Elemeno called out.

Eytea and the Bealstillan stranger both jumped hard enough to scatter the ankle-high stack of crystal fragments. The smoky humanoid faced her squarely and scolded her in Bealstillan. But something about their tone was less than accusatory. It was almost jovial. Sarcastic at the very least.

Perhaps she was being more quickly accepted than she thought. This one was taking to her well enough.

"Eytea!"

She apologized, more in body language than words, and headed off to her mother.

"What is...?"

She trailed off as she saw what had her mother calling so urgingly. Galo had also found his way down here along with a companion that she couldn't recognize at this distance. She looked back and excused herself, quite forgetting the language barrier in her excitement, and hurried off to catch up with him.

"Galo!" she remarked as they reached speaking distance, "Good to see you again. Who's your...?"

She stopped as mutual familiarity foisted shape upon his companion. It had been most of her life since the first and last time she had seen him. But only one person could have commanded reverence so unbefitting his frame and stature.

"Chieftain Sage Gijin," she managed, "Pleasure to see you again. Despite the circumstances, I mean."

"Ahh. Eytea. It's been a while," Gijin said, "Galo told me what happened. We've also discussed Sinkua's plan to cheat Phoenix's limitations."

"Do you think it's possible?" she asked, "If he doesn't get back, could a piece of his ruby really let me use Epesol to cut a way out?"

"You've reached the same conclusion, then?" Gijin asked, "That Sinkua intends to return here?"

"It's wishful thinking, if I'm being honest," Eytea said, "Just, someone said it didn't look like any reincarnation he'd seen, so I'm hoping, y'know, maybe."

"Well, it's a hope worth holding. Mortvill has a similar theory."

"Thank you. That actually helps to know," she said, "But Epesol with a piece of the Phoenix Ruby. Feasible or no?"

Gijin shrugged. "I'm sorry, but that's not for me to say. I'm not the infallible Hybrid authority you might think."

"Yeah, he just knew more than anyone else we could trust," Galo said, "Turns out I knew more about our history than him."

Gijin laughed and elbowed him.

"Okay, fine, it wasn't quite me," Galo confessed, "I'm actually the reincarnation of Metkhal, his son from before he was trapped in copper."

"Well, isn't that just wild?" Eytea bemused, "You can consult yourself about your family history, and I have no history at all."

"…Sorry?"

"No, that's on me," Eytea sighed, "Sorry, I've been trying to help the Bealstillans, but most of them are standoffish, and I don't know if it's because I'm the Odin Hybrid or a Hybrid at all or because pretty much everyone sees me as a shapeless blob."

"I, um…" Galo fumbled, "Wait. Why would you look shapeless?"

"I didn't get to tell you this earlier, but I didn't have any past lives," she said, "I didn't know for sure until later. But well, I'm guessing you've figured out how this place works."

Galo nodded. "There could be billions of souls here, but only a few knew you through one degree or less."

"Right. Even if these Bealstillans can distinguish people from their later lifetimes, they probably didn't know me."

"I'm sorry," Gijin interjected, "How did you conclude that they're Bealstillans?"

"Freja told us that's what they were speaking."

"What is she doing here?" Gijin asked.

"Same thing as the Valkyries," she said, shrugging, "Trying to figure out what they're doing here. Except now she's trying to figure out what the Bealstillans are doing here. The Valkyries are also looking for Epesol and my engagement ring."

"It sounds like a lot happened since we split up," Galo said, "Show me what you're working on, and I'll join in while we catch each other up."

"That sounds like the best thing," Eytea said, "Oh! And later I can show you my home!"

"Your... home?" Galo puzzled, "Sure. While we're at it, maybe you could tell me how and where you managed that?"

The ground rattled. The thorny grip subsided.

"Sin—"

The tension throughout his body subsided as dried brimstone flaked away.

"—kua!"

Thunder barreled through the clouds, rattling the ground again.

"Sinkua!"

His eyes flared as they opened. He took a lungful as quickly as the thunder sucked it out of him. He doubled over as he gathered his senses.

"Sinkua!" Phoenix called, her voice finally coherent, "Look up. Straight ahead."

Halfway to the horizon, Odin sat upon Sleipnir with his spear held aside.

"I was foolish to think you would grow in your solitude," Odin bellowed, "All you have grown is more insolent. Is this your gratitude for my tending to your resurrection?"

"Hey, we finally have something in common," Sinkua called back, "I regret resurrecting you, too."

Odin struck the ground with the butt of his spear. Lightning struck several points around Sinkua, singing the ash and dirt to flakes of brittle glass.

"Sinkua! You leave me no choice but to cast judgment upon you," Odin announced as he brought his spear to his shoulder, "Stand still."

"Phoenix?" Sinkua beckoned, "What's happening? Why can't I move?"

"Just go with it."

Odin rode forth, holding the spear steady despite the aggression in Sleipnir's gallop.

"Why can't I move?!" Sinkua shouted, "Did that bastard just paralyze me?"

Phoenix remained silent. Sinkua stared down the dual threat of Odin and Sleipnir. But as they neared, he and Sleipnir made just enough eye contact to catch what he could have sworn was a knowing glance.

"This won't hurt," Phoenix said, "But you need to trust me."

"What won't—"

Before he could finish, Odin hurled the spear with a thunderous bellow, both hard enough to shake the ground. Bewildered despite Phoenix's promise, Sinkua felt nothing as the spear passed through him with no more disturbance than a fluid rippling of his flesh.

Odin leaned as he closed in. Sleipnir narrowed his eyes. Sinkua braced himself, still immobilized. The spear punctured the ground far behind him.

"He's giving you what you want," Phoenix said, "But you'll need to be quick once we cross."

"I'm changing the terms," Sinkua said, "There's one more thing."

He fixated on Sleipnir, hoping Phoenix took the same cues from the look in his eyes.

Odin swiped at Sinkua, only for Sleipnir to lose his footing the instant before contact. One misplaced hoof set the beastly equine stumbling and jostled Odin off balance.

Sinkua's paralysis relented. He struck Odin's forearm and rolled his hand around to lock him in an underarm grip. But as Sinkua dug his feet in and pulled back, Odin resisted as Sleipnir regained his footing.

Instead, Odin lifted Sinkua with Sleipnir having scarcely lost his stride. But Sinkua controlled the grip and pressed his feet on Sleipnir's side. Sleipnir kicked and bucked as he ran. Odin pointed straight ahead. Sinkua followed his hand to find a portal rippling around the head of the spear.

It looked like sheets of crystal through stained glass. But with a twist and flick of Odin's wrist, the portal darkened and crackled. Smoke and faint screams seeped through.

Fist engulfed in flame, Sinkua lunged at Odin. Sleipnir bucked hard, giving Sinkua a boost of momentum. Sinkua's fist met hard straight across Odin's face. He rammed him as he came atop Sleipnir's back and pulled his arm into a hammer lock.

With one more effortful buck, Sleipnir discarded Odin, and Sinkua released his arm to let him fall.

"I take it that's the Netherworld?" Sinkua asked, as Sleipnir showed no sign of stopping or changing course.

"You take it correctly."

"Can we get to the other place from there?"

"It's not impossible."

"That'll have to do."

An amalgam of pain like suffocation, starvation, drowning, and hundreds of hot knives and electrical prods bore down on Sinkua as he passed through the portal. His mind swallowed by torment, the moment stretched and compressed into both years and an imperceptible blink in nonexistent time.

Sinkua only realized it had passed once Sleipnir knelt to let him off. He paused to take stock.

The black sky crackled and pulsated with sickly red flashes. Noxious puddles and fumes seeped from a ground that both burned and froze long idle feet. Nigh palpably dense noise rattled him to his bones. And fractalized smears swept the edge of his periphery with neither pattern nor purpose.

Sleipnir huffed and nudged him. He turned to see the horse with his head lowered.

"Thank you," Sinkua said, "Poor guy. I guess you really wanted to get away from Odin, huh?"

He rubbed Sleipnir's nose, but as he made contact, a voice flowed into his thoughts.

"Thank you as well, Sinkua," it said.

"Sleipnir?" Sinkua thought, leaving his hand on the horse's face.

"Yes. This is the only way I can speak to you," Sleipnir said, "I am pleased that you picked up on my intentions."

"What do you plan to do now?"

"Something has changed in Odin."

"You mean he's not always a self-righteous blowhard?"

"Hah!" Sleipnir guffawed, "Not so much as this."

"So, you think he's been... what? Corrupted?"

"I can only hope the change is external. That should prove easier to counter than a change of heart."

"Can Phoenix and I do anything to help?"

"Carry out your plan. Returning Eytea to the living world may serve to sus out the root."

"Well, it's nice to hear you believe in my plan," Sinkua said, "What are you going to do?"

"The change started while we were in the Yggdrasil Void," Sleipnir said, "Much of Odin's ability to cross realms is my own. Thus, my first methods are to be exploratory."

"Can you take me with you?"

"I'm sorry but no. My journey cannot take me through the tsoran afterlife," Sleipnir insisted, "But I can do this for you."

Sleipnir's skin glowed around Sinkua's hand. Sinkua's eyes warmed as his periphery shimmered. When the light settled, the fractal smears persisted. In fact, they stretched into the fore of his sight, whirling and snaking as they converged into a tangled mess.

"The rivers in the tsoran afterlife connect to the Netherworld," Sleipnir explained, "But only by seeing clearly here can you perceive them with constant certainty. The task of reaching and passing through them, however, is yours. Appealing for the aid of a beastkin would prove wise, were you able to find one."

"Wow," Sinkua gasped, the complex splendor distracting him from the pain for perhaps a second, "Thank you, Sleipnir."

"I take my leave now," Sleipnir insisted, "Do send any pertinent developments my way. I will reciprocate."

Sleipnir galloped off on a slight upward trajectory. But as he vanished into the darkness, that dim sense of hope faded.

Not because Sleipnir was gone. Rather, it was a voice, unfamiliar but shaking his subconscience with rusty fingernails.

"Well, well. Of all the places we could meet again," the voice said, "Although, strictly speaking, we never quite met the first time."

Sinkua steeled himself as he turned around.

"But I've long thought of you as the son I never had."

Chapter 6

Though sallow and emaciated by the Netherworld, this man exuded an air of familiarity. His eyes had a certain glimmer of assurance behind layers of spite and neglect.

"As I thought. You don't remember me. You were quite… catatonic in my presence," the man said with flashes of another form flickering, "And you would only hear me referred to as The Scout."

"Kabehl," Sinkua grumbled, his stomach folding in on itself, "Eytea's father. In genetics anyway."

"I am no father to that abomination!" Kabehl bellowed, "I was saddled with raising her and had no say in the matter."

Scarcely had the last word left his mouth before Sinkua delivered a backhand punch across Kabehl's jaw. But they both cried out as both their bones shattered. Blood filled the new gaps in Kabehl's mouth as Sinkua's arm hair became caked in crimson.

"Best not to give in to your anger here, boy," Kabehl said, "I've been putting up with it a lot longer than you."

Sinkua considered explaining the cost of his powers of resurrection, but he soon decided otherwise. Better to let this leech believe he was more seasoned at enduring pain.

The flickers of another form endured for longer, almost a full second at a time now. Coarse fur covered his legs. He had horns like a ram's. And though Sinkua couldn't be sure, his feet looked rather more like hooves.

"Ahh, the pain's getting to you, isn't it?" Kabehl goaded, "Fucking with your memories? Which version of me are you seeing?"

Sinkua's thoughts receded. A feminine voice spoke reassuringly as he entered a state of wakeful sleep. But he didn't recognize it as Phoenix's.

And he couldn't understand it.

"Kervatus," she snipped, "Of course you ended up here."

"I know not what you speak of, Miss Aroka," the hooved man said, "I had only the best intentions for my people."

"Far be it from me to dictate the affairs of fauns," Miss Aroka conceded, "But enslaving your kin to satyrs isn't what I'd call the best intentions."

"What a foul word. Slaves," Kervatus dismissed, "They were a detriment to faunkind. More for the greater good that they live among the satyrs. How the satyrs integrated them was their own prerogative."

"You knew damn well what they would do with them!"

"And what if I did?" Kervatus challenged, "Look at you, casting judgment on me as you stand in the same fuckforsaken Netherworld."

"I'm here by my descendant's accord," she insisted, "Odin judged us falsely."

"Oh, I'm sure a Fjarthursk Elder God has nothing better to do than meddle in the affairs of an Azzelegna and a Harkzanian," Kervatus snipped, "Tell me, Fetzikzi. Did Pluto tell you to judge me? Or is Hades still shoving his nose anywhere but his own fucking business?"

Sinkua called out a warning from the back of Fetzikzi's thoughts. But with the language barrier undamaged, he could only brace for reciprocity as she scorched Kervatus's leg fur with a sweep of her hand. The back of her hand boiled, the sensation dulled to feel, to Sinkua, reminiscent of punching the barrier around the Triad Titan.

Sinkua focused on the recent memory of breaking his hand against Kabehl's jaw. Fetzikzi grumbled something incoherent, but her discontentment and understanding were both clear.

She relinquished control, fading into their shared subconscious space, while Sinkua resurfaced. He glimpsed the faun Kervatus before he gave way to Kabehl.

"Curious. I hadn't seen him before," Kabehl said, "Tell me, boy. What did you do that Odin would send you here?"

"Let's just say we didn't see eye to eye."

"Did you let his precious Hybrid die?"

Sinkua's throat tightened. He clenched his jaw and fists. Smoke wafted from his shoulders.

"How did you—?"

"Lucky guess," Kabehl said, "You sounded guilty when you called me her father."

"Well, the bastard let on that I gave him plenty of reasons to hate me over my lifetimes," Sinkua said, "Failing Eytea is the biggest reason I hate myself. But he doesn't give her the same priority."

"You ignorant ass," Kabehl scolded, laughing, "Do you even know what she is? What she truly is?"

"Oh, I understand her far better than you ever tried to," Sinkua snapped, "You were too busy trying to see your reflection in Mortvill's ballsack to be bothered with her or Elemeno."

"It's almost endearing to see a monster try to appeal to emotions," Kabehl deflected, "The way you emulate humanity is almost indistinguishable from the real thing."

"Keep running your mouth, Kabehl. See where it gets you," Sinkua said, "Just know I've got a shot at getting out of here, so only one of us will be stuck with the injuries I'm willing to share with you."

"Oh, I'm sure you do," Kabehl said, "But you should know there's more to Eytea than either of you realize."

From the back of his mind, Fetzikzi pleaded through visual memories not to give in to his curiosity. If Kabehl was as much like Kervatus as she thought, it was best not to give him any more of a soapbox.

Sinkua persisted despite this.

"She told me about the dreamwalking the day we met," Sinkua said, "It's how we found Nikasu."

"Part of much grander machinations," Kabehl said, unmoved by the assertions, "Odin had her forged to secure his legacy against Pandora. But she was always doomed to fail. And to bring about her own destruction."

"Well, she brought Odin out of the Yggdrasil Void. And Ozzera killed her," Sinkua said, "So, so much for your stupidass prophecy."

"She hasn't even attempted to fulfill his purpose for her. And her being dead is a nonissue."

"Why are you telling me this? If you saw me in captivity, you should know I'll try to stop it."

"That's why I'm telling you, you arrogant ass," Kabehl said, "The only pleasure left to me is hearing about the madness of a world too blind to understand my vision. And what better than stories of a dimwitted incarnation of the chronically failing Phoenix Hybrid challenging fate and the will of an Elder God?"

"Shit in a shoebox, you're a mouthy little fuck," Sinkua derided, "But I've got nothing to prove to you. I'm off to 'challenge an Elder God,' whatever the fuck that means. You can just wait here and stew in your stupid choices."

"Nothing you do will matter," Kabehl said, stepping aside as Sinkua approached to pass, "You could tell her everything. Her eventuality will remain inevitable."

The air thrummed so palpably that Sinkua strained his neck when he looked up to the rivers. The ground softened and hardened as he walked, taking his foot to the ankle and locking it in place until he jostled free. He ballparked each step at about ten seconds, as much as he could rely on his sense of time.

"Fetzikzi?" he thought.

No response.

"Miss Aroka?" he said aloud.

"She can't hear you," Phoenix said, "It doesn't work that way."

"What do you mean?" Sinkua said, "We talked to each other with Kabehl and the goat man."

"That was a faun named Kervatus. And that's why you could convene with her," Phoenix said, "You can't call on your prior selves on a whim."

"Well, that's a bitch," Sinkua grumbled, "I was going to ask her about Odin's Hybrid in her time."

"You're wondering if she had insights about what Kabehl said?" Phoenix guessed, "About Odin's legacy and Eytea?"

"For one, yeah."

"He wasn't Kervatus's son."

"... What?"

"That's the other thing you wanted to know, right?" she asked, "If Kabehl and Kervatus were both the father of an Odin Hybrid?"

"I was more wondering if he always chose a woman," he said.

"You wanted to know if you were a lesbian in a prior life?" she asked, snickering at his bashfulness, "Well, you were, but not as Fetzikzi. You've also been a gay man and even asexual and pansexual."

"The gay man was Tetsen Drukoa, right?" Sinkua asked, shuddering at a sudden change in temperature, "I picked up on it when I was talking with Eytea and Lhangat. I was engaged to his son, right?"

"Yes. Kanet Lhangatssen," she said, "Odin left Gungnir with him before he entered Yggdrasil."

"So, that's what the spear is called."

Viscous fluids roiled from the ground, eroding the soles of his feet in a sensation between chewing and burning. His eyes rolled back as he choked back the urge to vomit. But just as his bones were exposed, the sinew reconstituted, and his flesh grew back.

As soon as he started to grow accustomed to any extreme in the air, it would change. The shifts were often so great as to strike him with a sense quite like motion sickness.

"Something is bothering me," Phoenix said after a prolonged silence.

"I thought you couldn't feel the air from in there," Sinkua guessed, "Or is it how empty this place is?"

"I did think we'd find more people here, but that's an issue for another time," she said, "No, it's the fact that you and Fetzikzi Aroka could convene at all."

"But you said it yourself. It's because she knew a past version of Kabehl," he reasoned, "We have a shared connection."

"Yes, but you're here in your physical body."

"What difference does that make?"

"Your past incarnations taking conscious prominence should only be possible without a body. As should seeing other people's past incarnations," Phoenix explained, "As you are, Fetzikzi shouldn't have been able to talk to Kervatus."

"And yet, they spoke at length," Sinkua realized, "Kervatus even saw me as Miss Aroka. So, what do you think it means?"

"I don't know and could rationalize any number of theories," Phoenix said, "But I'm worried that this portends more of your past life memories spilling out."

"It sounds like the Phoenix Ruby wasn't one of my better plans."

"Well, you didn't think any of your future selves would break me out and assimilate me."

"Would or could?"

"Both, but more the first."

"So, what do we do about the memory leak and shifting incarnations?"

"Short of being careful who we speak with, I don't know that there's anything we can do," she said, "The shifting is only an issue in the afterlife though. We'll make as short of work of your plan as possible and look into the memory leak once we're back."

"Is that what you were talking about when you said we'd need to be quick?"

"I'd love to tell you it was, but you're too good at telling when I'm lying for your comfort."

The air clamped his throat as Sinkua chuckled, the very environment spiting any sign of amusement.

"What was it, then?"

"The tsoran afterlife includes four spatial dimensions. You won't be able to see clearly or navigate," she warned, "The longer you spend there, the more susceptible you'll be to madness or immobility."

He hadn't considered that aspect of the afterlife. Honestly, he wasn't sure if he had even been aware of it. He had been able to see and navigate the tsoran afterlife and had rationalized it all in a three-dimensional mindset.

Now, he'd be a sheet of paper looking for pebbles in a refrigerator box. Or like Phylus shooting with only one eye.

An epiphany began to set in, more of a slow burn than a sudden realization. Those goggles had caused Phylus to see and interact in four dimensions and restored his depth perception after he lost an eye. They were effectively an extra eye.

He sat on the festering ground as it clamped his knees.

"What about Lhangat?" he asked, "I mean, what if we can find him?"

"To what end?"

"He knew Tetsen and met me as Sinkua," he explained, "When he was talking to Tetsen, it felt like both of us were in control. Or conscious prominence as you put it. Maybe we could recreate four-dimensional sight."

"I suppose it wouldn't hurt to try," Phoenix said, "Tetsen was a sight shorter than you. I can't say with any confidence that it would work, mind you. But you won't need to find Mister Leyessen. Galo will do."

"Really? How?"

"He's the reincarnation of Metkhal, son of Takmet and close friend of Tetsen Drukoa," she said, "I don't know why they didn't speak when you and Galo found each other, but working through the silent treatment should prove easier than finding Lhangat again."

"Galo just sort of stayed off to the side when I was talking to Eytea and Lhangat," he recalled, "I guess he felt Metkhal surfacing and didn't know what was happening."

Empowered by a plausible workaround, Sinkua pushed himself upright. As much as he had to subsist on the faintest of hope, it did nothing about the fact that he had sunken to halfway up his thighs. The screams grew louder as he wriggled against his confines.

Noxious fumes pierced and clamped his throat from within. His vision throbbed and thrummed. He closed his eyes, fighting for control of his senses, but the pulsations permeated his mind's eye.

One arm began to move through no will of his own.

"Trust me. I know your intentions," Phoenix said, "The air isn't affecting me."

That hand settled upon the ground with firm pressure. The ground shifted and roiled to swallow it down to the wrist. It then became hard and brittle.

His other hand came ablaze as it lifted, then hammered the hardened ground. Fragments of heated stone sprayed from the point of impact, semi-liquefying into scalding gelatin.

Sinkua drew in a sharp breath, fortified by this minor victory. He had almost unbound his thighs. He pounded the side of the hole, but it did little to release his knees. With the ground creeping back up his quads, he surged milystis through his fists as he bombarded his confines with sledgehammer punches.

He paused as the screaming grew louder and now more distinctive. It wasn't a single voice after all. There were several. More than he had time to count.

Silhouettes cropped up along the horizon, dotting the expanse with an uncountable stretch of figures. They rattled in time with the screams.

"What are those things?" Sinkua asked, freeing his knees.

"Integrated souls," Phoenix said, taking control of his arms as he stopped in his stupor, "Those who fail for too long to prove worthy of reincarnation become a feature of this place."

"It turns old evil souls against the new ones?"

"Not the finest point you could put on it, but yes," she said, "And there's no reasoning with them. They have no autonomy left to them."

With the silhouettes closing in, he and Phoenix broke his legs free of their caustic confines. Toxic soil stung against his exposed sinew, but he had little time to wait for his skin to reconstitute.

"Can I fight through them?" he asked, "Or am I going to have the same problem I had with Kabehl?"

"There's no reciprocity with them," she assured, "But they also don't experience pain, and dismemberment will do little to hinder them. If any part of them can move, they will persist."

"So, it's a matter of numbers and tenacity," he said, "I'll break through and make a run for it."

"That would be wisest. Not even you could kill them. They'll reassemble from themselves from each other's parts," she said, "Failing that, this place will rebuild them."

As endodermis poured into his calves, Sinkua shuffled onward. The wall of silhouettes had now stretched across all horizons, surrounding him. The longer he waited, the more tightly they would close ranks. But the sooner he charged, the more fatigued he would be when he reached them. And it was all but impossible to judge distance here.

The nearest silhouettes gained the faintest of faces. None of them looked entirely human. But the more pressing matter was that this threshold was the best sign he could hope for.

Sinkua choked back a war bellow as he charged the line. He drew his morningstar and unbound the chain, spiked ball bouncing and swaying in his wake. A spike of milystis from Phoenix set it aflame.

His own scattered shadows danced around his feet. The oozing noxious substance sizzled under his milystic fire. Soft ground hardened and fragmented into patches of igneous rubble.

The uncountable screaming silhouettes became throngs of gnashing and snarling creatures. Their very flesh was, in a word, uncertain. Deepest blackness served as a backdrop for negative iridescence. Limbs sprouted from places they ought not to have and bent in ways they had even less business doing so.

But they all had a sense of core presence, as though to show what they had last been. Still none of them looked entirely human. This gave Sinkua the slightest pause.

"Focus!" Phoenix snapped.

An arm of rippling void lashed at him. He choked back his fear that this had been the fate of the activated just soon enough to pivot around the arm. Sinkua whipped his fiery morningstar at the assailant, goring and searing the anti-iridescent torso.

As Phoenix had warned, it showed no signs of pain. A second swing took a chunk out of a leg, toppling it. But just as it fell, another set of appendages snaked under Sinkua's arm.

He pivoted into it, clasping the appendages and stretching them across his chest. They sizzled and boiled against the heat coursing along his keraunographic scars. He twisted and wrenched the limbs until they broke away from their body with a most sickening snap.

Faces both mammalian and reptilian, as well as many he couldn't classify, swarmed him. Their breath enveloped his head and trickled down his neck. Ice cold and boiling hot all at once. Cloyingly sweet but sour with rot. Palpably thick yet so thinning the air as to trouble his breathing.

He swung his morningstar through the densest gathering, leaving an aerial trail of flames through neither his nor Phoenix's will. Their breath, apparently, was flammable. Punching through the trail to deliver a blazing uppercut to a reptilian biped left him with burns on his hand.

Once it subsisted on their breath, the fire was no longer his own.

Two swings of his morningstar created two rings of fire around himself, scorching any creature that breached it. As much as this threshold held them back though, he couldn't move forward either. The longer he stalled to weigh his options, the more tightly they closed in.

He took his chances on shuffling forward and deploying two more rings, overlapping the first pair. Gritting his teeth, he lunged through the first two rings, but the pain of even so brief of contact was enough to knock him backward.

His back struck the other side of the fiery barrier, crying out as his skin sizzled for a second time in disorientingly rapid succession. He dropped to his hands and knees.

The creatures kicked at him, anti-iridescent limbs roiling as they reshaped into more flexible forms. But as quickly as they had noticed his vulnerability, Sinkua figured out an opportunity.

Shielding himself with milystic heat, he lunged under the first barrier. Any creature that dared grab at him had their skin all but boil on contact. He passed the next barrier with a second lunge, and with a third, he tackled a bird-headed cat.

Black steam hissed out as he pressed into its malleable flesh. But as his hands found the ground behind it, he became lightheaded.

Phoenix seized control to pull him to his feet. Three swings of his morningstar created just as many rings of fire. A shot at the ground scattered the gored creature at his feet..

"That isn't sustainable," Phoenix said, "but it got us some ground."

"What the fuck?" Sinkua grumbled, "How could I not get us through these things?"

"I did warn you," Phoenix reminded, "They're impossible to incapacitate for long, considerable as your strength and resilience are."

"What? No. I know that," Sinkua refuted, "I mean I should be able to figure out how to get past them. I'm the plan guy. I've always been the plan guy. Sure, they could be better, but I get results. And with less damage than other people would."

Phoenix chuckled.

"… What's so funny?"

"That's the most credit you've ever given yourself," she said, "You always fixate on your failures, but now you're realizing what you've accomplished in spite of them."

"What can I say? Being in a stalemate with the Netherworld has a way with my perspective."

"Well, as soon as you're ready, I have a plan."

"What are we gonna do?" he asked, "Wait. Can they understand us?"

"They have no sense of language," she assured, "We're going to spread fires and force them to scatter."

"Sounds like a start," he said, "But they'll close in once the fires go out."

"We'll need to hurry then."

"Can we keep the fire anchored to us?"

"Possibly," Phoenix said, "To what end? So, it doesn't hurt you?"

"Well yes, but I was thinking more for stealth," Sinkua said, "If they still sense our milystis in the fires, they should lose track of us."

"I don't know that that's how their senses work," Phoenix cautioned, "But it's worth hoping for."

Chapter 7

Palms upturned, Sinkua closed his eyes and channeled milystis down his arms, coalescing it in his hands. A faint glow flickered through his lower eyelids, dulling as the milystis concentrated in his fingers.

The malformed denizens gnashed at his heat barrier. With Sinkua preoccupied, Phoenix pulsated the threshold to keep them at bay in his stead.

Sinkua opened his eyes. His fingers trembled with glows of the most brilliant shades of crimson. His head wobbled with a spike of fatigue.

"Gonna need your help with this."

"I've got you," Phoenix assured, "Deploy when you're ready."

Tethered by ten hair thin strands, Sinkua launched the milystic orbs from his fingertips. They bore perfectly circular holes through the creatures, leaving smoldering wounds that could have set the orbs ablaze had they lingered.

As his hands strained, Sinkua signaled Phoenix. The orbs halted. Clusters of snarling creatures stopped to face them. Those not near any orb kept their sights on Sinkua. But every one of them stood in silence.

"I… think it's working," Sinkua said.

"Seems like it," Phoenix said, her voice strained, "Listen, this is harder on me than I had wagered. Once I light these, it's up to you."

Sinkua drew the milystic strands to his torso, anchoring the ten orbs around his midsection. "I've got you."

Her will surge from the anchor points like palpable thoughts. Ripples rushed down the strands, exploding all ten orbs with violent brilliance.

Ten hordes of integrated beasts closed in on ten roaring balls of fire. Mistaking these for their quarry, they collapsed into each other with bodies disfigured by flames so intense as to all but have their own mass.

Sinkua gave his legs a once over. The flesh had reconstituted. He gritted his teeth and lunged through the rings of fire.

He took the only split second he had to swat the flames from his clothes before the Netherworld beasts noticed him. Those other milystic presences were strong and dynamic enough for standing decoys. But this one moved.

Sinkua shot a thought to Phoenix, asking if she could move the fireballs. Her silence told him she couldn't. Not with the strain she was already under.

Sinkua charged into the narrowing opening. The integrated closed in like a zipper, many risking maiming for half a finger of extra reach. Adrenaline contended with a spike in fatigue as he pulled the strands taut.

Dragged by his momentum, the fireballs carved clean through some creatures and scattered the rest with their blast impacts. The zipper broke with many dispersing in a stupor but many more closing in faster.

He ducked and weaved around grabbing hands, only taking up arms when it was absolutely necessary. He fixated on his earlier lament. He was the plan guy. He got results, and they usually came with less damage than other plans.

But not without any damage at all. Difference was, now the damage of an imperfect plan was his alone. He had long often taken the emotional scars upon himself, but the physical pain, he had always shared. If he took any at all.

He realized a deeper truth to Phoenix's words. That was the most credit he had ever given himself. But it wasn't just the stalemate or even being in the Netherworld at all. It was what was at stake beyond this place.

On the other side of the fractalized river, Eytea and Galo were waiting for him to find Vielle and bring them all back to life. Somewhere in this elaborate beyond, Sleipnir waited for him to regroup and confront Odin's corruption with him. Back in the living world, Nikasu clung to hope against the last of MalVek's forces.

As did whoever survived the plan to stop him from destroying The Veil.

Just as he had been made the catalyst in this mayhem, he had made himself the lynchpin in setting it right. Through it all, he saw in himself what he had seen in everyone else. Possibly what many of them had seen in him. It went beyond benefit of the doubt.

Sinkua finally had faith in himself.

Binding his thoughts with Phoenix, he grabbed the strands and swung the concentrated fireballs through the hordes. Phoenix cried out as he left ten blazing arcs converging to them along fiery tethers. Sinkua steeled himself as she shared the strain of withdrawing the flames.

He reached into the shared mental space to find his ancient incarnations of Tetsen Drukoa and Fetzikzi Aroka. Himself in the spiritual sense but their own people in personalities and memories. Different but one. Shaped from memories buried beneath his subconscience, Sinkua passed control of three of the tethers to each of them.

A hive mind within himself, three iterations of one Hybrid ripped through the forces of the Netherworld. But no matter how far they pushed, they were no closer to passing through. Those further from the voracious zipper created a moving wall, thus locking the Hybrid quarry in a battle of attrition with an opponent that no longer knew fatigue.

Three of the tethers wavered as he felt Tetsen's attention wander. From far off and aside came a booming sonorous voice in another language that Sinkua didn't understand.

A horned silhouette rushed in from that direction, growing at an alarming rate. Sinkua didn't sense fear from Tetsen, though. Quiet misgivings, yes, along with a touch of conditional trust. But no fear.

Sinkua perked up as he called out, "Arestor!"

Three meters and just as many quarter tonnes of solid bulk and momentum t-boned the horde. So great was the impact that he shattered denizens and created a shockwave that loosened limbs even at its weakest reaches.

Fetzikzi panicked and pulled her three fireballs between them and the charging minotaur. Tetsen pushed back though, tamping down his misgivings to force himself to trust Arestor, even in the Netherworld.

Indeed, Arestor slowed just enough to spare Sinkua and his memory alternates from the shockwave. The minotaur scooped him up under one arm, banked right, and snapped back to his unrelenting momentum.

The tethered fireballs bounced in their wake as Arestor plowed a path through the hungry hordes. No longer needing to preserve the milystic connection, Phoenix allowed herself to rest. The tethers came ablaze, igniting the collective breath of the creatures in ten rippling sheets and just as many snaking infernos.

At the back of the swarm, Arestor grabbed a creature by the inside of its torso and pitched it into the crowd as he fishtailed to a halt. The denizen struck another hard enough to shatter them both, scattering parts and denting the swarm. With decent distance on the integrated souls, Arestor set Sinkua down.

Sinkua dropped to his hands and knees and vomited. His arms trembled under the burden of staying upright. Short of getting back to his feet, he could at least hope to keep his face out of his own puke.

Fetzikzi faded into the white noise of his subconscience. Tetsen remained though, willing him through the language barrier to stand and face Arestor so Tetsen could speak with him. Sinkua dug deep for his last reserves of energy and forced himself to his feet. He closed his eyes to convene with Tetsen.

But no sooner had he reached him than he lost his focus to Arestor's voice.

"Sin… ku… a," he sounded out, hunkering to eye level, "Thank… you."

"You…?" Sinkua asked, "No. Thank you. Did you… learn Ouristihran?"

Arestor shrugged and shook his head.

"I think that's all he knows," Phoenix guessed, "We'll let Tetsen speak with him. I'll fill you in later."

"Fine with me," Sinkua said, "Lets me rest."

"These are dangerous gambits, Sinkua," Phoenix said, "I know you'll say they're necessary and they get results, and it's hard to disagree. But just know that you cannot depend on them for long."

"I'm aware," Sinkua said, "Thank you."

With that, he faded to the back of his own subconscience, nearer to Fetzikzi, and yielded prominence to Tetsen.

The Harkzanian flinched as he awoke into control. He panned the landscape, at once crackling and roiling, jumping and shrinking back as he saw the clamoring malformed creatures in the distance. They were closer than he thought.

Tetsen took several long tiptoeing steps away from them and, feeling his breath down the back of his head, steeled himself to face Arestor. Sure, any friend of Takmet and Metkhal was a friend of his, but he had never understood why the

Chieftain Family was friends with someone like that. The best reason he'd ever seen was that Fentak was friends with Arestor's parents.

"So. What's your deal?" Tetsen asked, "Metkhal piggybacked you into being remembered as a hero, so now I'm getting punished for thinking you're full of it? Or do you think helping me will score you a few reincarnation points?"

"I don't need help with that," Arestor said, "Could we speak Pukoqeyen? My Harkzanian is rusty."

Tetsen sighed and rolled his eyes. "Sure. Fine," he said in Pukoqeyen, "So what'd the new guy do to land us here?"

"I'm afraid I know nothing about that," Arestor said, "I hope I had nothing to do with it."

"Why would you have…" Tetsen trailed off, drawing back with epiphanic shock, "How much Elder God ass did you kiss that I'm still being punished for thinking you shouldn't be in the Trifecta?"

Arestor pinched the bridge of his nose. "It has nothing to do with that, Tetsen. Look around you."

Tetsen panned his surroundings with about as much patience as he had for this bull-headed manipulator.

"Looks like shit," Tetsen said, "What am I looking for?"

"The creatures! They're all beastkin."

"Yeah? And?"

"This new you? Sinkua?" Arestor led in, crouching to Tetsen's eye level, "He found my soul leaking out of my statue, and he tried to resurrect me to speed up the release."

So much of that shouldn't have been possible. All the metallurgists who had studied Takmet and Pahres had assured him that their souls were secure in the statues. Phoenix brought souls back to bodies. She didn't release them. And the Lechuatzulan masons had assured him that the reincarnation curse would depend on proximity. If he died far enough from it and any blood relatives, he wouldn't come back as the next born nor as the Phoenix Hybrid. But he had felt her in that shared subconscience.

He didn't know how long it had been, only that at least one new language had cropped up, but Phoenix had come back to him. Or perhaps she never left. Either he hadn't traveled far enough, or the masons had been mistaken.

That was another matter. He remembered leaving, but he couldn't remember any of his travels. There wasn't even a blur after his departure. Nor did he have any memories of his first time in the afterlife. Between leaving Masnethege and awakening in a new subconscience, there was nothing.

"H… How?"

That was all he could manage. For all his questions, he could only boil them down and choke them out as a single word.

Arestor shrugged. "I know fewer than ten words of their language, and Phoenix didn't bother to translate his plan for me."

"Right. Of course. Why would she?" Tetsen said, pacing as much to keep his feet from sinking as out of contemplation, "But how did I end up as the Phoenix Hybrid again?"

"What makes you believe I would be an authority on such things?"

"I don't!" Tetsen remarked, throwing his hands up, "But I don't remember anything after I left, and I'm hoping maybe something happened that might explain this."

"Something such as what?" Arestor asked, "Such as your reincarnation finding the Phoenix Ruby?"

"Sure. That or an error in their research or a manufacturing defect."

Arestor's expression flattened. He blinked hard. Tetsen just shrugged. Arestor sighed and tapped his own sternum as he tipped his chin down.

Tetsen's eyes widened with alarm. Not only had the Phoenix Ruby found its way back to him, he was so accustomed to the weight that he no longer noticed it against his neck.

His tension, however, deflated when he felt his chest and found nothing there. His brow flattened.

"Look down at it," Arestor said.

Tetsen rolled his eyes but did as he was told. The tension came flooding back when he saw an array of squiggly scars blooming from his solar plexus. In the center was another scar in the shape of a four-pointed star, same size as the Phoenix Ruby.

"Arestor," Tetsen beckoned, his voice shaky, "What happened? And while we're at it, how did I get so jacked?"

"I'll tell you as much as I know, but we need to walk. Come," Arestor said, "It's been approximately five thousand years since we sealed Pandora and Seriamus and became trapped in copper. Every one of your reincarnations since then could have been the Phoenix Hybrid, but none of them ever possessed the Ruby. Until Sinkua."

"The guy who tried to release you?" Tetsen asked.

Arestor nodded. "He was born as MeiLom, but..."

"Oh, is he a, ah, gender switcher? Like Motanos?"

"Transgender? No, he only changed his name," Arestor said, "Takmet escaped his statue and possessed his descendant, Gijin. He gave MeiLom the Phoenix Ruby and dubbed him Sinkua because it sounded like Tsenukoa."

"I suppose I should feel honored then," Tetsen said, "But if both of you were in statues all this time, how do you know what happened with the other reincarnations?"

"Oh that? Cedalion told us."

"Cedalion? He's still alive?"

"Well, not currently. But he was until recently."

"Amazing," Tetsen exhaled, "Is he still wearing that stupid mask?"

"Yes, even over here," Arestor said, "After he saw Sinkua vanish from the tsoran afterlife, he sent me here on a scouting mission."

"What about this scar though?" Tetsen asked, "Did I do something with the Phoenix Ruby after I left?"

Arestor looked at him flatly. "I never thought too much of your intellect, Tetsen, but I'm surprised you haven't figured it out."

Tetsen tamped down the urge to get offended and act on it. It wouldn't do far from any good here. "... Figured what out?"

"That's not your body," Arestor said, "It's Sinkua's."

"Wh... What are you saying?" Tetsen asked, his voice trembling, "No. That can't be right. We're in the afterlife. We should be switching off completely. But then... why else would I have this physique? This can't have come from being out at sea for a long time. Could it? No. ... Maybe? But the scars—"

"The scars are from the Phoenix Ruby," Arestor said, "We don't know why, but he destroyed it and reintegrated Phoenix into himself."

"That was stupid," Tetsen derided, "But that doesn't explain why I have his body."

"If I had to guess, it's because you don't have your own," Arestor said, "When he first came here, he had a plan to break himself and some other Hybrids out. But he dropped Epesol in the river and disappeared. But Cedalion suspected he would find his way back. That's what I was scouting for. Both Epesol and Sinkua."

"How did he get back, then?" Tetsen asked, "Hell, how did he disappear without reincarnating?"

"I don't know either of those," Arestor admitted, "But when I found him, he looked flat. Like he lacked substance. But he wasn't incorporeal."

The implication wasn't lost on Tetsen. The idea for the Phoenix Ruby only came about because she, like any Etherworlder, could change size at will. They existed in four dimensions, and so did Omphaloworlder souls. Tsoran and milystic alike.

But though it wasn't lost, Tetsen refused to accept the implication.

"Maybe the Netherworld just does that to people?" he grasped, "Maybe this place is four dimensions, but people stay in three. You know, like as part of the punishment."

"We both know that's not what's—"

"Or maybe this place has five dimensions!"

"Okay sure, but why would he look flat to me?"

"Because he... ah..." Tetsen stammered, "Because you can come and go as you please. It doesn't affect you, so..."

"Tetsen."

He was right to stop him, and Tetsen knew it. The harder he tried to deny it, the more desperate he felt. It was time to accept the implication. For as implausible as it was, no other explanation sufficed.

"Arestor?" he asked, "Are we... in a, you know... physical body?"

"I'm afraid so, my friend," Arestor exhaled, "Sinkua returned here alive."

"So, when you said this is Sinkua's body," Tetsen said, "you meant that literally?! Fuck's sake, I thought I just couldn't fully take over because of some Netherworld restriction."

"Nothing in my studies ever hinted toward that being an effect of this place."

"Hey, that's right! You studied this stuff," Tetsen said, his voice rising and hastening, "What's going to happen to us? We're a physical being on a spiritual plane. That can't be good."

"I'm afraid I didn't study this phenomenon," Arestor apologized, "But I suppose, and mind you this is conjecture, that your body will degrade and release your spirit."

"But how are we even partially switching out?" Tetsen pressed, "That shouldn't be—"

Phoenix beckoned him from within. Tetsen closed his eyes to listen.

"There's a simple explanation for all of this, including your lost memories," Phoenix said, "But I don't think you'll like it."

"I... I need to hear it," Tetsen insisted, "What happened after I left? Did I find anyone else?"

"I'm sorry, but I don't know," she said, "When Tetsen Drukoa left Mberhan, that was his last memory that I was present to record."

Tetsen went rigid, staring into the distance. She referred to him in the third person, as though she was talking about him. Not to him.

"Phoenix," he beckoned, "What are you saying?"

"That is why you cannot remember anything beyond that point. You're not the real Tetsen Drukoa," she explained, "You're a composite of his memories of our time together. You've been slipping into Sinkua's id ever since he broke me out."

"I'm... I'm not..." Tetsen stammered, "I'm not even the preincarnation of this scab-picking meathead?!"

"The real Tetsen Drukoa is still part of Sinkua's soul."

"I'm just memories?!"

"If Sinkua loses this body, the real Tetsen will emerge when he meets—"

"I know how it works, you insufferable heap of sparks!"

"Drukoa!" Arestor bellowed.

Tetsen jerked into a sloppy defensive stance as he turned to face him. His shoulders trembled as one eye twitched.

"What do you want, you old cow?" he snarled, "How do I know you're not just a product of the real Tetsen's memories, too?"

"Because no matter how much I wanted to, I never did this to you."

With swiftness unbecoming of his bulk, Arestor buried his fist in Tetsen's borrowed abdomen. The mismatched Phoenix Hybrid doubled over and stumbled back, clutching their midsection.

"You asshole," Tetsen grumbled, "That doesn't mean—"

"If I were projected from his memories, I could only do things that you remember," Arestor insisted, "Now, what I was trying to say is that you should take this as a blessing."

"How do you figure?"

"How far do you think your bloodline has spread in the past five thousand years?"

"I... can't even fathom it."

"Exactly. Under your usual circumstances, you'd be lucky to have a full day before you reincarnate," Arestor said, "So while you may just be memories, you're the best chance Tetsen has had in a long time to be heard. One might argue that it makes you more the real one."

Tetsen regarded him for a moment. He huffed and shook his head, then shouldered past the Pukoqeyen minotaur.

"Come on," he urged, "Let's keep walking."

"Are you sure you're okay?"

"This Sinkua guy has done some stupid shit, but maybe he knows what he's doing," Tetsen said, "I can't do anything about being a shadow. But if he gets back to the living world, I'll see to it that this shit pit isn't the only life I get."

A gruff voice spoke in an unfamiliar tongue from the depths of his mind. Phoenix provided a translation.

"He says he'll do what he can," she said on his behalf, "For you, Fetzikzi Aroka, and anyone else he finds."

Chapter 8

Eytea brushed a spreading of shards and sand into a shallow pile. For a fleeting instant, they melded into a cohesive mass. As far as she could tell at least.

The crystals only melded where she was touching them. As soon as she moved her hand, the pieces dropped and scattered. So, the idea that they were melding was more a matter of feeling than sight.

Moving her hand more slowly didn't help either. In fact, she wasn't even sure she felt them melding in that case. And while some of the Bealstillans had warmed up to her, she couldn't ask any of them for a second opinion. What with the language barrier.

The more cohesive of groups they worked in, though, the taller and more persistent of mounds they could make. They didn't stay up all that long, but even a sliver of tangible progress kept hope alive.

Though she, her mother, Galo, and Gijin would have worked well together, Gijin had insisted they split up. He reasoned that the Bealstillans had a better idea of what they were after, thus each of them would be best off assisting.

By a small but undeniable margin, her mother's group managed the most persistent mounds. Perhaps her optimism was fooling her, but it looked like they even managed shapes more deliberate than sloping heaps. But they were still just as quick to collapse. Eytea attributed that to her mother's memory flashes.

A hand patted her upper back, reminding her both that she, well, had an upper back. She winced twice when she looked up and saw Galo, and she winced twice. The first was at his interloping between her and her mother.

The second came when she realized he had felt the same way when she first met him and Sinkua.

"Hey, I know you have a better sense for these things than I do," he said, "But I feel like we've been at this for days, and we're getting nowhere."

"Oh? You can tell it's been days?" Eytea teased, "I thought you lost your sense of time. You know. Like the rest of us."

"What? No, I mean..." Galo stammered, "I thought maybe you had figured out how to get a general idea."

"What, like with those trippy-ass clouds?"

Galo shrugged. "Maybe?" he said, "So, do you?"

"No. I hate to tell you this, but if the constant daylight ever starts sucking less, it hasn't happened to me yet," she said, "But I will have you know we are absolutely making progress. Case in point, I can do this now."

She ran her hand across a scattering of shards and sand, just fast enough to feel the fleeting melding.

"You've... found some new sensory trick?" Galo grasped, "Do you want to take some home? Maybe it'll help with your tangibility issues."

"That's... Maybe?" Eytea considered, "But that's not what I meant."

"Then what—?"

"The Bealstillans don't hate me anymore," she interrupted, "See? These ones aren't cowering."

As she swept her arm toward them, the dozen or so faceless spirits backed up the space of a step. Galo laughed, pulling her attention back to him.

"Yes, you're obviously a big deal around here," he said, "Look, maybe experienced ghosts don't get tired anymore, but I still do. Can we call it a day? You did say you want to show me your home."

"Oh! Oh, right. Of course," she remarked, "I just go so wrapped up in this that I sort of, um, forgot about that."

They called Gijin and Elemeno over, and the four of them made for the nearest ledge. Eytea rolled a bit of sand between her fingers and palm while they walked.

Truth was, she had hoped Galo would forget about her home if she went long enough without mentioning it again. She had meant to deny it if he asked. She would have questioned why she would tell him about a home she doesn't have. Or she could have just changed the subject. That might have been less antagonistic than directly gaslighting him.

But at his first passing mention, her defenses were down. She couldn't pin down why she wanted to deny him though. Embarrassment came to mind.

Sure, it was more than a mite sappy that she had built it for herself and Sinkua. Her mother noticing that didn't embarrass her though, and if anyone knew their relationship as well as her mother it was his best friend. The third chair was ridiculous, but she could laugh with him about that.

No, as best as she could figure, his confusion had made her uncomfortable. It teased the edges of standoffishness. She had spent the past however long searching her memories for anyone else disappearing into the ground.

On one hand, she might not have noticed because there were so few people she could perceive. On the other hand, the ability could have been exclusive to Hybrids or a subset of them. So, either the unique circumstance she wasn't used to kept her from seeing she wasn't alone, or the unique circumstance she was used to was alienating her. She sympathized that much more with Vielle's desire for the mundane.

His suggesting the sands could keep her tangible also tugged at her misgivings. It occurred to her she had remained tangible and relatively consistent. Sure, she was with him and her mother, but they were barely in shouting distance.

As they neared the edge, Eytea decided not to take the shards to the other side. They hit the ground far more loudly than she expected. More singularly as well. But by the time she turned to check, they had scattered to indistinguishable sand.

Still, she had heard them shatter, as surely as she had felt them cohere in her hands. It was almost enough to convince her she wasn't imagining it. That maybe she could show someone else even if just to prove it to herself.

Eytea and Galo flipped to the barren side together and waited for Elemeno and Gijin to catch up. Eytea wondered if Metkhal and Takmet might have any theories about her homebuilding skills. Though some part of her worried it might make them standoffish.

Well, Metkhal at least. Takmet and Gijin were more literally the same person than Metkhal and Galo were. She could guess what to expect from Takmet, but Metkhal was a wildcard.

As much as she wanted to keep mulling it over, the inevitable was already in motion and closing in. Besides, Metkhal was the only one who might have taken issue, and that was more that she couldn't say he wouldn't. Better to talk to Galo about his confusion than to assume he was put off. Were she honest, all she ever feared was what the answers to her abilities might portend.

Or that she wouldn't get any answers at all.

"Where exactly is your home?" Galo asked, "Is it far?"

"Well, no. But also, yes?" Eytea puzzled, "I can get to it from anywhere. I just assumed I have to be on this side."

"Wait. Then how is it far from here?"

Eytea shrugged. "I've never walked past it," she said, "or stumbled across it."

Now it was Galo's turn to shrug. "If you say so."

Eytea crouched and hovered her palm above the ground. She closed her eyes and thought of her home. With visions fortified in her mind's eye, Eytea slammed her palm against the ground and dragged it toward herself. The ground parted and, as she opened her eyes, filled with fractalized light.

"My home is in there," she said, "Come on. I can't hold it open for long."

Without waiting for acknowledgement, Eytea bounded through the hole.

"Interesting arrangement you've gotten yourself," Galo said, announcing his entrance, "The television and record player look older than the ones you had when we first visited. Is that right, Miss Elemeno?"

Elemeno nodded. "It is," she said, "These are more like the ones we had when she was little."

"I never would've expected you to be nostalgic for your childhood," Galo said to Eytea, "But I'm not here to judge your choices."

"It's not really nostalgia. I don't know what to call it," Eytea said, propping against the arm of her chair, "It's more like I didn't realize just how bad things were back then."

"But you do now," Galo said, "You're really able to live here and not think about all the things you overlooked as a child?"

"I wouldn't say that. But meeting you and Sinkua was the start of the happiest time of my life," Eytea reminisced, "Even when things were rough and bloody, I wasn't alone. I had a sense of purpose and community. Sinkua is all the best parts of that rolled into one with the candor for me to know it's real."

"He certainly does keep his heart on his sleeve," Galo chuckled, "At least with the negatives."

Eytea laughed with him. "You get it," she said, "I think I just wanted to combine the naïve happiness of my childhood with the best part of my adulthood. If I could bring him here, it would all feel more real."

"Well, I suppose it falls to me to address it," Gijin said.

Eytea grew tense. She had hoped he could explain her crafting ability. Or at the very least assure her she would come to understand it. Instead, he sounded poised to ask her about it. Confront her even.

He sounded annoyed. She didn't even know he could do that. But if she had ever thought to imagine what that would sound like, it would've been just like that.

"What manner of monstrosity is that in the corner?" Gijin asked.

Her tension deflated. "Oh that?" Eytea laughed, "I was trying to make a chair like the one my grandparents had, so my mom would have a place to sit."

"But you last saw it when you were small," Gijin finished, "Thus the result has scaled with your current size."

"Yes, sir," she said, bowing her head, "You seem to understand how these homes work. Do you think—?"

"I'm afraid not, young lady," Gijin said, "I could no better postulate as to its nature than you."

"What about you, Mom?" Eytea grasped, "Did you pick up on anything in your visions?"

"If I did, it didn't stick around," Elemeno said, "I'm sorry. I know it's been bothering you, but I haven't come up with any new ideas."

"Galo," Eytea beckoned, "Can you ask Metkhal?"

"We don't speak the same language," Galo fumbled, "Besides, I can't just draw him out at will."

"Metkhal," Takmet said, the tonal shift announcing the reversion, "Nataji kongea naveve."

Galo's eyes rolled back in his head. His face faded and what emerged in its place was unfamiliar. With just a few words from his father, Metkhal had shown himself.

Elemeno leaned on the opposite arm of Eytea's chair, and they watched Takmet and Metkhal converse in Mberhali. With no grasp of the language though, they could only speculate from body language. But they both thought it best to keep their interpretations to themselves.

Eytea did at least, and she assumed her mother felt the same way. The more she thought of other reasons for her mother's silence, the more she fidgeted with her fingernails. Not thinking about it did little to help.

After a bit, Takmet resumed to the form of Gijin, and Metkhal yielded prominence to Galo.

"What did he say?" Eytea pleaded, "He looked… annoyed? Bothered? I don't know. Or was that normal body language for your ancestors?"

"Eytea?" Galo beckoned, "It's not like you to get this worked up. Are you okay?"

"No, I'm not okay!" Eytea cried out, "I got killed the morning after I got engaged, and I've been immaterial damn near this whole time. Because fuck-all of anybody can perceive me. Because I've had fuck-all of past lives. My mother-in-law was my only confidant, but then she disappeared because my fiancé can raise the dead but not Hybrids. Because fuck us, I guess. And now you're all being weird because I made a home for my fiancé and me. I've been alone since the moment I died, and every time I think I'm not alone anymore, somebody fucks off and ruins my afterlife again."

Everyone stared at her for longer than she liked. Her focus bounced among them, waiting for someone, anyone, to say something. Anything. Some kind of assurance that she wouldn't lose them, too. But the silence only grew thicker, more deafening, as it stretched on.

"… Eytea?" Galo beckoned, his voice soft and thready.

Eytea cast her gaze downward. Not like this. It shouldn't have been like this. Three other Hybrids had died, and he was the only one to find her and stick around. And where before, she had let him walk away, now, she was pushing him away. She closed her eyes as she brought her hands to her face.

"Eytea, your—" Galo called out.

Eytea cried out and jumped back as one eyelid sizzled against her hand. She looked to Galo with fearful bewilderment.

"I'm sorry," he said, "I tried to warn you. Your finger is, um, glowing."

Indeed, she saw a bright red band around her left ring finger, right where she had worn her engagement ring. Pensive, she tapped it with her thumb, wincing as she found it hot to the touch.

"This feels like his milystis," she said, almost breathless, "It's like the ring rubbed off on me."

"Do you think you could use pyromancy now? Maybe only with that finger?" Galo guessed, "Grandfather. Any thoughts?"

"I'm afraid I'm unfamiliar with this phenomenon," Gijin said, "The Phoenix Ruby was the first of its kind, and Tsenukoa never gave anyone a piece of it."

"I don't feel like I could," Eytea said, "So I probably definitely couldn't revive anyone with it either. It took that outburst just to get it heated up."

"What about Epesol?" Elemeno chimed in.

Eytea perked up at the mention. "Hey that's right!" she exclaimed, "We might not have to find the ring now."

"Do you mean," Galo said, "that if Arestor finds Epesol, you could cut a way out? Assuming Sinkua was on to something."

"And he usually is," Eytea said, "More often than he gives himself credit for."

"Well yeah, that too," Elemeno said, snatching everyone's attention with her flippancy, "But I meant maybe you can find it now."

Eytea's expression flattened. She looked back and forth between Galo and Gijin, hoping one of them understood what her mother was on about. Close as they had been in life, the woman had just lost her.

"I'll bite. How do you figure?"

"The Dragon Family swords resonate with their owner's milystis. You have a piece of Sinkua's milystis in your finger," Elemeno reasoned, "So maybe, and I might be grasping at straws here, you can feel that resonance in your finger depending on how close you are to Epesol."

Eytea, Gijin, and Galo all exchanged thoughts distilled down to eye contact and body language.

"You may be on to something, Miss Elemeno," Gijin conceded, "It's conjecture, of course, but it's both worthy and harmless to pursue."

"Sinkua never told me he felt different if he was holding his sword or not," Galo said.

"He would only mention it if he thought it was important," Elemeno deflected.

"It also would've been in his whole body," Eytea added, "I'd be more likely to notice it with it just in my finger."

Galo let out a small laugh. "Well, I suppose any hope is worth reaching for," he conceded.

"Of course!" Eytea remarked, "We'll just quit our jobs as sandcastle contractors to play four-dimensional hot-and-cold. No big deal."

"Oh, we'll go pro circuit before the month is out," Galo added, "You can count on that."

"As joyous as this realization is," Gijin chimed in, "Do you still wish to know what Metkhal said?"

"Maybe," Eytea said, "Was it useful?"

"It could give you an answer," Gijin said, "But that might lead to more questions, as is the wont of answers in the pursuit of knowledge."

Eytea sighed in defeat. "Fine. Let's hear it," she said, "You know, Galo, I'm glad the whole buzzkill thing isn't a permanent fixture."

"Metkhal thinks you're something more than a Hybrid," Gijin announced, "Not an Etherworlder in your own right, mind you. However, only the Etherworlders have ever been able to freely craft from the crystals. All you've built here has been from a mineral aggregate containing those very crystals."

"I must admit," Arestor said in staggered Harkzanian, "I was wrong about you."

"I don't doubt that," Tetsen said, coughing as he snickered to himself, "But if you don't mind... What were you wrong about?"

A sharp pain shot through his borrowed torso as Arestor smacked his shoulder with a firm laugh. The beastkin hit with force entirely at odds with his jocularity. Tetsen couldn't tell if that was his nature or an effect of the Netherworld.

"Your reason for trapping Phoenix in that ruby," Arestor said, "It wasn't just meant to transfer her to Pandora, was it?"

Tetsen stared at the ground as they walked. Visions of Sinkua's memories showed him that this mentally fragmented descendant had seen the flaws in his vision. Pandora was beholden only to herself and would thus have been under no obligation to withdraw when he returned Phoenix. His only assurance was her word, and the word of a Trickster Goddess, rather the Goddess of Chaos, was perhaps the ficklest thing known.

"It wasn't for that. It never was," Tetsen said, "That's just what I told the Lechuatzulan crafters. If Pandora or Seriamus —"

"You don't remember the crafters' names?"

"I chose not to learn them. I didn't want to risk leading Pandora or Seriamus to them."

"I did not give you credit you deserve."

"No, I guess you didn't," Tetsen said, "So what do you think my real reason was?"

"You, ah..." Arestor said, trailing off into consideration, "You were being attacked... No... Invaded? ... No. Your past memories. The other your memories."

"I think the word you're looking for is 'intruded,'" Tetsen said, "The memories of my past incarnations were intruding on my own thoughts and memories." He craned his neck to glare up at Arestor. "Just like I'm doing to Sinkua, right?"

"Well, it certainly sounds antagonistic when you put it like that."

Tetsen sighed and shook his head. "It's fine. You're right though. Twelve lifetimes of memories was pushing her limits."

"A drawback of an immaterial body, I suppose?"

"You suppose right," Tetsen said as an amorphous black structure came into view, "The structure of the Phoenix Ruby let her compartmentalize the memories."

"It lets her do what?" Arestor asked, rubbing his chin.

"The design of the ruby lets her put the memories in different places," he called back, "Sorry. I forget you're not quite fluent in Harkzanian."

Arestor chuckled as he took a couple of long strides to catch up.

"It's no bother," he said in Pukoqeyen, "Despite the circumstances, I am pleased that we are coming to understand one another better."

Tetsen flattened his expression. "You had to switch to Pukoqeyen on me didn't you?" he asked, "Is this your way of getting back at me?"

"Perhaps," Arestor said, shrugging, "Though I do wonder if a memory composite of Sinkua was released from the Ruby as well."

"If it was, I can't tell it apart from him," Tetsen said, "I can't imagine having identical copies of a memory would do much. Might make it harder to forget things, if even that."

"Yes, I suppose that would be redundant," Arestor said. He grabbed Tetsen's shoulder and pointed to the black structure. "Now then, see that pile of junk? That's our way out."

"What's so special about it?"

"What? Nothing. It just isn't flat. If we climb it, we can reach the river."

"Can I pass through it with a body?"

"You couldn't even without a body. To wit, only we beastkin have ever managed it, and our results have been, well, mixed."

"What do I do, then?" Tetsen asked, "Hold my breath and hope I fall through fast enough?"

"That would be far too reckless," Arestor deflected, "I'm going to shield you with my body and carry you through."

The ground sizzled Tetsen's feet as he stood regarding Arestor for longer than he should have. "You're going to hug me and do a cannonball into the ceiling river?"

"When you put it like that, of course it sounds ridiculous."

"No, it's fine," Tetsen said, chuckling under his breath, "We aren't exactly spoiled for options here."

Chapter 9

Eytea awoke to a most delightful cramp in the crook of her knee. It had been so long since she had such a stretch of materiality that she had forgotten the aches of sleeping in strange positions. She didn't miss the irony of having abhorred them in life.

Then again, back then she could ask Sinkua to work the knots out. He wasn't particularly good at it, but the effort was enough to help her loosen them throughout the day. And if the mood struck her, it wasn't hard to tempt him into making it a better morning for both of them.

Eytea's expression flattened at a stirring from the oversized chair. She had wandered so far into fond memories that she hadn't considered the sort of guests she was hosting. Particularly the sort that she shouldn't reminisce about her sex life in front of. Getting sentimental about her fiancé was one thing. Getting horny about him was crude even for her.

She propped herself on her elbows and looked to her mother. She was curled up like a cat, right down to the outstretched arms framing and burying her face. Eytea laughed to herself.

Galo and Gijin slept sitting up, leaning against opposite sides of Sinkua's armchair. Eytea smiled and nodded, exhaling her gratitude that they had respected her sanctity for that chair.

For a moment, she just enjoyed the quiet of it all. Sleep wasn't necessary in the afterlife. The illusion of their bodies ran so deep that spirits still felt fatigue. But all anyone needed was waking rest, making sleep a matter of comfort and personal enjoyment.

Eytea reflected on Metkhal's take on her crafting ability. She had considered that her being a new soul had something to do with it. Perhaps souls evolved, and this was a new trait.

Her being an advanced or specialized Hybrid could have worked on a similar logic. Hybrids had been dormant for centuries, but the genes of the Hybrid Chromosomes must have still evolved just as the rest of the genome had. Maybe this was just the outcome that she got stuck with.

Then again, she didn't have to be an anomaly. Galo could just as soon have been the weird one. Sinkua might have been able to do it, had he not been spirited away. Or bodied away, more aptly.

Knowing her, Nikasu would've shown up with a fundamental grasp on it. Eytea hoped she wouldn't witness this for several more years, of course. A good half dozen decades at least.

Vielle could have been honing the ability ever since she arrived. In fact, that must have been where she had been all this time. She felt insecure about not having the hang of it yet and had isolated herself while she practiced.

Eytea huffed and shook her head at how hard she was grasping. She knew where she stood, and she knew where Galo stood. That needed to be enough.

She reached toward the record player and thought about what music she wanted to hear. Nothing happened, much to her disappointment. If she had to be an anomaly for the time being, a bit of telekinesis with her constructs would've been nice.

Eytea hoisted herself out of the armchair to start the player the old-fashioned way. But as she reached for the knob, the base of her ring finger glowed, and she drew back.

Eytea held her hand up to the light and turned it about. She narrowed her eyes at the ceiling, as though she might see through if she squinted hard enough. She reached up and splayed her fingers out. Her face came alight as the glowing ring shimmered that much more brightly.

Her mom had been right. The mark was resonating. Arestor had found Epesol, and it was telling her he was nearby.

Better yet, Sinkua had returned. Epesol had led him to where she opened the door, and now he was wondering why the trail went cold in the middle of nothing.

For a moment, she considered waking her guests. Instead, she manifested a couple of her mom's favorite albums and two from Berinin before she went outside.

Tetsen stared up the scorched tangle of detritus. It radiated an inward pulsation that thinned the surrounding air with its discordant thrumming. He dragged his fingernails along a stretch. It was rough, felt not unlike bark.

An urging tugged at the rear of his conscience.

"You're sure this will hold us?" Tetsen asked.

Arestor winced as he crumbled a segment with a slap. "It's… going to need to," he insisted, "Rather, we're going to need it to."

Tetsen looked him over. "You've never used one, have you?"

He leaned a hand against the structure, only to pull back as that urging tugged harder. Tetsen narrowed his eyes at the tangled mess. It no longer appeared to thrum inward. Rather, it was more that the air of the Netherworld was suppressing it.

This thing wasn't supposed to be here, and he suspected that's what the urging behind his conscience was trying to tell him.

"… I noticed Sinkua," was all Tetsen caught of Arestor's answer.

"I'm sorry," Tetsen said, "What about Sinkua?"

"I was just saying I only dropped from the river when I saw him," Arestor said, "But other beastkin have escaped, and this is the only way up there that we've seen."

A second urging joined the first in the back of Tetsen's mind. He signaled Arestor to give him a moment. Tetsen closed his eyes to find two inner visions awaiting him. One was of a spiteful man with a winged child, the other, a cunning faun consorting with satyrs. The two overlapped.

"Sinkua and Fetzikzi think Kervatus must have escaped on one of these," Tetsen said as he opened his eyes, "He was reborn as Kabehl. Father of the Odin Hybrid."

Arestor tapped his fingers in various spots along the structure. "Is that all they said?" he asked, "Or did something else distract you before I mentioned beastkin?"

"It was Sinkua," Tetsen said, "He was showing me a girl named Vale. Or Veel. I think."

"Any thoughts on what she has to do with this?"

Tetsen shrugged. "He also showed me Yggdrasil in the middle of an enormous city. Entire buildings were made of metal and glass."

"Perhaps this Vale is the Yggdrasil Hybrid?" Arestor suggested, "He might believe she has something to do with this."

"I guess these do look like petrified tree roots," Tetsen said, "But that vision was obviously a dream. An entire city made of metal and glass? And how did Yggdrasil come back?"

"I can't speak on their advancements, but Pahres confirmed Yggdrasil's return," Arestor said, "He died before it happened, but he had set everything into motion. That's all moot though, because neither Yggdrasil nor its Hybrid can reach the Netherworld."

Tetsen felt that same urging again. This time, he didn't hesitate to give Sinkua a mind's eye audience. Tetsen's borrowed stomach turned at the manufactured visuals of a spoken memory.

"What if one was killed by an Etherworlder of death?" he asked. "Or its Hybrid?"

Arestor regarded him with cold steely eyes. Behind his shoulder, brittle threads wove into the cracks in the structure.

"That might make it possible, but I can't do more than speculate," Arestor said, "For now, we climb."

Lonely as it had been, Eytea had never found the afterlife quite so desolate as she did in that moment. She had internalized Sigrdrifa's disregard of this side as a wasteland, especially after working, or trying to work, in the crystal fields with the Bealstillans. Tenuous camaraderie was better than none, and isolation had made it all the sweeter.

But perhaps the most prominent root of that desolation was the darkness that now filled the sky. Glints and smears of light glimmered off the contours of the crystal clouds, looking like a stretched and warped night sky.

A voice called through the darkness.

"Glory be that we found you, Lady Eytea."

Eytea tensed as she tried to place the voice. And figure out where it came from. It carried both a maternal warmth and a guarded coldness in equal measures.

A streak of green flitted around the contours of a single cloud. A woman dressed in silvery blue feathers appeared with a winged trio close in tow.

"Lady Freja," Eytea exhaled, the tension melting from her shoulders, "Eir. Randgrid. Sigrdrifa. It's good to see you."

"Yes, I should suppose you have much to ask," Freja said as she approached, "Not the least of which would pertain to this darkened sky, yes?"

"Any number of the Etherworlders of day and night or sun and moon has emerged from our afterlife," Eir interjected, "We believe some proceeded to the Omphaloworld, but we have not been able to track them with any certainty."

"The Fjarthursk Dagr and Nott were likely not among them," Sigrdrifa added, "We would have been better able to follow their movements."

"So, we have days and nights now? Does that mean we'll have a sense of time?"

"Not in the capacity that you did in life," Freja assured, "That mercy will remain intact."

"Fabulous. Hey so, um, weird question," Eytea said, "But I guess that's all any of us have got. Anyway, um… do Etherworlders make green flashes when they emerge? Or is that like your calling card for announcing yourself?"

Freja put her back to Eytea in turning to consult the Valkyries. They spoke in hushed and rushed tones in what Eytea figured to be Fjarthursk.

"We are not aware of a green flash," Freja said, "I suppose you saw it shortly before both times that we have now spoken?"

"Yeah, and I even saw a few before I met the Valkyries for the first time," Eytea said, "I thought maybe you ladies had something to do with it."

"Not as far as we are aware," Freja said, "Now. Can we assume Sinkua has returned to you?"

"What? No. Why would you assume that?" Eytea asked, "I thought he was out here because my ring finger was flaring up."

"As though with Phoenix's milystis?" Eir asked.

"Yeah. I thought it was reacting to him being nearby."

"This is most curious," Freja professed, "I was not aware that the Lechuatzulans could facilitate the sharing of milystis."

"No doubt an unintended consequence," Sigrdrifa added, "Why would they craft the means for Pandora to more easily pilfer powers?"

"We should hope it was intentional. Otherwise, it might be as simple as holding a piece of the stone," Randgrid countered, "Now, Eytea, as to why we thought Sinkua was with you, Freja sensed Sleipnir traversing these realms without Odin. We thought he might have delivered Sinkua through the rivers."

"Why through the rivers? Can Sleipnir not come here himself?"

"Sleipnir banished himself from this realm that he no longer be tempted reunite orphans and deceased children with their families," Randgrid said, "The rivers connect this tsoran afterlife to the Netherworld."

"Eytea, did Sinkua indicate which Etherworlders he chose to resurrect?" Freja asked, "I have yet to see pattern or logic to his methods."

"Normally I'd say it always looks like that, that he always knows what he's doing. But I don't think I can this time," Eytea confessed, "I think his plan only went as far as bringing Odin back. After that he just took whoever Phoenix could get a hold of."

"He may have thought Pandora would lose their powers," Sigrdrifa suggested, "A foolhardy assumption. Many of our people sided with the Goddess of Chaos."

Eytea shrugged. "You mean she wouldn't?"

Eir nudged Sigrdrifa. "This is the first time any of us has returned from the dead."

"That may explain why some proceeded to the Omphaloworld, while others, such as myself, remain here," Freja said, "Some did have the fortune of reclaiming their powers from Pandora."

"Well, when Sinkua gets back, I'll ask him if he has any ideas," Eytea said, "But for now, I've got company over, and I'm sure they're waking up and wondering where I am."

"I'm sorry. You have… company?" Freja asked, "Might I ask where?"

Eytea sighed and pinched the bridge of her nose. Figuring a demonstration would beat an explanation, she excused herself and put her back to them.

Deep in the subconscious space, Sinkua and Fetzikzi shared visual memories of Kabehl and Kervatus. He and Kabehl had committed similar atrocities, exploiting and trafficking sentient lives.

Sinkua pondered if Kervatus had made Kabehl the sort of person he was. After all, Fetzikzi's tendency to act on her anger reminded him of his own temper. It stood to reason that prominent traits of past lives could imprint on new ones.

Then again, she was quicker witted than him. And Tetsen's temper was more like indignant impatience. Even if Kervatus had imprinted on him, Kabehl chose to embrace those tendencies.

Fetzikzi receded as Sinkua's awareness expanded. The walls of his mind drew near. Tetsen receded past him in the split second before Sinkua filled his conscious presence.

He awoke enveloped in the musculature of Arestor's limbs. Arestor let out winces and yowls as water rushed around them. What bypassed the minotaur's shielding sizzled as it splashed over Sinkua's flesh.

A brief reprieve left him feeling like he was floating with no sense of orientation. He grunted as they hit ground, the impact shaking him in Arestor's clutches as they bounced in directions beyond his vocabulary. After a dragging moment's rolling, they settled, and Arestor stood up with him.

The ground rippled with dull prismatic light. The sky was a boundless sea of roiling fractals. Other islands were vague shapes, only distinguishable through a disorienting balance of hard focus and blurring his eyes.

Sinkua collapsed forward and vomited. Bile seeped into the contours of the ground, further dimming its light. He reached into his subconscience for Tetsen. Whatever contempt Tetsen held for him, for his circumstances, or toward Metkhal for validating Arestor, it all had to be put aside. Otherwise, none of them could go any further..

Eytea parted the ground to see her mother groping the wall on the other side of the fractalized light. They stopped and stared, interrupting each other with an awkward apology.

"Just get out here, Mom," Eytea called through, "Bring the guys, too."

Elemeno emerged. "Just how long did you intend to leave us in there?" she exhaled.

"Oh!" Gijin gasped, "Oh now this is a most curious sight. What has happened while we slept?"

"I assure you this bodes well," Eir said as she approached, "All your questions will be answered in—"

"You must be Freja," Galo said, looking past Eir as though he didn't realize he had interrupted her, "Eytea mentioned you."

Freja cocked her head, her jaw slack with bemusement. "Metkhal?" she asked, "How did you come to befriend this neophyte soul?"

"Actually, Your Grace, I believe he goes by Galo now," Randgrid offered.

"He doesn't go by Galo," Sigrdrifa corrected, "He is Galo."

"Lady Freja," Metkhal said, lowering his head, "I'm sorry I couldn't do more for you and your husband."

"Oh, don't lower your eyes to me, young man," Freja insisted, "Nothing good comes of blaming you or anyone after their sincerest of efforts. Besides, you and your descendants safeguarded Gungnir, yes?"

"We did. That and other relics," Metkhal said, "We couldn't assume Kanet Lhangatssen could keep it safe. Not with so much of Fjareskjon underwater."

"No, even so seafaring a people as the Fjarthursk had their limitations," she said, "So tell me. This other face I'm seeing. Is he this Galo that the girls spoke of?"

"He is," Metkhal said, "I reincarnated in the same generation as Eytea."

"And this is Takmet with you, yes? When did he escape the copper?"

"Shortly before Galo was born. He posed as his grandfather, Gijin."

Freja put a hand to her chest. "Oh my. That is quite the ordeal for an Omphaloworlder," she professed, "I see. So, he's the reason I'm seeing Metkhal and Galo?"

"Yes, it can be… disorienting. But I like to think we're getting used to sharing control," Metkhal said, "We're even picking up each other's language. Watch this."

"Eytea!"

She jumped at her name being called in a thick Mberhali accent. No clue what Metkhal wanted to, or could, talk to her about, Eytea acknowledged him with a shrug.

"Do you have the mango juices?"

Eytea cocked her head and stared agape. She laughed and shook her head as she looked to Gijin for an explanation. Metkhal returned to his conversation with Freja.

"It would appear that my old son has been learning from my new grandson," Gijin said, "He's just, well, showing off for an old friend."

"Oh my gosh!" Elemeno gasped, "He totally has a crush on her!"

"What? No!" Gijin refuted, subtly nodding to her, "He could never be with her. He knows that."

"Is it really that unheard of for Etherworlders and Omphaloworlders to fall in love?" Eytea asked, "I mean, I get we have different lifespans, but—"

"It is when the Etherworlder's spouse is one such as Odin."

Eytea smacked her lips. "Well," she said, "she didn't mention that."

"I implore you to pardon the exclusion," Freja interjected as she drifted nearer, "My betrothment was not relevant to our past exchanges."

"Especially not once she knew his condition had become suspect," Eir added, "We know what conclusions Omphaloworlders might draw from that."

"Indeed. But on the topic of suspect behavior," Freja said, "What sorcery was that with the ground? Did I see a furnished living quarters?"

"You did, but I was hoping you'd understand what I did. Would've hoped harder if I knew you were Odin's wife," Eytea said, "All we've got is a working theory."

"Which is?"

"Metkhal thinks I'm a sort of extra evolved Hybrid. The idea is that the crystal sand has seeped toward this side, and I'm able to make stuff out of the mineral composite," Eytea explained, "You know, like how you Etherworlders built things from the crystals themselves."

"I see," Freja said, pausing to consider, "Well, speaking of which, some Shrines have been restored alongside their Etherworlder. We believe some of our kin bound them to their lives. I certainly wish I had had such foresight."

"Did Khepri and Nut return?" Gijin asked, "Or Liza and Mawu? Is that why it appears to be nighttime here?"

"Ones such as them, yes, but we do not yet know who," Freja said, "Now Eytea, do you understand the implications of this theory? Odin was firm on the divide between Etherworlders and Hybrids." She shot a quick glance to Metkhal. "Why do you suppose he would permit his own Hybrid to acquire a power so similar to one unique to we Etherworlders?"

A throaty voice rumbled through the darkness. "Because she's his failsafe."

Chapter 10

Eytea whipped around at the sound of his voice, thready and subdued as it was. Staggering from the darkness came the wispy vision of her betrothed. Unstable and frail of depth, he clung to a minotaur of such domineering stature as to rival the man's father. Eytea's chin quivered as her mouth hung agape.

Calling out his name, she ran to him. Sinkua pushed away from the minotaur, his depthless form rolling into her arms.

Eytea held him as firmly as she could bring herself to, fearing she could crush him, he looked so frail. He gasped and hacked into her shoulder, acrid moisture running down her shoulder blade.

"What happened?" she choked out, "What happened to you?"

"Ga—"

"Please. Please tell me you'll be okay."

"Galo."

"Don't worry about Galo. Galo's okay," Eytea insisted, "I can't lose you like this, okay?"

"Take me," Sinkua exhaled, "to Galo."

"It's okay," she said, "You don't need to apologize."

"It's… not," he grunted, wriggling out of her grasp.

He staggered away, wobbling and swaying as he moved toward the others. Eytea hustled after him, but a meaty hand grabbed her shoulder.

Her eyes scaled the massive frame of the minotaur at her side. He was even taller than she had thought. But despite his fearsome presence, there was warmth in his eyes.

"Galo ma waned kemekened," he said, "Meba aw rah marem."

"I…" Eytea stammered, "I don't know what you just said."

The minotaur put his arm around Sinkua and walked with him. Slow and unsteady as they were, that minotaur kept him upright and never left his side.

Eytea's throat tightened as she watched them converge with Galo. She had long known him to be the type to risk himself for her well-being. For any of them. And she'd have done the same.

But to see him like this, so much on her behalf, cut deeper into her composure than she knew she could feel. Her mother had told her about his spiraling depression. Her death had been painful. Excruciatingly so. But he had to live, knowing he had fallen just short of saving her.

She was finally seeing what that truly meant. He had returned to the afterlife for her. But she had to watch him wither away.

Then there was his assertion. He had called her Odin's failsafe. It almost sounded like an accusation.

But she couldn't be mad at him. He couldn't have intended any of the malice she heard. Not in the state he was in. Stupefied and frustrated as she was, she couldn't even be sure there had been any malice in his voice.

The minotaur obstructed her view of Sinkua and Galo. She steeled herself for whatever grim spectacle might lie beyond him and pushed herself a meter off the ground.

Instead, she gasped into a puzzled smile as she found Sinkua upright and robust. Glimmers of another face flickered with fully green eyes on Sinkua's jawline. When she saw Galo's and Metkhal's faces in a shared presence, Eytea began to understand.

"Sinkua," she sighed, nuzzling his shoulder as she hugged his side. She looked up at his eyes and smiled. "Who's your friend?"

"This is Tetsen Drukoa," Sinkua said, "Most of him. It's a long story. Sorry if I worried you."

"What? No!" Eytea scoffed, slapping his chest, "Okay fine. Maybe a little."

She rubbed his arm, smiling as she shook her head. There was so much to tell him. So much to ask him. But she could only bask in the moment.

"Tetsen Drukoa," she said, "Kanet Lhangatssen's boyfriend, right?"

"Yeah. You met his father," Sinkua said, "Tetsen and Kanet were both friends with Metkhal, too."

"Metkhal and Takmet called him Tsenukoa as an honorary Mberhali," Galo provided, "That's where Gijin got the name Sinkua from. Few millennia in copper, and he got the name mixed up."

"Right. Right. I feel like you mentioned that at some point," Eytea said, "So what's going on here? I mean, I get why both of you have, well, both of you out. But what was happening to you before? And why are you okay now?"

"Phoenix brought me back from the dead, which I think she could only do because I used the dagger. I'm not sure. Anyway, Odin came to take me to Nikasu, so we could go after MalVek," Sinkua recounted, "But I refused."

"You should have gone," Eytea said, "You could've come back for us later."

Sinkua shook his head. "It was a trap," he said, "I told Odin that Nikasu and I wouldn't stand much of a chance against MalVek. I said we'd be better off with you two and Vielle. But that was a lie. The first part, I mean. Judging by how we fared against Pandora and that I killed her Hybrid, I'm sure she and I could've handled MalVek."

"Well now—" Galo cut in.

"If barely," Sinkua assured, "Truth is, I was afraid of Odin. I couldn't risk him being there when we confront MalVek."

"For what reason might you be afraid of Odin?" Eir asked.

"I'm sorry. Who are you?"

"Eir. De facto leader of the Valkyrie," Eir said, "These are my sistren, Randgrid and Sigrdrifa."

"We serve Odin in the afterlife," Randgrid added, "by selecting his next Hybrid."

"Well, I can't put this gently, but your boss is up to some sketchy shit."

"We feared as much," Eir confessed, "We understand he still spoke broken Ouristihran after several weeks in your world, yes?"

"Yeah," Sinkua said, "but I never found that suspicious."

"Fjarthursk Etherworlders only need a little exposure to become fluent in a language," Eytea said, "He should've had it down by the end of the day."

"It's like the old bastard's finally losing his mind," Sigrdrifa said, "But then what did tip you off?"

"Since you work closely with him, why don't you tell me why you're suspicious of him?" Sinkua insisted.

"He chose a new soul to be his Hybrid," Sigrdrifa said, "At least one of his usuals was up for reincarnation within a decade of Eytea's birth."

"But he was in the Yggdrasil Void when she was born," Sinkua puzzled.

"Exactly!" Sigrdrifa remarked, "It's as much as a matter of how he chose someone new as why."

Sinkua let out a long huff, his eyes wide. "Well, this circles back to why I was how I was when I showed up," he said, "Odin threw me into the Netherworld. Alive."

Every set of eyes jerked to face him. Even the minotaur's, though he was probably just reading the room.

"What the fuck?!" Eytea blurted.

"Yeah," Sinkua said, "I'm here in my physical body."

"He used Gungnir's Judgment on you, yes?" Eir asked, "Where he throws his spear and—"

"Yeah," he said, coughing.

"We only just met, but you do not at all strike me as deserving of such judgment. None of the Hybrids of Phoenix have," Eir said, "And you are no beastkin."

"Well. That's something to unpack later," Sinkua remarked, "But no, you're right. Gungnir didn't think so either."

"It tried to send you here?"

"I think so. Odin changed the portal."

"And he chose not to strip your soul," Eir added, "He wanted you to have your body in the Netherworld."

"He also tried to take credit for Phoenix and I resurrecting."

"An absurd assertion, to be sure. That has nothing to do with him."

"Right? I mean, the guy's a blowhard, but—"

"It's threat management," Galo interrupted.

"Beg your pardon?" Eir asked, "Could you elaborate?"

"Odin has to have noticed that other Etherworlders have been coming back," Galo said, "And my brother has never been subtle about his misgivings about people."

"I see. You believe Odin meant to prevent a meeting of the minds," Eir said, "Binding the informant to three dimensions in a four-dimensional world would be an effective countermeasure."

"Sucks for him that he didn't anticipate Sleipnir turning on him," Sinkua said, "Or Arestor feeling like he owed me one for trying to help him."

"Or Tetsen Drukoa lending you his eyes so you can see clearly?" Eytea asked, "That's what's happening, right?"

"More or less," Sinkua said, "Phoenix carries the memories of all her Hybrids. They've been, ah, leaking out as memory imprints. As long as Galo is nearby, Tetsen can copilot." He turned to Galo. "Of course, that means you have to deal with Metkhal copiloting with you. Sorry about that."

"It's no bother," Galo insisted, "We've already had some experience with this. You know, since Grandpa and Takmet are the same person."

"Have you met any of your other past selves?" Eytea asked.

"Just a woman named Fetzikzi Aroka. No honorary Mberhali name as far as I know," Sinkua said, "She knew a past incarnation of Kabehl. He was a faun, which is this sort of weregoat, named Kervatus. He sold other fauns to satyrs. Whatever those are."

"Once a trafficker, always a trafficker," Eytea muttered.

"Well as much as we can't trust any version of him, he said something worth looking into," Sinkua said, "He says Odin created you as a failsafe against Pandora."

Eytea stared at him for a few dragging seconds. A couple of hard blinks and a shake of the head later, she finally spoke. "The hell does that mean?"

"Beats me," Sinkua said, shrugging, "He just said you're supposed to secure Odin's legacy against Pandora, but you'll fail and self-destruct."

"So, he didn't choose a new soul from the Yggdrasil Void," Eytea said, "He made a new soul and sent it to the Omphaloworld. However the fuck that works."

"Kabehl did say he had you made, so he might have given the order before he went into the roots."

"Which means he has an accomplice," Galo added.

"Has or had. We can't say for sure," Sinkua said, "But all the more reason to make quick work of getting out of here."

"Had, yes. I hadn't considered that," Galo said, "Even if we knew who his accomplice was, we don't have a timeline for when any of the Etherworlders died."

"I'm afraid we'd be inadequate counsel in that regard," Randgrid said.

"It's MalVek all over again," Sinkua said, "Whatever Odin's intentions are for Eytea, we don't know how far back his scheming goes."

"So, what do we need to do to make this happen quick?" Eytea asked, "Find Vielle and get the sword, right?"

Opacity flowed from Sinkua's face and into Tetsen's. Arestor and Tetsen spoke in what Eytea figured was the same language Arestor had addressed her in. After a moment, Arestor gestured his farewell and walked away as Tetsen relinquished opacity.

"He's gonna go back to the Netherworld to keep looking for Epesol," Sinkua said, looking past Eytea's shoulder, "But speaking of Vielle, I think Arestor climbed an Yggdrasil branch to get us out of there."

"Pahres did say it spans reality," Galo said, "That could include the afterlife."

"That side, anyway," Eytea said, glancing back to see what had caught Sinkua's attention, "It might have restricted itself from coming here, like how Sleipnir did."

"So he's not tempted to take people back to the living world," Sinkua asked, to which Eytea nodded, "Well, I don't think that branch was supposed to be there. It felt burnt and petrified."

"Do you think maybe Vielle forced it through there to help you?" Galo asked.

"Something like that," Sinkua said, narrowing his eyes at another snatched glance, "I think she's trying to lead us to her."

"I've been seeing green flashes," Eytea said, "I bet she has something to do with it."

"Yeah, she might. Checking up on you could be how she found out about Galo and me," Sinkua said, "Hey, so who's the woman in the bird coat?"

"Oh, that's—" Galo began.

Eytea shushed him and subtly shook her head. "I'll go talk to her."

She left the four of them in two entities to discuss their next move as she hurried to catch up with Freja. She hadn't noticed it until she caught Sinkua looking her way, but Freja had been distancing herself from the gathering.

A tinge of envy pulled at her conscience. And with Sinkua in his body, she couldn't assume this was what he felt when other men's eyes skimmed her a bit too much. No, this was all her own, hard as it was to rationalize.

Freja's ethereal grace was undeniable, a perfect complement to Sinkua's crassness. Sure, she was married to Odin, so she had no room for further courtship. Especially not an Omphaloworlder, much to Metkhal's chagrin.

But with Odin compromised, maybe corrupted, Freja could have sought other companionship. Perhaps with the man who had been uncovering her husband's schemes.

Whether Sinkua could even want her was neither a question nor an issue. Freja was a Etherworlder of fertility and love, a literal sex symbol. Anyone of a proper orientation could have wanted her, and Sinkua was no exception. Eytea knew, if she felt that way about women, she would've found her attractive, too.

She forced a stern expression as she came up alongside Freja.

"Hey, what's wrong?" Eytea asked, "I just saw you wandering off. Are you trying to avoid us?"

"Not all of you," Freja assured with an almost pitying smile, "Just him."

"You mean Metkhal?" Eytea asked, "Because he has a crush on you?"

Freja let out a boisterous laugh. "My lingering would indeed stir some… discomfort in him," she said, sounding almost boastful, "But no, he's not the one I speak of."

"Good, because that wasn't his last lifetime crushing on someone he can't be with," Eytea said, "Galo went through it, too. Not with an Etherworlder. Just a classic boy meets lesbian story."

"I have sensed a much-requited love within him. I suppose that happened after your passing."

"Must have. Good for him," Eytea said, "So I guess you're avoiding Sinkua, then?"

"I am indeed."

"Is it because he confirmed the Valkyries' suspicions about Odin?"

"Nothing so weak-willed as that," Freja insisted, "I've had adequate time to steel myself for so uncomfortable a truth. No, this is for his sake."

"How so?"

"It's because of what he called memory imprints," Freja said, "Every one of his incarnations, up through Tetsen Drukoa, was personally familiar with me."

"And he already said they've been leaking out."

"Precisely. I fear that my speaking with him could worsen the matter," Freja said, "In fact, I implore you to keep him clear of any Etherworlders here."

"What about the Valkyrie?"

"If he's ever met them, it's likely been brief and only on this side."

"Oh. Right. Of course," Eytea said, nodding vigorously, "Hey, so that stuff about me being Odin's failsafe? I'm sorry if it's a sore subject, but—"

"If there's merit to it, there's merit to Metkhal's theory about you," Freja interrupted, "I am uncertain as to what manner of failsafe you might provide to his legacy. But if he intended for you such a purpose, he may have granted you powers beyond those of a typical Hybrid. And if he is corrupted, that may have informed such a decision."

"Corrupted…" Eytea said, letting the aftertaste of the word linger, "Does that mean I'm a mistake? Or a threat?"

"Oh, perish the thought, my little neophyte," Freja guffawed, "Whatever intentions he had for your soul, you were born of Omphaloworlder genetics and influence. Nature and nurture, I believe they are called. Your free will is your own and your life and afterlife to your choosing."

"Thank you. I… needed to hear that," Eytea said. Her expression flattened as realization struck, and she looked up to meet Freja's eyes. "So, you're saying fate is bullshit?"

Freja laughed again. "Yes, I suppose I am," she said, "We Etherworlders have our hopes and intentions for you Omphaloworlders, but loath as some are to accept it, we cannot force you to align with them."

"Well in that case, you should look into The Avatars of Fate," Eytea suggested, "Maybe there's a connection between them and what happened to Odin."

"Thank you. I will keep your advice in mind," Freja said, "And if I might offer some in kind?"

"Yes. Please do."

"Seek the Famidraget Shrines. If the Phoenix Shrine is among them, Epesol may find its way there."

"Should we tell Arestor to call off the search in the Netherworld?" Eytea asked, "I mean, if we can catch up to him before he goes in the river."

"I would not advise it," Freja said, "My advice is largely postulation, and I know not how the sword being in the Netherworld might factor into it."

"Fair enough," Eytea said, "Well thank you. We'll look into it."

Eytea took only a couple of steps before realization stopped her.

"Hey, one more thing."

Freja turned with a look that blurred quizzicality with annoyance.

"Can I tell Sinkua about you?"

"Yes as long as he keeps his distance from me."

Eytea hurried back to the others before Sinkua thought to approach Freja. But by the time she got back, the crowd had dispersed.

"Hey, what'd I miss?" she asked, "And where's everyone else."

"Takmet went to check on Pahres," Galo said, "He wants to get the Trifecta back together considering the news about Odin."

"The Valkyries are off looking for Fjarthursk Etherworlders and seeing who's ready to pick their next Hybrid," Elemeno said, "So just back to work."

"Okay. So, it's just the four of us," Eytea said, "Six with Tetsen and Metkhal."

"Seven with Miss Aroka," Sinkua added.

"Right. Can't forget her."

"So, who was that woman?"

"Freja. She's the Fjarthursk Etherworlder of love and fertility. And Odin's wife," Eytea said, "She said she has to keep her distance, so she doesn't stir up your other incarnations."

"Damn. Might've been good to have an Etherworlder along," Sinkua said, "But I see where she's coming from."

"She actually said for you to avoid Etherworlders while you're here. The Valkyrie are safe though," Eytea said, "Oh! But she did say that Epesol might end up at the Famidraget Shrines. But I didn't get to ask what Famidraget is."

"Odin called Drakougeneospa Husefamidraget," Sinkua said, "It's the House of the Dragon Family."

"You think Famidraget means Dragon Family?"

"Or maybe House of the Dragon," Galo chimed in, "Probably not House of the Family. That's a little mundane."

"Right?" Sinkua said, chuckling, "Well I hope you two know where there are any shrines at all, because I've seen fuck-all but rocks and a river."

"They're on the underside of the islands," Galo said, "The crystals are the remains of them."

"Great. Good. It's a start," Sinkua said, "An Etherworlder is our best shot at finding specific shrines, though, and I can't ask them for directions."

Eytea looked down at her hand as a faint glowing warmth emanated from her ring finger.

"We might not have to," she said, showing him her hand.

Sinkua narrowed his eyes at it. "Is that... from the engagement ring?" he asked, "Did you find it?"

"Sorry, no. I had a, um, a bit of a meltdown earlier, and it started doing this," Eytea said, "We think the ruby left an impression on me."

"Which we could use to find Epesol like a game of hot-and-cold?"

"Exactly!" Eytea beamed, "That's how I explained it to Galo. Four-dimensional hot-and-cold. I first came out here because I thought it sensed you nearby."

"Well, the logic tracks, so it's worth a shot," Sinkua said, "Phoenix lived in the Ruby, and Epesol reacts to her milystis." He turned his attention to her mother. "Did you want to go back with us? After what happened, I feel like I should at least offer."

"Oh, you know I don't blame you for any of that," Elemeno insisted, "But I'll have to think about it. Tell me how it feels when you're crossing over, if you could. For all we know, it might not be safe without milystis."

"That's a good point. I hadn't thought of that," Sinkua said, "It's probably safer if I just revive you after I get back."

"Well thank you for considering me, but I'll need time to decide if I even want to go back," Elemeno said.

"In the meantime, we should look for victims of The Avatars of Fate. Especially those of MalVek and The Harvester," Galo said, "They might have intel we could take back with us."

"Great idea, brother," Sinkua said, "If we're lucky, maybe we can take them back with us, too."

"Only if you think you can handle it," Eytea said.

Galo and Metkhal flashed wolfish smiles. "The people of Ouristihra will be their own cavalry."

Chapter 11

As he looked out over the sea of roiling clouds, Sinkua's every thought traced back to the base of Yggdrasil. Bolstered by everyone's assurances, he extended one foot off the edge. But he drew it back with a sharp exhale of stockpiled little gasps. Same as the countless times before.

A hand found his shoulder. He closed his eyes and focused on gathering the little gasps into steady breaths. Tetsen spoke to him in fractured Ouristihran, peppered with Harkzanian.

He had seen that memory, his suicide attempt at Yggdrasil. So, with Sinkua's eyes closed, Tetsen described the view not for parallels to that moment, but as one of artistic splendor shared across many generations of friends.

Sinkua opened his eyes and cupped his hand over Eytea's.

"Sorry," he exhaled.

"It's okay," she said, "It'll become natural after a few times."

"I'm the one who should apologize," Galo said, "I should've known what this would be like for you."

"But what were you saying just now?" Eytea asked.

Sinkua turned sharply, his mouth slack with confusion. But his furrowed brow soon gave way to wide-eyed realization. Tetsen hadn't been speaking in his mind.

"Shit," Sinkua spat, "That was the other guy."

"Tsenukoa?"

"Yeah. I started meditating, and he took the front seat."

"The restrictions are weakening," Phoenix said, "Smaller changes in your conscious state are allowing the others to take prominence."

"Did I just say something in a woman's voice?" Sinkua asked.

Eytea, Galo, and Elemeno all shook their heads.

"Is Fetzikzi trying to come out?" Eytea asked.

"No. She's just observing for now," Sinkua said, "Phoenix said something. I had to make sure she didn't use me to say it."

"Sinkua," Elemeno beckoned, placing her hand flat on his back, "Did I ever tell you the name I used when I helped rescue Nikasu?"

Sinkua thought on it for a moment. The tension left his shoulders, and his breathing evened. Whatever her angle was, his pondering had cast off his misgivings at least for a moment.

"I'm actually looking for an answer, you know," Elemeno insisted, "If you can't remember it, I probably didn't."

"Oh! Sorry. Guess you didn't then," Sinkua said, "What was it?"

"Teyaku."

Elemeno looked at him expectingly. She was proud of this alias, and it must have had something to do with him. But she just gestured ever more emphatically as he failed to see the relevance of it.

Fetzikzi tugged at the back of his thoughts, drawing his attention inward. She saw the relevance of the name, and he was embarrassed when she spelled it out. He chalked it up to distress and overthinking.

"A piece of her name and a piece of mine," he said as he emerged from his inner dialogue, "Teya from Eytea and ku from Sinkua."

Elemeno beamed. "I knew you'd get it eventually," she said, "Now I came up with that name because I was doing what you two would've done if you could. I needed to be the kind of person who would put herself in danger to save someone from the worse of it."

"The difference is that stepping off the ledge doesn't endanger you," Galo said, "But the longer you wait, the more danger Nikasu might be in."

Sinkua nodded vigorously. "You're right. You're both right," he said, "You're absolutely right. I should just… step off… into the abyss. Because… that will… save… my little sister."

He took a decisive step toward the edge, only to wince and pivot away yet again. But before he could say anything, Eytea grabbed his hands and turned him the rest of the way around, standing between him and the edge.

"You tried to kill yourself because you weren't able to save me."

He swallowed and nodded.

"And you thought Galo had abandoned you."

"Y… Yeah."

"And that my mom hated you."

He nodded once more.

"Well now that we're all with you, you know two of those weren't even true," Eytea said, "And you can make up for the other one, but we have to go to the flip side first." She tightened her grip on his hands. "But I gotta say, even if it doesn't pan out, all the effort is… pretty hot."

She cupped his hands over the sides of her breasts and moved her own hands to his waist. Sinkua's vision smeared and warped as Tetsen retracted toward Miss Aroka. His stomach churned in stark contrast to where his hands were taking his mind, and he slumped forward.

Eytea pressed herself against him, pinning his arms in the posture of a perverted tyrannosaur, and fell backward. Over the edge and onto the crystalline expanse of the flip side.

A messy landing knocked them apart, and Tetsen resumed his post in dual prominence. Eytea rolled a ways further before coming up on her hands and knees, panting through laughter.

"You should've seen the looks on your faces!" she said, "Tsenukoa was like, 'Oh no! Boobs! My not-favorite thing!' And Sinkua was all, 'Heh heh. Nice. I missed these.' And then, 'Oh no! I can't see shit!'"

Sinkua folded his arms and shook his head, failing to stifle his laughter.

"Are you done?" he asked.

Eytea's laughter sputtered out. "Um. Let's see. Then I flipped you over the edge. And now we're here. So… Yeah. Guess I am."

Sinkua looked out over the field of coarse crystalline sand. "Weird," he said, "They're not the mountains I remember."

"Rude!" Eytea gasped, looking down her shirt, "Absence makes the hands grow hornier, huh?"

"Oh, shut up," Sinkua laughed, "If anything, they're better than I remember. I'm talking about the crystals. They looked like upside-down mountains when I was dead here."

Elemeno and Galo with Metkhal joined him at his sides.

"They were, but they were Shrines back before Pandora nearly wiped out the other Etherworlders," Galo said, "As best we can figure, those crystals fused into mountains, and everyone since just came up with their own explanations for them."

"We figure they fell apart so their Shrines could be rebuilt when the Etherworlders started coming back," Elemeno said, "Unless maybe the Bealstillans have something to do with it."

"What do you think they'd have to do with this?" Sinkua asked.

"Hey that's right, we never got to tell you. Sorry, there's been a lot happening," Galo said, "A bunch of souls reverted to incarnations who spoke what we later learned was Bealstillan. They all gathered over here and started trying to build with the crystal sand.

"Freja thought Bragi was playing a practical joke," Eytea said "He's the Fjarthursk Etherworlder of the literary arts."

"Amirione was one of them," Galo said, "He'd just told me he was glad The Geneticist was dead. The shifting matter state was supposed to be a cure for his bulletproof bones. Which was a cure-gone-terminal for a terminal brittle bone condition. Which was what first led him to The Avatars."

"Shit," Sinkua spat, "You mean The Hunter was being—"

"No, he sought them out," Galo interrupted, "He wanted to spend whatever time he had left working with them."

"Still an asshole then, but now also kind of an idiot," Sinkua said, "But I think the Bealstillans were my doing."

"Sinkua," Elemeno said, "You caused a mass identity crisis. Don't you think you're being a little too nonchalant?"

"No need to be harsh with him," Galo insisted, "We both know he's been trying to not be so hard on himself."

The two of them shared a long stare, which became flattened looks of annoyance.

"Well, if you're done impersonating each other," Sinkua said, "Galo's right. And Elemeno, you probably are, too. Come on. Walk and talk. Eytea, take point."

"Sorry about that, brother. It's the nature of this place," Galo said, "I guess your body exempts you from it."

Sinkua thought back on his brief disembodied time here. As best he could remember, people who knew each other would either pick up the other's behavior or the other's feelings toward them. Foisted mimicry or foisted empathy.

His mutual contempt with Kabehl was useless in telling whether that held in the Netherworld. Fetzikzi and Kervatus were little more help. But Kabehl's resignation ill fit someone who so ardently cheated death.

"Seems like it," Sinkua said, "But as I was saying, I think I triggered what happened with the Bealstillans. After Odin left me behind, I found what was left of the village. I gathered up the remains of Pandora's victims and had Phoenix try to revive them."

"Why? It's not like you could've brought any of them back," Eytea said, "So what were you trying to do?"

"I know. Even if there weren't time constraints, they all must've reincarnated several times," Sinkua said, "I was hoping the tension from pulling at their souls would create a, um... portal into the afterlife."

"It's, well, not the worst reasoning," Galo said, "but that was reckless even for you."

"I know. I was desperate. Phoenix thought the worst that could happen was souls starting to unravel."

"Like what happened to Arestor?" Galo asked.

"Yes, but only while she was pulling. And she insisted she was only guessing, and it probably wouldn't happen," Sinkua said, "Neither of us thought it would cause the ones here to revert like that."

"Is that what brought Odin back to confront you?" Eytea asked, "Or did he not care because they weren't Fjarthursk?"

"Neither as far as I know," Sinkua said, though this did shine a different light on Odin's corruption, "I blacked out and went brimstone. Everything's cloudy between then and when he came back, but I think I went back to the annex."

"How?" Galo asked, "The underwater bridge was incomplete."

Sinkua shrugged. "In any case, I remember feeling souls fading out and... I don't know.... turning back on? It was like a dimmer switch for tsora."

"Sounds like you were resurrecting and killing the people who died when MalVek was sending you to The Veil," Galo suggested, "Must've been horrifying for them."

"Yeah," Sinkua sighed, "But that's my problem. You two don't need to stress over it."

"Should we expect Odin to be waiting for us on the annex when we get back?" Eytea asked.

"I don't know where we'll pop out, but I wasn't on the annex when he found me," Sinkua said, running his fingers along the beginnings of a crystalline pillar, "I went back to Bealstilla. Seriamus came to mind just before I came to my senses."

"Pandora's Hybrid," Galo supplied as a preemptive courtesy to Eytea and Elemeno, "It might be a good thing that Odin interrupted you when he did. Intentions and awareness aside, it sounds like—"

"I got desperate enough to try reviving the motherfucker of all Hybrids to open a portal here," Sinkua interrupted, "Don't worry, I already kinda hate my brimstone self for that one."

"You remember what I told you, right?" Galo asked, "On Borret's ship?"

"Yeah. I won't forget."

Eytea nudged his side. "What did he tell you?" she asked in hushed tones.

"He can commit me if he thinks I need it."

They walked in silence for a stretch, trying to let the growing scenery overshadow that revelation and his realization that came with it. For the first time, Sinkua truly considered the conundrum he had put himself into.

There was no reason to believe Odin had anything to do with his resurrection. The most logical conclusion was it was because he had released Phoenix with the dagger and sacrificed her and himself in tandem. But if he had died any other way, he probably would've reincarnated by now.

For all he knew, his bluff about Nikasu being pregnant with Galo's child was true. He could've been awaiting rebirth as his best friend's son and his own nephew.

Instead, he was clinging to this life. This life who had been, and could still be, manipulated to juggle the lives of strangers. All because, somehow, better people would be hurt if he let go.

And were he to save Galo, Eytea, and hopefully Vielle, his own return could land him in a padded prison. But maybe that was what he deserved. After all, the surest way to avoid it was to leave them behind. They couldn't commit him if he was the only one alive.

He took a measure of solace from that fact though. That was a line he wouldn't dare cross, and that told him he was still in his right mind.

Sinkua receded and let Tetsen take point. He could still hear the others, but they sounded distant. And only Tetsen could speak. So, while Tetsen more fully immersed himself in Ouristihran, Sinkua floated in the muffled earshot space between his companions and Fetzikzi.

Galo, Eytea, and Elemeno discussed the partially built shrines. Some grew before their eyes while others were being reassembled by, presumably, Bealstillans. As best they could figure, the ones that were growing were bound to their Etherworlders. Sinkua made a note to ask what that meant later.

His focus was on translating for Tetsen and Fetzikzi. Not that he spoke much Harzkanian. But he knew a handful of words and could at least give them that much to work from.

"It is quite lovely though," Elemeno said.

"We don't have time for sightseeing," Galo reminded, "But yes, it is. I wonder if this has anything to do with the Lechuatzulan's stonecrafting or the Quircois's metallurgy."

"I'm sorry. Who?" Eytea asked.

"Ancient Lenguardians and Kirtsians," Galo said, "The Lechuatzulans made the Phoenix Ruby, and the Quircois made Epesol and the rest of the Dragon Family swords."

"Not ArcNosian ancestors. Interesting," Eytea pondered, "Hey Sinkua? Do any of the other yous..."

She trailed off as she turned to face him, finding that Tetsen's was the more prominent face now. Tetsen winced and shrank back at her turning to him with unbridled curiosity and enthusiasm.

"What? Tsenukoa? You don't..." Eytea fumbled, "Wait. You can't understand me. Sinkua! Can you tell him he doesn't need to be scared of me?"

Sinkua considered what memories could best convey this. Or convey it at all. He couldn't portray her as harmless, but assessing her character from the harm she could and had done required context.

Before Sinkua could try to calm him though, Tetsen started speaking Harzkanian at Eytea. He pointed an accusing finger, then grabbed his wrist hard enough to shake it. Tetsen pointed at Eytea's breasts, then shook his head as he swiped his hand before his throat. He pulled his arms in and shuddered.

Eytea stood with her mouth agape. Elemeno and Galo waited aside, exchanging mutterings.

"Oh? ... Oh! Oh gosh! I am so sorry!" Eytea sputtered. She reached a shaky hand toward his shoulder but hesitated and withdrew. "I... I just wanted to startle Sinkua. I didn't think... I didn't think about what it would do to you, Tsenukoa."

Tetsen made sudden eye contact. "You... like... those name?" he asked. Sinkua corrected him.

"That name?" Tsenukoa doubled back.

"Metkhal's father. Takmet called you that, right?"

"Father... Patera?" Tsenukoa asked, gesturing up and over his shoulder. He mirrored it on the other shoulder and asked, "Mitera... Mather?"

"Mother," Eytea corrected, "Galo's grandfather. Patera patera?"

Tsenukoa chuckled "Pappos."

"Galo's pappos," Eytea said, "named Sinkua after you."

Sinkua presented his memory of meeting Gijin as a child. He showed Tsenukoa that his birth name had been MeiLom, but the Chieftain Sage, hosting the soul of Takmet, dubbed him Sinkua as he gave him the Phoenix Ruby.

Tsenukoa gave Eytea a once over. He sighed and shook his head. He put his fist to his collarbone, then clutched Eytea's shoulder only long enough to give a begrudging nod. He shouldered past her to continue their expedition.

Sinkua resumed control just long enough to turn and address her.

"He guesses you're cool," he said, "As long as you don't make him grope you again."

Eytea let out a small laugh. "I won't," she said, "I promise."

"I don't suppose you can ask if he knows what the Famidraget Shrines look like, can you?" Elemeno asked, "No, of course not. He doesn't have those memories."

"The only one with any memory of the shrines is Metkhal," Galo said, "But most of them were sand when he was here, and he can't remember if he ever found the Phoenix Shrine."

Sinkua consulted Phoenix as the rest of them continued speaking. He heard only notions and fragments of their conversation. Elemeno hoped that finding the Dragon Family Shrines would jog Metkhal's memories. It would only help if Metkhal had seen the Phoenix Shrine though. And it left them relying on Eytea's ring finger to find the Dragon Family Shrines.

"Hey, it's a place to start," Eytea assured as Sinkua came out of his inner dialogue, "Tsenukoa? What do you know about this place? Did you learn what the Phoenix Shrine looks like?"

Tsenukoa looked at her with the blankest of bewilderment.

"I'm joking. It's a joke," Eytea said, "Of course you can't answer that."

"Phoenix can't help. She's never seen it," Sinkua said, "She doesn't even know what designs made it into the books."

"I thought she was bound to your mind though," Galo said, "She should have memories of everything that was put in the books."

"She distanced herself for certain moments. Writing in the books being one of them," Sinkua said, "It was a matter of courtesy. And how she's been able to keep the others of me at bay."

"Leviathan did the same thing when something was bothering me."

"Okay but for now, we've got my ring finger to track down the Famidraget Shrines," Eytea said, "and when we get there, Metkhal might recognize the Phoenix Shrine."

"There's another among you who might know," a disembodied voice said, announcing itself from indiscernible depths.

Sinkua took point as Mortvill emerged from behind a crystal column. Dark lines in his mask showed where it had been mended. This was the one he had killed. The Harvester. His mask must have been bound to his soul.

"Elemeno," The Harvester said, "I long suspected there was something more to you. Now, freed from the fetters of a body, I see it well."

"Don't think you can intimidate her just because she's dead," Eytea scolded, "She held up The Geneticist at gunpoint. And broke The Scout's neck."

"I know her exploits better than you realize, child," The Harvester said, "This matter is between your mother and myself. I implore you to stand aside."

"It's okay, Eytea," Elemeno said, "I can handle myself."

Sinkua exchanged knowing glances with Galo and Eytea. Metkhal looked poised to intervene as well. Sinkua receded to consult Fetzikzi through visual memories. Other voices became distant and hollow.

"Elemeno," The Harvester said, "I wonder if you might enlighten me."

Elemeno swallowed hard and squared her shoulders. "What do you wanna know?"

"Do you know the two most powerful forces at humankind's employ?"

Her eyes widened with an epiphanous smile. "Well, it sure as hell isn't venture capitalism."

"Not at all," The Omnimath said, laughing, "I'm glad I found you, Elemeno. Or would you prefer Teyaku? Or Picuarus?"

"Elemeno will do," she said, "What about you? Mortvill? Or Omnimath?"

"My title does not so define me as to become me. Unlike The Harvester," he said, "Call me Mortvill."

Sinkua's stomach folded in on itself. He hadn't killed the founder and of The Avatars of Fate. He had slain the leader of The Coalition. And on his most ambitious infiltration mission, no less.

Sure, he had had his disputes with The Coalition. But they weren't his enemy. Manipulative self-important nuisances, yes. Nothing worth killing over though.

But something didn't add up. Mortvill came to kill him and take the Phoenix Ruby, just as The Harvester would have done.

Sinkua couldn't comprehend why The Omnimath had still kept up the façade. He must have had something in mind for the Phoenix Ruby, but Sinkua, Tsenukoa, and Fetzikzi were all at a loss. Their only clue was that it was something The Omnimath couldn't have accomplished before MalVek caught on and caught up.

Their best guess was that Mortvill was trying to keep it away from MalVek. But killing Sinkua for it would have made it harder to protect the Phoenix Ruby. They were, once again, at a loss.

"Look at my eyes, Miss Elemeno," Mortvill said, "and all will become clear."

A horrifying realization struck Sinkua as Mortvill reached for his mask. Mortvill had, if the stories were true, lived so long that every one of his past selves might have known him. Seeing his face here could shake loose any or all of the memory imprints, just as Freja feared his meeting her might do.

The mask came down.

"Skata!" Tsenukoa shouted.

Sinkua plunged into his own subconscience and took shelter behind Fetzikzi and beyond sight and sound.

Vertigo swept over them, and everything went dark.

Chapter 12

Elemeno looked down at herself. She was smaller now. Darker, too.

"Jehgoro!" a small voice called out.

She looked toward the voice through no will of her own. On the one hand, she had no control over this body. On the other hand, moving her head so quickly didn't ache her neck. Not the worst tradeoff.

"Jehgoro. There you are," the other child said as he caught up, "I thought we were meeting at the north end."

Jehgoro looked over his shoulder to an ornate stone fountain. Elemeno couldn't help but share in his smile, both at the grandeur of the fountain and his childlike wonder.

"Sorry Nayon," Jehgoro said as he hopped down, "I like how the water smells here."

"You're weird," Nayon said with a laugh, "Come on. The best ones'll be gone if we don't hurry."

Elemeno wondered what they were talking about. She considered probing Jehgoro's mind to find out.

Briefly.

Fact was, she was at a loss as to how this arrangement worked. Or what it even was. But Jehgoro had yet to react to her, so he probably wasn't aware of her presence. Still, digging around in his mind felt intrusive. Especially when all she needed to get answers was to wait.

Jehgoro and Nayon weaved around the other park visitors. Jehgoro's eyes kept flicking toward a cluster of shops just past the northeast corner. His thoughts hastened, and Elemeno picked up an anticipatory taste of papaya and sugarcane.

The two boys scrambled up to a stall.

"Detonde! Hi!" Nayon called out.

The woman jumped, nearly spilling the tray in her hands. Elemeno chuckled, being reminded of many such moments with her Eytea. Detonde turned around with what Elemeno knew was a partially forced smile.

Detonde was what the boys would've called an older woman, though Elemeno was even more so. Just a bit, or at least so Elemeno told herself.

"Nayon. Jehgoro," Detonde said, "You boys are just in time."

"Really?!" Nayon asked, his posture perking up.

"We beat the crowd?" Jehgoro asked, matching the gesture.

Detonde guffawed, and their bodies deflated. "Of course not," she laughed, "All the best papaya candies are already gone."

Jehgoro turned to Nayon. "I'm sorry. I should've been where I said I'd be."

"Well maybe if this one didn't oversleep so much," Detonde said, gesturing to Nayon, "But don't be hard on yourselves. There's some left, just not the best of them. Five beads for three pieces."

The boys rummaged through their pockets, but they only came up with four beads. Elemeno couldn't tell what they were made of, but they looked hand-carved with little concern for uniformity.

"We don't have enough," Jehgoro said, "Could we get two for four beads, please?"

"Do you know that that's a worse deal?" Detonde asked, "You know your arithmetic, yes?"

"Yeah, but I'm not trying to haggle," Jehgoro countered, "Three beads for two is worse for you than five beads for three. And what would we do with one bead left?"

"Save it for a time like this," a fourth voice cut in.

Jehgoro came alight with an excitement Elemeno wasn't familiar with. This man was special to Jehgoro. Almost like a much older sibling. Perhaps a cousin. Except the admiration felt one-sided.

"Well look who it is," Detonde teased, "See, Nayon? You keep oversleeping, and you too could grow up to do sleight of hand for spare beads."

"Oh, you give me too much credit," the man guffawed. With a flick of the wrist, flames popped from the back of his hand. "If I were that good at sleight of hand, I could just steal the beads. Most of you wouldn't miss them."

Jehgoro stepped back, his mouth agape. Elemeno realized that trick was a common one for this man. It was what he said that startled Jehgoro.

"I'm joking!" the man said, tussling Jehgoro's coarse curls, "At least about stealing. I could. But I wouldn't."

"You shouldn't have to," Jehgoro protested.

"Yeah, you should be politer to him," Nayon said, "He saved our moms' and dads' lives."

"He probably saved yours, too."

Detonde hunkered down to their eye level.

"That's the story he runs with. And your parents run right alongside him," she said, "But I was there."

"So were they," Nayon said.

"So, they know he wasn't the only one in good health when the rest of us began to recover," Detonde said, "Not the only one working on a cure either."

"It's pointless to argue about this. It doesn't matter who believes my story," the man insisted, "What really matters is whether I can chip in my last bead for the small piece."

"Sure!" Jehgoro remarked.

Jehgoro took the man's bead and handed all five to Detonde. Meanwhile, the man turned to address Nayon, crouching to eye level.

"There's nothing wrong with busking, you know," he said, "If you're good at something and it helps people, it's good to do it."

"Even if it only helps by making them happy?"

"Especially so!"

The man accepted his share from Jehgoro, the smallest of three pieces of papaya candy. A woman called out from a ways behind Detonde's stall.

"Hurry up!" she said, "You know I can't stand this heat."

Jehgoro's expression flattened at the sight of her. She was lithe and pale with billowing black hair.

Elemeno jostled, and her vantage point went black.

Sinkua scrambled to his feet and dusted himself off. The carpet felt thicker than he remembered. Looking aside, the ottoman was shoulder high. He looked down at himself, expecting to have landed as a child. He was still an adult though.

The room stretched toward every horizon, seeming to double back and overlap with itself. The furniture changed as it went, in size, color, and even presence itself. The carpet changed color as well, become dingier and more muted. But there were brief patches of revitalization.

But then there were the dark spots. The shadowy regions that smelled of smoke and bile. Bloody tendrils reached out, infecting all they touched. All, that was, but for one exception. A patch of dusty wood flooring with junkyard furniture was unmarred.

"Nice place," a woman said from above his shoulder.

She was a few years his senior and considerably larger, being scaled to the ottoman.

"You must be Miss Aroka," Sinkua said.

"None other," she remarked, "Well, in here anyway. My mom's also Miss Aroka. So are her sisters. And their mom. Just call me Fetzikzi, okay? What about you?"

"What about me?"

"Do you prefer Sinkua or MeiLom?" Fetzikzi clarified, "And do you have a family name?"

"Whichever you like better," Sinkua said, "And no, nobody has them now. By the way, how did you learn Ouristihran so fast?"

"I was about to compliment your Harkzanian," Fetzikzi said, laughing, "Phoenix must be translating for us. But anyway, I'm glad we got you down here."

"Yeah. Thanks for the assist," Sinkua said, pacing around the ottoman, "So. Is this what you looked like at the end of your life?"

Fetzikzi looked herself over. "No, I had about ten maybe fifteen years left after this," she said, "No ring, so Jandruug and I weren't married yet. So, no kids either."

"Married? Kids?" Sinkua stammered, "How did you break the curse? Which iteration are you?"

"Fourth. And it's more of a disconcerting pattern than a curse," Fetzikzi corrected, "We do always end up with the Odin Hybrid. And our reincarnation condition means we can't be with them in the afterlife."

"But that would happen no matter who we're with," Sinkua said, that fact just then occurring to him.

"Exactly! And Hybrids tend to attract conflict," she said, "But nothing's stopping us from starting families. Not even knowing about the so-called curse would always hinder us. Hell, I bet you would've rushed into it out of spite."

Sinkua laughed. "Probably," he said, "So I guess Odin just calls it a curse because he takes it personally."

"That's the best I can make of it."

Sinkua looked to the roiling void of a ceiling. "What do you think they're talking about?"

"He must have recognized her from several generations ago. Maybe from when he first came here."

"The hell are you talking about? He came here about thirty years ago."

"I'm sorry. I said too much," Fetzikzi backpedaled, "It's not my place to discuss it. But you know he's crazy old though, right?"

"Yes, of course," Sinkua said, "What can't you discuss?"

"If I told you that, I'd be discussing it, you doofus," she laughed, "Okay, if you know he's old, it shouldn't shock you to know he knew the first of us. If he thinks Elemeno has info on our Shrine, he probably recognizes her from back then."

"Oh wow, the first Phoenix Hybrid, huh?" he remarked, "I wonder if his memory imprint is in here."

"Probably not. As I understand, she wasn't bound to him long. Not a lot of memories to build from," she said, "But it's already risky with three of us. We shouldn't dig up more if we can help it."

"Do you know his name?"

"Could I have your pardon please?"

Elemeno followed within as Jehgoro turned to find a man in a black tunic a few paces behind him. He had the same complexion as that lithe woman.

"You want my pardon?" Jehgoro puzzled.

"Sorry. I still am learning your language," the man said, "Beg your pardon?"

"That's more like it. What did you need, snowman?"

"I look for a woman with skin like mine. I heard she lives in here?"

"Sure, if by 'lives in here' you mean she leeches off Ajaveo," Jehgoro said, "But she speaks Bealstillan way better than you."

"Ah! That answers my other question. But I don't think you would've known if I asked it," the man fumbled, "I shouldn't have brought it up."

"Brought what up?"

"Ajaveo has something I'm looking for. I mean I'm looking for him because he has something. But I don't need something."

Jehgoro pinched the bridge of his nose. "Look, snowman, do you want me to take you to Ajaveo or not?"

"Oh! Yes please. That would be splendid. By the way, can I ask of your name?"

"Jehgoro. You?"

The man took a long pause as they walked through the plaza. "Pesmenas," he said at last.

"Weird name. How far north are you from?"

"Um, pretty far," Pesmenas said, chuckling nervously.

"Harkzan?"

"Around there."

Galo spun Mortvill by the shoulder as he pulled his mask down. Elemeno stood by with her eyes glazed over, while Sinkua lay nearby, functionally asleep.

"What did you do to them?" Galo demanded.

"I understand you have questions, and for that, you have my transparency," Mortvill said, "But while your concern has merit, they are unharmed."

"Answer his questions," Eytea said, flanking him.

"Elemeno is in a memory of a previous incarnation as a Bealstillan," Mortvill said, "This past self helped me find someone I was looking for."

"What about Sinkua?" Galo asked.

"The person I was looking for was his first incarnation. The first to be the Phoenix Hybrid at least."

"They realized you could've met all of them," Eytea said, "Knocked themselves out to keep from seeing your face."

"A sound deduction," Mortvill said, "They both ought to come around shortly."

"Okay, but if my mother was Bealstillan, why didn't she change?"

"My working theory is that it's because he — that being her prior self — did not die in Bealstilla."

"The Veil obstructed the memories of the people behind it," Galo said, "That's what you're getting at, right? Their reincarnations couldn't access that incarnation in the afterlife until The Veil was down?"

"That is the best I can surmise of it, yes," Mortvill said.

"And if Mom's past self wasn't behind The Veil," Eytea said, looking to Galo, "what Sinkua did wouldn't have affected her."

"What did Sinkua do?" Mortvill asked.

"He tried to revive a bunch of Bealstillans to make a tangible hole between here and the living world."

"That's as reckless as it is illogical," Mortvill said, "But it's useful to know that the change was more than a matter of time."

Seeing Elemeno and Sinkua looking so restful, Galo's thoughts wandered back to the flashes between dying and waking up here. He had reconciled the piggybacked memories of Metkhal's last conversation with Tsenukoa. But he was finally piecing together what had come after that.

It had been this simultaneous pressure and tension. Nothing and everything. A constricting void of intangible tangles, formed of conceptual details and incomplete memories. He was the only complete entity within the reach of perception. Something at what he had reasoned as the center might have also been whole, but he couldn't get close enough to be sure.

Mortvill had taken his soul. But that shouldn't have been possible. Then again, Sinkua shouldn't have been able to resurrect his mother. That led him to a hunch, but the soulscape had been too erratic for his memories to have an answer.

"What did you do with Vielle?"

Jehgoro sat at the top of the beach, hugging his knees as he watched the evening tide. They were running late. Assuming he had heard them correctly, that was.

Overheard, Elemeno reminded, forgetting that this past self was unaware of her.

That snowman. Maspanas. Posmantas. Whatever his name was. He was much more interested in Ajaveo than the woman he had said he was looking for. Jehgoro supposed it made sense. She was apparently his lead on Ajaveo.

But to have loitered about town for half a moon cycle bordered on fixation. He had spent a lot of time pacing the graveyard like he was waiting for something. Something other, or more than, a moment alone with Ajaveo.

The snowman must have taken an interest in Ajaveo because of how he had saved everyone's lives. That was why that woman latched onto him as well. Judging by how Manpesos or whatever regarded her, her reasons must have been less than noble.

Assuming, of course, that his intentions for Ajaveo were any better. He did at least bother to introduce himself to the locals. That put him in far better graces than the pale woman, even if Jehgoro couldn't remember his name.

Still, if Ajaveo's exploits had brought them from so far north, he had to wonder how far the news had spread. And how much it had been exaggerated.

Jehgoro sprang to his feet at the sound of sand rustling under footfalls. He had been watching the wrong dock. Seeing two men talking on the darkening beach, he rushed to the northwest beach.

"Ajaveo!" he called out.

The two men went silent as they looked to him. He was right. Ajaveo was talking with that Harkzanian man. Jehgoro doubled over, catching his breath as he caught up to them.

"Ajaveo," he gasped, "Where are you—?"

"Breathe, child," the snowman said, patting Jehgoro's upper back, "Your friend is—"

Jehgoro wrenched his hand away. "Don't touch me, Pementus!" he scolded, "You're trying to take Ajaveo away!"

"Pesmenas."

"Shut up!"

A pair of hands spun him around by his shoulders. Ajaveo hunkered down to eye level.

"It's okay, Jehgoro," he said, "Pesmenas and I are going on a trip to help people."

"But you already help people here."

"Yes, but I gave the best help I could before you were born. Other places need that help, too."

"What if I need that kind of help?" Jehgoro protested, "What about Nayon? What if you don't come back?"

"It'll take some time, but I'll do my best to make it back," Ajaveo said, "But Pesmenas says we're going to look for other people like us. So maybe we'll find someone to fill in for me so I can come home sooner."

Jehgoro flashed a smile. "I like the sound of that," he said. He looked to Pesmenas. "So, uh, how are you—?"

"He doesn't dress the part, but he's sort of like a shaman," Ajaveo provided, "When I can't save people, he gives them directions to The Paradise Waters."

"Is that what he was doing in the graveyard?"

Pesmenas nodded. "It was," he said, "A disconcerting number of your dead got lost on the way. An increasingly common occurrence the nearer I came to Ajaveo in my travels."

Jehgoro had to admit his Bealstillan had gotten a lot better.

"So, one of you saves bodies, and the other saves souls," he assessed, "Does that mean you're looking for a third who saves minds?"

"We just might be," Ajaveo said with a chuckle, "Who knows? If we find a lot of us, we just might start our own community dedicated to helping people."

"If that happens, I'll come see you myself," Jehgoro asserted, "If there's other people that can save people like you do, then I need to meet them."

"In that case, you'll need these."

Ajaveo fished some things out of his pocket and pushed them into Jehgoro's hand. Six beads.

"I can't take these. What if you need—?"

"Those are only good here," Ajaveo said, "But if you're going to come looking for us, you'll need a friend and snacks for the trip."

"Yeah, I guess," Jehgoro said, "But what do I do about the pale lady? Should I tell her where you went?"

"She never deigned to talk to you, and I don't see that changing now," Ajaveo sighed, "But if she does, play dumb. Not too dumb though."

"I could say you went a different way."

"That should work. Tell her we went northeast. She'll think we're checking out Ippatsuru," Ajaveo said, "Whatever you do, just don't let on that we talked before I left."

"You and Nayon look after each other," Pesmenas said, "Ajaveo and I will do as such."

"I endeavored to make her death quick and painless," Mortvill said, "I apologize if she suffered overlong."

"You know that's—"

"Wait!" Eytea cut in, "You killed Vielle?"

Mortvill reached under his mask to rub the bridge of his nose. "Yes, I—"

"You?" she interrupted again, "As in The Omnimath? Not The Harvester?"

Mortvill regarded her for a moment. "Yes," he said at last, "And my reasons coincide with what I assume you, Galo, mean to ask about."

"Did you take her soul, too?" Galo demanded, "Are you keeping us from finding her?"

"I've been seeing green flashes," Eytea added, "And Arestor brought Sinkua out of the Netherworld on a petrified Yggdrasil branch."

"Vielle is clearly trying to contact us. So where are you hiding her?"

"As much as I wish I was hiding and could thus return her, this has nothing to do with me," Mortvill said, "Yggdrasil Hybrids and Dryads have a different afterlife."

Elemeno awoke in the subconscience of a much taller Jehgoro. Bealstilla had comparably sprawled. Bazaar stalls were now sturdier structures. She couldn't place specifics, but the fountain in the plaza looked reinforced. More ornate, even.

This all followed a quick flash of darkness. Those childhood experiences felt like they were both a moment and uncountable years ago.

Jehgoro looked upwind as an acrid odor swept through. Smoke rose from northern horizon on the other side of the strait. The tree line collapsed to leave a single figure. Jehgoro tugged the strap on his scabbard.

"Where do they go, then?" Galo asked, "And how is she signaling us?"

"You only assume those flashes are her doing," Mortvill reminded, "She is, however, almost certainly responsible for the petrified branches in the Netherworld. Yggdrasil connects to all planes of both spirit and body, and Vielle now resides inside it."

"Inside? The same way that Odin was inside?"

"There is some overlap, yes. The Dryads had to grant him entry," Mortvill said, "But his would have been a singular presence, isolated and limited. Theirs and hers, while centralized, are more immersed and broader."

"Sort of like Sinkua being here in body instead of in spirit?" Eytea asked.

"If that helps you understand, yes," Mortvill said, "They move energy throughout Yggdrasil, even encouraging what fruits grow where."

"So, all those times that Vielle used Yggdrasil for recon and communications, she was, what, commanding the Dryads?" Galo asked.

"The Dryads were acting upon her will, yes," Mortvill said, "The ones from before and up to Pahres's time were most likely restored when Vielle planted Yggdrasil."

"Why kill her, then?" Eytea asked, choking on the words, "If you wish you could bring her back, why'd you do it in the first place?"

"Simply put, to give her better control."

"She had plenty of control!" Galo protested, "Do you have any idea what she did from outside of Yggdrasil? Not to mention all she was and could've been that had nothing to do with whether she was a Hybrid!"

"I do apologize, Galo, and I understand if you'll always resent me. Just know that my choice was pragmatic. There was no malevolence in my actions," Mortvill said, "The Dryads need leadership. Centrality. Best that it's someone versed in the current ways and affairs of Ouristihra."

"I get the whole tactical pragmatic thing," Eytea said, "But I would've rather found my friend waiting for us when Sinkua takes us back."

"I understand that. I truly do," Mortvill commiserated, "I have people I've been away from for most of their lives. And countless more that I've lost in the wake of my longevity. Every loss, however, has and will serve a greater purpose. I'll see that Vielle's death is not in vain."

"Why are you talking so candidly about this?" Galo pried, "When we were alive, you were always so cryptic about everything."

"Before I infiltrated The Avatars of Fate, I told The Coalition to work toward full disclosure with the Hybrids and anyone you trusted," Mortvill explained, "I also intend to ask Sinkua to bring me back as well. I'll lie low until the others are ready to go home."

"Just give us time to say our goodbyes to Spril, okay?" Eytea insisted, "His coaching was a big part of how I survived as long as I did. And he's just fun to hang out with."

Mortvill let out a small chuckle. "You don't need to justify your request," he said, "Nor explain the nature of friendship. But I do ask one thing of the two of you."

"What is it?" Galo asked.

"Do not tell Sinkua why I killed Vielle," Mortvill pleaded, "I saw the trouble in his eyes when he realized which of me he had killed, but he would not take well to learning I treated her soul like a chess piece."

"We can play dumb if he asks why we think you did it," Eytea said, "But if he asks you, we can't promise we can get him off the topic."

"That'll do. Thank you," Mortvill said, "Never mind that I had my own war much more in mind than how it might benefit you."

Fetzikzi reflected on their family history. The journals. The murals. The sprawling family tree. The expanding house. But despite being made of memories, she could no better isolate the one she wanted than she could control her pancreas when she was alive.

"There were these books. Back in my time," she said at last, "I don't know how much longer the tradition went on for. I mean, how would I?"

"All of us up through Tetsen wrote one," Sinkua said, "Journals about ourselves and the Dragon Family, right?"

"Yes! Are they still around in your time?"

"Sort of. All the old books were preserved and recently translated, but I never got to write one."

"That's a shame. But I guess you didn't have anyone to teach you about the tradition," Fetzikzi said, "Anyway, the first of us probably put his name in his, but honestly, I don't remember much of it. Man, that makes me sound bad, doesn't it?"

Sinkua shrugged. "I never read yours, and I don't feel worse for it," he said, "Hell, if you feel bad about not reading your great-great-whatever-grandfather's journal, you must've been a pretty okay person."

Fetzikzi glowered at him. "You couldn't even read mine, you lump," she said, "But yeah, I get your point. He wasn't my great-anything-grandfather though."

"When did we branch off into nieces and nephews?"

"Third one. Second was his granddaughter. Third was her nephew or once removed cousin," Fetzikzi said, "I forget which."

"Was Odin's Hybrid the mother of his children?" Sinkua asked, "Or did that start happening later?"

"Oh! That actually came up a lot behind closed doors. Very hush-hush stuff," Fetzikzi said, "So don't quote me on this, but apparently our first didn't fall for the Odin Hybrid. No, no, no. Odin chose our first's lover as his first Hybrid."

"Hold up!" Sinkua remarked, "You mean Odin arranged the whole thing between us and his Hybrids?"

"I didn't say that," Fetzikzi said, putting her hands up, "I did not say that. I may or may not have strongly implied it. But what I really said? First one? Totally all him."

"He wanted to keep Phoenix close," Sinkua deduced, "But I don't know what he was like back then, so I can't say why."

"Sure, but he created soulmates and got mad at us for making each other sad by, um… What was it?" Fetzikzi said, "Oh! Right! Not dying and reincarnating at the same time."

"The audacity of us!" Sinkua laughed, "Still having emotions in a diplomatic marriage. That wasn't diplomatic when we got together."

"It's worse when you consider Odin is married," Fetzikzi said, "He has an actual fucking wife. And kids, so he was actually fucking his wife. But he gets all taken aback when we and his Hybrids get feelings for each other even though he set us up."

"Sounds just like him."

Fetzikzi looked up to the amorphous ceiling. "Sounds like you'll be okay to wake up soon. I think Mortvill, as you call him, is about to wake Elemeno up."

"As I call him?" Sinkua asked, "What do you call him?"

"His name."

"No shit. I thought Mortvill was his name."

"What?!" Fetzikzi laughed, "That's obviously an alias. It's Harkz-cois, means town of death."

"Harkz-cois?" Sinkua asked, "Harkzanian and Quircois?"

"Yeah. You really didn't pick up on it?" Fetzikzi asked. Sinkua shook his head. "Wow. The languages really died out, huh?"

"I thought you already got that, but yeah," Sinkua said, "So what is Mortvill's real name?"

The silhouette rushed across the strait, her feet carving a rising wake. The woman had seen through the ruse, and now she had returned to take everyone involved to task.

Except nobody knew where Ajaveo was. None of them had heard from him since he left. Jehgoro steeled himself and held his machete forth.

Locusts erupted from her throat as she screamed. Jehgoro shielded his face, and the ravenous bugs chewed at his shirt as they scrambled past.

Once clear, Jehgoro looked up to settling shockwave echoes. The pale woman had banked hard toward the plaza, leaving an oozing trail of lava as her footfalls melted the cobblestones.

Jehgoro whipped around to find countless buildings already collapsing from more kinds of damage than he could assess. Smoke and dust billowed from the plaza and outlined the roads.

Nayon's house was still standing. If barely. Pock marks in his roof were growing so quickly that Jehgoro could almost see the upper deck. He called out to him as he pounded out a hard sprint.

Visibility was all but nonexistent. And the echoes of that woman's shrieks made it impossible to hold on to a sense of direction. Jehgoro let decades of memories and instinct carry him, his machete drawn and ready.

A familiar figure caught his eye. But before he could say anything, a shadow stretched over him. He spun and slashed, missing the pale woman by several meters. She stopped drifting back just long enough to look him over with equal parts disdain and disinterest.

Her focus moved beyond him. She was looking for his backup. Or easier prey.

Jehgoro's eyes widened with sickened epiphany. The pale woman fixed her stare where he had been looking when she rushed in.

"Nayon! Run!"

A silhouette rippled the smoke as it fled. The pale woman blazed past, checking Jehgoro's shoulder like a slung stone to a sapling. He whipped his machete after her, a useless gesture, and pounded out a diverging path.

A shockwave off to his left grabbed his attention. The woman clutched Nayon's neck with her arm as sand rained around them. His eyes were glassy and body limp. Jehgoro rushed the clearing, only to be yanked back by the third step.

He whipped around to strike down her accomplice, but a runic broadsword deflected his machete. Pesmenas, of all people, grabbed his shoulder.

"What are you—?"

"You jackass!" Pesmenas scolded, "What if I had been your parents? Or Detonde?"

Jehgoro shook his head. "Why aren't we helping Nayon?"

Pesmenas gestured to the clearing. Announced only by a split-second glimmer, Ajaveo erupted from the smoke with a runic broadsword of his own. His eyes glowed green, and flames lapped and coiled around his body. The pale woman discarded Nayon aside and put her focus on Ajaveo as he devoured the gap.

"Wh… What happened to—?"

"We call him a Hybrid," Pesmenas said, "Phoenix had to merge with him. For both their safety."

"Both their..." Jehgoro puzzled, "From her?!"

"Pandora is the biggest threat to peace between the mundane and mystic worlds. Merging is an attempt to keep her from getting stronger," Pesmenas said, "I may have to do the same with Tiamat."

"I think she already found a mystic to merge with."

"No. She is the mystic," Pesmenas clarified, "She's from the Etherworld. Mystic world as you call it."

"She's what?!" Jehgoro shouted, "Are you, too?"

"Yeah. They sent me to apprehend her."

"Shit lotta good that did."

"I'm aware of my failures, boy," Pesmenas scolded, "Do you want refuge or—
"

A blood-curdling scream cut him off. The smoke and dust scattered to reveal Pandora, her arm behind Ajaveo's back with her shoulder in his sternum. Blood hit the cobblestones as the new green glow of Ajaveo's eyes faded, and his body went limp.

Jehgoro cried out in protest. Pesmenas covered his mouth and pulled him back.

"Ref... Refuge... I... I want refuge," he stammered.

"I thought so," Pesmenas said, "I'm sorry you—"

"Nayon!" Jehgoro exclaimed, "We have to get Nayon."

"Both of you would die!" Pesmenas shouted, "This city is doomed. If you go after him, the legacy dies, too."

"Bullshit," Jehgoro snapped, "Other people emigrated. They're the legacy."

"Look around. Everyone else is trying to run," Pesmenas said, "Because they're scared. And reasonable. As you should be."

"Of course I'm scared. But they're all dying face down."

"Because they don't have me."

"Because they turned their backs."

Pesmenas pressed his forearm to Jehgoro's chest. "Listen to me," he said, "We can't fight her."

"I have to try," Jehgoro choked out, holding back tears, "Nayon's like a brother to me. I can't."

Pesmenas lowered his arm as someone called out to Jehgoro. They both turned just as a blood-soaked arm grabbed Nayon by the neck and pulled him into the smoke.

Jehgoro called back as he rushed past Pesmenas. But with a dull impact to the back of the head, Elemeno's sight went black.

Chapter 13

"Who the hell are you?"

Mortvill, as much as he could be called that, checked his mask and turned to face him. Sinkua narrowed and flared his eyes. Tetsen, in secondary prominence, followed suit. Their attempts at a better view of his face, however, proved fruitless.

"Another of you spoke of me," Mortvill deduced, "Who was it? Was it you, Tetsen?"

"I need a name," Sinkua thought, "Quick."

Phoenix shot back with the name of an Ippatsuranu ancestor. Their seventh. Hopefully not too obvious, picking from the center of the bookshelf.

"Tenzu Tamanoro," Sinkua said, "Now answer the question."

Eytea nudged Galo. "What's he talking about?"

"Mortvill isn't Mortvill's real name," he said, "Metkhal can't remember. Didn't talk to him much."

"Ah, Tenzu-Kun!" Mortvill remarked, "He was one of my favorites, despite the cultural diaspora. Or perhaps because of it."

"That's… great?" Sinkua shrugged, "Quit stalling."

"Yes of course. Would you mind if I spoke with Tenzu-Kun?"

"Phoenix?" Sinkua thought, "Can you —"

"No. Too risky," she cut off.

It had been too obvious after all.

"You got me," Sinkua said, "It was Tetsen here."

"Oh, well that's simple enough, what with him already present," Mortvill said, "The residents of Drakougeneospa knew me as Cedalion. Same as what Miss Aroka told you, yes?"

Sinkua nodded. "Did Takmet tell you about her?"

"No, Arestor did. He said her and Tetsen's memories are running loose in your subconscience," Mortvill, or rather Cedalion, said, "As to my new name, it was necessary to avoid suspicion. Your mother-in-law certainly understands the need for aliases. As you ought, MeiLom."

"Hold on," Eytea interjected, "Why'd you need an alias if only residents of Drakougeneospa knew your name? Pandora wasn't one, was she?"

"I should say not," Elemeno said. The younger Hybrids faced her sharply. "Something certainly had her feeling slighted when she came back to Bealstilla."

"Oh? What did you see?" Cedalion beckoned.

"Hey! Don't sidetrack me!" Eytea protested.

"I would never," Cedalion said, "I assure you, you'll find this quite pertinent."

"Sorry, I'll just be a moment," Elemeno said aside to her, then returned her attention to Cedalion, "I was a young man named Jehgoro. There was an older man named Ajaveo. He was the first Phoenix Hybrid."

She recounted the pale woman who latched onto Ajaveo. She told of his leaving and Jehgoro giving her a bad heading at Ajaveo's behest.

She spoke of the pale woman's vengeful return. And of learning her name. Pandora.

"I don't think Ajaveo made it," Elemeno concluded, looking to Cedalion, "The only reason Jehgoro survived was because of you. Pesmenas."

"I certainly helped his chances, yes," Cedalion said, "Pesmenas roughly translates to Fallen One in Harkzanian. I thought it fitting with my being an exiled Etherworlder."

Sinkua gave a hard blink, consulting Tetsen and Fetzikzi in that brief time. Neither of them had known that about him.

"Must not have been a very important one," Sinkua goaded, "No one else in Drakou picked up on it, did they?"

"Not to mention becoming the Hybrid for another Etherworlder," Galo added.

"So, what'd you do to get exiled?" Eytea added, "Must've been pretty stupid, huh? I mean, you're still doing time for it."

Cedalion's mask shifted. "Mine was a self-imposed exile."

"Uh huh. Because you were embarrassed?" Eytea taunted, "At how stupid you were?"

"Rather a crude take, but I suppose you're not wrong," Cedalion said, "Hephaestus forged Pandora according to Zeus's specifications. After what transpired from his creation, Hephaestus gave the Omphaloworld Hephaeseum and Hephaestite that they might craft the means to stop her."

"Okay," Sinkua said, drawing it out, "What does that have to do with you?"

"There's nothing to be gained from further pursuing my ire," Cedalion insisted without a hint of spite, "You're already getting answers.

"I was one of Hephaestus's servants. His teacher, in fact, until he surpassed me. At that point, I became his assistant," Cedalion said, "In fact, I aided with forging Pandora. After Hephaestus cast himself into his forge, I formed a pact with Tiamat, and we fled the Etherworld.

"The descent was far more detrimental for me than for her. She used the tsoran ether to patch much of the damage to herself. I became her Hybrid soon after the destruction of Bealstilla."

"I've met Pandora. If I made someone like that, I'd kill myself, too," Sinkua said, "But I just assumed she was, well, born. Not crafted. I didn't know that was even possible."

"I was crafted," Galo reminded, "Technically anyway."

"That's different. You grew from blood and water, probably both milystic. She's made of super etherore."

"Most of us were born from sexual reproduction," Cedalion said, "Pandora wasn't the only one to be forged though. Phoenix was as well, by Ptah and Hephaestus. Ptah was disappointed that Phoenix didn't vote to found the Dragon Family in Dagiliz. Not enough to betray us, mind you. I doubt anything could. His loyalty to Bahamut wouldn't allow it."

"Harkzan is ArcNos, right?" Elemeno asked, "Which one is Dagiliz?"

"Eprilen," Cedalion said, "Tiamat would like to have settled in Pukoqet. Now Poravit. But she understood that it only fit her well out of the four of us."

Sinkua consulted Tetsen as he panned the crystal field for anything resembling a heading. He also hadn't known Phoenix was forged. Or that she had two countries of origin.

Sinkua found the whole thing almost poetic. Phoenix's parents, for lack of a better word, represented Harkzan and Dagiliz. Present day ArcNos and Eprilen. The homelands of his sister's parents. Part of him wondered if Nikasu might have been a better fit for Phoenix.

Vielle had the same Eprilenese mother and a father who became influential in ArcNos. Not the same parallel of parentage, but her conception and incubation had been artificial. Probably the closest thing to being forged with Omphaloworlder technology. She wasn't of Dragon Family blood though, as far as he knew. Never mind that her getting Phoenix could have put him with Yggdrasil, and he couldn't fathom putting up with all those voices.

His face tightened with realization.

"Tell me something, Cedalion," he said, "Why did you kill Vielle?"

Eytea and Galo drew back, distancing themselves from the conversation. Sinkua flicked a sidelong glance at them. Maybe they knew something. But they could just as well have known his question could lead to violence.

"What brings this on so suddenly?" Cedalion asked, "We need to look for the Phoenix Shrine."

"Yeah, that's why you put my mother-in-law in a Bealstillan flashback. To get a lead," Sinkua said, "But it doesn't make sense for you to kill Vielle. You helped make sure she planted Yggdrasil. And you can't seize control of it. And it sure as shit wasn't in self defense. So, what?" His fingertip rippled as he jabbed Cedalion's sternum. "The fuck? Did you do it for?"

"Sinkua!" Eytea called over, "This isn't a good time."

"I hate to say it, but she's right," Galo said, "Elemeno confirmed he's The Omnimath. We can work out why he killed Vielle after he helps us find the Phoenix Shrine."

"Sinkua, dear, you've already avenged her," Elemeno said, "Knowing why he did it won't let you do anything more for her."

"I know all of you mean well, but he does indeed have a right to know," Cedalion said. He paused and cocked an ear. "Though I'm sure he'll have rather I had a much better reason than I do."

"Drop the canned empathy bullshit," Sinkua scolded, "You're stalling."

"I did it for the same reason as anyone with more power than authority," Cedalion said, "I was under orders."

"Orders?" Sinkua grumbled, "Who's fucking orders could you have possibly been under?!"

Sinkua threw a clumsy haymaker. Cedalion ducked it with no visible bother.

"MalVek and The Harvester had an arrangement," Cedalion said, "MalVek would correct The Harvester's method of breaching The Veil in return for The Harvester eliminating anyone MalVek said. No questions. No hesitation."

Sinkua looked him over. He was right. He did wish he'd had a better reason. But it wasn't just that it was a pathetic moral justification. Lashing out just didn't feel right anymore.

Throwing that punch did nothing for Vielle, and it would've done just as little if it had landed. In fact, he suspected no amount of violence he could visit on Cedalion would change a thing. Perhaps all the death and killing had finally numbed him.

Or, far more likely, his vengeance of her wouldn't find satiation until MalVek was dust and ash.

As much as he wanted to hold on to his anger, he knew Cedalion hadn't had a choice in the matter. The soldiers he had killed had been following orders. Whether out of loyalty or fear didn't matter. They were there, and they died because someone else, someone they feared more than the Subtransit Resistance, said so. Sinkua had long since let go of his hatred of them.

Sure, Cedalion by any name was considerably more formidable than any of them. But with MalVek having bested Galo and Leviathan, Cedalion defying him was about as dangerous as CreSam's firing squad refusing his orders. Not to mention Cedalion needed to keep his cover.

That said, even if Sinkua had understood the stakes it wouldn't have gotten any mercy out of him. Cedalion's reasons for killing Vielle aside, he was trying to kill him and take Phoenix to Pandora.

That was still a mystery, why Cedalion thought he was better suited to complete Tsenukoa's plan. But Sinkua decided not to pursue that line of questioning just yet.

The bottoms of his feet tingled as he came out of his introspection. His focus returning, he now stood in the doorway to the old cabin. Toward every horizon stretched iterations of their lawn across the seasons and years, splitting and folding back on themselves.

Sinkua's eyes went distant. His face became so pale that his skin glowed like a paper lantern.

Eytea gasped sharply as Tsenukoa's face became as distinct as Sinkua's. She lunged for them, reaching low just in time to catch Tsenukoa and some woman, presumably Fetzikzi Aroka, across her arms. The woman took prominence, smiling up at Eytea with mischievous eyes.

"Efkaaristas," she said, "Ala... denesai typomas."

Eytea could only stare in dumbfoundment as Tsenukoa emerged into prominence.

"She says, 'Thank you.',," he provided, "'But not you are the type of ours.'"

"What? I…" Eytea stammered, "Oh! Sorry!" She helped them upright and took a long step back, feigning nonchalance. "Sorry. I wasn't trying to… You know."

"How well can you understand us, Tetsen?" Elemeno asked.

Tetsen stared at her with equal parts focus and distance. Eytea suppressed the urge to simplify the question for him.

"Better than her," he said at last, "Still I have yet trouble."

"I think the more pressing matter is what happened to Sinkua," Galo cut in, "Cedalion can translate for any of us."

"I thought that was obvious," Elemeno said, shrugging, "He had to check out of the conversation before his anger got the better of him."

"If that's what it was, he wouldn't have collapsed," Galo argued, "Something happened to him."

"He is well," Tetsen said, "He fell behind us, and…"

He trailed off into a loss for words. Understandable seeing as his knowledge of Ouristihran was barely rudimentary. He excused himself to speak with Cedalion in tones as hushed as the accents were thick.

"Sinkua, I'm afraid," Cedalion said at last, "is literally lost in thought."

"Meaning what, exactly?" Galo said with a decisive step toward Tetsen and Fetzikzi, "These two buried him? Sure, they're putting up with it, but I doubt they're happy with the arrangement."

"Stay your hand, Galo," Cedalion urged, "Your friend was reflecting on what I said, and he got stuck in his memories and subconscience."

"You mean to tell me that thinking too hard can cause these changes now?" Galo said, "And you expect me to not be worried?"

"He never said not to worry," Eytea empathized.

"I never said not to worry," Cedalion said almost in unison with her, "Just know these two did nothing of malice."

"I think it's like a pulley," Elemeno provided, "Sinkua is at the top when he's talking to us. But if he goes into his memories for too long, Tetsen and Fetzikzi rise to the top."

"That… isn't the worst analogy," Cedalion pondered, "Sinkua is, as much as anyone ought to be, every aspect of his mind. But sharing that space with these memory imprints, as Mister Drukoa just told me, has made navigating his own thoughts and memories more hazardous."

Eytea recalled how quickly he had collapsed, in both senses, when The Omnimath removed his mask. She thought back on how quickly Tetsen had retracted when she put his hand on her chest. It wasn't just that his mind was harder to navigate.

"It's getting worse," she blurted out. Everyone turned to look at her. "They're all moving in and out more easily than before. Which sounds good, but now it's so easy that they're doing it when they don't mean to."

Cedalion spoke aside with Fetzikzi and Tetsen. She couldn't see his eyes, but now and again, he seemed to shoot a glance at her and Galo. Far less frequently, he looked toward her mother.

"What are they saying?" she asked as he faced her.

"As much as Mister Drukoa would love to take over this idiot's body — his words, not mine — not only can he not, this wouldn't be a good time for it," Cedalion reported, "As to Miss Aroka, she tried to help Sinkua back to the fore, but taking his place that they not collapse took precedence."

Galo looked down at himself. "Metkhal, you need to talk to your friend."

"Hey yeah, now that I think about it," Eytea said, "if Sinkua can, well, fall in that easily, what's stopping Tetsen from pulling him down? Or holding him down? He obviously doesn't like him."

"I can no better assert an answer than any of you," Cedalion said, "These circumstances are unprecedented."

Galo's eyes went wide. "He's... unraveling," he choked out.

"Excuse me?" Eytea recoiled, "He's what?"

"When he found Arestor," Galo said, "his soul was still in the statue, but he was dead. His tsora was unraveling and leaking out."

"Oh shit!" Eytea gasped, "I didn't think it was that bad. You think his soul is coming apart?"

"I didn't say that," Galo asserted, "I didn't say it, and I don't want to think it. I just think that his mind —"

"It's his body," Elemeno interjected, "We're in the afterlife, but he's technically still alive. Nature has ways of correcting those sorts of contradictions."

"If that's the case, we might not have time to look for Vielle," Eytea said, "If we find her, wonderful, but we can't hang around much longer after we find Epesol."

"Well, I have a couple ideas as to what it might look like," Elemeno said, "Cedalion? Could you ask Fetzikzi if she's seen pictures of Detonde's market stall or Nayon's house? Adult or childhood."

Chapter 14

Metkhal closed his eyes and imagined the market stall as Fetzikzi had described it. Of course, he hadn't seen them in life, seeing as their destruction predated him by a few centuries. But he also couldn't recall anything resembling them. That was probably for the best, as it could've clouded his judgment of his afterlife memories.

Unfortunately, those were proving useless as well. Visions and communications from his past selves, now memories of memories, carried so many vague and minute resemblances that he couldn't be sure which, if any, were leads on the Phoenix Shrine.

Even if they had seen it, none of them had any reason to find it of note. They were wholly different people from him, scattered across the continent and largely devoid of dealings with Famujokoa. In fact, he didn't know if he and Galo were the only two, but he looked to be his soul's first Hybrid.

Not that it mattered if anyone between Galo and himself were Hybrids. Or if they had dealings with Famujokoa. Remembering his time piggybacking on their afterlife was impossible, and they didn't have time to look for someone who knew any of them. Not that they had a workable way to do that.

All he knew for sure was that he did set out to find the Famujokoa Shrines to wait for Tsenukoa to show up. He had entered through the Leviathan Shrine, so Tsenukoa should have come through the Phoenix Shrine. He had wanted not just to see his friend one more time but to ask what he found beyond the sea.

But he couldn't remember what Tsenukoa said he found. So, either he never found the Famujokoa Shrines, or the Phoenix Shrine wasn't among them.

After all, she had roots in both Harkzan and Dagiliz. That fact seemed to have fallen to obscurity well before Famujokoumba. Ptah couldn't have been happy about that.

Now, after countless centuries of reincarnation, he and Tsenukoa had found each other. He could ask about the other side of the sea. And the Phoenix Shrine.

Except he couldn't. This memory copy, this next best thing, knew nothing beyond Tsenukoa's departure.

Fetzikzi Aroka wasn't quite so limited. Her memory copy was of her entire life. Unfortunately, just as with Tsenukoa, she had no recollection of her time in the afterlife.

So, he couldn't ask either of them about the Phoenix Shrine, and if he could, he wouldn't need to. Not so urgently anyway.

He opened his eyes and faced the group. His best hope was that Fetzikzi had forgotten something.

"Sinkua," he called out, pausing to sort out his Ouristihran syntax, "Fetzikzi of Aroka I would speak with?"

Sinkua argued back with absolute disrespect for Metkhal's limited grasp of the strange monolanguage. Argued, so he assumed, more by his inflection than by comprehension. Metkhal couldn't even be sure if he lost the thread by the fourth word or the seventh.

Metkhal pinched the bridge of his nose and waved Sinkua off. But this reincarnation of his friend powered forth like he thought he'd been fluent for years.

Knowing he could slip seamlessly into Mberhali, he spoke instead with Cedalion.

"I have no idea what this guy's rambling about," Metkhal bemoaned, "He sounds defensive. Is he always like that?"

"Often, from what I've seen. But also often with good reason," Cedalion said, "He thinks it's unnecessary for you to speak further with Miss Aroka, on account of his instability."

"I have more questions for her," Metkhal said, "Which, yes, might exacerbate his condition, but the sooner we find the Phoenix Shrine, the sooner that won't be a concern."

"I'm sorry, but I need to know that you have particulars in mind," Cedalion insisted, "not just exploratory questions."

Eytea interjected in Ouristihran, but she at least had the decency to only address Cedalion this way.

"What did she say?" Metkhal asked.

"Her ring finger isn't getting dimmer, so we aren't moving in the wrong direction."

Metkhal regarded her flatly. After a moment, he sighed and shrugged. "It doesn't help, but it's not the worst news," he said, "But I do have particulars in mind."

Cedalion looked him over, his mask betraying nothing of intentions or misgivings. Metkhal tamped down his anxious impulses, returning the same speculative body language.

"Very well then," Cedalion conceded, "I'll have him call her forth. I know you're not one to be satisfied with a relayed answer."

Cedalion spoke with Sinkua in Ouristihran, far too quickly for Metkhal to pick up any of it. Meanwhile, Eytea and Elemeno conversed in hushed tones. If they were trying to keep secrets, it wasn't from him. They knew how limited his knowledge was. The two sentences he had spoken in their language were a strain, and he lacked confidence in his syntax.

Sinkua's face lost opacity, giving way to that of Fetzikzi of Aroka as Tsenukoa vanished.

"How well do Harkzanian you speak?" she asked in fragmented Mberhali.

Metkhal chuckled. "Better than you speak Mberhali," he said in Harkzanian, realizing how he must have sounded speaking Ouristihran.

"Oh good," Fetzikzi sighed, now speaking Harkzanian, "Sorry if it's rude to say, but your language gives me a headache. But I never had any motivation to learn it, so I guess it's no surprise that you speak mine better than I speak yours."

"Cedalion doesn't like me asking you forth again so soon," Metkhal said, his eyes going distant as he concentrated on his fluency, "So I'll get right to it."

"Of course. We don't want the host coming unwound," Fetzikzi said, "What else do you need to know?"

"Were there design concepts for any other Famujokoa Shrines in Ajaveo's journal?"

"Not that I can remember. And honestly, I don't even know if he settled on Detonde's stall for the Phoenix Shrine."

Metkhal muttered an expletive. "What about building it somewhere else? Did that come up?"

Fetzikzi cocked her head, the translucent image of Sinkua following after a slight delay. "Somewhere else from where?"

"Not all Etherworlders in collectives build their Shrine among that collective. Some build theirs in the nation they're beholden to instead," he said, "Take Tiamat. Hers could be with the Dragon Family or with the Pukoqeyens."

"Sure, I get that," Fetzikzi said, "But Phoenix is beholden to Harkzan. Which is where the Dragon Family was established."

Now it was his turn to cock his and Galo's turns to cock their heads with the same delay as she and Sinkua.

"You do know that Phoenix is also Dagiliši, yes?"

Fetzikzi's eyes widened. "She is?" she asked, "That explains so much."

"Could you elaborate?" he beckoned.

"I had never had any business with Dagiliz, but when I was twenty, Phoenix practically begged me to go there," she said, "That's where I met Jandruug. He had moved there from Fjareskjon six months before. I always assumed he was why Phoenix wanted me to go there."

"Fulfilling the compulsion between you and the Odin Hybrid," he said, nodding toward Eytea, "But unless you remember Odin consulting Phoenix shortly before that, I don't see how that could be her reason."

"No, you're right. That would be putting too much stock in the whole thing being destiny," she said, "I was just telling Sinkua how Odin started the whole thing."

"Fascinating stuff, I'm sure, but you'll have to tell me some other time," Metkhal said, "So with all this in mind, do you think we should be looking for the Dagiliši Etherworlder Shrines?"

Fetzikzi of Aroka gave it a moment's consideration. "Absolutely."

Sinkua was all the more careful to keep Galo in sight as they traversed the crystalline landscape. Well, on the moments of him that flickered through Metkhal's prominence. Knowing how delicate, how volatile, his mind had become, he feared his depth, in both perception and presence, could follow.

Tetsen argued for uprooting a third memory imprint. His logic was that they could better handle another collapse if they didn't all have to surface. He specifically nominated Tenzu Tamanoro, Tenzu-Kun as Cedalion had called him, under the reasoning that Sinkua having heard of him would make it easier. If only slightly.

Sinkua maintained that it would do more harm than good, no matter who it was. Still, the more he strained to focus on the flickers of Galo, he was loath to admit that he wanted to try.

Even having such thoughts was dangerous, even if he didn't entertain it. Tetsen could perceive those thoughts and thus tempt him further. But that could've been for the better, so long as Sinkua could resist. After all, it kept Tetsen from delving into his deeper and more private thoughts.

Eytea's hand pressed against the small of his back, assuring in its firmness. "Tell me something, babe," she said, "Do you think he knows what he's doing?"

Sinkua shrugged. "If Galo trusts him, I'm willing to see it through," he said, "Your milystic ring can only do so much."

"Yeah. I guess you're right," she said. She held out her hand, furrowing her brow as she moved it side to side. "But it isn't like you to let someone else take the lead on."

"It's like when I delegated jobs to deal with the motorcycle cavalry," he reasoned, "I just have to hang back and wait for someone else to finish theirs."

"Well, when you put it that way," she said, then pinched his oblique, "You want a map to doodle on, pumpkin head?"

Sinkua laughed and nudged the side of her breast. His vision and balance both faltered. Both returned, along with Tetsen's secondary presence, as he drew back sharply. The deeper thoughts became harder to hide.

"But you said you trust Metkhal because Galo trusts him, right?" Eytea asked.

"Yeah and because your mom does," Sinkua said, "She became an even better judge of character after you died. And she got more brazen about calling people out on their bullshit."

"Hah! Yeah, she told me the stories," she said, "But what about Cedalion?"

"What about him?" he countered, "I only trust him as far as I need to."

"Can't say I blame you," she said, "Hell, just knowing what he did to Vielle has me on my guard. I get that he was following orders and couldn't get out of it, but I want him to have had a better reason. Except I can't think of one."

"That's saying a lot, coming from you," Sinkua noted, "I'll go along with calling him Cedalion for now, but I feel like he's been playing everyone since he first came down from the Etherworld."

"He's too much of a control freak for how guarded he's always been," Eytea pondered, "Which I guess makes some sense, but it's also shady, you know?"

"Odin reminds me of him," Sinkua said, "Well, he was more self-important than guarded. After a while, he started being both."

"Did he really try to strangle Leviathan?"

"Her proxy, actually. But there's —"

Metkhal called out to him and asked to speak with, as he called her, Fetzikzi of Aroka.

Elemeno called for Jehgoro in the back of her mind. No answer. She told herself that he couldn't answer, rather than wouldn't. But the longer the silence went on, the harder it was to convince herself.

He had known Cedalion. Briefly, yes, but it was enough that seeing his face pulled Elemeno into his memories. Just knowing he was nearby should have been enough to keep a line of contact, regardless of whether Jehgoro learned his real name or only knew him as Pesmenas.

"What's on your mind?"

Her daughter's sudden voice pulled her out of her introspection.

"Eytea. Hi," she said, stalling to sort her thoughts, "You've got enough troubles without bothering with mine."

"Oh hush. Don't talk like you're too good to talk about it," Eytea said, "Is it Jehgoro? What's he saying? You want me to beat him up?"

"No! No," Elemeno refused through waning laughter, "Well... Maybe? We'd have to get him to come out first."

"And then I'll beat him up," Eytea said, shaking her fist, "That'll teach him not to be so difficult."

"If children were that easy, there'd be a case for corporal punishment," Elemeno said, "So what were you and Sinkua talking about?"

"He thinks Cedalion's still using an alias," Eytea said, "Don't mention this around him, but I think he might be a smidge paranoid."

"I... don't necessarily agree with him, but I can't blame him for feeling suspicious."

"Oh, don't get me wrong, I get where he's coming from. But Cedalion has to run out of ruses eventually, right?"

Elemeno shrugged. "Maybe? Not necessarily."

"I'm just worried that if we do get the clear and irrefutable truth, Sinkua would stay suspicious."

"Well, whatever the case, make sure Sinkua knows to go along with Cedalion's story for now."

"He already said he would."

"That shouldn't surprise me," Elemeno said, "He told you to tell me the same, didn't he?"

"Actually no, I think he assumed you already knew," Eytea said, "He's been talking about how shrewd and bold you've been."

"What can I say? I picked up a few things from you two."

"Oh please," Eytea scoffed, "The only reason I was comfortable confronting and then leaving with him and Galo was because of how you dealt with Kabehl."

"How's that?" Elemeno asked, "Rolled over and took it until you were strong enough to fight back?"

"No. Toughed it out until you were ready to put him in the dirt," Eytea said, "But that's not my point. I'm not talking about doing what you did."

"If you say so," Elemeno said, "Anyway, I can't blame Sinkua for still feeling suspicious of Cedalion, and neither should you. I saw enough with The Coalition to know we shouldn't fully trust his story without corroboration."

"I guess Fetzikzi and Tetsen don't count," Eytea said, "Not for Sinkua anyway. He's worried that every version of him got duped."

"Well, if Cedalion gave them all the same story."

"So, what did you think of Odin?"

"What about him?" Elemeno asked, "BeiLou got to know him better than I did. So did Nikasu."

"I… don't know," Eytea fumbled, "I get where Sinkua's coming from. You know, about taking credit for his resurrection and holing up in the mines while everything went to shit. But the stuff that Kabehl told him?"

"You don't think it's feasible?"

"More that it's weird for him to take him at face value."

"Well," Elemeno said, "It must say a lot about Odin if Sinkua puts stock in Kabehl. Especially with an idea like that."

Eytea's eyes wandered, and Elemeno thought it best to let them. The young woman had always been clever. Frightfully so. She might have said too much for her own good, but too much for The Avatars' own good felt more apt.

Partial structures tugged at the nesting doll memories. Bases and frames bore passing resemblances to Bealstillan buildings from Jehgoro's childhood. Elemeno latched on to these similarities, but they were all too vague to draw him toward prominence.

Someone called out from across the way, his voice ringing with indirect familiarity. Jehgoro stirred in the furthest depths of Elemeno's consciousness.

"Well shit! He's getting the old crew back together," the man remarked, drawing nearer, "He even brought Kabehl's old cow along for the ride."

With Sinkua and Galo occupied as former selves, Eytea shielded the group from the encroacher. She took particular care to block his view of Elemeno.

"Stay your hand, ranch girl," Amirione said, "It took a lot of work to get back like this. I'm not risking it fighting any of you."

"What do you want then?" Eytea demanded.

"To deliver a warning," he said, "Not a threat. I got no stakes here. But. Galo left me to mine while I got myself sorted. So, I'm returning the half-assed courtesy."

"I already know about Kabehl and Kervatus," Eytea snipped, "Thanks though."

"Same, bitch, but they got fuck-all to do with it," Amirione bit back, "I'm talking about Pahres. He's…"

He trailed off, rippling and flickering as he fixated on Metkhal and Fetzikzi.

"He's… what?" Eytea asked.

Amirione grumbled and grit his teeth in faltering synchronicity with a translucent other self. This most recent incarnation lost opacity.

Elemeno sank into her own subconscience in time with Amirione's fading. Eytea shouted. "What about—?"

"Nayon?" Jehgoro interrupted, the last presence of Elemeno's mouth shaping the name.

Amirione and Nayon, in a split second of equilibrium, thrust a shared hand at the fading form of Fetzikzi Aroka.

"What the fuck is he doing here?!"

Sinkua's focus wavered between Metkhal and the tessellated amalgam of damaged memories in his subconscience. The strain of trying to understand Harkzanian and the fluctuating vantage point made him a strange new kind of nauseated. The one distractible sliver of his mind wondered, if he threw up, where it would go. Or if that was even possible.

But he couldn't risk leaving this cusp of consciousness, straddling secondary presence and subconscience. Succumb to rest, and Miss Aroka would lose her sense and presence of depth. Fully commit to being the second set of eyes, and he would lose sight of Tetsen.

"Sinkua," his voice resonated from the depths, "You and I need to talk."

"Tetsen," Sinkua answered, masking his discomfort at Tetsen's timing, "Come up here. You know I can't leave this spot."

Tetsen rippled and sank into the fields of Sinkua's memories. Sinkua consulted Phoenix, affirming that she would translate. Tetsen manifested before him with an unmoving and stern look. He was just opaque enough to ensure that he wasn't trying to be a tertiary presence to Miss Aroka.

"You're hiding something from me," Tetsen opened, "From both of us actually. But you're more concerned with keeping it from me."

"We're all allowed our secrets, Tetsen," Sinkua countered, "You of all people are in no place to be standoffish about it."

"Oh, now what's that supposed to mean?" Tetsen snarked, "Because you've been such a gracious host, I can't be suspicious of your secrets?"

Sinkua leaned closer, spoke lower. "No," he said, "Because I know the conditions of your cooperation."

"Conditions that you agreed to," Tetsen said, "But all you've done is circle the fucking drain."

"Because of you, you insufferable twat!" Sinkua shouted, "You recede at the slightest discomfort. We can't get our bearings because you're not copiloting. You're just along for the ride when it's convenient for you."

"Well, if I'm such a burden, why don't you bury me and have Fetzikzi copilot?" Tetsen challenged, "Oh! That's right. You can't because you need Metkhal."

"You just admitted that you're only useful because of him. Not the biting comeback you think it was," Sinkua said, "Believe me, I would love to put Miss Aroka on permanent copiloting duty. But besides needing Metkhal, I can't leave you unsupervised."

"What do you even think I'm trying to do?"

"You obviously don't trust me, so you're trying to bury me because you think I'll renege on our deal."

"That's absurd," Tetsen insisted, "Sure, it's hard to trust that you'll do what you promised. Much less that you even can. But I know I can't destroy you. That would be suicide. But if you become a threat to the rest of us, yes, we will bury you."

Sinkua snickered. "Nice to see you're finally being honest," he said, "In that case, I've been on the lookout for Lechuatzulan craftspeople. You can be sure Eytea is looking for them, too. I think you can guess why."

"Do you really mean to trap me in a crystal to assuage your paranoia?" Tetsen guffawed, "And why would she want to trap me? We're on good terms now."

"I never said she did, but it's very telling that that was your first thought," Sinkua said, "But no, I'm not doing this because I'm paranoid. I'm doing it to protect myself and the other incarnations from you if you keep being a spiteful cuntbiscuit."

"Oh look! The utilitarian is pretending to care about his prisoner," Tetsen snarked, "Do you even realize the opportunity you—"

Sepia shadows swept over them, halting their arguing into a stunned stupor. The darkness funneled through a point of light at some unknowable distance. A voice reverberated from all around.

"What the fuck is he doing here?!"

The point of light closed.

Jehgoro awoke among nebulous spirits. How long he had slept, he couldn't be sure. Time was illusory while he was little more than a concept. But life feeling so distant, so disconnected, it must have been centuries since he died.

He had no concept of who any of these spirits were, what they meant to each other and to the latter self who had called upon him. Their words were strange, almost alien in their unknowability.

One spirit shielded him from someone of substance. Certainly trying to keep that latter self from reverting to him. An understandable concern, but Jehgoro was glad for the moment of wakefulness. He beckoned the spirit aside, and it complied with a trembling that spoke of uncomfortable resignation.

"What the fuck is he doing here?!" came a familiar voice, interlaced with another in the alien language.

His old friend, the one he failed to save, stood before him with flickering uncertainty. Jehgoro approached hesitantly.

"N… Nayon?" he asked, "I think we're the strangers here."

Nayon turned to him, his presence stabilizing as his latter self receded.

"Not you, Jehgoro. I've got words for you, but they can wait," Nayon said, his voice no less harsh, "This pud-flicking cockroach."

Jehgoro followed Nayon's pointing finger to a nebulous spirit and someone with a depthless but consistent presence. Ajaveo stood dumbfounded and disoriented. The other spirit moved in front of him, and an amorphous glimmer gave him depth and thus balance.

"I… I don't…" Ajaveo stammered, "Boys? Where are we?"

"Don't play stupid," Nayon scolded, "How did you get to be on this side after what you did?"

"After what I...?" Ajaveo asked, "Do you mean Phoenix?"

"Phoenix? What's Phoenix?" Jehgoro asked, "Is it what you saved Bealstilla with?"

"It is, but—"

"That must be why he's here," Jehgoro said to Nayon.

" —but I don't remember why I have it," Ajaveo continued.

"You have it so you can save people," Nayon reminded, "But you fucking betrayed us!"

"What? No. I mean... Not its purpose. I mean how I got it."

"You said a strange man gave it to you," Jehgoro said.

"I remember that," Ajaveo said, nodding, "Well, I remember saying that. But... I... don't remember being given it. Actually, I... can't remember anything before I had Phoenix."

"Do you remember betraying us?" Nayon scolded, shadowy tendrils wisping around his hand, "Keep dodging that and see what happens."

"Are you talking about Pandora?" Ajaveo asked, "That woman who followed me around?"

"That bitch you led back to us to test her new powers on!" Nayon shouted, "And you were no better with all the collateral you caused!"

"Nayon?" Jehgoro said, "I know you saw me. And I'm sorry. But—"

"I know you tried," Nayon sighed, "Fuck you kinda for failing. I guess. But fuck Pesmenas harder for taking you away." He thrust a finger at Ajaveo. "And fuck you even harder for bringing Pandora back to Bealstilla!"

"Nayon. You have every right to be upset," Ajaveo said, "But you've misunderstood my role in what happened."

"I watched her kill my family. Every time I intervened, she threw me aside. But she was careful to keep me alive. Do you know why?" Nayon said, "She took me in as a slave. I thought maybe she'd share her powers like Phoenix did with you. But oh no. No. No! I wasn't worthy of that. Wanna know what I was to her?"

"Um, what—"

"Fucking! Bait!" Nayon shouted, the tendrils surging more aggressively, "She took me to Kyojinomachi to lure someone more deserving."

"Nayon, I am so sorry," Ajaveo professed, "Were the Kyoji... merciful?"

"I think she chose that place because of us," Jehgoro cut in, "When Ajaveo left, we decided I'd say he went toward Ippatsuru if Pandora asked."

"Oh, you know most of those giants are as civil as anyone else," Nayon said, "But the civil ones didn't interest her. No, the ones she wanted were eager to violate me in ways I still can't talk about."

"Nayon, I don't expect your forgiveness. I could never truly empathize with what you went through," Ajaveo said, "But I need you to understand that when I came back, I was—"

"Enough of you!"

Nayon swept his hand at Ajaveo, erupting the shadowy tendrils. They snared Ajaveo and branched toward Jehgoro and the gathering of nebulous spirits. The ground churned and reverberated as it and they passed through each other. Darkness flooded in from directions both perceptible and otherwise.

Jehgoro, Ajaveo, and their latter selves' companions, fell into the Netherworld.

Chapter 15

Eytea scrambled to her feet as something noxious seeped and smoked under her butt. She spread her wings to hover just above the ground.

"Is everyone okay?" she asked, "We're all here, right?"

"'Okay' might be too strong a word for, well, any of this," Galo said, "But I'm here."

"As am I," Cedalion assured.

"Why can't I see my mom anymore?" Eytea worried, "This spirit is her, isn't it?"

"Ah yes, I suppose you can't perceive him," Cedalion said, "Jehgoro surfaced, and he isn't receding."

"So, he went from not talking to her to not getting out of her way?"

"Truth told, I don't know that this is by his will."

"This new face that Sinkua's copiloting for," Galo said, "Ajaveo?"

"Yes," Cedalion said, "First Phoenix Hybrid. Rather disconcerting that his memory imprint has surfaced."

"I think I can fix this then."

Galo approached Ajaveo with Sinkua as a secondary presence. He beckoned Metkhal into prominence, and they called to Tsenukoa.

Despite his intentions, Tsenukoa pulled Sinkua back and placed himself as the secondary presence.

Ajaveo's face tightened as he stammered in Bealstillan. The shapeless Jehgoro called over to him in a garbled voice. Ajaveo spun to face him, his voice rising and quickening as he gestured to the others.

Galo and Metkhal whipped him around by the shoulder. This time, Metkhal called for Tsenukoa while Galo beckoned Sinkua. With as much fear in his eyes as they had reluctance in theirs, Ajaveo receded as Sinkua and Tsenukoa emerged in tandem.

"Sinkua?" Galo asked, "Are you back with us?"

"What happened?" Sinkua stammered, "Did you get me back? Thank you."

"We'll figure it out once we're better sorted, but yes," Galo said, "More pressing, Elemeno needs to see you."

"Mom's old self came out," Eytea said, "Now Jehgoro either can't or won't let her resurface."

Eytea stood before Jehgoro, looking into where his eyes ought to have been. Galo and Sinkua flanked her, with Metkhal and Tetsen in tandem. The three of them spoke past Jehgoro, hoping their talk of shared memories and inside jokes might reach Elemeno.

They talked about Galo and Sinkua arriving in Ferya and first meeting her and Eytea. They sidetracked into realizing it was the only time that both of the boys had been at her house together.

Galo reminded her how she had helped rescue Nikasu. Eytea reminded her how she faced down and outlived two Avatars of Fate. Sinkua reminded her about bringing Luvros to him.

Jehgoro's face rippled with shadows of Elemeno's presence. Her voice seeped through his, strained and thready.

Sinkua's and Tetsen's eyes rolled back, and Ajaveo erupted forth, tamping them down into a shared secondary presence. His head jerked and eyes shifted as he rambled in Bealstillan.

"He wants not to go," Metkhal said, "He has fear."

Everyone stopped speaking, save for Ajaveo. Apparently picking up on the silence, he joined them shortly.

"Which one?" Eytea asked at last, "Ajaveo or Jehgoro? Or both?"

"Ajaveo more," Metkhal said, "He forgot most of life and has not understanding."

"He's afraid of disappearing," Eytea exhaled, "And that's keeping Jehgoro here."

"I think so," Metkhal said, "He may be keeping Jehgoro here until he has answers."

"Well, I have answers. But I don't think he wants to or should hear them from me," Eytea considered, "Do you speak Bealstillan or just understand it?"

"I have ability to speak a little."

"Can you assure him that he won't vanish? He'll be safe with Fetzikzi," she urged, "And Phoenix can explain his memory loss."

Metkhal nodded, then spoke to Ajaveo in Bealstillan. It didn't take long for their exchange to move from stern debate to jovial banter and emphatic gestures.

Ajaveo's face rippled as Northlander shadows seeped through.

Sinkua and Tsenukoa stood before a roiling luminous wall. The Netherworld lay beyond it, murky and illusively distant. Either of them using their visual talent made it all the more so.

This was far worse than being a secondary presence.

"We need to put a put in our spat," Sinkua said, "This guy's gonna fuck everything up if we don't rein him in."

"As remiss as I am about it, I actually agree with you," Tsenukoa said, "Mind you, I'll still be waiting for you to renege on our agreement."

"Die again waiting. I don't back out on promises," Sinkua said, "But for what it's worth, the crystal idea first came up because I might need one to move you into your own body."

"I don't believe you."

Sinkua shrugged. "I don't need you to. I just—"

"Hold on!" Tsenukoa blurted out, "Metkhal's trying to talk to him."

Tsenukoa closed his eyes to focus as Sinkua went tight-lipped. Between the muffling of the barrier and his recent conscious volatility, Sinkua thought better than to listen in with him. Not to mention that he knew exactly zero words of Bealstillan anyway.

Tsenukoa soon opened his eyes as he let out a long exhale. He looked back and down into the fractalized expanse of memories.

"Fetzikzi!" he called out "Fetzikzi Aroka!"

"You even speak Bealstillan, huh?" Sinkua asked, "I'm impressed. So, what's the plan?"

"I only know a few words and common phrases," Tsenukoa said, "This is more like an instinct that Metkhal and I have with each other."

"You're on the same wavelength," Sinkua said, "like Galo and me."

Tsenukoa called for Miss Aroka once more.

"I don't know that word," he said, "Wavelength. Phoenix didn't even translate it. But I think you get it."

Elemeno awoke as though from an amalgam of dreams. The last thing she could remember was calling out to someone. But not the name. That, as well as everything since, was cloudy. It was like fragments, perhaps pieces of fragments, of memories stitched together with a distorted sense of time.

But where she woke up had her wondering if she ought to have stayed asleep.

She sighed with an inquisitive cadence. "Oh, we've wound up in the Netherworld, haven't we? Well, isn't this just the worst luck?"

"Good to have you back, Elemeno," Sinkua said.

"You gave us all quite a scare," Galo added, "We weren't sure we could get you back from behind Jehgoro."

"It was more that Ajaveo was keeping him in your way," Eytea said, "By the way, how'd you get him to cooperate?"

"Metkhal proposed your idea."

"Damn right, he did."

Elemeno laughed hard enough to almost distract herself from the sudden spike in temperature. The air so thickened as to burden her shoulders.

"Any of you care to fill me in?" she asked.

"Nayon came out of Amirione, which brought Jehgoro out of you," Sinkua recapped, "Which brought Ajaveo's imprint out of me. He can't remember most of his life, so he's afraid he's gonna disappear."

"Fetzikzi agreed to get him up to speed and keep him company in their subconscience," Galo added, "He shouldn't be alone, even if it wouldn't cause him to fall back into the collective."

"Well, I'm glad everything's worked out. But are you sure you're okay, Sinkua?" Elemeno asked, "This must all be becoming quite the burden."

"We're, ah…" Sinkua pondered, "We're managing. For now."

"Despite the necessity of my actions," Cedalion said, "I must apologize. Ajaveo would not have surfaced had I not first brought Jehgoro out of you, Miss Elemeno."

"Oh, that's no bother," Elemeno dismissed, "Your foresight doesn't mean enough here that you should've seen this coming. Besides, your insights about the Phoenix Shrine are priceless."

"But they're worthless if we can't get out of here, sorry to say," Sinkua said, "Which we stand little chance of without Arestor."

He gestured upward, and they all craned their necks to follow. Some unknowable distance into the inverted abyss, yellowish fractalized light glistened through the darkness.

"That's the underside of the river," he said.

"Which Arestor can pass through, but we can't. Probably," Galo said, "Do you know if it's because he's a beastkin, or is there more to it?"

"More to it. He said only beastkin have pulled it off, but even they've had mixed results," Sinkua said, "Tsenukoa didn't ask him to elaborate."

"How do we go about finding Arestor, then?" Elemeno asked.

"We have a better chance of him finding us," Cedalion said, "When Sinkua first vanished, I sent Arestor to scout both sides for either him or Epesol. With any luck, he's still watching for the latter."

"So, you sent Arestor to help Sinkua and Takmet to help Galo," Eytea said, "What did you have Pahres do?"

"Pahres will help as needed and able, but I have no reason to expect him to look for us here."

"Well in the meantime," Sinkua said, "I need to give you all a rundown on how to handle ourselves here."

His first point was to not stand still for long. Between the rapid softening and hardening of the ground and the itch of scar tissue snaking up her calves, Elemeno found it hard to argue.

They walked nowhere in particular as he continued. This caustic wasteland had no visible landmarks. Given the volatility of the landscape though, she doubted they'd be permanent anyway.

His warning about the air explained the earlier sudden heatwave. Density, temperature, humidity, any of it could change without warning.

"There is one thing I haven't made sense of," Sinkua said, "but I'm not sweating it. I'll let you all know if it comes up."

Silence dragged. Elemeno cast a sidelong glance at Eytea, hovering a few centimeters off the ground to spite its spiteful fluctuations. She sidled up to her and nudged her with her elbow.

"Do you know what he's talking about?"

"No, but I'm okay with it," Eytea said, spinning to drift backward, "It doesn't matter how this place works. Either I go down fighting, or someone like him carries me out."

Elemeno furrowed her brow, then turned her attention to Sinkua.

"Could you perhaps elaborate?" she asked, "I feel like I should know what you're talking about, but it won't come to me."

"What? I just mean that I've got it covered. I shouldn't need to get any of you involved," he said, "But you know the forced empathy thing?"

"Yes, we feel toward others how they felt about us?"

"Right. Well, that doesn't happen over here," Sinkua said, "But I feel different, and Kabehl acted different from what I heard about him."

"Different how?" Elemeno urged.

"It was like he… thought less of himself," Sinkua said, "But not exactly. He thinks everything that went wrong after he died was because people didn't listen to him. But he had also kinda resigned himself to his fate."

"He gave up on himself," Galo chimed in, "He thinks he has nothing useful to contribute."

"Not anymore, at least," Eytea added.

"That's how he saw us," Elemeno said, "Maybe that's what it is. You see yourself the way you saw other people."

"I guess that makes sense," Sinkua pondered, "Vielle would call him a textbook sociopath."

"Lucky we all thought well of the people around us," Galo said, "Well. Mostly. Honestly, I'm surprised you all trust my judgment enough to draw that conclusion."

"Which is why we should," Sinkua insisted, "You're questioning your own trustworthiness. Just like you did with your aunt and uncles. That means Elemeno's right."

"Someone needs to keep an eye on Cedalion," Eytea said, "We don't want him slipping into his disposable humans era."

"I'm managing quite fine on my own, thank you," Cedalion said, "That stage of my life is centuries behind me."

"Well, in those centuries since you started giving a shit," she said, "did you maybe learn why this place is so empty?"

"Arestor explained it to us," Sinkua said, "Nearly all the souls here are beastkin or the human reincarnations of escaped beastkin."

"Maybe that's why they all died off," Eytea suggested.

"Might have something to do with it," Sinkua said, "Anyway, the people who don't or can't get out become part of the environment."

"Do you mean to say," Elemeno said, swallowing as she sorted her thoughts, "that this place is made of dead beastkin souls?"

"Something like that but not entirely," he said, "Creatures can take shape out of the ground. They can reassemble themselves from each other's scraps. Like the biomechs but worse. Lucky for us, they're the exception to reciprocal injuries."

"Reciprocal injuries?" Galo asked, "You never mentioned that. Do you mean that if I try to hurt you, I'll get hurt instead?"

"Not instead. Also," Sinkua said, "So maybe reciprocal isn't the best word. Miss Aroka punched Kervatus and shattered his jaw along with her own hand. Everything does grow back though."

"That just means we can relive that pain as many times as the Netherworld wants," Eytea said.

"So. Now that we know who and what to look out for," Elemeno said, "Now what? Just wander and hope we cross paths with Arestor."

"Yeah, as far as I know," Sinkua sighed, "Maybe scout for another Yggdrasil root."

"The rest of you wait here," Eytea insisted, "I want to check something."

Eytea gave a single glance back as she thrust herself upward. The others were milling about for the sake of their lower halves, talking about she knew not what.

They all had overlapping past lives. Souls parting and reuniting across multiple incarnations. Even The Scout and The Hunter got in on it, and she knew if they found other Avatars, the same would be true of them.

But not her. Being a neophyte soul hadn't bothered her much. Not enough for her to let on, anyway. But the more she heard about their previous shared lives, the more out of place she felt.

Then there was what Kabehl or Kervatus had said about Odin's plans for her. She put next to no stock in either of them, but hearing how Odin behaved made it hard to write it off.

The air thinned as she ascended. But then it thickened. Thinned again. A powerful gust swept through. The temperature spiked.

That was the other thing. Those changes did affect her flight of course. But that was it. No matter how the air fluctuated, she breathed with the same natural ease. She could feel the changes in temperature, but she was little more than aware of them.

Eytea stopped to reconsider beneath the shimmering river. If she backed out, she wouldn't have an answer. She'd have to go on wondering if it was another aspect of the Netherworld that didn't affect her. But she wouldn't have to worry about keeping the others' trust in her.

Well, Cedalion's at least. Her mom and the boys, she was certain would stick with her. As certain as she could be. But Cedalion, guarded as she'd known him to be, there was no telling how he'd react to her being immune to the river. Everyone else, she could just say it didn't work.

If she persisted, she'd have answers. That and, were her suspicions true, a workable way out. If she could dredge up the strength to carry Sinkua again, she could carry all of them.

Then again, carrying them to the river was only half the problem. There was still the logistics of getting them through. Her wings were big but not that big. Cocooning more than a small child would have been impossible.

The Valkyrie and Freja came to mind. They might have been able to help. Finding them would an ordeal unto itself though, and she loathed the thought of leaving the others behind.

Eytea swiped her hand through the water.

Sinkua only realized he was staring when caustic tendrils slithered along his hamstrings. He wriggled and swatted his way out, cursing the fact that nobody had warned him. They had all been just as preoccupied. Not so much with staring, but with staying above ground without wandering off.

Eytea began descending just in time to distract him from thoughts that he deserved better. Somebody ought to have mentioned to him that he was sinking. Even if he hadn't been the one to teach them about the Netherworld, it was a basic courtesy. Sure, they all had themselves to look after, but he was the only one being eaten by the ground.

"I'm impressed," Tetsen said, "You're even more insufferable in the Netherworld."

"I have a bad habit of being the last to give up on people," Sinkua defended, "It bothers me when people don't reciprocate."

"Or maybe the whole standoffish ass bit is just that. A bit," Tetsen said, "You think everyone else deserves better than you do. Step."

Sinkua wrenched his feet out of the roiling brimstone and paced about.

"And now that you see yourself as you see others," Tetsen continued, "you're a narcissistic bumblefuck. And I learned about Narcissus in my history studies."

Sinkua narrowed and flared his eyes as Eytea drew nearer. Her eyes were distant, her expression flat. Unnaturally so. It looked forced.

"Something's wrong," Sinkua said, "She's poker-facing too hard."

"Wow, you can pick up on nuance," Tetsen snarked, "Honestly, I'm as impressed as I am surprised."

"The fuck is that supposed to mean, Tetsen?" Sinkua challenged, "Read the damn room. Something went wrong on her recon. Nobody has time for your pettiness."

"I can leave it alone, I suppose," Tetsen said, "I do have a point to make, but it can wait."

Eytea staggered as she landed on unstable ground, bracing against Sinkua with her entire upper body. Sinkua's vision flattened and bubbled as Tetsen pulled back for personal space.

She couldn't have been privy to his inner dealings with the memory imprints. But the timing was too perfect for him not to wonder if she knew what she was doing.

"What'd you find out?" he asked.

"I, um…" Eytea said. Her eyes darted, panning the gathering, as she smacked her lips, "I can't pass through."

"Bummer. Well, it was worth a shot," Sinkua said, nudging the crook of her elbow as he started walking, "I hope you didn't hurt your hand."

"What? Oh! No. It's fine," Eytea said, "Nothing broke. It just stung. Like a hard slap."

"Maybe I'm out of line here," Galo chimed in, "But was that all? You gave up because it felt like a slap?"

"Seeing as I barely touched the water, yeah."

Sinkua spun on his heel to face her, walking backwards as he spoke.

"You okay?" he asked, "You seem defensive."

"Yeah, well he seems offensive," she deflected, "Ask him why he can't just take my word. "

"Even a neophyte ought to know this place brings out the worst in everyone," came another voice. One of fading familiarity and memories of betrayal. "And that miserable pawn has long been plagued by doubt."

Chapter 16

"Did you ever visit Ippatsuru?" Fetzikzi asked, "Or did you think Pandora would be watching it too closely after your deception?"

"It did cross my mind. Her watching it, I mean," Ajaveo said, narrowing his eyes at the taut fabric aglow with moving images, "But we eventually made our way over there."

"I figured you did," she said, shrugging as he cocked his head at the sheet and gestured to her, "You must've written about it in your journal."

"I did. But what made you so sure?"

"I heard Tenzu Tamanoro, third after me, was Ippatsuranu," Fetzikzi recalled, "Your stories must have inspired someone between me and him to visit Ippatsuru."

"I don't know about that," Ajaveo said, "We only went to establish contact. And maybe find more people like us." He paced along an irregular array of cobblestones and slushy mud. "Keep in mind that the House of the Dragon Family was in its infancy."

"True. You did pioneer the whole Hybrid thing," Fetzikzi said, "But I wonder who his parents were. And how long did they stay in Ippatsuru? It must've been a while since he puts his family name first. Cedalion even calls him Tenzu-kun."

"It is quite curious," Ajaveo concurred, "If this Sinkua get new bodies for us, perhaps we can read Tenzu-kun's journal and learn for ourselves."

"I hope so. His or, um… Mister Vlazir's might have the story about how Tamanoro's…"

She trailed off as the air rippled and darkened. The ripples tightened as the darkness condensed. Fetzikzi's tongue pressing into her palate as they took the shape of a human silhouette.

"Oh shit," she muttered, "I think maybe we shouldn't talk so much about the other usses."

Galo's jaw clenched at the sound of that voice. He dug his fingers into his leg, bracing and willing himself to face him. After all the warnings Sinkua had given as to the nature of the Netherworld, he had to steel himself for whatever monstrosity his abuser had become.

That and for reciprocity of whatever violence his instincts might dole out.

"Prophet," Galo said with as much indifference he could muster, "Scurrying around in dark recesses is a… suitable look on you."

"I follow the path of Nidhogg. You who follows that of Leviathan are much the same," The Prophet said, pacing and gesticulating, "Though I delight to hear you still so revere me as to call me as I was Named."

"Oh. No. It isn't like that," Galo said, "Calling you Pahres would be disrespectful to the real Pahres."

Enamel flakes fell from The Prophet's mouth as he ground his teeth. "Do not mention that inter—"

"And sure, I could give a nickname, but you're not worth the effort."

"Calling him Fuckstick might get boring after a while, anyway," Eytea chimed in, "Heya, Fuckstick. Did your superiors ever tell you how much effort they put into killing me?"

"More than they put into saving you, I'm sure," Sinkua added, "Fuckstick."

"I will not tolerate such indignation!" The Prophet bellowed, "Not from those who would—"

"Then walk away, Fuckstick," Galo said, "Huh. You know, I thought you were right, Eytea, but it don't see it losing appeal anytime soon."

"Lord Harvester!" The Prophet beckoned with a sweeping gesture to Cedalion, "How did you fall so far as to fraternize with such lessers? What manner of machination could you be devising?"

"Curious. Neither The Harvester nor The General told you about me?" Cedalion said, "I was as he in flesh and history and little else."

"Ah. The Coalition's Imposter," The Prophet muttered, "An externalization of the battle I lost. Should I thus assume you to have been responsible for my usurping?"

"I had nothing to do with that. Not directly."

"Legends spoke that Yggdrasil might bridge the temporal rivers," The Prophet said, "I was buried within my own mind once that Dryad held the seed."

"Vielle's not a Dryad," Sinkua interrupted, "Fuckstick."

"Do you mean to tell me, Imposter, that you and he intruded upon this stream by dissimilar means?" The Prophet continued, ignoring Sinkua's prodding.

"I mean to tell you that I didn't help the other Pahres take over your mind and body," Cedalion reiterated, "I only gave him refuge from The Avatars of Fate."

"The real Pahres never lost confidence in his family," Galo said, "And he sure wouldn't have betrayed the Trifecta. Not even when Yggdrasil was reduced to a seedling. Fuckstick."

"What faith is deserved by so meddlesome a construct as Yggdrasil?" The Prophet challenged, "We and Etherworlders are meant not to cohabitate. Should we need their intervention to inhabit this world, then this world was not intended for us."

Galo looked him over. His posture and thus conviction was unwavering. Some of MalVek's more knowledgeable followers had been aware of what the Era of Chaos might portend. But they saw it as an evolution they would take part in. The Prophet was the first to celebrate it as something that would remove him just as anyone else.

He shot a glance aside at Sinkua, signaling him to be ready to intervene. Just in case. Instead, he found him with his eyes glassy and rolled back. Probably a sensory defensive meditative state, he figured.

"If Yggdrasil is meddlesome for stabilizing the Omphaloworld, why did you try to use Leviathan to destabilize it?" Galo challenged, "And don't say you were balancing things out. The only reason we used Yggdrasil was because of what you did with Leviathan."

"Yggdrasil's meddling long predates that of—"

"We could be at this for eons," Cedalion interrupted, "And while I do have that sort of time, I would rather spend it in different company."

"Phoenix came here to save a dying community," Sinkua said, pacing and gesturing as though re-acclimating to physical presence, "Zeus's reaction was to send Pandora. Not to bring her home. But to take Phoenix's power for herself."

"And sunder the Omphaloworld as recompense," Cedalion added.

"You're right that someone up there meddled with this world to keep it together," Eytea said, "But someone else severely overreacted trying to undo it."

"The Era of Chaos was never a corrective measure," Elemeno said, "It's vain justification for genocide. It's manipulative."

"I don't fully understand the connection between the Omphaloworld and the Etherworld. And don't act like you do either," Galo said, "But it sounds like someone up there wanted us to die off, and when someone else helped us, they used that as an excuse to kill us."

"Fools!" The Prophet bellowed, sweeping his arm out in a grand gesture, "Bastards and fools, every last one of you!"

"Actually, my father came back into my life," Galo corrected.

"I was always on good terms with mine," Elemeno added.

"You think you can manipulate me just because I'm stuck in this pit?!" The Prophet challenged, "My punishment is undeserved. But keep in mind that it is taking five of you to manipulate one of me."

"I possess thousands of years of human experience," Cedalion said, "Much of your knowledge came from my other self, and I outmaneuvered him and infiltrated his master's operations."

"Oh, but we are not within the human experience now, are we?" The Prophet challenged, "I straddle comprehension to see both worlds with an all but unique insight."

"Do you think you're a fucking Nether-Hybrid?" Sinkua chortled, "You've seen the creatures that grow out of the ground here, right? I don't know what kind of powers you think you have, but that's what you have to look forward to."

"Oh, but what better way to manipulate the machinations than to become part of them? Isn't that right, Imposter?" The Prophet said, "Born under Yggdrasil and cast unto Nidhogg, I have become as Ratatoskr!"

He dug his feet into the caustic brimstone Arcs and bolts of black lightning flickered up around him as he drew back into a challenging stance. Eyes dark and glassy, he fixed his glare on Galo.

"Only by embracing Leviathan's true calling might the wrath of the Netherworld embrace you," he continued, "For naught but their interloping are they and you with them to be consumed by it."

That word resonated in Eytea's mind. Nether-Hybrid. Surely, he just made it up. But that might have been the best title for her.

Assuming Odin was corrupt when he created her. And that he created her.

But that was assuming he even needed to be corrupted for her to be a Nether-Hybrid. If Zeus was petty enough to create Pandora to pursue Phoenix and undo her work, Odin could be just as underhanded and destructive.

All speculation aside, it was a good explanation for why she didn't feel anything in the Netherworld. Of all the warnings Sinkua had given, none of them affected her. She still took him at his word though. After all, everyone else was clearly experiencing the things he had talked about.

But not her. Even the river felt tepid. That didn't do them any good though, seeing as she had no way to escort them through it. And with no way to get back in touch with them, doing recon on the other side was too big a risk.

All her speculation and mulling collapsed though as black lightning erupted from where The Prophet had stood half a blink ago. Eytea launched forth with an electrical burst of her own. She snapped her hand up and grabbed him by the side of the neck on a perpendicular trajectory.

She dragged The Prophet along the roiling brimstone, tissue and bone shredding as his ankles carved a gulley. Eytea planted her feet, stopping cold, and slammed The Prophet into the ground.

"Eytea!" Sinkua called out, "You can't—"

He trailed off into a stupor as Eytea stood and faced him. She was unscathed.

She could see the calculation behind his eyes. There was no suspicion. No pity either. Were she a Nether-Hybrid, he saw her as neither a victim nor a villain.

No, that calculation was reassessing his knowledge of the Netherworld.

"You're too late," The Prophet grumbled, still pinned under her hand, "I've called forth the denizens."

Eytea looked back along his trajectory. The cracks swelled with obsidian and caustic substances. They took on the shapes of vaguely bodily entities, messes of limbs, bestial heads, and torsos with little care for form and barely more for function.

Eytea leaned down within a whisper's distance. "When you see Nidhogg," she exhaled, "Tell him he'll have to answer to me."

She launched to her feet and stomped on The Prophet's neck. Luminous smoke erupted alongside blood and bone. The light left his eyes as fast as the color left his face, and his entire presence went limp.

Ridiculous as dying in the afterlife was, it was the only way she could think of to stop him from summoning more of those creatures. She knew he wasn't dead. No more than before anyway. But she could make him as good as such, even if just to buy them some time. And perhaps make him wish that he was.

The first creature to break away charged at Galo with limbs flailing and teeth gnashing. Before Eytea could even think to react though, Galo launched an absolute bullet of a kick through the frenetic mess of appendages. His foot met mass with a sickly thwack, launching the thing back at its brood, and withdrew unharmed.

"He's right," he called over, "No reciprocity with these."

The horde scattered to separate and swarm them.

"Don't hold back!" Sinkua commanded.

With his words still resonating, the brood was upon them. Though long in disuse, the morningstar on Sinkua's back was the only weapon among them. The only customary weapon, at least. Most of them had milystis and combat experience to call upon. That left only her mother for Eytea to worry about.

Some faceless tripedal swiped a half-winged arm at her. Eytea caught it by the wrist in a piercing grip, releasing a burst of milystic lightning into the puncture wounds. With a firm tug, she snapped the arm off and whipped around to bludgeon another closing in from behind.

Tendrils snapped from the sever and latched onto the stricken creature. Reintegrated and thus reanimated, the limb wrenched from her grasp and swiped its craggy claws across her face. A forward thrust of her wings launched her back and beyond reach.

The scratches were gone by the time she landed.

Galo scattered and suspended icy caltrops with a swipe of his hand. He bounded and danced back, baiting the denizens nearer. They shambled with no particular direction, but the more he moved about, the more a sense of cohesion emerged.

But though they more or less advanced on him, the caltrops were neither the trap nor defense he'd intended. No, if anything, they were a distraction for the Netherworld creatures.

Galo snapped his fingers, and a single caltrop flattened and widened. That got their attention, even if only for a split second. And when a flick of his wrist ripped it through luminous tar flesh, that attention followed.

They didn't track their prey by conventional senses. They sensed milystis.

Unfortunately, one glance at Elemeno showed him his relief was as brief as it was presumptuous. She held them off with quick hard jabs and a shielded face, but her tsora was scarcely less a target than his milystis.

Only one thing to do for it.

He focused on every trace of moisture. The humidity behind the fluctuating air pressure. The liquid in the seeping sludge. The concept of hydration in this illusory body. The ethereal steam trapped in the brimstone ground.

Galo anchored it all with his milystis. He was all that remained of Leviathan, the tsoran extension of her power. And he reached into the greatest depths of that power to seize control of the very notion, the very concept, of water itself.

The denizens around him shriveled and decayed. The ground dried. The air fell still and silent.

Watery motes of shadow and iridescence whipped along just beyond the contours of his body. Collisions became connections, stretching into branches to form a latticework shell in the swollen shape of himself. As it tightened and adhered to him, it grabbed the attention of the creatures setting upon Elemeno.

But it wasn't enough. Just as quickly as they set their sights on him, the nearer quarry took their attention right back. He had to draw them off.

He willed the latticework shell to break and fold into itself, starting from the middle of his back. It worked its way to the front of his body, coalescing over his solar plexus. He cupped his hands just beyond the edges of the tangled mass of shadowy iridescence. The pulsations of his own milystis binding with the concept of Netherworld moisture thrummed the bones of his illusory body.

The creatures skulking about Elemeno turned to him with greater earnest and longer focus. He squeezed the Nether-milystic mass, condensing it all the tighter.

"Elemeno!" he called out, his voice strained and thready.

She looked to him, eyes wide with equal parts excitement and fear.

"Duck!"

Sinkua cracked the first in striking distance with his morningstar, ripping trails of brimstone blood from a serpentine neck. He erected a pillar of flame with a swipe of his hand and, shielded for now, turned his thoughts toward Phoenix.

She didn't answer. She should have been able to. He could sense her in the depths of his subconscience. She was simply, it seemed, refusing to.

"Tetsen," he beckoned, "Can you see her?"

His depth perception bowed inward, settling into partial flatness. A couple of hasty fireballs and another swing of the morningstar held off whatever breached the faltering barrier.

"Not from here," Tetsen said as Sinkua's depth perception normalized, "Same plan as before?"

"Yeah. You on board?"

"I'm not thrilled," Tetsen said, "But I'm willing."

Sinkua looked to the others. Eytea had no trouble standing her ground. In fact, he could almost swear she recovered from her injuries unusually fast. But it was so rare for any of them to even land a hit that he couldn't be sure. Especially not at a distance. But that was a nonissue at the moment anyway.

Cedalion was even less cause for concern. He all but baited the denizens toward him since they deteriorated at his touch. Sinkua pondered if he actually came from here.

Elemeno handled herself just as well as Sinkua had expected. Not with nearly the focus and power of the rest of them, but far better than strangers would've assumed.

But any ground she was losing became of no concern when he checked on Galo. By the darkly radiant shell, he looked to have realized how the denizens tracked their prey.

Sinkua swept his arms out, launching a ball of fiery milystis from each of his fingertips. He upturned his hands up, and all ten erupted into whirling masses of flame larger than his body. A luminous red string set out in pursuit from each fingertip.

As they made contact, Sinkua's senses blurred.

Galo unleashed a resonant war cry as he threw his arms back and launched the Nether-milystic mass with a pulsation from his chest. Churning water shifted through every state as it plowed forth, consuming ambient moisture in its path.

Elemeno hunkered down. The watery mass shattered the first denizen it struck. Then the next several after it. The very wake of its momentum discarded those in the fringes, flinging them into and through their cohorts.

Creatures piled atop one another, breaking and rebuilding with no sense of their original forms. As the torrential blast broke through the back of the crowd, the first to come upright gave chase.

Elemeno got to her feet and mouthed her gratitude. Galo slumped over and braced against his own knees as the ambient moisture normalized.

From off in Sinkua's direction came a rumbling bellow and a rush of heat. Galo closed his eyes, and the sightless vision pulled at itself.

Eytea found a glimmer of hope in Galo seizing control of the waters of the Netherworld. He had performed similar feats when they were alive, freezing columns of ocean water and such. But Netherworld water had to be different on some intrinsic level.

And if he could control it, maybe that meant she wasn't alone. Maybe Leviathan, regardless of her morality, had roots in the Netherworld. Obviously, Galo felt the fluctuations in the air though, which meant the river was almost definitely caustic to him. But any ties he might have had here made her that much less isolated by her own origins.

The horde closed in on her, grabbing and gnashing ever more tenaciously. Though the wounds, rare as they were, healed all but immediately, the pain persisted much longer. As Eytea rammed and ripped her way through, a corner of her mind wondered if her quick healing drew their ire. Or maybe it was her being a Nether-Hybrid.

A rush of heat tugged at her intuition.

Eytea pulsed out a lightning orb to clear an armspan of breathing room. Netherworld abominations crackled and burned, brimstone flesh turning to sludge and sizzling against the ground. She rushed forth and grabbed a straggler by the throat, clamping down as Galo's attack scattered the horde around her mother.

The heat scattered and swelled.

Those on the fringes scattered. A wingbeat put Eytea half her height above the crowd. Her mother was out of harm's way but seemed to realize she was out of her depth to help the others. Cedalion, of course, was as much in danger as concerned with aiding the rest of them.

Galo had worn of himself out protecting her mother. But he was largely out of danger as well. The massive fireballs around Sinkua kept the swarming hordes in distinct clusters. The orbs moved as though anchored to him, emphasizing his growing sluggishness.

Eytea slammed her feet into the ground, throwing up rubble with a blast of electricity. She rushed the flailing horde, grabbing a creature under two of its arms and driving it into the ones behind it. Their torsos broke against each other, tendrils snaking from break points to reintegrate with whatever they could reach.

She pulled the two limbs away as she pivoted aside and around, bashing yet another creature with quick shocks upon impact. Eytea wove through the brief clearing scattering sparks as she thrust her wings. She choke-slammed a denizen with an impact surge that arced through the last line of them.

She pushed through the horde just in time to see Sinkua collapse on the caustic ground. The orbs had become fiery silhouettes. And as their tethers diminished, two more emerged on thicker strands.

Chapter 17

Awakening in a tessellation of incongruent landscapes set Tamanoro scrambling through his last memories. Everything was distant and disjointed. Nothing he could recall lined up with this place.

Establishing a sense of time was impossible. His most recent memories felt like they were an immediate eternity away. And while this place appeared to be outdoors, the sunlight was, in a word, inconsistent.

"I guess we can't ignore you into going back inside, huh?" came a voice.

It was rare to hear Ippatsuranu spoken so well with a Harkzanian accent. He recalled being raised to avoid Northlanders, especially Harkzanians and Azzelegna. But if the alternative was being alone in this strange place, he could cast off his misgivings. Especially if she was fluent in his language.

And hopefully as much a looker as she sounded.

"You speak Ippatsuranu very well," he said, turning to face her, "Where did you study?"

"Dagiliz," she said, "I met my husband there while I was studying abroad."

He gave her a once over. Northlander or not, she was undeniably attractive. Even if he were more spoiled for options, she would've been worth a second look. Cultured, too. Being trapped here might have had its perks.

"Ah, you were married?" Tamanoro asked, "Well I don't know where we are, but I don't think there's a way out. And I might dare say your husband has no knowledge of your whereabouts. Much less that he or anyone could find us anyway. Do you get what I'm saying?"

"What? Oh! … Oh, this is embarrassing," she said, "Mostly for you. It's just… awkward for me. You do understand who I am, right?"

"Yes, you're from Lekazonoryu," Tamanoro said, "Well, Drakougeneospa to you. But I would hardly say we're related. We clearly come from divergent branches."

"We're not even the same distance from the trunk, kohai," she said, rolling her eyes, "You really don't get it, do you?"

"Ko… Kohai? What gives you the right?" Tamanoro recoiled, "You're far younger than me. And clearly out of your depth! Do you even—"

The woman flicked her wrist, and flames manifested from her hands. Just as he could do. She also had green eyes. Just as he did.

Granted, a lot of Hybrids in Lekazonoryu had green eyes. And a lot could manifest and manipulate fire. But only one had green eyes and pyromancy.

"What trickery is this?" he protested, "What the hell is this place to imprison me with such a fraud and a tease as you?"

"Tamanoro. Tenzu-kun," she beckoned, "Please tell me the entire House didn't become as stupid as you after I died."

His eyes widened. She knew his name. And she was already dead. Which meant he was dead, too. All that talk of an afterlife from Cedalion and Tiamat, and this was all it was.

"Who are you? How do you know who I am?"

"I've been trying to tell you that since you started hitting on me," she said, "My name is Fetzikzi Aroka. I'm, in a sense, you."

"Fetz… I've read about you! You were in my uncle's journal!" Tamanoro exclaimed, "You helped take down the faun trafficking ring!"

"Yes I suppose I did," Fetzikzi said, "I was also the Phoenix Hybrid. Just like you were. Which means you are my reincarnation. It also means that I'm your great great blah blah blah aunt or something like that."

"Oh? … Oh! Right!" Tamanoro remarked, "Oh man. That's awkward. So embarrassing. I can't believe I flirted with you. You're old as shit!"

Fetzikzi's expression flattened. "Way to miss the point, kohai."

"Would you stop calling me that?!"

"Would you stop being an idiot?"

"Fine. Fine!" Tamanoro said, throwing his hands up, "So what are you supposed to be my conscience or something? I have to answer to my elders until I'm ready to be reincarnated as my own grandson or nephew or whatever?"

"If that were the case, don't you think there'd be a lot more of us?" came another voice.

This one was male. Southlander, probably. But he couldn't place the exact accent.

"Okay who the hell are you, and why didn't you speak up sooner?"

"My name is Ajaveo. The first of us," the man said as he stepped into view. A Southlander indeed. "As to your other question? Because it was funny. I was a busker, so I do love a good show."

Tamanoro pinched the bridge of his nose. "Ajaveo and Fetzikzi Aroka. Where the hell are we? Cedalion and Tiamat never said our afterlife was like this. Are the other four of us here?"

"We should hope not," Ajaveo said, "The three of us are here by accident."

"Each one presenting more danger than the last," Fetzikzi added.

Tamanoro sighed and hunkered down on an unfamiliar piece of furniture.

"Okay," he said, "I'm gonna try to shut up while you two explain what the hell is going on."

As they spoke, the imperceptible boundaries bowed and warped as though someone was squeezing his peripheral vision. Darkness flickered now and again. Disorientation came in fits and flashes. Swells of firelight came not quite from above and below so much as from the concept of vertical directions.

Fetzikzi spoke aside to a light in the notion of the depths. A voice rippled through Tamanoro's thoughts. It sounded like Phoenix's but meek and distant. The light subsided to the dullest of glows.

"So, I'm about five and a half millennia in the future?" Tamanoro asked, "And both of your Ippatsuranu just got worse because Phoenix isn't translating for you anymore?"

"Would you rather try to speak Bealstillan?" Ajaveo asked, "But yes. I'm still coming to terms with it all myself."

"I guess being a… what was it? Memory imprint?" Tamanoro asked, to which Ajaveo nodded, "Yeah, I guess that would be hard on you. Fetzikzi, you said we're made from Phoenix's memories, right?"

"That's right," Fetzikzi said, "Ajaveo here and Tetsen Drukoa up there took it the worst. One was missing his first several years, the other the last few."

"And up there is…?" Tamanoro asked, "Tetsen Drukoa and Sinkua?"

"More or less," Fetzikzi said, "This is Sinkua's subconscience. His conscious state and Mister Drukoa are up there because it takes two people to navigate the afterlife. But the more of us that Phoenix lets out, the harder it is for anyone to stay up there."

"One time, Sinkua thought too hard trying to remember something, and he fell in here," Ajaveo added, "Now that you're here, that might happen even more."

"Not that it's your fault," Fetzikzi assured, "It could've been any of us."

"Well, that does make me feel better," Tamanoro said, "But what happens if Sinkua's plan works? Or doesn't work?"

"Obviously, we can only guess. But I've had the most time to think about it. Except for Tetsen of course," Fetzikzi said, "If it fails, we'll try to become part of Phoenix again."

"Wouldn't we need to find a Lechuatzulan stonecrafter?"

"Someone who knows their ways at least. Now if it succeeds, we're hoping to still be here, as in his subconscience, but in the living world," she went on, "He told Tetsen that he'd try to get us our own bodies."

"How is he going to do that?" Tamanoro asked, "Does Cedalion have something to do with it?"

"I don't know. If he does have a plan, he's keeping it well guarded," Fetzikzi said, "Honestly, it wouldn't surprise me if he only said that to shut Tetsen up. Sinkua needs him to cooperate, and he's been, well, difficult."

"Yes, it might all be a ruse," Ajaveo said, "But with good intentions. He didn't mean to deceive. He simply made a promise that he didn't know how to keep."

"If that's the case, I'm sure he's been trying to come up with a way," Fetzikzi said, "He called himself the plan guy. So, if he didn't have a plan, he's been working on one."

Tamanoro's periphery bowed deeper than before. The glow from above thinned as it stretched downward. An urging tugged at his sternum.

"So, a broke man with a get rich quick scheme promised the world," he said, "The whole thing is ludicrous. I can't blame Drukoa-san for being suspicious."

"Neither can I, honestly," Ajaveo said, "But like I said, I don't believe there was any malice to it."

"It was more of an intention than a promise," Fetzikzi reasoned, "He promised to look for a way to make it happen."

Tamanoro sighed as he hefted himself to his feet. The ground swelled and shimmered, the momentum flowing through his body.

"Well as cynical as I am about the whole thing," he said, wincing at another tugging at his chest, "I suppose protesting won't do any good."

"It would just make things worse," Fetzikzi said, "If we lash out, we risk—"

The ground erupted in brilliant notions of shades of luminous red. The imperceptible boundaries rushed toward them, hazy light from above spreading to the widths of his peripheral vision.

Silhouettes woven of fiery yarn and green threads rushed past him from below. He tumbled end over end, rolling up to join in their mad charge. His body no longer felt like his own. Tamanoro looked at his hands.

He had become like them.

And with a flash of darkness, he stood on brimstone and brackish sludge.

The fiery figures kept the hordes at bay while Eytea hurried to Sinkua's side. But with their absolute lack of coordination, they stood little hope of gaining any ground. In fact, aside from the two more strongly tethered ones, they seemed just as confused by their own presence as Eytea was about them.

Eytea hunkered down beside Sinkua. For the first time, a Netherworld stench bothered her. The caustic sludge melted his flesh into the texture of chewed taffy, relenting only as seeping blood boiled against the oily amalgam.

She flipped him onto his back, hoping anything but his face burning would smell less bad. Sinkua's mouth was slack, eyes distant. Tsenukoa's body flickered and jolted. The shimmering reminded her of Laboratory 1341, the strangest and worst reason she'd ever been nostalgic for life.

Flitting and warping, Tsenukoa centered his face and looked to her urgingly. He appeared to speak as much so, but Eytea couldn't hear him.

The faces of the flaming silhouettes became more distinct. Especially the two with the strongest tethers. Eytea called out to the more feminine one.

"Fetzikzi?" she asked, "Fetzikzi Aroka?"

The figure turned to her with an emphatic gesture. Same as Tsenukoa, she looked to speak just as emphatically. But again, same as Tsenukoa, Eytea couldn't hear her.

"It can't just be me," Eytea muttered.

"What can't just be you?" Galo asked, startling her with how he'd chosen to announce his presence.

"Can you hear them?" Eytea asked, reining in her composure.

Galo watched the feminine one speak and gesture for a moment, then shook his head.

"Were you afraid it was something to do with you not being affected by the conditions here?" he asked.

Eytea winced and laughed nervously. "Did everyone notice that?"

Galo shrugged. "Probably?" he guessed, "For now, what do we do about these?"

"I think," Eytea said, sorting her thoughts, "these are his other past selves. The memory imprints. That one answered to Fetzikzi Aroka."

"Son of a bitch," Galo exhaled, "He only had three in rotation. The rest just popped out all at once?"

"I think so. And I have no idea what to do about," she fretted, gesturing with broad emphasis, "any of this. What are we supposed to do? Keep them from wandering off? I don't know what language they speak. Hell, I can't even tell them apart besides those two."

"Fetzikzi and Ajaveo," Galo said. He looked down at Sinkua.

"Anything coming to mind?"

"Yeah. I need you out of his line of sight, okay?"

"Um… Yeah. Sure," Eytea said, getting to her feet, "Is there anything I can do in the meantime?"

"Maybe if you figure out which one is Tenzu-kun," Galo said, "it'll help you tell the others apart."

Sinkua lay so still that Galo's first instinct was to check his pulse. Metkhal pulled at him, moving in time with Tsenukoa's thrashing. Galo kept Sinkua centered in his line of sight, hoping it would anchor Metkhal and thus keep Tsenukoa still as well.

The situation wasn't getting better. He dismissed Eytea. Two people holding Sinkua's presence and one holding Tsenukoa's must have been creating uneven tension. Probably. He knew he was spitballing. That much was easy to admit to himself. But she didn't need to know that.

He closed his eyes and focused inward. Metkhal's presence was erratic and scattered.

"Metkhal!" Galo called, "Kinachondela?"

Metkhal hesitated.

"Shuk hapa!" Galo shouted, "Nini kufanya?"

The thrashing halted. Metkhal coalesced from his own ambient leavings, looking equally confused and offended. Just as Galo had intended.

"What in fuck is nini kufanya?" Metkhal asked through laughter, "Shuk hapa, I understand. Maybe what your accent makes shuka hapa."

"I thought you might stop if I butchered Mberhali enough."

Metkhal pinched the bridge of his nose. "You're as impossible as Tsenukoa," he said, "If we still can talk after we escape with Sinkua, I do not let you forget nini kufanya. Every day I ask, 'Galo. What doing?'"

"I'll look forward to it," Galo said, "But right now, we need to get Tsenukoa to settle down so he can pull the others back in."

"I was trying, but I can't keep up," Metkhal said, "I think he lost control."

"If you take over, can you get through to him?"

"It is better possible that way."

"That's as good as I can hope for," Galo said, "Okay. I'm gonna fall back. But be ready to switch out in case either of you starts to break away. Elemeno will pull me up if she notices trouble."

Galo forced his thoughts to drift as he sank deeper into the lesser presence. It wouldn't do to have Metkhal know he feared that he or Tsenukoa could permanently take over. He didn't know if it was possible, and he trusted Metkhal wouldn't even if he could. But Tsenukoa, not so much.

The hordes focused more on the fiery silhouettes than anyone else. Eytea realized how Galo's attack had cleared her mother of danger. It was less to do with the damage his milystis caused, impressive as it was, and more a matter of the diversion it caused.

She thus had two reasons to keep her distance as she paced among the flaming figures. To avoid notice by the Netherworld beasts and to not startle the silhouettes.

The more Eytea looked over the milystic figures, indeed the more distinct they became from each other. But with all the burdens she had let pile up, it was an embarrassing stretch before she realized she had no frame of reference for what anyone looked like.

Nobody stood out as looking like a Tamanoro or a Tenzu-kun, whatever either of those looked like. Process of elimination fared little better. Their fiery skin had no indication of complexion, and their dynamic texture made facial structures difficult to discern. She also didn't know how old any of them were when they died or what age they would present as. That left eliminating the women as her best shot at thinning her options. But just as with nationality, their being made of fire made gender difficult to guess with any confidence.

A surge of warmth ran from her shoulder to between her wings. She jumped, arching her back, and turned around. Fetzikzi stood behind her, arm half cocked.

"I… don't know what to do," Eytea stammered, "Galo said to find Tamanoro, but I don't know who he is."

Fetzikzi mouthed something, still muted, and pointed to another silhouette.

"You can hear me?" Eytea asked, "And understand me?"

Fetzikzi gave a half shrug and a waggling of her hand. Eytea assumed she just understood the name and pointed him out. Fetzikzi pointed to her hand.

"You want my…?" Eytea said, trailing off as epiphany struck, "The ring?" She pointed to her finger.

Fetzikzi nodded excitedly.

"I can help you if I find the ring?" Eytea asked, gesturing for anything she could think of a gesture for, "Should I go find Eir? Maybe she found the ring, and she's looking for me."

Fetzikzi shook her head and rolled her eyes, smoke billowing as she sighed. She grabbed Eytea by the wrist. Eytea jerked back on impulse, but Fetzikzi held her grip.

But her touch didn't burn. It was actually a comforting warmth. Fetzikzi moved her grip to hold Eytea's hand. The base of Eytea's ring finger glowed as Fetzikzi pressed her fingertip against it.

And the flames subsided into a human complexion.

Eytea withdrew her hand. The flames swept back in. She took Fetzikzi's hand again, and her presence became clear.

"Bores nama akouses?" Fetzikzi asked, "Hore du mejg?"

"I can't understand you," Eytea said, "But I can hear you."

Fetzikzi tugged her hand and pointed to the other one with a strong tether. Her own had become nearly opaque. It looked like a rope of the entire spectrum of shades of red with green accents. She spoke at length and urgingly, either ignoring or not realizing the language barrier. But a single word, a name, was all Eytea needed.

Ajaveo.

She followed Fetzikzi and waited as she and Ajaveo worked through a lesser language barrier. Fetzikzi lifted Eytea's hand, and Ajaveo took it as well, pressing his thumb to the base of her ring finger.

The flames pulled back, revealing a translucent middle-aged Southlander.

"Now what?" Eytea said, still gesturing her intentions, "Do we restore the others just like that?"

Fetzikzi and Ajaveo consulted each other. After a moment, Fetzikzi shook her head and pointed to her wrist.

"Wait?" Eytea asked, looking at her own wrist and tapping her foot.

Fetzikzi nodded.

"Tsenukoa!" Metkhal called out.

He thrashed less violently, his translucency becoming consistent. But, despite Metkhal's presence, it persisted.

"Listen to me," Metkhal continued, "Focus on my voice."

Tsenukoa settled for a split second, making a glimmer of eye contact. As soon as Metkhal began to speak though, the thrashing resumed.

Metkhal called his name twice more, once beckoning, once urging. He talked about their shared memories. He asked about Kanet. About Cedalion. About the Lechuatzulan stonecrafters.

None of it worked. Short on options and shorter on time, Metkhal spat an expletive and clapped Tsenukoa on the jaw.

Tsenukoa stopped. With Metkhal's hand pressed on his cheek, he settled into opacity. The scatterings coalesced.

"Metkhal?" he gasped, "They... They all got out. All of us. They all—"

"I know. Eytea's talking to them," Metkhal said, "I don't know what Galo's plan was. Assuming he had one."

Metkhal's eyes wandered as he spoke. One of the memory imprints approached Eytea. His hand involuntarily relaxed.

"Don't!" Tsenukoa fretted, grabbing his wrist, "Don't. They're trying... They're trying to pull me out."

Metkhal apologized and moved his hand to Tsenukoa's shoulder.

"Can you go back into his subconscience?"

Tsenukoa closed his eyes, his face tightening. He flickered in fading translucency, but it proved unsustainable.

"Sorry. No," he said, "I can't go any deeper than this."

Metkhal tightened his hold on Tsenukoa's shoulder as he panned the area again. The imprint that had approached Eytea was now distinct and leading her to another.

"Eytea looks to be on to something," he said, "I think you'll need to take control of the body."

"What about Sinkua?"

"He should wake up once all of you are together again."

"Not that. I mean..." Tsenukoa stammered, "He can't be pulled out, but—"

"You're worried he won't be able to come back up?" Metkhal asked.

"And that he'll blame me for it."

"If either one happens, we'll work through it when the time comes. Not taking over would be worse."

Tsenukoa sighed in resignation. "Okay. Fine. I'm holding you to all of that. But okay. What's the plan?"

Eytea watched with a growing helplessness as Tsenukoa's translucent form thrashed throughout Sinkua. Despite her best effort to eavesdrop on Metkhal, just for some sense of progress, she couldn't pick up anything at her distance. It was just as well, seeing as she knew very little Harkzanian and even less Mberhali anyway.

She tugged their hands to get Fetzikzi's and Ajaveo's attention, only to hesitate as she searched for the right words.

"Mejg... get Tamanoro?" she asked as she made a gathering motion.

Fetzikzi shook her head. "Ikke 'mejg,'" she said, "'Jeg.' Et nej."

Ajaveo cut in, apparently to argue with Fetzikzi. Eytea was pretty sure that she had attempted a word of Fjarthursk and even more sure that she had gotten it wrong. So, while Fetzikzi and Ajaveo argued, Eytea made a mental note to ask the Valkyrie for help with the old Feryan language.

"Fetzikzi!" a voice called out.

Ajaveo and Fetzikzi's argument stopped cold as all three of them turned to the source. Sinkua with Tsenukoa's face approached in forceful limps, like a marionette in weighted shoes. A second limb flickered with every movement of an arm or leg, the two forming complementary opacity.

"Is he...?" Eytea puzzled, "Is Tsenukoa walking Sinkua over here?"

Fetzikzi and Ajaveo looked at her, then at each other, and shrugged.

Tsenukoa called out to Fetzikzi again, waving her over as he said something most likely in Harkzanian. Fetzikzi tugged their hands, and the three of them hurried over to Tsenukoa and Sinkua.

"Eytea," Tsenukoa said, bracing on her shoulder, "How did... you?"

"The ring. From the Phoenix Ruby," Eytea said, hoping he could follow simple phrases, "It left some power in me."

Tsenukoa gave a puzzled stare, eyes narrowing and head bobbing as he tried to understand while keeping himself and Sinkua upright. Eytea looked to Fetzikzi urgingly. This was worse than Sinkua falling into his own subconscience. His body was becoming both deadweight and immaterial.

Fetzikzi spoke quickly, needing only a few words to clarify. Tsenukoa nodded, then pointed to Eytea's finger.

"May?" he asked.

Eytea raised her hand, bringing the other two with it. Tsenukoa joined in, finding a bit of space on the base of her ring finger with the tip of his thumb. The disparate flickering stopped, leaving Sinkua's body, consistent and mostly opaque, with Tsenukoa's face.

But not that arm. Sinkua's fell to his side, while Tsenukoa's remained outstretched and translucent. Tsenukoa spoke with Fetzikzi and Ajaveo. Fetzikzi moved her hand to his wrist. Ajaveo to hers.

"You're sure?" Eytea asked.

Tsenukoa nodded and released her hand to grab Ajaveo's wrist. He closed his eyes, and his face disappeared behind Sinkua's, silent and still. His arm aligned and vanished as well. The translucent forms of Ajaveo and Miss Aroka flowed into Sinkua's body, the collective illuminating with each merging.

Tsenukoa's face appeared once again, and he patted Eytea's back.

"Come," he said, "Walk with."

He awoke in a pool of absolute blackness. Darkness stretched beyond every horizon in every direction, both perceivable and less than such. This was more than the absence of light. The very concept of light no longer existed.

That was except for a single spark at some unknowable distance above him. Or straight ahead. Floating in such nothingness, he had no concept of his own orientation. For all he knew, he was hanging by his ankles.

Thoughts like that kept him tethered. Kept him anchored. If he let his mind wander or go blank, he could feel himself fading. But by deliberating on things, especially his own presence, he persisted.

Not that he had anything to persist for. Not that he could think of anyway. He knew there had to be something. Otherwise, this instinct to survive didn't make any sense. If there was nothing, no purpose to fight for, he would have vanished already.

A purpose to fight for.

That for which he fought.

That which drove him to fight.

His mind raced down a chain of associations until it arrived at a dagger. That dagger had come from someone important. That someone led him to other someones. Every one of them and so much in between, someone and something to fight for. Everything that threatened them, something that drove him to fight.

There was a necklace. A medallion. With that came power. Within that came companionship.

The point of light swelled into a ring.

That companionship carried knowledge. Knowledge of others. Others became companions.

The ring became multiple points.

Companions who were both quite and little like him.

The points of light swelled and shaped.

Companions who were his kin in spirit.

The points of light became human silhouettes.

The last pieces snapped into place. Sinkua remembered everything that led him here. He and Tetsen had tried the anchored orbs technique. But it was more than they could handle. They lost the other memory imprints. And Sinkua had fallen so deep beyond unconscious that Phoenix could no longer reach him. Not with her mind so fragmented and scattered.

But somehow they had found their way back together and back to him. Tetsen could have used the opportunity to take over his body. But he chose to save him.

To trust him.

Sinkua pushed himself upright, orienting with the memory imprints, as they descended toward him.

Tetsen Drukoa was the first to become distinguishable, his hand coming alight as he reached down. Next was Fetzikzi Aroka. Then came Ajaveo, the one who started it all.

The fourth, he didn't recognize, but as the man reached his hand down, a name and origin flashed through Sinkua's awareness. Tenzu Tamanoro of Ippatsuru. One after the other came the rest.

A Pukoqeyen woman named Verazeh Jesham. A man from Sikaj by the name of Ibaš Qufik. A woman from Ippatsuru called Saniro Himarahi. An Uzhlatsin man named Chelok Vlazir. Hajima Tenzu was another Pukoqeyen woman. A Gobheodais man by the name Rhobhan Porywyd. Motanos Kuvrach, an Ëžoraci man. A Mberhali woman known as Dhamurasit. And a woman from Azzegnos, Boglia Drogera.

Their thirteen outstretched hands formed a ring of red milystic light with threads of green. Sinkua reached for them, his hand glowing in kind. The light from his stretched upward as theirs converged and funneled. The two beams, green threads weaving with one other into an elaborate array of ropes.

The darkness gave way to light as he rose. When he reached the midst of the circle, standing among every prior Phoenix Hybrid, they lifted him above their heads.

And as it all diffused in the growing light, Sinkua awoke.

Chapter 18

His first sight was a simple chandelier. That ring of lights overhead made Sinkua wonder if the whole thing had been a dream. Tetsen Drukoa, speaking within his thoughts, assured him it had all been real.

Sinkua sat up and realized he was draped across an armchair in a modest living room. He panned the room, finding as much assurance as answers. Eytea was curled up in a matching armchair. Elemeno sat in a comically oversized older model. Galo lay on a hammock near the TV table. Cedalion sat against the wall with his head back, snoring.

Sinkua stretched to nudge Eytea with his foot. She stirred only briefly before settling back into sleep. He slunk across the chair for better reach and, this time, poked her ear with his big toe.

"Wake up, thundertits," he grunted.

Eytea slapped his foot and flipped upright, mouth agape with laughter. She looked down her shirt, then back at him.

"Thundertits?!" she exclaimed, "That's a new one."

"Are you really gonna look me in the eye and tell me you've never, not even in private, shot lightning out of your nipples?" Sinkua insisted, "Just because you can?"

"Have you shot fire out of yours?" Eytea asked, rising from her chair.

The others stirred.

"I've shot fire out of everything," Sinkua said, "Sometimes not on purpose."

"You know they have pills for that, right?" Eytea teased as she came to his chair, "You know. Unintended releases. Burning when you pee. You should talk to Ophalin about it when we get back."

They stared at each other for a long moment with Eytea standing over him. The two of them burst into laughter, and Eytea threw her arms around him.

"It's great to have you back," she said.

"Yeah. About that," Sinkua said, pulling back and holding her shoulders, "How did we get back here anyway?"

"Remember how we had that run-in with The Prophet?" Eytea asked. Sinkua nodded. "Well, the other Pahres showed up. Sort of."

"Sort of?"

"Yeah, I'm gonna let him explain," she said, "Pahres! Come on out!"

Pahres entered from a second room that Sinkua figured was a recent addition. He was undoubtedly the same person in body as The Prophet, but his face was softer. Not in structure, but in how he carried it.

"Sinkua. Hello," he greeted as he crossed the room, "I thought it best not to be in sight when you awoke. I understand you endured quite the ordeal."

"That's… putting it lightly," Sinkua said, "How did you get us out? Or even find us? Well. Sorry. I guess the first thing I should say is thank you."

"The other Pahres and I share a psychic link. Some might say bond, but that implies a measure of symbiosis," Pahres said, "But I digress. When Eytea so brutalized him that he ought to have died, were that possible here, I became acutely aware of his location."

"Which brought you to us," Sinkua said, "And getting us out? Can you pass through the river like Arestor?"

"Recall you that I am the son of an Yggdrasil Hybrid, yes?" Pahres asked, "This affords me the ability to convene with the Dryads within the roots. I asked that they provide you an exit."

Sinkua gave a sidelong glance, then looked to Eytea. Galo and Elemeno both sat up. He had questions, but he wasn't sure where to start or what he was after. It was just that something didn't add up.

Something was missing.

"The Dryads are in the roots?" he asked, "Meaning Yggdrasil is their afterlife?"

"It is," Pahres said, "Were you not made aware of this as a friend of Vielle?"

"Nobody mentioned it," Sinkua said, "So she must've been responsible for getting Arestor and me up to the river."

"I should suppose this means it was she who answered my call as well," Pahres said, "The roots shielded us for safe passage."

"I'm a little surprised you slept through all of it," Galo said as he rose from his hammock, "Eytea and I had to carry you."

"Come to think of it," Pahres continued, "I should have realized an Yggdrasil Hybrid was in control. So weighty and delicate a task is rather much to ask of Dryads."

Sinkua mulled over this new information. Dryads spent their afterlife in Yggdrasil. They moved energy and information through the roots. They willed new growth. The Yggdrasil Hybrid served in some sort of leadership role.

Hybrid or Hybrids. He didn't know what happened to the old one when a new one showed up, and he wasn't about to ask.

What mattered was that there was no use in looking for Vielle. They wouldn't find her and thus couldn't bring her back.

But her being within Yggdrasil granted the Dryads greater control. They could push roots into the Netherworld. They could cocoon people to carry them through the river. They could even look for specific people. It thus stood to reason that they couldn't be hijacked, like MalVek had done, anymore.

Sinkua nudged Eytea aside and got to his feet. He crossed the room to stand over Cedalion. The Tiamat Hybrid still lightly snored. Sinkua considered waking him.

Briefly.

Instead, he stomp-kicked his face hard enough to dent the wall with the back of his head. Cedalion cried out and sprang up into a defensive stance, scattering crystal dust from the wall.

As he found Sinkua glaring at him, Cedalion straightened his mask and put his hand on Sinkua's shoulder. "I suppose you've —"

Sinkua wrenched his hand aside and pinned him to the wall by his solar plexus. "Her life wasn't yours to take!"

"You're not entirely wrong," Cedalion said, "Though her passing will prove a boon to us all."

"I hope it hurt like hell when I killed you," Sinkua said, "I hope you felt the death of every soul I ripped out of you."

"Would it ease your fury to know that I did?" Cedalion asked.

He pushed forward, rising from the wall with surprising ease. Surprising not for the display of strength, but because Sinkua didn't move. Sinkua looked down to see his wrist vanished into Cedalion's chest with a ring of glimmering ripples.

Sinkua yanked his arm back and put some distance between them. He touched his fingertips to each other. They felt solid.

"Pahres?" he beckoned, "Is this an effect of this part of the afterlife?"

"Could you elaborate?" Pahres asked.

"Like the forced empathy thing. Or the reciprocal injuries in the Netherworld," Sinkua explained, "Do people become, um… pass-through-able if they hurt people here?"

"The word you're looking for is 'immaterial,'" Pahres provided, "And no. I'm not aware of such a phenomenon."

"I have a theory," Galo said, "Do you remember, well, coming apart in the Netherworld?"

"Is that what happened?" Sinkua asked, "Tetsen and I tried to replicate a technique that I had used with Phoenix. We sent out fireballs on milystic tethers."

"Yes, but why the tethers?" Galo asked.

"Safety. The creatures' breath is flammable. So once my fires aren't connected to me, they can cause me some serious harm," Sinkua explained, "Anyway, when Tetsen and I did it without Phoenix's help, I felt this weird rush and then blacked out. Next thing I knew, my other past selves were pulling me out of a pit, and then I woke up here."

"The others escaped in the fireballs. Or maybe as them. All but Tsenukoa. Ajaveo and Fetzikzi Aroka were the only ones with any control. The rest mindlessly fought the Netherworld creatures," Galo explained, "They're all back in you now."

"That's a story for another time," Eytea added.

"Right, you two can catch up on that later," Galo agreed, "In any case, I assume Phoenix has the whole thing sorted now."

"That explains why I can't hear Miss Aroka or Ajaveo anymore," Sinkua said.

"I'd say so," Galo said, "All that to say, deploying and recalling your past selves? I think it's causing your body to, well, come apart."

"That or you've overstayed your welcome," Eytea added, "But that'd be quite the coincidence."

"This could be what Odin was after when he sent you here alive," Elemeno said as she dropped from the oversized armchair, "Maybe not exactly this, but he probably knew something like this would happen."

"Which'll be useful when we get back," Sinkua said, "but it doesn't really help now."

"Yeah. No. It doesn't," Eytea said, "If you become completely immaterial, we won't be going back."

"So now we're short on time."

"And we don't even know how short," Galo added.

"And what happens to you if you become completely immaterial?" Eytea asked.

"I'm afraid we have no way of knowing that," Pahres said, "It is thus imperative that the lot of you find the Phoenix Shrine with the utmost of haste."

"Obviously," Sinkua said, he turned to Eytea and Galo, "Did either of you get to ask the memory imprints about that?"

"I'm sorry," Eytea said, "With the language barrier and everything that was happening, I didn't even think to ask."

"I might have some useful insights," Pahres said, "Mind you, I have yet to see the Phoenix Shrine as far as I am aware. But I did have many a fraternization with The Dragon Family."

"You think maybe you've seen what it was based on?" Sinkua asked.

"I can only promise that it is quite possible," Pahres said, "I ask only for time to search my memories."

"Metkhal told me Phoenix is both Harkzanian and Dagiliši," Galo said, "So we have a third location for it."

"If we're gonna check the Dagiliši Shrines, we need to split up and somehow find each other later. We don't have time to cover that much ground together," Sinkua said, "Which one is Dagiliši?"

"Dagiliz is present day Eprilen."

"I have an idea," Eytea said, scratching the back of her hand as she approached a wall, "I should be back soon."

Eytea focused her thoughts on the Valkyrie as she raised her hand to the wall. She visualized the three of them individually and collectively. Her thoughts wandered to Sanngridr. But as Eytea knew so little about her, the thought was as passing as Randgrid's mention of her.

At first, she had considered focusing on Freja. But knowing the sort of psychic bond between the boys and their Etherworlders, she feared that might alert Odin to Freja's whereabouts. Or worse, her suspicions.

The passage opened to an unfamiliar expanse of the crystal fields. Nearly all the structures she could see looked to be complete.

"Lady Eytea!" someone called out.

Eytea turned to see three winged figures cresting the horizon. One waved broadly. She hurried to meet them midway.

"Lady Eytea," Eir repeated, patting her on the shoulder, "What brings you out here?"

"Your search for the Phoenix Shrine oughtn't bring you this way," Sigrdrifa said.

"Are you lost?" Randgrid asked, "Were you separated and now seek aid in finding your companions?"

"What? No. I, um… I came out of my home here. I was looking for you ladies," Eytea said, flummoxed by the barrage of questions.

"Your aim is a bit off," Eir said, "But I suppose that's to be expected, given your inexperience."

"Sanngridr popped into my head," Eytea said, "I think that knocked me off course a bit."

"A reasonable supposition," Eir said, "So then what did you need from us?"

"Well first off, where exactly is this?"

"These are the Fjarthursk Shrines. Freja has asked that we locate Odin's Shrine," Eir explained, "Know that this is our burden alone, lest you offer to help."

"Yours is to be ready to confront him when Sinkua escorts you back to the Omphaloworld," Randgrid added, "All of us wish you the best in that endeavor."

"That's reassuring. Any developments I should know about?"

"Bearing in mind how they remember him, the other returned Fjarthursk Etherworlders suspect Odin of corruption," Eir said.

"Unfortunately, there's no consensus as to the nature of it," Sigrdrifa added.

"Yes, theories abound, but answers do not. It thus falls to you to sus them out," Eir said, "Now again, why have you sought us out alone?"

"We still don't know what the Phoenix Shrine looks like, and now we have three places to check," Eytea said, "But we're short on time, so we need help searching those places."

"Can we assume you have a lead on its appearance?" Sigrdrifa asked.

"Pahres is working on it. His mother was the Yggdrasil Hybrid, so he associated with some people in the Dragon Family," Eytea said, "But I just didn't think to ask any of you because you would've told me if you knew."

"Where do you need to check?" Randgrid asked.

"Dragon Family Shrines, Harkzanian Shrines, and Dagiliši Shrines."

"Oh yes, Hephaestus and Ptah created Phoenix together," Eir said, "My apologies. We spoke so little with Ptah that his involvement slipped our minds."

"Bridges and water," Eytea said, shrugging.

"But may I ask what you mean by being short on time?"

"Sinkua's past selves. The memory imprints? They got loose. As in outside of his body as spirits on milystic leashes. We got them back in, and they're with Phoenix now. But he keeps becoming, um…" She thrust her fingers in and out of interlocking. "You know. Incorporeal."

"Having an Omphaloworlder body in the afterlife indeed has strange consequences," Eir said, "It was all thirteen of them?"

"How did it happen?" Randgrid asked.

"It was. The short answer is excess milystic exertion," Eytea glossed over, "Fortunately the mark that the Phoenix Ruby left on me was able to stabilize them."

"Are we thus to assume that he can no longer consult any of them about the Phoenix Shrine?" Eir asked.

"Only Tetsen Drukoa, and he's said as much as he knows."

"Well, we haven't found the ring, but we have noticed a curiosity that might interest you," Sigrdrifa said, "You recall asking about a green flash, yes?"

"Yeah, we're pretty sure that's Yggdrasil's doing," Eytea said, "Like it's some kind of milystic residue from the roots trying to enter this place."

"Well, we've come to notice the flash as well, and it coincides with trace senses of Phoenix's milystis."

"You think the flash has something to do with Phoenix?" Eytea asked, "Not Yggdrasil?"

"We can't say Yggdrasil has nothing to do with it," Sigrdrifa said, "But we suspect it's a beacon to lead Phoenix to the ring."

"Not dissimilar to how Epesol resonates with Phoenix," Eir said, "The ring may be calling out, so to speak, with these green flashes."

Eytea sat on the notion for a moment. If the flashes were a regular occurrence, they could go after the ring, then use that to home in on the Shrine. Possibly. But as things were, she doubted the extra trip would save them any time.

"Well, if you're right, then we're probably also right about it being Yggdrasil," Eytea said, "As I understand, Vielle planted it near where I died. But that doesn't help us find the Shrine or the ring though, does it?"

"No, I suppose not, but sometimes we must let knowledge be its own assurance," Eir said.

"Could it be Epesol?"

"Plausibly, though that would suggest Yggdrasil is less likely to be involved," Eir said, "Now as to your request for help searching. I can only promise the aid of the Valkyrie, but our work here must take priority. I can, however, ask Ratatoskr to assist you."

Eytea's eyes widened. "Hold on. Ratatoskr?"

"Yes. You are familiar?"

"Other Pahres said he'd, quote, become as Ratatoskr. Then he did some black lightning thing and summoned a bunch of Netherworld creatures," Eytea recounted, "That's what led to Sinkua being in the shape he's in now."

"Who, might I ask, is Other Pahres?" Eir asked, "Pahres is helping you identify the Phoenix Shrine, is he not?"

"There's two of him. Technically their names are backwards because I think the one we call Pahres is from some kind of alternate reality. Or timeline," Eytea said, "But Other Pahres was The Prophet in The Avatars of Fate and put a lot of work into bringing Pandora back. So, the new one gets the name, and the old one gets called Fuckstick."

Eir snickered, her air of dignity briefly wavering. "I suppose these Avatars of Fate are what became of Vuordevaltene?"

Eytea gave a half shrug and just as noncommittal of a nod.

"Well as it were, Ratatoskr is an impartial messenger," Eir assured, "The unscrupulous often try to foist their own morals upon him."

"Okay. If you trust him, I will, too," Eytea said, "Which Shrines will you ask him to search?"

"Harkzanian and Dragon Family."

"Both? Wow. Thank you," Eytea professed, "You're sure he can cut it?"

"Absolutely, Lady Eytea," Eir insisted, "Between his speed and their proximity, he could search both in the time you take and yours to search the Dagiliši Shrines. Possibly even report to you there."

"Color me impressed. And would he know how to find the Phoenix Shrine?"

In a nigh undetectable blur, Eir scooped up Eytea's hand and jammed a fingernail against the base of her ring finger. Eir withdrew with a mote of red milystic light floating on the tip of her nail.

"He can with this."

"Ow! Shit. Could you warn me next time?"

"I cannot imagine there would be a next time, but yes I can promise that."

"Right. Okay," Eytea said, rubbing the translucent prick mark, "So he'll check Harkzan and Dragon Family, and the rest of us will check Dagiliz. And the ring or maybe Epesol is trying to find us with the green flashes. Is there anything else I should know?"

"This might be a longshot," Randgrid said, "But Tiamat also has a dual nationality. Pukoqeyen and Dagiliši. Judging by how opening your door apparently works—"

"You think if I focus on both Phoenix and Tiamat, it'll open where they overlap?" Eytea asked, "You're right. That is a longshot."

Randgrid furrowed her brow at her.

"But it's worth a shot," Eytea continued, "Now I thank you ladies and ask that you share that gratitude with Ratatoskr. I need to get back inside."

With the radio playing a Dirty Frog broadcast composited from Eytea's memories, Metkhal and Pahres sat swapping memories of their own. They had lived at the same time, Metkhal having been a young adult when Pahres worked with his father in The Trifecta. But neither had much recollection of having known each other.

They had more of a connection, in fact, through the Dragon Family. Metkhal's friendship with Tetsen Drukoa put him in the circles of several other members. Though none were so close as Tetsen as to earn an honorary Mberhali name. Pahres's dealings, however, were often more formal and businesslike but just as varied.

Both found themselves invited to cultural events, whether as a diplomatic relation or a plus-one.

"Do you recall their funeral processions?" Pahres asked, "Should I remember correctly, the décor included depictions of their Shrines."

"Depictions or intended depictions, yes," Metkhal said, "But they never had a funeral for Tsenukoa as far as I know. And Boglia Drogera died before I was born. So, I never saw anything about the Phoenix Shrine."

"I was too young when Signora Drogera passed to attend her funeral," Pahres said, "But the ones I did attend, the Shrine art included those of other Family members."

"Yeah, now that I think about it, you're right," Metkhal said, staring at the wall in contemplation, "Who do you have in mind?"

"Kuzaro Tracholos."

"He and Tsenukoa were very distant cousins."

"I know, but the Bahamut Hybrid's funeral was a vastly adorned affair," Pahres said, "I can't recall if Phoenix's was among the Shrine artwork, however."

"I'm pretty sure it was, but I'm having trouble remembering it," Metkhal conceded, "We might need to ask Tsenukoa about it."

"Asking him to switch with Sinkua will be a last resort," Pahres said, "Did you ever meet Zadid Onabyuni?"

Yanked from his contemplation, Metkhal's brow furrowed and expression flattened. He turned to meet Pahres's eyes as he tried to make sense of the question.

"Who the hell is Zadid Onabyuni?" he asked, "The Dragon Family didn't even have an Onabyuni branch."

"He was Kuzaro's successor, the new Bahamut Hybrid."

Metkhal watched Pahres's face. He saw no sign of deception or malice. Whatever Pahres seemed to be selling, he wasn't selling anything.

Master Tracholos's passing had been the beginning of the end for the Dragon Family. There wasn't a Bahamut Hybrid successor, because there wasn't a Bahamut for a Hybrid to be bound to. Pandora had seen to that shortly after dispatching Master Tracholos.

Metkhal thought it best to let Pahres elaborate though. After all, if it was real enough to him to alter his memories, there could have been something useful at its core.

"I guess I wasn't close enough to know about Master Onabyuni," he said, "Tsenukoa began distancing himself from the Family soon after Bahamut and Master Tracholos's funeral. So, I rarely heard about new births."

"New births?" Pahres asked, "Zadid came as all Bahamut Hybrids did. As an adult."

Metkhal cocked his head and an eyebrow. "I... wasn't aware of this," he said, "They just knock on the front door and tell everyone they're the new Bahamut Hybrid?"

"That's quite the oversimplification, but I suppose you're not wrong," Pahres said, "Instead of choosing a soul due for rebirth, Bahamut takes a living adult and moves them to the House of the Dragon Family."

Metkhal leaned over the back of his seat.

"Cedalion!" he called over, "Did you catch all that?"

"I did," Cedalion responded, "I also recall neither Zadid nor an Onabyuni branch of the Dragon Family."

"What are you implying?" Pahres asked, "Do you think I would lie to either of you about such things?"

"No. Not this version of you," Cedalion said, "You believe this history so completely that it must have been real for you."

"Could this be where my and The Prophet's paths diverged?"

"I believe so. Whoever Zadid Onabyuni was, he must have been the catalyst."

Chapter 19

Fjarthursk clamor poured in as Eytea opened a passage to her home. Pahres and Metkhal sat conversing in Mberhali. She gave herself a little mental pat on the back for recognizing it with such certainty. Cedalion chimed in from the other end of the room. Sinkua, meanwhile, meditated with her mother keeping watch over him.

"Pahres?" she beckoned, "Any progress?"

"Apologies, Eytea. We believe it was depicted in certain Dragon Family funerals, but the discussion went astray," Pahres said, "You might ask Tetsen about Kuzaro Tracholos if you feel safe letting him come forth."

"Did anything good come of meeting with the Valkyrie?" Cedalion asked.

"Yeah, and I need your help with something," Eytea said, "But how'd you know I was looking for the Valkyrie?"

"I heard people speaking Fjarthursk when you opened the door," Cedalion said, "You went to their Shrines, yes?"

"I did. And now I need you to tell me about Tiamat," she said, "I mean on a personal level."

"To what end?"

"The Valkyrie are getting someone to search the Dragon Family and Harkzanian Shrines. Which just leaves us with the Dagiliši Shrines," she said, lingering into a pause that stopped just short of awkward, "That's where... you and Tiamat come in?"

He just stared at her, his face unreadable behind his mask. She gestured emphatically, puzzled by how he wasn't picking up on her meaning. This man had thousands of years of human experience on top of however long he had lived as an Etherworlder. Her intentions couldn't have been any more obvious.

"What does that have to do with Tiamat?" he asked at last.

"Phoenix and Tiamat are both half Dagiliši," she said, "Randgrid thinks if I focus on both of them when I open the door, it'll split the difference and put us near the Dagiliši Shrines."

"Oh! I'm sorry, but I'm afraid that's a misconception," Cedalion said, "Tiamat isn't Dagiliši. She's Sikaji."

"Sikaji? Is that Ivarian or Tanelenese?" Eytea asked, "And I thought you said she was Pukoqeyen."

"By adoption, yes," Cedalion said, "As for Sikaj, it's between Eprilen and Poravit."

"Wait. But that means—"

"Yes. It's at the bottom of the sea now," Cedalion said, "And not unique in that regard. But Sikaj was destroyed long before the cataclysm, and its Etherworlders became part of the cultures of Dagiliz and Pukoqet."

"And now there are misconceptions about who went where," Eytea said, sighing with resignation, "Well shit. Is there anyone else I could use?"

"Kuzaro Tracholos was the Bahamut Hybrid," Pahres said.

"Ah yes. Bahamut did indeed integrate into Dagiliši culture," Cedalion confirmed, "We could tell you about Bahamut until you mistook him for an old friend."

"I'll leave you and Metkhal to that," Pahres said, "I am, after all, uniquely qualified to be the safest to ask Tetsen about Kuzaro."

Puzzled, Eytea watched Pahres approach her fiancee and her mother. She looked back to Cedalion and Metkhal and cocked her head back over her shoulder.

"The hell does he mean by that?"

"Nothing to worry over," Cedalion said, "He is correct though."

Sinkua sat with his legs knotted and his hands on his knees. Eyes closed, he fixated on each point of contact between any two parts of his body.

He breathed in time with Elemeno, both her instructions and the sound of her own breath. His mind wandered to her difficulties. Balancing her presence with Jehgoro among so many presenting as their Bealstillan predecessors. And himself with Ajaveo only dormant by choice.

His hands sank into his knees like gelatin. He snapped his thoughts back to both the notion and actuality of his own physical touch. Corporeality returning, his knees pushed his hands to their surface. A stirring in the recesses of his mind calmed to a dull murmur.

A shadow settled over his eyelids.

"Sinkua?" someone exhaled, just above a whisper.

He opened his eyes. Pahres sat hunched over in front of him, hand poised but hesitant to tap his shoulder.

"Pahres. Hey," Sinkua said as he got to his feet, "Did you figure it out?"

"We're working on a lead. Eytea will fill you in," Pahres said, "For now, would you mind if I spoke with Tetsen?"

"What about?" Sinkua asked, "I mean, I don't mind. We've gotten good enough at switching off that it shouldn't be a problem. But if he knew what the Phoenix Shrine looked like or where to find it, he would've said so."

Pahres explained the Dragon Family's funeral artistry, particularly that the Bahamut Hybrid's funeral may have included depictions of the Phoenix Shrine. The Bahamut Hybrid's power secured their position as the highest authority, while the Phoenix Hybrid was held in the highest esteem for being both their founder and the first Dragon Hybrid.

"You think maybe if you two talk it out, you can remember the décor at Kuzaro's funeral?"

"I do," Pahres said.

It was a reasonable enough plan. From what Sinkua knew of the Dragon Family, it would've been strange for the Phoenix Shrine to not appear in most funerals, especially those for the more esteemed members.

Sinkua closed his eyes and, as his eyes rolled back, slipped through the boundary of his own subconscience.

Eytea looked first to Metkhal. "So… What do you remember about him?" she asked, "Did you talk to Bahamut or, um, Kuzaro Tracholos much? Or were you just friends with Tetsen and Phoenix?"

"I was Chieftain Heir in Master Tracholo's life," Metkhal said, "My with him talks were mostly business. Sometimes had friendly talks but not much."

"Hey! Your Ouristihran sounds even better now. Keep it up," Eytea said, "What was he like when he, you know, talked business?"

"Generous. But careful," Metkhal said, "He asked Bahamut before makes offers or answers questions."

"Bahamut had a top-down perspective of time," Cedalion said, "The futures he saw were only possibilities though, so it would've been difficult for him to create a paradox. Even so, Bahamut was wary of accidentally sharing future knowledge, even before the fall of Sikaj."

"Why?" Eytea asked, "If paradoxes weren't much of an issue, I would think he'd want to use that power to help people close to him and his Hybrid. So why was he so guarded about accidentally mentioning the future?"

"He believed it best that we experience time sequentially," Cedalion said, "He saw the stress that too much future knowledge put on his Hybrids and sought to minimize it."

"That part of his power was isolated in his sword, was it not?" Metkhal asked.

"Epeceles. The Sword of Celestiality," Cedalion said, "But yes, Bahamut did have his chronomancy isolated as a matter of security. At least as much as the best Quircois smiths could manage."

"So, he just didn't want to stress people out by mentioning things that hadn't happened yet but probably would?" Eytea asked, "But also might not happen?"

"You have a knack for oversimplifying these things, but yes. Bahamut didn't come to be so revered by throwing his weight around," Cedalion said, "He knew power gained by force and intimidation was unsustainable."

"Yeah, I've seen it fail enough to know that, and I died younger than he probably ever was."

Cedalion chuckled. "An interesting way to put it, but yes, he had millennia more life experience than even me," he said, "Fact is, had he survived Pandora's wrath, I might not have strayed so far."

"Well, I don't know about that. Not after, well," Metkhal said, cocking his head aside, "You know."

"Not after what?" Eytea pried.

"Not a matter for mixed company," Cedalion insisted.

"No. Absolutely not," Eytea argued, "We're all entitled to secrets, but if you're dangling this many in front of me, you're keeping too many. So, what does Pahres have to do with how you handled Bahamut's death? And why is he uniquely qualified to talk to Tetsen?"

"Fine," Cedalion conceded, "Pahres remembers another Bahamut Hybrid appearing after Kuzaro Tracholos died."

"Appearing," Metkhal emphasized, "Not being born."

"But how could there be another if Bahamut's power was in Pandora's Box?" Eytea puzzled.

"That exactly is the issue," Metkhal said.

"The past he remembers is, beyond a certain point, different from ours," Cedalion said, "We've yet to determine exactly when that point was."

"Wait. So then," Eytea said, trailing off in pondering, "Does that mean he really is from an alternate reality?"

"That's been my working theory since his dichotomous nature first manifested," Cedalion said, "Trouble is, I have no explanation for how this alternate reality came to be. Only that Yggdrasil facilitated his crossing over."

"That's saying a lot, coming from you," Eytea said, "But if his past is different, wouldn't he be least qualified to talk about the funeral with Tetsen?"

"He seems to remember Kuzaro the same as we do. So, we're working on the assumption that his reality diverged after the funeral," Cedalion reasoned, "But since Tetsen didn't know this particular Pahres—"

"He can't flip Sinkua and Tetsen to the point that Sinkua needs help resurfacing," Eytea said, "At least he shouldn't."

"Precisely. Only Sinkua knew this Pahres, so Tetsen can only surface if Sinkua allows it."

"Okay, glad we got that cleared up," Eytea said, clapping once, "Back to Bahamut, then?"

"Of course," Cedalion said, "He found the Omphaloworld charming and quaint. It is indeed a sight smaller and more than a sight less, well, dimensional than the Etherworld."

"The Etherworld has more than the four here?"

"Far more," he said, "But he admired what the Omphaloworld did within those limitations. He often insisted on traveling by traditional means so he could take in the scenery."

"Walking instead of flying?" Eytea asked.

"Flying instead of spatial bending," Cedalion clarified, "His top-down view of time also gave him a top-down view of space, and he could bend both to move himself and others between distant points."

"You mean to tell me there was a Dragon and Hybrid who could teleport and time travel?! And they lost to Pandora?!" Eytea exclaimed, "I mean, yeah, I've heard your story. But you figured out time travel long after you gave in to Pandora."

"I'd appreciate you not rubbing that in any further," Cedalion said, "It may be their restraint with those powers that cost Kuzaro Tracholos and Bahamut their lives to Seriamus and Pandora. That is not, however, mine to speculate upon. Much less judge."

"No. No. You're right," Eytea said, "Still. To think they had that kind of power. No wonder the rest of the Dragon Family looked up to them. I just assumed they could see futures and remember the past perfectly."

"They could, but when he saw how much happier his Hybrids were when they weren't constantly seeing possible futures, Bahamut endeavored to appreciate the present more," Cedalion said, "He would often talk about the possibilities within events that he was looking forward to. Most people thought he was preparing us for what might come. I knew better, having known him for a time in the Etherworld."

"What was it really?"

"His emphasis wasn't at all proportionate to the likelihood."

"He was trying to give everyone else more of a sense of anticipation?"

"Close. He was trying to give himself one by fooling his own sense of probabilities," Cedalion said, "He envied others for the wonderment of uncertainty that he could never have."

"Wow. That's kinda sad," Eytea said, "Charming, too. Y'know, that someone so powerful would look up to more primitive beings."

"He was an interesting creature to be sure."

"Phoenix reminds me of him," Metkhal said, "If things were better, I think she would enjoy staying this long here."

"She would indeed," Cedalion agreed, "Her power comes with such a burden that Ptah and Hephaestus may have been ill-advised in forging her capacity for emotions."

"Were Phoenix and Bahamut friends in the Etherworld?" Eytea asked.

"Phoenix wasn't there for long, but yes," Cedalion said, "Bahamut had been indifferent to the affairs beyond his region of the Etherworld. But that changed when Phoenix came out resembling a Dragon."

"Was she the first forged Dragon in the Etherworld?"

"To my knowledge, yes," he said, "In fact, it was Phoenix and Bahamut's fast friendship that led to my meeting with Tiamat."

"It sounds like he never actually wanted to be alone," Eytea said, "But making excuses was easier than putting effort into relationships."

"That sounds like him," Metkhal chuckled, "Both of them really."

"Yes, you're not wrong," Cedalion said.

Even without a physical description, Eytea felt like she could picture Bahamut with the clarity of a casual acquaintance. Rather than ask for one though, she nudged Cedalion and Metkhal into gossiping about day-to-day life and notable memories with Bahamut and Kuzaro.

"Tetsen? Mister Drukoa?" Pahres beckoned in Harkzanian as the faces shifted, "Can you hear me, Tetsen?"

"What? Yes. I'm here," Tetsen said, blinking away the fatigue.

His eyes snapped wide at the sight of Pahres, and he scrambled into the sloppiest of defensive stances. Pahres sat back and pinched the bridge of his nose, waiting for Tetsen to get his thoughts in order.

"Sorry," Tetsen exhaled at last, "The man who attacked us looked just like you."

"Well, there's a good reason for that," Pahres said.

"Is he your twin brother?" Tetsen considered, "Strange that I never knew you had a twin."

"I don't—"

"But come to think of it, Galo implied his name was also Pahres," Tetsen interrupted, "Who exactly are you, then?"

"Both of us are Pahres," Pahres said, "But I remember someone who Metkhal and Cedalion insist never existed."

"Who?"

"Does the name Zadid Onabyuni mean anything to you?"

"Sounds Sikaji. So, I don't know how it could."

"He succeeded Kuzaro Tracholos," Pahres said. Tetsen's face twisted with equal parts confusion and offense. Pahres went on, "That's not far from how Metkhal reacted. It's as though I experienced a different history from everyone else."

"That sounds like Janus's work," Tetsen said, "Or it could have been Zurvan. Bahamut would've been capable, but the timing is questionable."

"I'm not concerned with how it happened at the moment," Pahres said, "I needed to ask you about Kuzaro's funeral."

"What about it?" Tetsen asked, "Do you need to know if you remember it differently?"

"No, I'm confident that I diverged after Kuzaro's death. Less so but still hopeful that it was after the funeral," Pahres reasoned, "That said, what do you remember of the décor?"

"Rather a lavish affair. Garish, some would say, but it's what we all would have expected for the Bahamut Hybrid."

"What about the Shrines?"

Tetsen blinked hard and tilted his head as he stared at Pahres. "You think maybe the Phoenix Shrine was depicted there?"

"I hope so," Pahres said, "It may be the only Dragon Family funeral that you and I can brainstorm about. Rather, the only one that might have included the Phoenix Shrine."

"I'm sure it did, but the details of that day are fuzzy," Tetsen said, rising to pace about as they conversed, "I was busy planning my search for the Outer Lands."

"And to separate from Phoenix?"

Tetsen nodded. "I assume the Tetsen you knew did the same?"

"At the time of Kuzaro's and Bahamut's deaths, yes."

From there, the two spoke extensively about the elaborate affair that had been Kuzaro Tracholos's funeral. The event had begun and been planned as solemn and mournful but quickly became a celebration of his life.

Bahamut was honored alongside him, but there had been an air of hopeful denial. In fact, those attending had been careful not to mention Epeceles out of an almost superstitious fear that it would lead Pandora to the last Bastion of Bahamut's powers.

Once they had established the atmosphere of the event, more and more specific memories manifested and found their place. Before long, Pahres and Tetsen each came to their own conclusion about how the Phoenix Shrine had been depicted. And where their conclusions overlapped, they found their answer.

As Sinkua returned to prominence, Eytea called everyone back over to her side of the room. Metkhal drew back to a secondary presence behind Galo.

"Okay. Pahres?" she said, "Tell me you've got good news."

"Tetsen and I have determined that the Phoenix Shrine is a stone bench draped with a thatch blanket," Pahres said, "in front of a one-eighth wedge of a fountain."

"I've seen the ruins of that fountain," Sinkua said, "So now we need to figure out where it is. How'd your idea pan out earlier?"

"I asked Eir if she and the other Valkyrie could help with the search. They can't, but she's going to ask Ratatoskr to check the Dragon Family and Harkzanian Shrines," Eytea said, raising her hand in anticipation, "I know we all heard The Prophet invoke his name, but Eir insists he's an impartial messenger."

"Her word's good enough for me," Sinkua said, "So that leaves us with the, uh… Dagiliši Shrines? Is that right?"

"Yeah. Ratatoskr's gonna report to us there."

"Assuming he's on board," Galo pointed out.

"Yes naturally," Eytea said, "Now, thanks to some things I learned from Randgrid, Cedalion, and Pahres, I have a plan to get us there quickly."

"Great! We just might still pull this off," Sinkua remarked, "So what's your plan?"

"Nah-uh," Eytea refused, brushing his nose with her fingertip, "You always played your plans close to the chest. Now it's my turn."

"Actually, it occurs to me that Pahres and I ought to convene with the rest of the Trifecta," Cedalion said, "I ask that you first open a door near Takmet's location."

Chapter 20

Simulated daylight shimmered almost blindingly off the crystalline sand as Eytea led Sinkua, Galo, and her mother out of her home. Stone buildings trimmed with gold and black materials speckled the rippling horizon.

"Whatever your plan was, I think it worked," Sinkua said, rubbing Eytea's back, "We at least landed near some shrines."

"So. Ptah's Shrine. What do you kids think?" Elemeno said, hustling forward to walk in their midst, "Is it the fanciest one because he can or the simplest because he has nothing to prove?"

"We'll put wagers on that after we find the Phoenix Shrine," Galo insisted, "But my money'll be on modest."

"Because it's what you would do or what you think Ptah would do?"

"You might as well place your bet now, 'cause I'm sending you back first, Galo," Sinkua said, "Nikasu needs you the most out of any of us."

Galo stared at him, dumbfounded. He blinked hard as he looked for the right words.

"I.. ah…" he stammered, "Are you sure? I mean. Thank you. But… that didn't even cross my mind."

"Of course I'm sure," Sinkua said, "You were right that the whole idea was a desperate gambit. It was stupid to leave Nikasu alone."

"I wouldn't say it was stupid," Galo said, "Desperate, yes, but those were desperate times."

"You don't have to sugarcoat it," Sinkua insisted, "I assessed the risks, but my assessment was stupid. You've been the most rational about what we're up against. You should be first to regroup with Nikasu."

"Well, if you're going to insist."

Scarcely sooner had they entered the community than shrines of countless shapes and sizes surrounded them and stretched to every horizon. Some were obvious enough what they were modeled after. Others looked to be amalgams of influences, like they were based more on dreams than deliberate thought. Just the same, some had an obvious entrance, while others could only be assumed to have one at all.

Crowds of spirits moved along the complex tangle of roads. After some wandering, the group found a placard engraved with pictograms by one of the shrines. Metkhal emerged and identified it as the Dagiliši written language.

"This is the Renenutet Shrine," he said, "She helped with good harvests."

"An agricultural Etherworlder, huh?" Sinkua said, "I bet people in Ferya would like to have her around."

"She does sound a bit like Freja," Elemeno said, "Maybe a cross between her and a Dryad."

Metkhal gave a noncommittal shrug before fading back to return Galo to prominence.

"So, Mom," Eytea said, "Do you wanna go back with us?"

"Oh, I don't know," Elemeno said, eyes wandering along the meandering road, "I haven't given it much thought. I hadn't considered that it would be an option."

"Why wouldn't it be?" Sinkua asked, "If I can open a portal like I said, all of us can go back as easily as one of us."

"If that's even possible, do you really think you'd be the first Phoenix Hybrid to do it?" Elemeno challenged, "I'm sorry. I know you mean well. But you can't think you could overcome life and death that simply. That you could just open a door and a bunch of us walk out of the afterlife."

"Well... No... I guess not," Sinkua fumbled, "It's more like, I—"

"What about the consequences of resurrecting one person when you were alive?" Galo interrupted, "I realize what you went through to kill Mortvill, but this is different. We don't know how much worse it could be here. Or forcing it to work on Hybrids."

"Plus, dear, you're putting effort into staying material," Elemeno said, "We love that you have this scheme to bring us back, but, well—"

"I think we all just assumed," Eytea said, "that there was more to it cutting a hole with Epesol."

Sinkua winced and shook his head, fingertips rippling through his legs as he walked.

"No. You're right. All of you are," he said, "I don't know what kind of blowback I'll be dealing with. And there's no way I could just cut open a portal. I was, I don't know, overselling myself so maybe the actual plan would sound more workable. And maybe so I wouldn't psych myself out."

"Hey, we didn't mean to bring you down, brother," Galo said, putting his hand on his shoulder, "But what is your actual plan?"

"Epesol can be used to revive people," Sinkua said, "To put it way too simply, I'm gonna stab you with it."

"If it was just a matter of using Phoenix's power on us, couldn't you have done that when you first got here?"

"I couldn't do it that way when I was alive, so why would it work like that here?" Sinkua challenged, "Besides, using Epesol lets Phoenix get inside and work at her full strength, and we need every advantage we can get."

"I guess you have a point," Galo conceded, "The 'no Hybrids' rule is probably because different milystises in one soul won't cooperate with each other."

"Milystic interference?" Sinkua asked, "Yeah I could see that."

"And since ethermaterials can allow for perfect flow—" Galo began.

"Epesol can inject your milystis into us," Eytea said, "without interfering with our own."

"Um. Yeah. Obviously," Sinkua guffawed, "Of course I thought it through exactly like that. Inject my milystis into you and force yours to play nice. It wasn't just because I could pull souls out of Cedalion when I impaled him."

They all shared a good long laugh, culminating with Elemeno patting him on the back.

"Well however you came up with it, it sounds like you had a good plan in mind all along," she said, "But next time, just sell your plan as it is."

"Next time?" he asked, "So you are going with us?"

"I haven't dismissed the idea," Elemeno said, "I don't have to tell you how dangerous the living world has become. And the people I love the most are in the worst of that danger, but there's only so much I can do."

"Well, I think you can do plenty."

"And the world can get better when we get rid of the people who are making it that dangerous," Eytea added, "You deserve to experience that better world."

"There will always be garbage people vying for power," Elemeno said, "But I appreciate the kind words."

"Is there any way we can talk you into come back with us?" Galo asked.

"I just need time to decide. This place is getting very interesting and a lot less dangerous at least on this said," she said, "But I'll tell you what. I'll tag along with The Trifecta. I've buddied up pretty well with Takmet and a bit with Pahres. I'm sure they wouldn't refuse a familiar fourth set of eyes and hands."

They searched the town of shrines in growing silence as the conversation faded to sparse banter and observations. Sinkua mostly listened, saying less and less as the search progressed. As Elemeno had said, he needed to concentrate just to stay material.

He felt lucky to have plenty to think about. He accepted Galo's reasoning for how using Epesol on them would work. The mechanics weren't worth dwelling on and even less worth speculating about. Knowing any more would have to come firsthand. Same for finding out if it was even possible. If it wasn't, he'd think of something else. Assuming there was something else.

But he didn't know why he had reduced his plan to something so absurd as cutting a hole out of the afterlife. Aside from that one incident with Galo, they had always trusted that he knew what he was doing. Or to at least have good intentions and a workable idea.

He could have told them he planned to use Epesol on each of them one by one. Sure, it would've sounded, well, exactly like it sounded. Like he was asking for help finding his sword so he could stab them. But nobody could assume it would hurt. At the very least, they couldn't assume he had to impale them.

They probably wouldn't have felt anything if he was quick with his milystis. It also stood to reason that he would only need to break the skin, or the spiritual approximation, with the tip of Epesol.

Recalling that their skin, their very physicality, was illusory troubled him. Epesol was only in the afterlife because he was effectively dead, and it was bound to his soul. Its corporeality might have also been illusory, which would mean that it would hurt. A lot. And it might not have even worked on him on account of his actual body.

A stumble and drop rattled him out of his introspection. He took rapid stock of his surroundings. Not only had he fallen several meters behind, he had also sunken to his knees.

He called out to Galo.

All three of them apparently realized in that moment that they had gotten ahead of him. Safe to assume, he figured, that it had just happened. Galo hurried back and pulled him up onto solid ground by his forearm.

"You good?" Galo asked, "What happened?"

"I was um…" Sinkua said, hesitating to explain for fear of reliving the consequences, "I got too introspective. Kinda slipped out of the moment."

"Well, be careful with that. We don't want to find out what happens if you go too translucent."

"Yeah, wouldn't want you to vanish, would we," came a fifth voice, "little Hybrid?"

The man stood from a stone pedestal as Sinkua and Galo turned to see him. His form was approximate and his face vague as he approached.

"Masfaru?" Sinkua asked as certainty set into his features, "You're looking surprisingly… What's the word?"

"Two-handed?" Galo said.

"Yes! That's the one," Sinkua said, "So. What the hell are you doing here?"

"Me?" Masfaru scoffed, "What am I doing here? I've been here. You're the one who just showed up."

"Eh whatever," Sinkua shrugged, "What do you want?"

"What I want is for you to…" Masfaru snapped, trailing off in bewilderment, "What happened to the anger? You remember what I did, right? And what you did?"

"I have my reasons. Not that I feel like explaining most of them," Sinkua said, "But what am I supposed to do? Kill you again?"

"Well no, but you're being surprisingly civil."

"Well for one, I found out we're cousins. At least by blood."

"And you still didn't—?" Masfaru started.

"I also ran into Kabehl and Amirione," Sinkua cut off, "Kabehl's in the Netherworld. Amirione's on this side. You can guess which one at least had decent intentions."

Masfaru stalled, looking him over with his jaw slack. His eyes flicked over to Galo, then to Eytea and Elemeno. But he didn't look to be sizing them up. It was more like he was expecting, perhaps hoping, the whole thing to be a joke.

"Hey why does it look like you have two faces, but one's all blurry?" he asked.

"I don't feel like explaining," Sinkua said, "Look I don't care what you were after when you joined The Avatars of Fate or how much you knew. But I'm guessing AinZun had a lot to do with it."

"How do you know about AinZun?" Masfaru asked, "The Engineer promised me she wouldn't get directly involved."

"That's curious," Elemeno chimed in, "Did you always call your mother by her name?"

"Bitch, am I laying on a couch?" Masfaru snapped, "Do you have a clipboard that I can't see?"

"Fine, fine. Backing off."

"I'm not here for you anyway," he said, turning to Sinkua, "Back to you. Where the fuck were you?"

"Where the fuck was I when?" Sinkua asked, "After I killed you? I was trying to protect what was left of my family. If it wasn't for SenRas, there might not have been anyone left."

"SenRas? The asshole who orphaned AinZun?!" Masfaru shouted, "I hope the only reason you know about her is because she killed him."

"Sorry. Other way around."

"You haven't come across her here?" Galo asked.

Masfaru thrust a finger aside at him with the briefest flick of eye contact. "Get the fuck out of my face, you insufferable jungle whelp."

Galo stared at him for a moment, his expression going from flat to a scowl.

"Sinkua?" he said at last, "I'm gonna have to try to kill your cousin. Just know that it isn't personal, but I'm also not asking permission."

"Yeah. Sure. Knock yourself out, brother," Sinkua said, "I'm fascinated to see how it would even work."

"I can't believe you," Masfaru grumbled, "You forgave SenRas. You call this asshole your brother."

"They've both more than earned my respect," Sinkua said, "So what's your point?"

"But you knew we were cousins. You knew what AinZun was like," Masfaru continued, "And you never fucking came back for me!"

"I'm… sorry?" Sinkua puzzled, "I didn't know I was supposed to."

"You act like family's so fucking important," Masfaru spat, "But you killed and bailed on the one who needed you most."

"No, CreSam said he was in too deep to be saved. Still looking for him here though," Sinkua said, "But since you insist that… Hold on. When did you find out I can resurrect the dead?"

"What does it matter?"

"I thought that was privileged information. MalVek kept a lot of stuff under wraps until it factored into his plans."

"Who the hell is MalVek?"

"Exactly," Sinkua said, "So when and how did you find out?"

"I don't know," Masfaru said, "Sometime after I came to these shrines."

"This is gonna sound like a stupid question," Sinkua said, "But did you already resent me when you came here?"

"I guess," Masfaru said, "I tried to relate to you. I gave you a reason to let me live. I thought you'd realize I was in over my head."

"If it was all an act, you played it way too well," Sinkua said, "I'm not even convinced now that you wanted out. I never forgot what you did. And I sure as shit haven't forgiven you."

"I didn't want out. Or your forgiveness. I wanted someone to level me out. Keep me in check."

"Keep you in check? You killed a man for what was under his house. There was nothing to keep in check."

"You know damn well what those drugs did!"

"You can't..." Sinkua said, trailing off in sickening realization, "Oh shit. They had us both on the same stuff, didn't they?"

"Yes. Idiot. It's about time," Masfaru scolded, folding his arms, "I thought you'd figure it out when I told you about the failed lab experiment and how we'd met before that day in Berinin. But no. You just bashed my face in. Asshole."

"Look. We're working on a sort of spirit heist. Trying to skirt the rules and get the three of us out of here," Sinkua said, nodding aside to Galo and Eytea.

"Oh, shit yeah!" Masfaru exclaimed, "Does that mean you could send me back, too?"

"Why do you assume you're part of it? We're only family by blood. I chose to make them my family, and you flung shit at Galo and Elemeno just for talking to you," Sinkua reminded, "No. Listen. When I get back, I'll look for your body so I can try to bring you back. No promises it'll work. I don't know how much you've decomposed."

"Are... Are you sure?" Masfaru asked, "Let's be real. I could be pulling one over on you. What's stopping me from going back to The Avatars?"

"The fact that they're dead," Sinkua said, "MalVek didn't replace the ones we killed. Didn't factor into his plans. And there's no place for you in what he's built."

"That's not for you to —"

"No place that you'd want," Sinkua interrupted, tapping the crook of his elbow, "Trust me."

"Ah. That bad, huh?"

Sinkua just nodded.

"Fine. I guess that's more than I can ask for. All things considered."

"So did someone here tell you about my power?"

"Yeah. I don't remember who it was," Masfaru said, "I needed someone to talk to, and, you know, after a while, anyone perceptible will do. Especially if they look, you know, recent."

"I know what you mean," Sinkua said. He cocked his head toward Eytea. "The only ones she can perceive are recent."

"Sounds rough," Masfaru said, giving her the slightest chin tilt and even less eye contact, "Anyway. Turned out some of them had hard feelings about how they died and you not helping them."

"Did they also learn about Phoenix here?"

"Probably, but I don't know who from."

Sinkua excused himself and turned to face Eytea, Galo, and Elemeno.

"This is the right place," he said, "People who resent me for not reviving them are being drawn here, even if they don't know I could've revived them."

"Who do you think told them about Phoenix?" Galo asked.

"My first thought is KalChi. Not that it matters."

"Should I have the Valkyries call off Ratatoskr?" Eytea asked.

"No. I know it's impolite, but we can't risk the delay," Sinkua said, "We'll split up to search. You go with your mother. Galo, you're with me. Throw up a signal if you find it."

"You know, you can cover more ground with three parties," Masfaru said, "Tell me what you're looking for, and I can, you know, keep an eye out for it. Like a show of good faith. Maybe, you know, earn that trip?"

Sinkua looked him over, then looked back to Eytea. She shrugged and nodded.

"Sure. Can't hurt," Sinkua said, "It's a blanket on a bench in front of an eighth of a decorative fountain. Like a pie slice."

"Great!" Masfaru said, clapping once, "Okay. I'll, um… I guess I'll just throw something in the air and yell if I find it."

Chapter 21

Elemeno drifted aside from the conversation. Masfaru telling her off didn't bother her. She'd heard worse from stronger. Even lived with it for twenty years.

But she didn't excuse nor forgive it either. Whatever his problem was, it was between him and her son-in-law. If he didn't threaten her or hers, she could stay out of his.

After all, her reluctance to go back had almost everything to do with how dangerous her life had become. She'd fulfilled her goals behind joining The Coalition. She had given even more meaning to her daughter's death and helped put the hurt on MalVek's schemes.

Truthfully, she had set out to hurt The Avatars' operations. The power shift only happened to coincide with her making her move. So, she ended up with a bigger target on her back than she had expected. Hence she doubted she could keep dealing with the consequences.

Returning with three of the four dead Hybrids might have given her the sense of safety she needed. But then again, it might have only made matters worse, especially if there were witnesses to her returning alongside them.

All that said, she wasn't about to recreate her problems in life by stoking conflict in the afterlife. Here she had the choice to walk away.

The shrine they had stopped at was a curious thing. Elemeno distanced herself from the conversation by trying to figure out what it was. Obviously, it was an animal head, but exactly what animal was hard to say.

It had horns for lack of a better word. They were straight and flanged though, and they stopped flat. It reminded her a bit of a jackal. The thing could've also been a dingo but with a hooked nose. The best she could conclude was that it was a predator-prey motif, because it looked like a tapir and something that ate tapirs.

A hand grabbed her shoulder.

"Mom," Eytea beckoned, "Come on."

"What? Oh!" Elemeno remarked, "Sorry I just checked out of that entire conversation."

"Same more or less," Eytea said, "We're splitting up to look for the Phoenix Shrine. You're with me."

"Good idea. What happened with what's-his-name?"

"Masfaru. Sinkua said he'll see if he can revive him when we get back."

"Why?" Elemeno asked, "He tried to kill both of you."

"It's a long story. I can kinda see why he offered," Eytea said, "But I also think he might've just said it to get him off his back. I hope so anyway. I don't wanna deal with him again."

"I guess we'll just have to wait and see," Elemeno said as they set out, "So this is the right place?"

"Seems that way," Eytea said, "People who resented Sinkua for not resurrecting them have been coming here, even if they didn't know about Phoenix."

They walked in silence, heads on swivels in search of the thatch blanket and stone bench. The pair wove around clusters of people in all states of shape and corporeality. Conversations in countless languages melded into a sea of polyglot noise.

Elemeno didn't miss the implication behind Eytea's reasoning. She hoped it hadn't occurred to Eytea, but knowing her, that was quite a distant hope.

In the hours between her death and Sinkua's, Elemeno hadn't made for this area. She hadn't had an impulse to go anywhere in particular. So, if she didn't feel entitled to resurrection, she might not have had the survival-like instinct to want it at all. In fact, she might have wanted to not be revived. Subconsciously anyway.

Besides, someone had to keep Kabehl from climbing out of the Netherworld.

Near the horizon, Elemeno noticed someone looking just as familiar as she did out of place. She was tall and radiated elegance and authority, even at a distance. Her stature was domineering and, at the same time, comforting. Her posture both intimidating and assuring.

And she was enrobed in silvery blue feathers.

Her face alight, Elemeno waved broadly. "Freja!" she called out, "Lady Freja!"

Freja looked annoyed at the abrupt calling. But that annoyance turned to pleasant surprise when her eyes crossed Elemeno's. Though it may have been her noticing who was with Elemeno.

"Eytea," Freja said, lowering her head ever so slightly as they came in speaking distance, "Well met that I found you here."

"Did you always know we needed to come here?" Eytea asked, "Don't get me wrong, I'm glad to see you, too. Always an honor."

"No, perish any thought that I might have led you on," Freja insisted, "The Valkyrie told me of your meeting at the Fjarthursk Shrines. Have only the two of you come here?"

"We split up with Sinkua and your boyfriend at the jackal tapir shrine," Elemeno said, "They figured out that this is the right place."

"Your banter is charming, dear, but I ask that you not refer to Metkhal as my boyfriend. Odin is wont to jealousy on his best days and doesn't always pick up on humor," Freja said, "But what, might I ask, is a jackal tapir?"

Elemeno shrugged. "It looked like a jackal with a tapir's nose. And flat horns."

"Oh! You speak of the Set Shrine," Freja said, her eyes wide, "You would do well to stay clear of him. Set is violent and unruly."

"An ally to Pandora?" Eytea asked.

"An ally to himself," Freja said, "His loyalty endures only as long as his temper."

Elemeno exchanged a quick knowing glance with Eytea. That they had found Masfaru there wasn't lost on either of them.

"Well now, I was looking for you for two reasons, but I already have an answer to one of them," Freja continued.

"Were you going to ask if this was the right place?" Eytea asked.

Freja nodded. "Ratatoskr felt no sign of Phoenix's milystis among the Harkzanian or Famidraget Shrines."

"Well, I'm glad to hear he already finished searching," Eytea said, "I felt a little bad that we don't have time to tell him it's here at the Dagiliši Shrines."

"Don't have time? Did something happen?" Freja asked, "I thought Sinkua was stable with Galo nearby."

Eytea invited Freja to walk with them while she recounted the events in the Netherworld. Now and again, she rubbed the base of her ring finger. She glossed over the details of how they got there, namely Cedalion causing Elemeno, Sinkua, and Amirione to tap into their Bealstillan incarnations. The meat and potatoes was the run-in with Pahres, rather The Prophet, and Sinkua and Tetsen's tactic against the hordes.

And how horribly it backfired.

"Pahres engaged you, but Pahres saved you?" Freja asked, "Quite curious that your assailant and savior shared a name."

"They're technically the same person," Eytea said, "The one who attacked us is the original. The other one's memories diverge after Bahamut died."

"An interloper from another reality come to correct the sins of his past?" Freja asked, "I've never known such things were possible even for the temporal Etherworlders. Though it might explain the ordeal with Odin."

"You think he's corrupt because he's... How did you put it?" Elemeno said, "An interloper from another reality?"

"If this other Pahres could cross realities, I see no reason an alternate of my husband could not as well."

"What about being pushed into another reality?" Eytea asked, "Wouldn't it be easier for an Etherworlder to resist it?"

"It would also be easier for an Etherworlder to survive it," Freja countered, "But we've digressed all the further. If his corruption occurred while he was in the Yggdrasil Void, it would be reasonable that he was, in a word, replaced."

As he and Galo walked away from the strange shrine, Sinkua compartmentalized his thoughts and pushed all but one aside. Doubts about his plans, whether to look harder for his father, whether they'd get back in time to help his sister. None of it mattered. Not enough to risk incorporeality.

The only thing that mattered, the only thing worth spending thoughts on, was finding that shrine. A thatch blanket. A stone bench. A pie slice of a fountain. And when he found it and Epesol with it, he would stab his best friend.

With, of course, the most benevolent of intentions.

"So do you trust him?" Galo asked, breaking the long silence.

"Masfaru? I don't know. I'm trying not to think about it," Sinkua said, "I'm just focusing on finding the shrine. Can't let my mind wander too much."

"Yeah. I get it," Galo said, "Well if you don't mind my being candid, I think he's putting you on."

"Well, he is actually my cousin. Our mothers were sisters," Sinkua said, "I don't think they ever met though. They had different fathers."

"I know. I mean about the cry for help," Galo said, "And about being a victim of those treatments. Remember when we ran into him Ferya?"

"All too well."

"He was proud of it. With how he was talking, you'd think he helped develop it."

"Well, it doesn't matter."

"Why's that?"

"I just said I'd look into reviving him," Sinkua said, pivoting to face him and take a few steps backward, "How's he going to hold me to that?"

Galo stopped walking. "Sinkua?" he asked, "Did you lie to an Avatar of Fate to get what you wanted out of him?"

"Lying and out of him are strong words," Sinkua said, waving him along as he turned back around, "I said what he wanted to hear so we could get back to searching."

"And to confirm that this is the right place?"

"Sure. That too."

"Your grandfather would be so proud of you."

"I know, right? It's like I learned from the best," Sinkua said, "Speaking of him, have you noticed we haven't seen him here?"

"Yeah, I guess we haven't."

"Maybe he doesn't resent me for killing him."

"Brother, I could've told you that," Galo said, "Grandpa also never mentioned coming out this way."

"Elemeno wasn't drawn here either," Sinkua said, brow furrowing with encroaching realization.

"Kinda makes you think maybe not everybody holds it against you, huh?"

"Kinda. Almost."

Flaring heat pulled at the back of his thoughts. He paused, only to feel it again as soon as he proceeded. Several roads crossed and converged here. He looked down one and felt it yet again.

Sinkua gathered this to be Phoenix sensing and zeroing in on Epesol. Neither a conscious effort nor an instinct. But more of a natural attraction, like milystic magnetism.

Galo had kept on the same heading they'd been on. Sinkua called over to him, only to be surprised by someone calling from behind his periphery.

"Hey there!" an older woman beckoned, "I remember you."

She looked vaguely familiar. If they had crossed paths, it must have been brief. But it was a significant enough moment for her to remember him. It must have been something personal.

Perhaps something in a confined space.

"You're... the woman from the elevator," Sinkua deduced, "RoeZal? Is that right?"

"Yes. RoeZal," she said, "Sinku, was it? No. That's not quite right."

"Sinkua."

"Oh! Right. Well, you look older, so you must have escaped. That's splendid to know," RoeZal said, "What about Biroe? Do you know what happened to him?"

"He helped me get out of the city. After he avenged you of course."

"Oh, did he? Well, I'm just honored to hear that."

"Yeah, we've been sort of friends, sort of allies since then," Sinkua said, "We kinda had a falling out a few days before I died though."

"Sinkua?" Galo cut in, "Who's this?"

"Oh sorry, brother. This is RoeZal. We met in the capital building after I delivered our declaration of war," Sinkua said, "Some soldiers executed her for helping me escape."

"You don't find it weird that she's here?" Galo asked, "She doesn't seem to resent you."

"Resent him?" RoeZal recoiled. She turned to Sinkua. "Why would I resent you?"

"We think people I either got killed or failed to save have been drawn here to the Dagiliši Shrines," Sinkua said, "I found out I can resurrect the dead a few months before I died."

"Resent is a strong word, but if I felt it, it wasn't for you," RoeZal said, "My days were only as long as they found me useful and compliant. Helping you just happened to be the figurative straw."

"You mean you..." he hesitated, "don't... blame me for getting you killed?"

"Of course not! There were so many things beyond your control," she said, "We were both in a bad place at the wrong time. That's all."

"I could've taken a different elevator," Sinkua said, "Or I could've kept fighting. It's not like they could've overwhelmed me."

"Sinkua," RoeZal urged, "You made the best choice you could have. You're right. Nobody there was a genuine threat to you. But when you saw someone who looked sympathetic, you chose to stop fighting and leave instead."

"But it cost you your life."

"So? I'd had a long life!" RoeZal remarked, "It had been a good long life until CreSam and his band of bastards took over. But what're you gonna do?"

"I could've stayed and protected you."

"And what? Get shot, too? Burn down the building?"

"I didn't mean—"

"You know what I think?"

Sinkua waited in silence for a long stretch. Apparently she expected an actual answer.

"That I, um..." Sinkua fumbled, "... didn't put you in the elevator."

"Well, no you didn't," RoeZal said, "But the person who resents you most of all? I think it's yourself."

"Ma'am, I've been trying for years to get him to realize that," Galo said, "But someone we bumped into earlier told us he and some other people who resented him for not saving them learned about his power here."

"Resented him or resented the circumstances?" RoeZal challenged, "You boys seem clever. You especially. So, I thought you'd be smart enough to know that there's not always someone to blame. Sometimes bad things just happen. And sure, maybe it's comforting to point the finger at someone. But that doesn't make it right."

Sinkua's mind raced back to the marauders on the Southland Sea.

"Shit does happen," he said.

"Look, if what happened with us was a common occurrence for you, I'm sure someone held a grudge," RoeZal said, "But what if they didn't come here out of resentment? What if it was hope?"

"Hope that I could revive them?"

RoeZal shrugged. "Not my place to say," she said, "But I should let you boys get back to what you were doing."

"Thanks. We are kind of on a time crunch," Sinkua said, forcing nonchalance, "But it was good to bump into you, RoeZal. Definitely better than last time."

"One more thing if you don't mind," Galo said, "Have you seen a shrine that looks like a wedge of a fountain?"

RoeZal rubbed her jaw as she considered the question.

"With a bench in front of it?"

"Yes, with an old blanket on it."

"Keep on this road," she said, "At your heights, you ought to see the top of the fountain by the time you need to turn."

As they continued, Sinkua now looked out for something more than the shrine. By RoeZal's reasoning, he could find anyone who died knowing him. It didn't matter if they resented him and possibly not even if he tried to save them.

If he found CreSam, he could offer another second chance. The stakes back in the living world had escalated, but circumstances were better for him. What with The Avatars being dead, and his wife being alive again. They'd just have a bigger age gap to account for.

Finding SenRas, well, was more a matter of wanting to apologize. Not that Sinkua thought he didn't deserve to be brought back. The only reason he hadn't tried was because he needed to conserve his strength. No, it was more that he knew SenRas might not want to return.

He had spent over forty years atoning for the transgressions of his young adulthood. He had died trying to stop his grandson from ushering in the Era of Chaos. If SenRas wanted to rest, he had more than earned the right. And if he and XalRut had found each other, he would have deferred to her judgment anyway.

Of course, if his grandfather had been sent to the Netherworld, Sinkua knew he would dive through the river and burn that place down to get him out. Unfeasible as it was.

But whether either of them had come here was just speculation. Masfaru and RoeZal had both made good points about this place, but that was all he could do. Speculate. Too much of that, however, like too much introspection, risked immateriality.

People who had died on him came out here. Anything beyond that wasn't worth stressing over.

Besides, some of them might have been better off staying. If beastkin had the potential to safely cross the river, Kervatus and thus Kabehl could escape the Netherworld. And bring The Prophet with him. The afterlife, thus, would need protectors, such as the Haprianite Coastal Patrol officers and combatants from both sides of the ArcNosian Civil War.

"I just thought of something that none of us are gonna like," Sinkua said, breaking the long silence.

"Yeah?" Galo asked, rubbernecking around fragments of a sandstone monument, "Worse than anything else we've gotten into?"

"I don't think there's a comparison," Sinkua said, "But Elemeno's not going back with us."

"Shit. You're right. I guess she wouldn't," Galo said, "Grandpa probably feels like he's done enough, and I think he's happy to be Takmet again. I can't imagine Arestor is eager to go back either."

"True, but that's not what I was thinking," Sinkua said, "Remember, Kabehl was a beastkin in a past life. What do you think would happen if he got out and brought The Prophet with him?"

"I hadn't even considered that," Galo admitted, "That could be disastrous for everyone. Maybe even the entire ecosystem of this place."

"Yeah, and if we're realizing this now, they figured it out yesterday," Sinkua said, "I'll be that's why Cedalion went to meet with The Trifecta."

"To ask them to stay behind?"

"And protect this side from The Avatars in the Netherworld, yes."

"Which means Elemeno stays, too," Galo said, "You're right. None of us like that. Eytea's gonna hate it."

"I don't know if I should bring it up to her," Sinkua said, "Maybe I should just wait and let her mom break it to her."

"That's probably the right thing to do. Knowing her, she figured it out shortly after her mom said she'd tag along with The Trifecta."

The road wound on and on, looping and folding back on itself until it overlapped in ways that ought to have violated spatial logic. With Tetsen's help, Sinkua could still perceive and navigate four dimensions as though they were three. But trying to have any sense of direction made him starkly aware of that extra dimension.

Logically, these roads must have been tunnels they were walking on top of. Or inside of. Maybe both. Perhaps they would've looked like lines if Tetsen receded. He wasn't sure, and he wasn't willing to find out.

So, he was quick to give up on rationalizing the structure and even more on trying to keep track of where they had been. If RoeZal had been right, they'd find a junction somewhere near where they saw the top of the fountain.

Around when the sky began to dim into a simulated sunset, they found a stone bench with a thatch blanket draped over it. Behind was a surprisingly functional pie slice of a marble fountain.

Despite Phoenix's status, her shrine looked quite pedestrian compared to her neighbors'. There was no sense of reverence. Nothing to isolate or elevate it. She wasn't a construct who saved the Omphaloworlders. She wasn't the first to bind with one. And she sure as anything hadn't had wars fought over her. Not according to what her shrine said about her anyway.

Rather, it so blended into the community that she could only be seen the same way. As part of the community. No matter her history or her burdens, Phoenix was, before and above all else, their kin and their neighbor.

Sinkua and Galo waited on the bench. Eytea and Elemeno arrived soon after.

"Is this the place?" Eytea asked as she joined them on the bench, "Looks like it. And check out my finger!"

The base of her ring finger shimmered brightly enough to give her entire hand a slight red tint.

"Where's Epesol?" Elemeno asked.

"Probably behind me," Sinkua said, "I don't think it'd appear out in the open."

Galo, Eytea, and Elemeno gathered around as Sinkua rose and turned toward the fountain wedge.

Galo braced against a faint rumbling. He stole a quick glance aside. Nobody else noticed it.

Despite only being enclosed on one side, the water stayed within the wedge. The only thing more difficult to explain than the meringue pie effect was how clear the water was. Not only did it churn with the spray of the fractional spout, sandstone residue also covered the bottom.

"I, um…" Galo said, "I don't see it in there."

"Neither do I," Sinkua said, "Maybe if I just…"

The churning and rippling obscured his forearm as Sinkua reached into the water. His arm tensed, and his face lit up.

He pulled back, hand erupting from the water with Epesol in his grasp. The water split as though sliced by the sword, spilled out, and evaporated. Spurts of steam sputtered from the fractional spout. By the time Sinkua had brought Epesol down to his side, the fountain wedge was dry.

"I wonder," Galo said, "Was the water protecting Epesol, or was Epesol holding the water together?"

"I don't know," Sinkua said, flipping the blade up to his shoulder, "Why don't I stab you, and you can ask your girlfriend?"

"Oh yeah? I have a better idea," Galo retorted, "How about you stab me, and I'll ask your sister?"

"Aw, I'm gonna miss this banter," Elemeno said.

She retracted her lips, her whole face tightening as they all looked to her.

"I just meant... Well —"

"It's okay," Eytea said, "I figured it out as soon as you mentioned the Trifecta."

"Told you," Galo said, nudging Sinkua.

"We just worked it out a little while ago. But yeah, it's about them," Sinkua said, "They won't go back."

"Kervatus might figure out how to escape the Netherworld," Galo said, "and bring The Prophet with him."

"Well, I didn't think of all that," Elemeno said, "But I had a hunch that they won't want to return."

"We'll all miss you. Mother-in-law," Sinkua said, "I'm glad we got more time. It's been, well... At least it's been memorable, right?"

Galo and Eytea followed with their last farewells to her.

Sinkua beckoned Galo a few steps aside. He aligned the tip of Epesol with his sternum and pressed it into the solar plexus.

The end of the sword vanished through ripples in his illusory body, the puncture wound a patch of translucency. Galo closed his eyes as heat channeled through him along branching serpentine paths. He became starkly aware of his own milystis as this warmth, or the concept thereof, wove and wrapped around it.

"It.... feels like —"

Sinkua shushed him.

Galo saw his strain through dimming and smoky vision. This wasn't just a matter of sticking him with Epesol and thinking about sending him back. Resurrections under common circumstances were taxing enough, and these circumstances were anything but common. No, this was a power that had triggered a war being used for purposes beyond its intentions.

None of Sinkua's predecessors had pulled off anything like this. Not because they lacked the ingenuity. Certainly not because none of them had the audacity. But because none before him had the right amount of both.

Galo became unaware of his fingertips as light bloomed from the puncture and pulled inward at his sternum. He looked down one arm, then the other, to find woven yarns of light, fraying at the ends. Galo had become a sightless vision, and he'd begun to unravel.

The ground rumbled again. This time, Sinkua almost faltered.

Autonomic tasks became concepts. They didn't happen manually. Nor did they happen to him. Rather, senses of need and fulfillment ebbed and flowed throughout his being.

"Do you hear that?" Eytea asked, her voice sounding like it came through molasses.

The light of the afterlife faded. Stretching to every hyperspherical horizon, Galo could see only the sightless visions of spirits and skeletal foundations of Etherworlder Shrines.

"Where's the Trifecta when we need them?" Elemeno sighed.

"Sinkua?" Eytea beckoned, "Sinkua! Hurry!"

"I'm... going as—" Sinkua grunted.

A fissure of shimmering darkness tore between foundations, making straight for the sightless visions of Sinkua, Eytea, and Elemeno. Sinkua bellowed an expletive with mind-rattling emphasis and clarity.

Then everything went dark. And silent.

Moments to hours later, the warmth of sunlight parted Galo's eyelashes.

Trouble had caught up with some of his greatest friends. But Galo had made it back. Despite his faltering faith, Sinkua had pulled it off.

All he could do now was look for Nikasu. And hope they would join him soon.

Chapter 22

"Fuck!"

Pale flames erupted from Sinkua, rippling translucency through the gathered onlookers as he fell back with Epesol. But the unraveling threads of Galo vanished through the puncture in his center.

That, at least, had been enough.

A cacophony of screams echoed and faded as people dropped into the fissure. The shimmering darkness enveloped them as they fell toward the Netherworld. The emanating stenches of brimstone and caustic sludge made their destination known.

Sinkua tumbled along the edge of the fissure, grasping for a modicum of purchase. Epesol fell from his hand, bouncing and along the walls as a crosswind carried it toward the horizon.

Sinkua slammed his white-hot hands against the edge and twisted to a halt, hanging into the pit. He looked for Eytea and Elemeno. The latter was nowhere in sight. Eytea, he found a blur of purple feathers in screaming pursuit of Epesol. He pulled himself up to the ledge and dug his feet in.

Two voices spoke together. One in Ouristihran, the other Tetsen identified as Azzelegna. They both emphasized and drowned each other out, making the one Sinkua could understand nearly incomprehensible.

Kabehl and Kervatus rose from the darkness, a single figure of two distinct entities. Their head was split into two faces like some bestial mitosis. Each arm branched at the forearm. And cloven hooves sprouted from under their heels.

Kabehl shouted Sinkua's name as Kervatus screamed for Fetzikzi. Sinkua sent a quick thought inward, urging Phoenix to keep her from hearing him.

"Blame yourself for your inevitability!" Kabehl roared, laced with Kervatus's Azzelegna shouting, "This is what happens to those who defy the Elder Gods!"

A third voice joined them, calm yet forceful enough to carry through the screams of falling souls.

"Judgment comes always for the noncompliant," he said, "Thus is the eventuality of deviance."

Caked in blood and head swaying on his flattened neck, The Prophet ascended on a brimstone latticework.

"Sinkua. You are not worthy to return as you are," he said as he reached eye level, "You have been named as anathema and impediment and thus are to be removed."

"Eytea has been judged unworthy!" Kabehl and Kervatus snarled, "A failed experiment to be aborted!"

"Is that really what the Elder Gods told you?" Sinkua mocked, "Because that would mean Galo is worthy."

"Your petulant defiance proves nothing," The Prophet argued, "It only serves to—"

"No, it proves everything. Well, everything that matters anyway," Sinkua said, "See, if this is the Elder Gods' judgment, either they were too late or they were okay with Galo going back. Neither of which track."

"Did that bitch Fetzikzi—" Kabehl snarled.

"Which means you dropped the trout on a pledge to your Elder Gods," Sinkua interrupted, "That or you're on another bullshit agenda with an even bullshittier justification. My money's on that one."

"Enough of you!"

The Prophet swept his arm in a grand gesture. The ledge rumbled from beneath Sinkua's feet to just past his stride length. Sinkua bounded aside. The rumbling followed. He stepped back from the ledge, and the ground he'd stood on crumbled.

His first thought was to wait it out. Physical body or no, such a feat had to be taxing on The Prophet. Willful as The Prophet was, Sinkua had to believe himself to be more stubborn. The Prophet couldn't have known how outmatched he was in a battle of attrition.

At least so Sinkua assumed until his knees ached too much to ignore. His thighs felt gelatinous, and his feet went numb. The Prophet, ever the disappointment, showed no signs of fatigue.

Sinkua stole a glance down the fissure at a sound like sandpaper scraping. Crystal sand was rolling down and accumulating on the walls. It stopped cold just before the enveloping darkness. Any that fell beyond that highlighted the crosswind that had taken Epesol.

Falling souls rolled along the wall as well, most stopping before they reached the darkness. Those not so fortunate vanished through the palpable black as the crosswind dragged them away.

Sinkua kicked off his boots and dove into the fissure.

"Yes, embrace your destiny," The Prophet goaded, "The consequence of your defiance is—"

Sinkua pitched a whirling fire orb at the underside of The Prophet's platform. The Prophet bobbed aside and shielded his face. Sinkua clenched his fist and exploded the fire into a cloud of black smoke.

With The Prophet blinded, Sinkua planted his feet on the wall and hit a sprint before his sense of orientation had shifted. He swayed toward the abyss as he ran, gravities of the two sides playing tug-of-war with his incongruous body.

That flaring pull in the back of his mind grew stronger as he ran. Epesol was still in this direction, and it hadn't fallen into the Netherworld. Hopefully.

Kabehl and Kervatus rotated to Sinkua's perspective and squared themselves in his path. Their guarding stance, he noticed, was sloppy, not taking advantage of their extra appendages.

Sinkua banked hard toward the ledge. Kabehl and Kervatus scrambled to follow, only to trip over their own legs. Sinkua whipped black smoke across their faces and, with his pursuers screaming bilingual expletives, crested the ledge.

And he dove back in.

He pushed out far to reduce the wall's pull on his momentum. Kabehl and Kervatus cleared their eyes just before Sinkua drop-kicked their conjoined faces. One foot for each, they crashed hard enough to snap their neck back.

Sinkua curled his toes to clutch Kabehl and Kervatus by their faces. With a spiteful grunt, he kicked out hard and, paired with his own momentum, launched them back toward the abyss.

As he pushed off and back to the wall, the enveloping darkness took Kabehl and Kervatus back to the Netherworld.

No matter how fast she flew, Eytea couldn't gain on Epesol. The steady flaring of her ring finger assured her she wasn't falling behind. But after every push she made, Epesol ricocheted off the wall to maintain its lead on her.

It was as though the abyss was trying to take Epesol to the Netherworld. She had heard Kabehl say something about defying Elder Gods. And while this certainly looked like punishment for his sending Galo back, she had to trust that Sinkua was clever enough, stubborn enough, not to take it to heart. Especially since Odin had judged him falsely by sending him there.

Eytea's sense of orientation shifted as the wall pulled at her. She felt like she was flying sideways. She drifted nearer, the pull from the abyss diminishing the more she closed in on the wall. Turning parallel to the wall, despite knowing she was sideways, she now felt like she was flying along the ground.

Just as with all surfaces in this place, the walls of the fissure had their own gravity. Even if Sinkua or her mother were to be pulled in, the walls would catch them. Hopefully.

That also meant that Epesol wasn't ricocheting. It was bouncing. It would settle if the wall's gravity could overpower the abyss's gravity. She just had to keep close until then, make sure nobody else got hold of it before she did.

That or catch it if the wall lost the tug-of-war. Looking into the abyss at that notion, she saw something that gave her both hope and an idea.

The sands weren't falling through the enveloping darkness. They gathered in the wind stream, shading it into an elaborate braid of shimmering hazy sashes. The gravity of the Netherworld couldn't hold them.

Eytea struck several points on the wall with a forked lightning strike, throwing up a cloud of crystal sand. She rolled upright and beat her wings forth as hard as she could. The gust carried the airborne sand to Epesol, coating it in the faintest dusting.

With Epesol now heavier to the wall, Eytea streamlined her body to wear down the distance. When she couldn't get any closer, she hurled two balls of lightning at the wall. One under Epesol, the other just past it. A cloud of crystal sand splashed up around the blade, which then bounced into the next cloud.

The bouncing shallowed and shortened. Eytea closed the distance that much more, but it still wasn't enough. In fact, it hardly felt like she was gaining on it at all.

The faster she flew, the harder the wall of wind resistance felt. If not for onlooking souls and sand on the wall looking like smeared blurs, she might not have realized just how much momentum she was building. Far more than she had ever realized she was capable of.

Crystal sand swirled up in her wake. Eytea stopped hard and turned upright, pulling those swirling sands forward with her redirected momentum. She braced on the wall and beat her wings forth repeatedly. The sand accumulated in a dense coating, and Epesol bounced one more time.

And stopped.

"You must be so pleased with yourself."

Sinkua whipped around to find The Prophet closing in, floating much nearer than he'd expected. As fast and far as Epesol had flown, he had to trust Eytea to recover it. His was to keep The Prophet from pursuing her.

"Not generally," Sinkua said, "But right now? Yeah. I feel pretty good about that one."

Sinkua dug his feet in, channeling milystis through his soles as he braced himself.

"Always with the clever retorts," The Prophet mused, floating a few meters out and above, "You should know that that wasn't my accomplice you eliminated."

"You really think they survived that?"

"Their survival wasn't my point, you contextually illiterate buffoon," The Prophet derided, "Accomplice implies they were my equal, and that, they were not. No. You merely discarded an experiment."

"An experiment?" Sinkua asked, "I guess it was just a matter of time until you bastards turned on each other."

"Call it as you like, but The Scout outlived his usefulness when he failed to control your father even with The Geneticist's help. Down there, it was only when he tapped into his life as an Azzelegna faun that he could even be a functioning nuisance," The Prophet said, "He was no longer so crucial to the machinations as you and he thought he still was. Nevermind the self-proclaimed rook of his preposterous chess metaphors."

Another voice called his name. Sinkua looked back to find Masfaru standing barefoot on the ledge, toes curled over the edge.

"How are you standing on the wall?" Masfaru asked, "Well nevermind. I'm here to make good on my promise."

"You're a little late for that," Sinkua said, "I had Epesol. Already sent Galo back."

"Hell yeah, cousin!"

"Don't interrupt me," Sinkua scolded, "But your old colleague opened the fucking mouth of the Netherworld to eat it and all of us. So, what promise do you think you're making good on?"

"I told you I'd help you find Epesol," Masfaru said, walking down the wall, "So let me deal with this prick. Go catch up with your woman. Get your sword back."

The ground shifted and rumbled with each step he took. The Prophet drifted out of both their reaches. As he passed him, Sinkua noticed a long sixth toe sprouting out of each heel, grasping the wall like a talon.

Masfaru stopped under The Prophet's platform and drew a pair of rods from his belt.

"Stay your hand, you miserable pawn," The Prophet commanded, "I see your intentions as clearly as your failure."

"Well, peeka-fucking-boo, little prophet," Masfaru goaded, snapping the rods out into bladed fans, "I see you, too!"

Spiderweb cracks ran through the wall with his first underhand swing.

"Masfaru, no!" Sinkua shouted.

Masfaru followed with a thunderous bellow and an overhand slash.

With a groan of effort, Eytea hefted Epesol across her shoulders and clamped down with her wings. The caking of crystal sand made it even heavier than it looked. But she knew if she wiped it off, the sword could get pulled back into the crosswind. Maybe even take her with it. So, she squared her stance and stomped out forceful bowlegged strides toward the ledge.

Eytea looked back in the direction she had come in. Sinkua had disappeared behind the horizon. Her mother, as best she could recall, had been thrown away from the fissure. She closed her eyes and formulated a plan as she walked.

Once she got up top, she would need to put some distance between herself and the edge. Perpendicular gravity, she figured, could interfere with her opening a door to her home. From there, she just needed to exit first near Sinkua, then near her mother.

She crested the ledge, her sense of orientation revolving as she dropped off and upward. When she could no longer feel the wall pushing on her back, Eytea let her legs crumple and dropped to a skewed kneel. Epesol hit the ground with a thunderous clang, and she lay back with the flat of the blade behind her shoulders.

No sooner had she closed her eyes than she felt a shadow stretch across her.

"Eytea?" an obstructed voice said. She opened her eyes to see Cedalion standing over her. "Thank the ether I found you."

"Cedalion," Eytea said, grunting as she pushed herself to sit up, hands back and planted on Epesol, "What happened? Did you find the Trifecta?"

"Yes but this chasm put a damper on our reunion," he said, "I need your help to get back to them."

"That's just as well," Eytea said as she got to her feet, "Sinkua did promise to send you back."

"Yes I suppose he did. Where is our fiery friend, anyway?"

Eytea cocked her head aside. "Back there," she said, "Fighting your late ex-employees."

"Pity of pities that my transgressions continue to haunt him," Cedalion sighed, "Very well. I'll have to trust the Trifecta to make right of their circumstances. Can you use your door trick to get to him?"

"I don't know, but probably not," she lied, "I'm afraid the perpendicular gravity from the wall will interfere."

"A reasonable fear, I suppose. Looks like we're walking for a stretch."

"Looks like it," Eytea said as she set off toward the Dagiliši Shrines, "Hey so I don't suppose you've seen my mom, have you?"

"Elemeno? Arestor has her," he said, "He saved her and a handful more souls from falling into the abyss."

"I'll have to thank him again," she said, "I thought she…"

Eytea trailed off as a shimmering dust cloud swelled up from behind the horizon. The ledge crumbled ahead of it, chunks of landmass scattering to float and tumble over the abyss. Eytea spat an expletive and slammed her hand against the ground.

Sinkua ran at Masfaru, reaching for his drawn back hand. In a moment of adrenalized reflexes, he swerved toward the ledge just as Masfaru's hand launched forth.

The ground shook with the swing of his fan, stone and sand pulsating from the spiderweb cracks. Thoughts and vision blurred as Sinkua pounded out loping strides along the crumbling wall.

Kinetic force exploded from Masfaru's body. Sinkua fell forward, curling his fingertips over the ledge as the wall crumbled against his underside. Masfaru's shockwave gathered the pulsating crystal sands and fed on the spiderweb cracks, culminating in a spiraling sandstorm.

The storm stretched and merged the cracks as it chewed the walls of the fissure. The Prophet rushed back all but hard enough to fall from his woven platform, shielding his face as the storm swept over him.

Sinkua strained for a better grip on the ledge. His focus faltered, mind clouding with stress. And the ground still quaked, ever larger pieces of wall falling out from under him.

He looked aside. The Prophet and his platform were gone. As was Masfaru, where he had stood now the center of a misshapen crater.

It was only then that Sinkua realized just how much of the wall had broken off. He no longer felt oriented as lying facedown. He was hanging from a ledge with room to sway.

But just as he thought to swing for momentum, the ledge gave out.

The ground opened into a sheet of fractalized light.

"Get in!"

"What the—"

Eytea grabbed Cedalion by the back of his shirt, dragged him into her home, and shut the entrance.

She flew up for a better vantage point, but even with the sandstorm palpably close, she couldn't put back in front of the horizon. Streaks of sand nipped her ankles. She had two options, and neither were good.

On the one, she could hover above the storm. Epesol was lighter than anyone she had carried in flight, after all. But she didn't know how long she could stay up with it, much less how long she'd need to stay up.

The other was to hunker down and use her wings as shelter. That was the less strenuous choice, but it had a similar problem. She didn't know how much she could or would need to endure.

It seemed illusory at first, but soon it was undeniable. The storm was growing as it approached. What had only gone just a ways off the ledge now stretched to the opposite side of the chasm.

In that moment, Eytea realized going around the storm would have been her best shot at getting past it. If only she had thought of it sooner. Now she knew she couldn't outrun the edge of the storm. Not with it being close enough to dust her belly even at her current altitude.

That left her only one option.

Sinkua flailed and twisted for a sense of orientation as he plummeted toward the abyss. The shimmering darkness swelled and pulsated as though to reach for him. Stones pelted him as the wall continued to crumble against the lingering winds of the sandstorm.

One struck his foot and felt like it grabbed him by the ankle. His orientation flipped from upside down to lying face down. He checked his feet to find that the stone had stuck. The other sole was coated in prismatic glass from melted crystal sand.

"I just wanted better grip," he mumbled with a chuckle of disbelief.

Most of the debris, he realized, was falling slower. Out toward the horizon, much of it had stopped well before the enveloping darkness. What hadn't slowed all had one thing in common.

They didn't shimmer.

Sinkua didn't grasp the physics behind it all, but the crystal sand was counteracting the gravity of the chasm. Or maybe the Netherworld's gravity didn't affect it as much as this side. Either way, looking upon those braided ribbons of sand just above the darkness made him realize how obvious it should have been.

The coatings on his feet gave him a shot at staying out of the abyss. If he could just stick to the coated debris, he could get himself back to solid ground.

He kicked to turn his head toward the abyss. A second stone stuck to his other foot, turning his orientation upside down with the enveloping darkness above his head.

Sinkua lunged toward the next piece of falling debris, but he couldn't gain on it. He rubbed the rocks he stood on, melting a layer of crystal sand onto his palms. On his next attempt, he and the debris both slowed their freefall and converged on each other.

Sinkua grabbed it with both hands and kicked off the other two before climbing atop it. The next one was further out, but a hard leap and all limbs forward narrowed the gap enough for the piece to swerve toward him. The collision set them tumbling with each other's momentum. He scouted for his next target as the wind whipped and flipped him along the chasm.

The flaring pull in the back of his mind maintained his sense of direction. Faint as it had become, it had finally stopped fading. Epesol had stopped, and as long as he stayed out of the abyss, he could catch up to it.

With any luck, of course, Eytea already had.

Eytea dropped fast enough to hit a crouch when she landed. She dusted her body with several handfuls of crystal sand, rubbing it into her skin, hair, and clothes. The sandstorm stretched well past the other side of the chasm.

She staked Epesol in the ground and wrapped the blade in her duster. Sand lashed at her face.

She tied the sleeves under one shoulder and over the other, strapping Epesol to her back. The sandstorm grew louder than her thoughts.

Eytea ran back down the wall.

Crystal sand whipped and whirled around Sinkua as he bounded along the debris. Shimmering stones hovered and tumbled along the top of the fissure in the wake of Masfaru's sandstorm.

Stomach acid lurched in Sinkua's throat as his sense of orientation shifted with each jump. He pounded out long strides along a larger piece and bounded to the next one in sight. Grabbing that one flipped him into a handstand. He vaulted off, launching all but blind at the next stone. His trajectory bent as the glass coating converged his feet and the nearest floating stone on each other.

The flaring in his subconscience grew stronger the further he ran. The wind grew stronger as well, tumbling and crashing the broken stones that much more violently. Never breaking his stride, Sinkua whipped off his shirt and tied it over his face, covering up to the midline of his eyes.

An acrid taste filled his mouth and overwhelmed his nostrils as he bounded along the stones in pursuit of the sandstorm. Sinkua fish hooked a gap in the corner of his mask and spat the blood and bile that had been gathering on the back of his tongue.

Soon after the sandstorm appeared on the horizon, silhouettes began taking shape.

Eytea shielded the side of her face with a wing as she ran along the lower reaches of the wall. Wisps of shimmering darkness reached out in handlike shapes to swipe at her. Epesol bounced against her back and buttocks as she ran, her ring finger flaring with every strike.

Behind the sandstorm, the chasm sprawled into an aerial wasteland. Stone detritus tumbled among swirling crystal sands. Silhouettes appeared in the sandstorm, but they were too scattered and obscured for her to make sense of them.

Eytea pushed out from the wall, wings spread and feathers splayed wide. For the dusting of sand on her body, the walls above pulled her toward the storm. While despite that dusting, the abyss pulled her toward the enveloping darkness. Eytea flew above the crosswind, straining to give in to neither.

Sinkua made out two distinct figures in the storm. One floated, never going sideways or inverting for long. The other moved erratically, bounding about with no apparent control over its orientation. The erratic one circled and rushed with the floating one to goad its movements.

A third figure emerged from the horizon, hovering low in the chasm.

The sandstorm calmed all too abruptly. Eytea looked up to find a clearing like a tunnel into the eye of the storm.

Masfaru jumped from stone to stone, circling The Prophet in a match of aerial cat and mouse. Dust and distance made it difficult to be sure, but it looked like Masfaru was grabbing the stones with his feet.

"Eytea!" he called down, "Keep going! I've got this guy."

"Masfaru?" she answered, "Are you a fucking Hybrid now?!"

Masfaru shrugged and slashed at The Prophet with a bladed fan. "Go! Sinkua's still back there."

Eytea had second and third thoughts about whether Sinkua should revive him. Not just if he should but if he even could.

His Hybrid status aside, someone this unhinged was hard to trust. Even with his good intentions. Countless people were suffering the collateral damage of his methods to get one person. And he hadn't even gotten them yet.

His being the Set Hybrid would've been the less reason to trust him.

Just before she passed the eye, Masfaru called to her once more. She turned over to see him still locked in combat.

"Sorry about that one time," he yelled, "You know? On the roof?"

Eytea sighed and shook her head. "I'm over it," she said, flashing a half-hearted thumbs up, "You've got that guy."

The third figure picked up speed once it passed the storm, devouring the distance faster than Sinkua. He soon noticed how the figure was gliding through the chasm.

It had wings.

Sinkua called out to Eytea as he ran. Conscious effort gave way to instinct, and he closed in on matching her speed.

She could see his face now. Eytea rose beyond the lashings of the abyss, weaving around the stones clattering in the wake of Masfaru's sandstorm.

A sandy stone hit her feet, twisting her sense of orientation. She ran along it and jumped to the next one. Never letting Sinkua beyond her periphery, she bounded from rock to rock, orientation shifting with every jump.

They stood upside down to each other. Each leaned to their own left as they ran, and they aligned in the middle, sideways to how they'd started.

The two cast off their ground as they leapt at each other. Eytea thrust her wings back and snatched Sinkua in her arms. His hands found Epesol on her back, his touch relieving her of its weight. The burst of momentum sent them corkscrewing onto another chunk of stone.

They found their feet and, with his hand on her back, made their way back to solid ground.

"Okay! That was…" Eytea trailed off, still dizzy from the orientation shifting.

"Yeah. Yeah," Sinkua said, nodding as he unwrapped Epesol from her back, "I think, ah, Masfaru? He's, um—"

"Right?!" she exclaimed, "That was weird."

The two fixed their clothes, she her duster and he his shirt.

"I'm thinking maybe I shouldn't," he said, twirling his finger and thrusting his thumb back, "you know."

"Oh! No. Probably not," she said, "Freja told me whose shrine that was. It's this sketchy guy named Set."

"Set? Just… Set?"

"Just Set."

"He's not with Pandora, but he's not necessarily against her," Eytea said, "Freja says his short temper makes him impossible to work with for long."

"Oh no!" Sinkua said, waving his hands in mock fear, "We can't keep a guy with anger issues around."

Eytea backhanded his abdomen. "You know what I mean, you goof," she said, "You've never turned on us when you lost your cool."

"That bad, huh?"

"And you saw what Masfaru did."

"Yeah. Really, even if he's not the Set Hybrid, it's hard to trust someone that reckless," Sinkua said, "Now. Let's find Cedalion so I can make good on our deal."

"Oh! Good news. For once. He found me just after I caught up to Epesol."

"That's, um, convenient."

She shrugged off the coincidence and pressed her hand to the ground. She had to give it the benefit of the doubt and keep her suspicions in her back pocket. The door to her home opened, and Cedalion reemerged.

"I would ask that you better warn me next time," he said, "But with any luck, there won't be a next time."

Sinkua pointed the tip of Epesol at Cedalion's sternum.

"So. Cedalion. What have you been up to?" Sinkua asked, "Did you and Takmet find Arestor and Pahres?"

"Pahres and I found Takmet and Arestor," Cedalion corrected, "Now I do appreciate your diligence. But if I could implore you to get on with this?"

That did little to quell Sinkua's suspicions. Cedalion's timing had been too perfect. It was like he had been lying in wait for Eytea and Epesol.

But that wasn't incriminating. The Harvester could have gotten this information out of The Omnimath, but The Omnimath could have come to investigate the fissure.

"And how are they doing?"

"Not bad. All things considered," Cedalion said, his voice quickening, "Now. Do you mind?"

His being in a rush was unusual. Not enough to call him on, but it was enough for Sinkua to keep pushing.

"Do they want me to send them back, too?"

"No. They've chosen to stay."

"Then I guess I don't need to worry about finding Elemeno," Sinkua said, slightly withdrawing Epesol, "She's staying with The Trifecta."

"I know. Arestor found her," Cedalion said, "He also—"

"Don't listen to him!" came a muffled third voice.

Sinkua lowered Epesol to his side and stepped back. This other person had a shirt tied over his face with swipes of translucency flickering about his bare torso.

"I tire of your hauntings, you miserable relic," Cedalion said, pushing Sinkua aside as he approached the interloper, "The Trifecta should have dealt with you as promised."

"Now why would they do that?" the other one challenged, "They know where their loyalties lie."

"Yes and they were to ensure that I could return to the living world and complete our mission."

Sinkua flared his eyes to better see through this interloper's shirt mask. Proving his suspicions, it was indeed the other Cedalion. Unfortunately, he couldn't see whether this one had The Omnimath's scar, and Sinkua was well aware of the risks that came with seeing his face that clearly.

"Hey, I never got to ask," Eytea chimed in, "Do you know if Tiamat's Shrine is still standing? I didn't see any that I'd guess were it, but a lot of the Dagiliši Shrines are still in ruins."

The first Cedalion regarded her with a calculating once over. The other's shirt mask flicked up with what must have been a knowing grin. Eytea had an angle, and only one of them realized it.

"Why would her Shrine be with the Dagiliši?" the first one asked.

The second shook his head. "Randgrid was mistaken."

Eytea flicked up an ephemeral grin. She had him.

"Are there any Sikaji Shrines left?" she asked.

"I'm afraid not."

The first Cedalion leapt back as Eytea shot a bolt of lightning at his feet.

"That's the real one!" she called to Sinkua, "This one's The Harvester."

Trusting her to keep The Harvester at bay, Sinkua approached The Omnimath. The real, as far as he was concerned, Cedalion.

"Looks like you've had a rough go," he said, gesturing to the translucent marks, "Those from Epemort?"

"Yes, and I'm getting quite lightheaded. If you don't mind."

"Sure. One question. How did I kill you?"

"You impaled me with Epesol and freed the souls I had taken."

"Impaled you to a tree, right?"

"To a rock."

Sinkua flashed a grin. "You passed." He brought the tip of Epesol to Cedalion's sternum. "See you when I get back."

Sinkua's thoughts and vision blurred as he wove his milystis around Cedalion's. Sounds became distant and muffled. The ground felt like memories of foam rubber. Through it all, Cedalion's tsora and milystis unraveled and coalesced into the hole in his chest.

Crimson splatters rippled along his translucent form. Sinkua looked down to find something sticking out of his chest. His sight and thoughts were too cloudy to make sense of it. He only knew the pain radiating through his being. When he looked up, Cedalion was gone. His consciousness was close behind.

No sooner had Eytea called out The Harvester than he broke away. He ran at Sinkua and Cedalion with Epemort drawn and ready, while she pursued with well-timed wingbeats fortifying her sprint speed.

But it wasn't enough. Eytea could only watch in horror as The Harvester drove Epemort through Sinkua. Blood poured from both sides of the wound. His opacity destabilized, flickering to show his prior selves.

She had spent so much time alone here. And despite everything they'd been through, now she faced going back to that solitude. Galo had returned to the living world. Her mother's condition was suspect. And Sinkua was disappearing.

Serpentine flashes of green light flared from the ground as she ran that much harder.

"Mortvill!" she shouted, jumping and twisting in the air, "Stay dead, you absolute bastard!"

Propelled by a hard wingbeat and a burst of lightning, she crashed both feet into The Harvester's collarbone. He collapsed backward, putting several steps between them. The green lights flashed more aggressively as she landed, snaking between herself and Sinkua.

Eytea moved in front of Sinkua. Epesol lay at his feet. Careful not to cut herself, she pushed Epemort out of his chest. His eyes, and those of the memory imprints, were distant.

She lifted Epesol to her chest, but not even the adrenaline of urgency could keep it steady to his solar plexus. Even if she could, she needed his hands on it. The mark from her ring wasn't enough. But when she grabbed his hand, she dropped Epesol at his feet.

With that touch, however, came a glimmer of stability. The Harvester had recovered as well, though, and he was closing the distance fast.

"Sinkua? Sinkua!" Eytea beckoned, "Stay with me. Pick up Epesol. Come on!"

The Harvester drew Epemort back, ready to impale Sinkua again and Eytea with it. Eytea pulled Sinkua's arms, urging him down and pick up his sword.

The Harvester lunged at them with black smoke streaming from his blade. Tendrils of green light erupted from the ground and bound his arms, stopping Epemort cold.

"Vielle?!" Eytea gasped.

Another green light erupted at her feet, launching a ring into her line of sight. As baffled as she was grateful, Eytea snatched her engagement ring and put it on. A familiar energy surged up her arm.

Eytea lifted Epesol as easily as she could her halberd. She put Sinkua's hand on it and, as he faltered and flickered, plunged it through his chest.

She turned him around and pushed her chest onto the sword as well.

Roughness sandwiched her sides, alerting her to something beyond the darkness. Eytea opened her eyes to a dense foliage canopy high overhead. Streaks of moonlight and diffused speckles of stars filtered through the leaves.

Sinkua lay with his head in her lap and his eyes closed. All but deathly still save for the shallowing rising and falling of his chest.

She sat catching her breath as she took in her surroundings. Looking over her shoulder, she found a massive tree trunk nearby. Eytea pondered whether they'd returned near Yggdrasil because she'd died there or because of Vielle's help.

"Eytea!" he gasped, throwing his hands around her neck and pulling her down.

"Yeah," she exhaled, "We made it. We're back."

"Where... Where are we?"

"Yggdrasil," she said, hugging him tighter, "Near the trunk."

His grip faltered. "This is, um... I mean...," he stammered, "Who... are we?"

"What do you mean?" she asked, "You just said my name."

"... Eytea?"

"Yeah. I'm your Eytea," she said, "Always will be."

"Is that why I know your name?" he said, leaning into the crook of her neck, "Does that mean you could, um... Do you know mine?"

She pulled back with a look of concern, only to gasp at the sight of him.

"Eytea," he pleaded, "That's all I can remember. And that's —"

"Your..." she stammered, "Your eyes. They're..."

They were just green as she'd always known. But now it was only where it would've been if not for that one set of chromosomes. Just in his irises.

"What?" he asked, pawing at his face, "What's wrong with my eyes?"

"Not a thing," Eytea said, pulling him into an even tighter hug, "MeiLom."

Epilogue

"Excuse us? How far does this cart go?"

"Depends how far you're looking to go."

"We're heading to Harkzan."

"Heading home, are you? Well, that'll cost you a pretty bit of coin."

"Stop in the Sikaji capital. We'll find something to make the rest of the trip worth your while."

"Sikaj? What could even be left there for you to promise me?"

"That's for us to worry about. But if we don't find anything, leave us. No skin off your back."

"Suppose not. Climb aboard. Might I know your names, miss?"

"It wouldn't do you any good."

"We'll be together for quite a stretch."

"No, I mean if you've never heard of me, it won't mean anything."

"Suit yourself then. What about your partner? Quite the silent sort, isn't he?"

"He doesn't speak Mberhali."

"Look I just need one of your names for the ledger."

"In that case, call him Zadid. Zadid Onabyuni."

Prior Incarnations

Current	Sinkua	Galo	Gijin	Elemeno
5000 YA	Tetsen Drukoa	Metkhal	Takmet[†]	
-1 generation	Boglia Drogera			
-2 generations	Dhamurasit			
	Motanos Kuvrach			
	Rhobhan Porywyd			
	Hajima Tenzu			
	Tenzu Tamanoro			
	Chelok Vlazir			
	Saniro Himarahi			
	Fetzikzi Aroka			
	Ibaš Qufik			
	Verazeh Jesham			
-13 generations	Ajaveo			Jehgoro

†body transfer

Prior Incarnations (cont.)

Current	Sinkua	Mortvill*	Kabehl	Amirione
5000 YA	Tetsen Drukoa	Cedalion		
-1 generation	Boglia Drogera			
-2 generations	Dhamurasit			
	Motanos Kuvrach			
	Rhobhan Porywyd			
	Hajima Tenzu			
	Tenzu Tamanoro			
	Chelok Vlazir			
	Saniro Himarahi			
	Fetzikzi Aroka	Cedalion** (1st known use)	Kervatus	
	Ibaš Qufik			
	Verazeh Jesham			
-13 generations	Ajaveo	Pesmenas*		Nayon

*alias

**original name

Nations of the Ancient World

Ancient Name	Current Name	Language Spoken	Real World Equivalent
Azzegnos	Tanelen	Azzelegna	Italian
Bealstilla	Bealstilla	Bealstillan	Haitian Creole/Fongbe
Dagiliz	Eprilen	Dagiliši	Egyptian Arabic
Ëžora	Ivaria	Ëžoraci	Balkan Romani
Fjareskjon	Ferya	Fjarthursk	Norwegian
Gobheodim	Quarun	Gobheodais	Irish
Harkzan	ArcNos	Harkzanian	Greek
Ippatsuru	Haprian	Ippatsuranu	Japanese
Khirabai	Ierodhes	Khirabaitha	Hindi
Lechuatza	Lenguardia	Lechuatzulan	Nahuatl
Mberhan	Berinin	Mberhali	Swahili
Pukoqet	Poravit	Pukoqeyen	Persian
Quiront	Kirts	Quircois	French
Sikaj	N/A	Sikaji	Arabic
Uzhla	N/A	Uzhlatsin	Russian

About the Author

Meticulous to the point of obsession and ambitious to the point of anxiety, E. A. Setser is a career author and publisher trapped in a wage laborer's body. He holds a degree in accounting, which has nothing to do with any job he's ever been hired for, but it probably helps with being the founder of Social Detriment Publishing. Maybe.

E.A. lives in Indiana with his wife Celia, their son Tavin, and their cats, Bast and Echo.

A Note From the Author

Thank you so much for taking the time to read this story. Developing it, as well as the series as a whole, has been a labor of love for years. So, it means a lot when somebody decides to try it, whether they're dipping a toe in or diving headlong.

Now, I'd just like to ask that you leave a review on Amazon. I do read reviews, at least for now, and take constructive feedback into consideration.

Oh, and tell your friends about it. Especially if you liked it. Which I'm assuming you at least sort of did if you read this far. Gosh, I hope you didn't hate this book and only put up with it because you were hoping it would turn out to be so bad that it's good. That would make this whole closing awkward.

Until the next one.

Erik (E. A.) Setser

www.ingramcontent.com/pod-product-compliance
Lightning Source LLC
Chambersburg PA
CBHW070607120726
47909CB00007B/2477